OTHER MEN'S HORSES

AND

TEXAS STANDOFF

ELMER KELTON

A TOM DOHERTY ASSOCIATES BOOK | NEW YORK

This is a work of fiction. All of the characters, organizations, and events portrayed in these novels are either products of the author's imagination or are used fictitiously.

OTHER MEN'S HORSES AND TEXAS STANDOFF

Other Men's Horses copyright © 2009 by The Estate of Elmer Stephen Kelton

Texas Standoff copyright © 2010 by The Estate of Elmer Stephen Kelton

All rights reserved.

A Forge Book
Published by Tom Doherty Associates
175 Fifth Avenue
New York, NY 10010

www.tor-forge.com

Forge® is a registered trademark of Macmillan Publishing Group, LLC.

ISBN 978-0-7653-9356-2

Our books may be purchased in bulk for promotional, educational, or business use. Please contact your local bookseller or the Macmillan Corporate and Premium Sales Department at 1-800-221-7945, extension 5442, or by email at MacmillanSpecialMarkets@macmillan.com.

First Edition: April 2018

Printed in the United States of America

0 9 8 7 6 5 4 3 2 1

Forge Books by Elmer Kelton

After the Bugles
Badger Boy
Barbed Wire
Bitter Trail
Bowie's Mine
The Buckskin Line
Buffalo Wagons
Captain's Rangers
Cloudy in the West
Dark Thicket
The Day the Cowboys Quit
Donovan
Eyes of the Hawk
The Good Old Boys
Hanging Judge
Hard Trail to Follow
Hot Iron
Jericho's Road
Joe Pepper
Llano River
Long Way to Texas

Many a River
Massacre at Goliad
Other Men's Horses
Pecos Crossing
The Pumpkin Rollers
The Raiders: Sons of Texas
Ranger's Trail
The Rebels: Sons of Texas
*Sandhills Boy: The Winding
   Trail of a Texas Writer*
Shadow of a Star
Shotgun
Six Bits a Day
The Smiling Country
Sons of Texas
Stand Proud
Texas Rifles
Texas Standoff
Texas Vendetta
The Time It Never Rained
The Way of the Coyote

Lone Star Rising
(comprising *The Buckskin Line, Badger Boy,* and
The Way of the Coyote)

Brush Country
(comprising *Barbed Wire* and *Llano River*)

Ranger's Law
(comprising *Ranger's Trail, Texas Vendetta,* and
Jericho's Road)

Texas Showdown
(comprising *Pecos Crossing* and *Shotgun*)

Texas Sunrise
(comprising *Massacre at Goliad* and *After the Bugles*)

Long Way to Texas
(comprising *Joe Pepper, Long Way to Texas,* and
Eyes of the Hawk)

CONTENTS

OTHER MEN'S HORSES

For Glenn Dromgoole
and Ron Anderson

1

Cletus Slocum stole Donley Bannister's best horse and crippled it. Now Slocum lay facedown in the dirt, as dead as he would ever be.

Bannister was known locally as a horse trader, finding them in faraway places and bringing them to the West Texas hill country for sale. He could recognize a good horse as far as he could see it, and spot a blemish from fifty yards. He loved horses as other men might love a woman. The blue roan, he thought, was one of the best he had ever owned.

The four Slocum brothers—three now that Cletus was gone—also had a reputation for knowing good horses, stealing them when and where they could. They had gone unpunished because law officers had not been able to bring a strong case to court. It was difficult to persuade a witness to testify against one of them, knowing that to do so was to invite an unfriendly visit by the other three.

Bannister did not wait for the law to act. He pursued Cletus across the rockiest ground along the South Llano River. He caught up with him when the roan stumbled and went down, breaking a foreleg. While witness Willy Pegg trembled and begged for his own life, Bannister put an end to Cletus's dubious career. He felt no remorse over the man, but his heart was heavy with pain when he shot the crippled roan.

Riding back to Junction, he stopped at a modest frame house he shared with his wife Geneva. While he hastily gathered a few necessities for travel, he told her, "I just killed Cletus Slocum. It was a fair fight. You stay put here till I come back. Don't try to follow me."

Thoughtfully, he left her some money. Not so thoughtfully, he neglected to kiss her good-bye before he rode away. Afterward, though she often thought about that oversight, he never did.

Andy Pickard stood in the open boxcar door, feeling through his boots the rumble of steel wheels against the rails. Wisps of coal smoke burned his eyes as he watched West Texas hills roll by at more than thirty miles an hour. He wished he were heading home. Instead, the train was carrying him farther and farther from his new wife.

He sometimes wondered why he had decided to rejoin the Texas Rangers. There were less stressful ways to make a living. He had had more than enough of farming, walking all day behind a plow and a mule, taking verbal abuse from a cranky brother-in-law. He wanted to raise livestock, for that was something he could do on horseback, but a decent start in ranching required money. He did not yet have enough. Rangering seemed his best option for now. He regretted that it often took him too far and kept him too long away from Bethel.

He turned to a stall where his black horse stood tied, feet braced against the pull of the train's forward motion. He said, "At least you're gettin' to ride most of the way. Bannister's horse had to take it all on foot."

The Ranger office in Fort Worth had received a wire saying that Donley Bannister was seen in the West Texas railroad town of Colorado City. Andy happened to be in Fort Worth to deliver a prisoner. He had been dispatched to apprehend Bannister and bring him back to stand trial for shooting Cletus Slocum.

At least the disagreement had been about something worthwhile, Andy thought. Too many men had been killed quarreling over such trivial matters as whiskey, cards, or dance hall girls. A horse was a different matter. A good horse might well justify a righteous killing.

Extension of rails across the state had given Ranger efficiency a strong boost in these early 1880s. No matter how fast he traveled, a fugitive could not outrun the telegraph, and now he had to contend with the railroad as well. Rangers could put their horses on a train and cover distances in hours that would otherwise keep them in the saddle for days. They could move ahead of a fleeing suspect and cut him off or at least rush to wherever he had last been seen and shorten his lead. That was Andy's mission on this trip.

To the best of his knowledge, he had never seen Bannister. He had a physical description of the man, however, in the handwritten fugitive book he carried in his pocket: tall, husky, with pale gray eyes and a small scar on his left cheekbone where a mule had once kicked him. Probably a bit crazy too. A kick in the head could do that to a man, and nothing could kick harder than a mule.

The train chugged to a stop at a siding beside a tower upon which stood a large wooden water tank. Andy climbed down to stretch his aching legs and beheld the largest windmill he had ever seen. He judged its wheel to be twenty feet across, maybe twenty-five. Locomotive boilers required a lot of water to produce steam. The windmill, vital to the railroads, had also done much to open up large areas of West Texas for settlement by farmers and ranchers. They provided water where nature had neglected to do so.

He had recently placed a smaller mill over a hand-dug well on acreage he had bought in the hill country west of San Antonio. Someday, when he had saved enough, he planned to resign from the Rangers again, build a house beside the windmill and move there with Bethel. It was a good grass country for cattle, and several people had brought in sheep. Andy had no prejudice against woolies. They seemed to thrive so long as their owner could fight off the wolves and coyotes and bobcats. These had a strong taste for lambs.

The thought of Bethel brought both warmth and pain. Stationed in a Ranger camp near a former army post town, Fort McKavett, he had rented a small house at the edge of the settlement. There she was able to grow a garden and raise chickens. He had spent nights with her when he was not away on duty. He realized this was not the customary way for a young couple to begin married life. Too often he had to kiss her good-bye and ride away without knowing when he might return. Looking back, which he always did, he would see her small figure standing there, waving, watching him until he was beyond sight.

He had warned her at the beginning that as a Ranger's wife she would spend many days and nights alone, waiting, wishing. But he wondered if she had fully understood how often she would have only a flock of chickens and a brown dog for company. He even wondered if he should have put off marriage until he could provide her with a more stable home. But both had waited a long time already, almost beyond endurance.

He hoped he could capture the fugitive quickly and get back to her. A dispatch had indicated that Bannister could probably make a strong case for self-defense if he had stayed in Junction and faced trial. But he had chosen to run, so he was playing hell with Andy's married life.

The train's black-uniformed conductor walked down the line after seeing that the boiler was properly filled. Pulling out his pocket watch and checking the time, he said, "We'll be pullin' out in a couple of minutes, Ranger. Ought to be in Colorado City in an hour."

"Good," Andy said. "The sooner there, the sooner I can get my business done and go home."

The conductor gave him a quizzical smile. "I'll bet you've got a young wife waitin' for you. That'd account for your constipated look."

Andy's face warmed. "I didn't know it showed."

"I know the signs from personal experience. Seems like I've been married since I was six years old."

Andy asked, "How do you handle it, bein' away from home so much?"

"Home these days is whatever train I happen to be on."

"You don't miss bein' with your wife?"

Thoughtfully the conductor said, "Son, the fire burns hot when you first get married, but then it cools down. There's times you start feelin' crowded. You look for a reason to get away for a while, and she's just as anxious to be shed of you."

"It won't be that way for me and Bethel."

"It will. Nature works it out like that to keep married couples from killin' one another." The conductor frowned. "You ain't told me, but I suspect you're after a man. Is he dangerous?"

"I just know that he's charged with murder."

"Then he's dangerous. And you're fixin' to tackle him by yourself?"

"He's just one man."

"If I was you, and I had a young wife waitin' for me, I'd find a safer way to make a livin'."

Bethel had not said much directly, but Andy had sensed that she felt as the conductor did. One of these days, when he could afford to buy more land and the livestock to put on it . . .

The train slowly picked up speed. Andy watched the telephone poles going by. A line had been strung alongside the tracks all the way from Fort Worth. It didn't seem logical to him that progress could advance much farther. Just about everything conceivable had already been invented.

Colorado City was mostly new, an offspring of the railroad as it had advanced westward. When the boxcar was centered in front of a loading chute, Andy led the black horse down the ramp to a water trough. A little Mexican packmule followed like a faithful dog. After both animals had drunk their fill, Andy rode up the street toward the courthouse. It was customary for a Ranger to call upon local peace officers unless there was a reason not to, such as a suspicion that they were in league with the lawbreakers. That was not the case here.

Andy introduced himself to the sheriff, a middle-aged man with graying hair and an expanding waistline. The sheriff said, "I got a call that you'd be on the train. I thought they'd send an older, more experienced man."

"I'm old enough. What's the latest about Donley Bannister?"

"Nothin' much more than what I wired your captain. I got wind that he'd spent time here playin' poker and puttin' away whiskey. Me and my deputy found his tracks and trailed him to the county line. That's as far as we had jurisdiction. I can take you to where we turned back."

"I'd be much obliged."

"I hope you're a good tracker."

"Not especially."

"Bannister don't seem to be tryin' hard to cover his trail. He likely figures he's already outrun whoever may be after him. I doubt he considered how hard it is to outrun a train."

Standing at a window, Andy let his gaze drift wishfully to a sign that said *Restaurant. Where the elite eat.*

He was not sure what *elite* meant. Schooling had been limited by a tendency toward fighting more than studying when other boys offered offense, which they often did. He had been taken by Indians when he was small and lived with them several years before being thrown back into the white world. Fellow students made fun of his Indian ways and his awkward attempt to relearn the language of his people.

Even yet, a Comanche word occasionally popped out of his mouth. Moreover, he sometimes had a flash of sixth sense about situations and events beyond his sight. To the Indians, these were visions; to Andy, they were a mystery. He had no control over them. They came unbidden. Often when he would have welcomed one, it would not come at all.

He had such a hunch now about Bannister. He felt it likely that the man was no longer in a hurry, probably assuming he had traveled far enough to be safe. Otherwise he would not have tarried in this town to seek after pleasure.

The sheriff said, "Why don't you walk over yonder and grab you some breakfast while I go saddle my horse?"

Andy said, "Suits me fine. There wasn't anything to eat on the train."

The sheriff started to turn away, then stopped. "See that dispeptic-lookin' gent goin' into the café? That's Luther Fleet. He's a tinhorn gambler. I heard that Bannister and him have done business together. He might tell you somethin'."

Andy said, "Thanks. I'll go talk to him."

Fleet sat at a table alone. Andy sized him up at a glance. Restless eyes and slick, long-fingered hands told him this was not a man to whom he would trust his horse or even his dog.

Andy said, "Mind if I sit down with you?"

The answer was a growl. "There's other tables."

"But you're sittin' at this one, and I want to talk with you."

"If you're lookin' for a game, it's a little early in the day."

"I'm a Ranger." Andy touched the badge on his shirt, handmade from a Mexican silver five-peso coin. "I'm lookin' for a man named Donley Bannister. I hear you and him are friends."

The gambler's eyes flashed a negative reaction. He said, "Friend? Not hardly. Him and me have done a little business together. I always came out on the short end."

"Do you know where he went when he left here?"

"He didn't share his plans with me, and I didn't watch him leave town. He could've gone north, south, east, or west. Maybe even straight up. Why don't you try straight up?"

Andy moved in closer and noticed a small bruise on Fleet's left cheek. It looked fresh. He asked, "By any chance, was that blue spot a gift from Bannister?"

The gambler involuntarily brought his hand up to the bruise and flinched. "He claimed I've been owin' him money."

"Do you?"

"Go to hell."

The man's attitude was enough to sour Andy's appetite, strong though it was. He moved to another table and sat with his back to Fleet.

As Andy and the sheriff rode out from town, the lawman asked, "Did you have any luck?"

"I'd've learned more talkin' to a fence post."

"Fleet's pretty good at fleecin' cowboys and railroad hands, but he's not good enough to go up against the real professionals. He'll welsh on the wrong one someday and get his lights blown out. I'd volunteer to sing at his funeral."

"I might be inclined to join you, if I could sing."

The tracks led north. The sheriff said, "Ain't a lot in that direction, not for a long ways. Ranches and maybe a mustanger's camp or two. Hunters killed out the buffalo. Indians stay pretty much to the reservations anymore, where they belong. There's no way of mixin' the white race with the red. Too many differences."

Andy knew the differences all too well, for he had lived in both camps. He said, "The Indians were just fightin' for their land."

"But before it was theirs, they took it away from somebody else. This land has been fought over by first one and then another since God finished it and took the seventh day to rest."

Andy knew the futility of arguing the Indians' point of view. He understood the white view as well. The dilemma was too much for a man in his late twenties to reconcile. Old men had difficulty with it, too.

After a time the sheriff reined up and made a sweeping motion with his hand. He said, "This is the county line, as near as I can figure it. From here it's for you to catch up or to give up."

"Rangers don't give up easy."

"I've seen some that wished they had. Don't take it for granted that your outlaw will surrender peaceably. Been many a good rider thrown off by a gentle horse."

Andy was unsure about his ability to stay on Bannister's trail to its end. He had known Indians who could follow anything that walked, but the tracking trait had eluded him despite his best intentions. Perhaps the fugitive would become complacent and stop somewhere long enough for Andy to catch up.

Toward dusk he smelled wood smoke and spotted a chuck wagon camp a short distance ahead. He judged that it was about the time for a cowboy crew to be eating supper. He rode warily toward the fire, knowing the cook would object to dust being stirred up near his wagon. The men were scattered about, squatting on their heels or sitting on bedrolls, plates in their hands. They paused in their meal to stare at him with curiosity.

A little man in a frazzled old derby hat walked toward him, a grease-stained sack tied around his soft belly. He gave Andy's badge a quick study, then gestured toward a line of pots and Dutch ovens near the fire. He said, "Tie up your animals and come get yourself some supper. What's left, I'll have to throw out anyhow."

"Thanks." Walking in, Andy gave each upturned face a glance. He tried to picture Bannister from the brief description that had been given him. He had been told more about the dun horse than about the man who rode it. He saw no one who unmistakably fitted his preconception, but he remained uneasy. A couple of men quietly arose and walked away from camp.

"You're in luck," the cook said. "Boss brought us some dried apples. Got cobbler pie for you to finish off with. Help yourself."

Andy held the tin plate in his left hand, leaving his right hand free in case of a challenge. None came, and he loosened up. He said, "That coffee sure smells good." The cook poured a cupful for him. Andy seated himself on a tarp-covered bedroll and attacked the supper. Rangers on a trail missed many meals. They seldom passed up an opportunity to eat.

He could feel the men's gaze fastened upon him, a few with suspicion, one with open hostility. Likely as not, some were wanted by the law for one thing or another. He decided the best course was to lay his cards on the table. He said, "I'm lookin' for a large man ridin' a big dun horse with a TR brand on its left hip."

No one spoke at first. The cook broke the silence. "May I make so bold as to ask what he's wanted for?"

"Seems like there was a disagreement over a horse. The other man lost the argument."

"Permanent?"

"Real permanent."

The cook shook his head. "I always said there's three

things it's dangerous to argue over: politics, religion, and horses. Women would make four."

Andy asked, "Has anybody here seen such a man?" He looked from one face to another but saw no sign that anyone would answer. Cowboys as a rule were slow to give a man away unless outraged by what he had done. Especially if they had done the same thing themselves, or had been tempted to.

The cook ventured, "Maybe the other man was a son of a bitch that needed killin'."

Andy said, "Just the same, I've been assigned to bring Donley Bannister in. The rest is up to the court."

The cook frowned. "Last time I was in court, the judge gave me ten days just for singin' too loud on Sunday mornin'. He counted the money I had in my pocket and fined me all of it. Ain't trusted any court since."

Andy recognized that he would not get help here, even if the men in camp *had* seen Bannister. He said, "I'm much obliged for the supper."

The cook said, "It'll soon be too dark to ride. You're welcome to stay all night. You can start off in the mornin' with a good breakfast in your belly."

Andy nodded his thanks. He wondered if the offer was made to allow Bannister more time to travel.

The cook said, "Look, Ranger, we've got nothin' against you. You seem like a nice young feller, but we've got nothin' against the man you're after, either. We don't poke our nose in when we've got no dog in the fight."

Andy understood the reticence. He said, "A man's got to follow his own leanin's."

He had no specific reason to distrust the cowboys,

though it was possible that one wanted by the law might fear Andy had come for him and do something drastic.

He slept fitfully, hearing everything that moved. When the cook arose to begin preparing breakfast, Andy rolled up his blanket and packed the compliant little mule. He was waiting with a cup of water when the coffee began to boil. He poured the water in to sink the grounds, then dipped into the pot. He could barely see first light in the east.

Shortly the cook shouted, "Chuck!" and the cowboys began rolling out of their blankets. Andy took a plate from the chuck box and filled it with fried steak, water-and-flour gravy, and steaming high-rise sourdough biscuits that burned his fingers. He still sensed the men watching him in silence, looking away if he glanced toward them. He could probably find one or two in his fugitive book, but he considered it an abuse of hospitality to eat at a man's wagon and then take him into custody.

He spent more than an hour finding what he thought were probably Bannister's tracks. The roundup crew and their horses had compromised everything within a mile or more of camp. But he finally came across the print of an iron shoe that seemed to be the same one he had followed yesterday. He lost it a while, then found it again. He wished he had Choctaw John with him. A half-breed, John seemed able to track a hawk in flight. But his home was far away. Besides, the state in its frugality disliked paying for outside help. It assumed the Rangers it hired should be able to do anything the situation called for. Sometimes they fell short, however. Andy had, several times. He had already found some of his limitations and knew there must be others yet undiscovered.

* * *

He almost overlooked the dugout. It appeared to be some ranch's line camp, cut into an embankment and roofed with cottonwood limbs covered by a deep layer of dirt. Only the chimney showed above the surface. He saw the smoke first, then several log pens, one with three horses in it. In the last glow of the late-afternoon sun he rode close enough to examine the animals. His nerves tightened as he saw that one was a big dun with a TR brand on its left hip. Exactly the description he had been given.

Dismounting, he drew his rifle from its scabbard and checked his pistol. He looked about but saw no one outside. Because the dugout was essentially a roofed-over hole in the ground, it was unlikely to have a back door through which a fugitive might escape. He saw one small window beside the wooden door. He circled around so he could approach the door without exposing himself to the window. The glass was so encrusted with smoke and dirt that he doubted anyone could see much through it anyway.

He gripped the rifle firmly, put his shoulder against the door, and pushed hard. He stepped through the opening and shouted, "Hands up!"

Two men sat at a small table, cards spread before them. Andy recognized Bannister from his description. The fugitive froze in surprise, his gray eyes wide. The other man made a grab for a pistol in its holster hanging from a peg in the earthen wall. Andrew tickled the back of the man's neck with the muzzle of the rifle. He said, "You heard me. Raise your hands."

The big man had not moved. He demanded, "What is this? If you've come to rob us, you've picked a damned poor place."

"I'm a Ranger. I've been trailin' you, Donley Bannister."

"Bannister? My name is Smith. John Smith."

"Half the men I ever arrested called themselves John Smith." Andy addressed the other man, who had a face full of brown freckles. "And what's your name?"

"It's John Smith too."

"I'll bet I can find your real name on my fugitive list, and it won't be Smith. I'm takin' you in on general principles till we find out for sure who you are."

"What am I bein' arrested for?"

"Playin' cards on Sunday will be enough to hold you a while."

"This ain't Sunday."

"How do you know? I don't see a calendar in here."

Andy flinched as cold steel touched the back of his neck. He heard a pistol hammer cock back. A gruff voice said, "Ease that rifle to the floor real slow, or we'll be scrubbin' your brains off of the wall."

Andy felt a paralyzing chill. *What a damnfool thing to do,* he thought. *Stepped into a trap with my eyes wide open.*

The man behind him said, "Lucky thing I went out to pee. I kept low when I seen this feller snoopin' around. Now that we got him, what'll we do with him?"

The freckled one said, "Ain't but one safe thing, Ches. Shoot him and bury him deep enough that he won't even raise up on Judgment Day."

Bannister shook his head. "Now, boys, killin' a Ranger is about the worst thing you can do. The rest of them will trail you plumb to China, if they have to. They'll hang you or shoot you down like a yeller dog."

"Not if they never know what happened to him," the freckled one said.

Bannister argued, "I already got one killin' against me, Speck. He had it comin', but I don't want to answer for another one."

"You don't have to be a part of it. You can ride off and pretend you never seen us."

Bannister looked regretfully at Andy. "Sorry, young feller, but you ought to've rode on by."

Andy knew the other two were serious. He said, "The sheriff knows I came this way, lookin' for you."

Speck said, "But there's nothin' to connect us with this camp. It's been deserted for a while. We just decided to stop here and rest our horses."

Sweat broke out on Andy's forehead. He saw no help in Bannister's face and no mercy in the other two men. They were going to kill him if he didn't do something.

He grasped the edge of the table and quickly tipped it toward Speck, spilling the cards, sending a bottle of whiskey rolling off. In the confusion, he dropped to one knee and grabbed the rifle. He did not get to fire it. A pistol shot reverberated in the small confines of the dugout. His ears felt as if they had exploded. The bullet struck his shoulder and spun him around. The rifle fell to the dirt floor. The heavy smell of burned powder stung his nose.

His shoulder afire, he heard Speck say, "Shoot him again, Ches. You didn't kill him the first time."

Bannister stepped in front of the pair, holding a pistol. "I told you what happens when you kill a Ranger. Be damned if you're goin' to make me a party to it."

Red-faced, Speck glared at him with an air of defiance. Through a haze, however, Andy saw that the larger man had him cowed. Bannister said, "If I was you two, I'd gather up whatever belongs to me and scat. You can put a lot of miles behind you before daylight. I'll find you if I need you."

Ches argued, "He came here to take you in. He could still do it."

"I ain't doin' this for him, I'm doin' it for me. They'll follow me to hell and back if I let you kill him. I already shot one man. You-all don't want to make it three."

Speck grumbled, "That's what thanks we get for splittin' our grub with you." He started to pick up Andy's fallen rifle.

Bannister said, "That ain't yours, Speck. Leave it."

Ches said, "You're makin' a big fuss for nothin'. Look at the way he's bleedin'. He's fixin' to die anyway."

"Maybe, but it won't be none of my doin'."

When the two were gone, Bannister set a wooden bar into place to prevent them from coming back through the door. He hung a coat over the window. "I don't know why I have to deal with yahoos like that. I wouldn't put it past them to try to shoot you through the glass. Now let's take a look at what they done to you."

Unable to remain on his feet, Andy slumped into a chair. He had trouble holding his head up or focusing his eyes. Bannister unbuttoned his shirt and slipped it down from the shoulder. "You're bleedin' like a stuck hog. Serves you right, stumblin' in here, all guts and no brains." He pinched the shoulder. "I'll bet that hurts."

"Damn right it does," Andy wheezed, his teeth clenched. Sick at his stomach, he felt the tickling sensation of blood running down his arm.

Bannister said, "If you die, it'll be your own fault." He

looked into a crude wooden cabinet near the small cast-iron stove and found a flour sack somebody had used to wipe dishes. He said, "You spilled most of the whiskey. Don't reckon you brought any more with you?"

Andy shook his aching head. He rarely drank whiskey. He wondered whether Bannister wanted it for the wound or for himself.

Bannister roughly felt around the wound, causing Andy to cry out in pain. "I don't think the bullet's still in there, but you need a doctor. Nearest one I know of is back in Colorado City. The way you've been bleedin', you might not get that far."

Andy struggled to keep his eyes open. "I'm not dyin', not if I can help it."

Bannister seemed torn by indecision. "You won't make it by yourself, but if I take you, the law is liable to grab me." His voice was angry. "I don't see why they won't leave me alone. The man I shot stole a good horse from me. Crippled him so that I had to shoot the horse too." He picked up the bottle from the floor and held it high. It was nearly empty.

Andy was too weak and nauseated to walk on his own. He clenched his teeth as Bannister helped him to a cot. Bannister said, "You ain't goin' to enjoy this, but try to hold still." He took a swig from the bottle and poured the rest of it into the wound.

Andy heard himself cry out just before he sank into a deep well of pain. Consciousness left him.

When he struggled back out of the darkness, the pain returned with a vengeance. Through a haze he saw Bannister tear the empty flour sack into three pieces. He used one to wipe away the blood. Another he folded and placed over the wound to stanch the bleeding. The third he used to bind Andy's shoulder as tightly as he could.

Bannister said, "I got shot in the leg once. Had to take care of it myself. They said I was lucky not to die of blood poisonin'. If you don't get to a doctor, you're liable to take blood poisonin' yourself."

Andy measured his words, for each required an effort. "It's a long way . . . back to town."

"You need to go, though. Otherwise you'll be startin' a brand-new cemetery here."

Andy tried to raise up, but vertigo gripped him. He dropped heavily onto the cot. His head felt as if it were being forcibly pushed through the thin cotton mattress.

Bannister grumbled, "You haven't got a chance in hell of reachin' there by yourself."

"Maybe after I've rested some."

"You ain't really started to feel that wound yet. Tomorrow you'll be runnin' a fever and beggin' the Lord to let you die. Someday some cow hunter'll find your bones layin' on the prairie along with them of the buffalo."

Andy thought of Bethel, and the pain this could cause her. She might always wonder what ever became of him.

Bannister said, "Dammit, Ranger, you came here hopin' to take me in. I don't owe you nothin', not a thing." His face flushed with frustration. "This day ain't brought me nothin' but bad luck."

"It hasn't been lucky for me either."

Bannister lifted the coat just enough that he could see through the window. "Dark outside. I think the boys are gone."

"Do you know who they are?"

"Sure, but I ain't tellin' you." Bannister frowned darkly,

wrestling with a decision. He demanded, "Are you a married man?"

Andy nodded.

Bannister said, "I was hopin' you wasn't. I don't want a widow-woman on my conscience. You lay still while I fetch up the horses."

"We're fixin' to travel?"

"We have to. You're in bad shape now, but you'll be worse in the mornin'. Once I find somebody who can help you, you're on your own."

Andy said, "You're on the Rangers' list. There'll be others come lookin' for you."

"You could say you shot me. Then they'd quit huntin'."

"But one day you'd turn up alive, and I'd be on the list too."

Bannister grumbled, "Some people have got no gratitude."

2

Andy's shoulder throbbed. He knew Bannister was right about one thing: if he intended to ride anytime soon, he had better get at it. The fever would come before long, and the hurting would be more intense.

He struggled but could not lift his right leg over the saddle's cantle. Bannister gave him a boost and said, "Do I need to tie you on?"

Andy could barely hear his own voice. "I'll do all right."

"You didn't do very good against Ches and Speck, and they're a pair of sorry specimens."

As the hours dragged on, Andy became disoriented. He was dimly aware that they were riding in a southerly direction. Daylight came, the sun rising on his left. He was leaning forward, holding to the saddle with both hands to keep from falling off.

Bannister had spoken little during the night except to ask periodically, "Think you can make it?"

Andy was not certain, but he mumbled, "I'll make it."

As the sun rose, Bannister was ill at ease. "I'm lookin' for that chuck wagon camp. It's got to be around here someplace."

Andy wondered if they might have passed it in the dark. The thought of having to ride horseback all the way into town left Andy in despair. He was barely holding on.

Bannister's voice turned hopeful. "Yonder comes the whole outfit."

Fever clouded Andy's vision, but he made out a dozen or so horsemen riding in a northerly direction. Bannister shouted and waved his hat. The riders altered their course. As they approached, Andy recognized some of the men he had seen at the chuck wagon.

The wagon boss rode up close and gave Andy a quick looking over. He asked Bannister, "What'd you do to the Ranger?"

"Nothin', except bring him here for help."

"As I remember the description, you're the one he was lookin' for."

"Unlucky for him, he ran into a couple of other old boys who suspicioned they might be on his list too."

The cowboys gathered around, curious.

Bannister said, "I'd like to turn him over to you-all. I've got places to go."

"We're busy with the roundup. What would we do with him?"

"Get him to town, to a doctor that can fix him up proper."

Impatiently the boss said, "I'm already shorthanded as it is." He glanced over the gathered cowboys. "Kid." He beckoned with one finger to a youth of perhaps sixteen. "You take the Ranger to camp. Get Cookie to look at that wound. Then you hitch up the hoodlum wagon and carry this man on to town." As an afterthought, he said, "Ask Cookie if he needs anything from the store. We don't want your trip to be a waste."

One of the cowboys said, "The kid ain't old enough for that much responsibility. I'll go instead."

"And wind up drunk for three days? No, the kid ain't lost all his innocence yet."

"He's liable to, if he goes to town by hisself."

The boss turned back to Bannister. "I won't ask you where you're headed."

"I'd just lie to you if you did." Bannister said, "Ranger, I've done all I can do for you. More than I should've. From now on you'd better have eyes in the back of your head, or somebody may put a bullet there."

Andy murmured, "Obliged. But you're still on the list."

Bannister had already turned away. Andy doubted that he heard.

Andy rode as if in a painful trance, his mind roaming aimlessly from Bethel to Bannister and to the pair who had wounded him. The kid finally broke into Andy's consciousness by saying, "Yonder's the wagon."

The cook helped the kid lift Andy down from the saddle. They eased him onto a bedroll. Cookie unwrapped the crude bandage and swore. "Was this the cleanest thing he could find? It's a wonder you ain't got blood poisonin' already."

Andy could barely remember Bannister working on him in the spartan dugout. "I expect he did his best with what he had," he murmured. He did not feel like talking.

The cook maintained a one-sided conversation. He fetched a bottle from deep within the chuck box. He said, "This ain't goin' to feel near as good as if it was goin' down your throat." He poured whiskey into and over the wound. He and the kid had to push hard to keep Andy down. He said, "It wouldn't do you no good if it didn't burn a little."

"A little?" Andy wheezed, struggling to get his breath.

"You need a sure-enough doctor. It's your good luck that there's one in town."

Andy thought he would be glad to have a little good luck for a change.

The kid unloaded supplies from the camp's second wagon to make room, then took Andy's roll from the pack-mule and spread the blankets in the wagon. He said, "It ain't no feather bed." He and the cook helped Andy up into the wagon. He lay on his back, his felt hat a poor substitute for a pillow.

The cook admonished the kid, "Don't you tarry no longer than you have to. And don't you forget that barrel of flour if you want any biscuits tomorrow." He turned his attention to Andy. "While you're healin' up, Ranger, you might give some thought to another line of work. Yours can get a man hurt."

Andy nodded. "Maybe I can do somethin' for you sometime."

"The best thing you can do for me is to forget everybody you've seen here. This outfit is already shorthanded. A Ranger raid would just about finish us off."

The cook tied Andy's horse and mule on behind. The kid clucked at the team, and the wagon lurched forward. Andy gritted his teeth against the pain.

He was dimly conscious of their arrival in town. He heard the kid ask someone how to locate Dr. Coleman. Shortly he found himself being half supported, half carried into a frame house. A strong voice said, "We'll lay him down on that cot."

A man in his thirties leaned over him with a stethoscope and listened to his heartbeat. Andy heard the kid say, "The feller that brought him to us said he didn't think the bullet is still in there."

The doctor said, "I'll have to find out." He poured ether into a wad of cotton and held it to Andy's nose. Andy fought it for a moment, then drifted off. He was only vaguely aware of the probing, though he continued to feel pain. When it was over, he peered up through a misty veil at the man who had operated on him.

The doctor said, "I found no bullet, but I took out a tiny chip of bone. You'll feel better now that I've cleaned the wound."

Andy did not feel better. He tried to lift his hand. It weighed a hundred pounds.

"Easy, young fellow," the doctor said gently. "You won't be going anywhere for a while."

"How long?" Andy managed.

The doctor shrugged. "Hard to say. I'll keep you here a day or two, then move you over to a boarding house where

I can look in on you till you're ready to travel. Is there any-body we should notify?"

"My captain. And my wife Bethel, down at Fort Mc-Kavett."

"I'll see that it's done."

The kid gave Andy a look of concern and said, "I al-ways thought I'd like to be a Ranger myself someday. After this, bein' a cowboy looks pretty good."

Andy hurt too much to smile. He said, "Most Rangers hardly ever get shot."

"Cookie is liable to shoot *me* if I don't show up before dark. Good luck, Ranger."

"I'll put in a word for you if you ever decide to join."

"Don't expect me any time soon."

When his head was clear and the fever had subsided, Andy started reading through his fugitive book, staying with it until his eyes went blurry from trying to decipher the pen-ciled notations. He thought he probably found a match for the two who had shot him. One appeared to be a cow and horse thief named Chester Lamplin, charged with murder. The one with the freckles was probably Francis Fuller, better known as Speck. He had half a page of charges against him, chiefly horse theft.

Andy was in his third day in the widow Kelly's boarding house when he heard a woman's voice from down the hall. Bethel burst into the room and threw her arms around him.

His heart jumped. He hugged her though it set off a sharp throbbing in his shoulder. "How did you get here?"

"In a fast buggy."

"By yourself?"

"Almost." She turned and nodded toward a tall, skinny man with a homemade silver star on his vest. "Len Tanner rode along with me on horseback."

Len's lopsided grin reached from one ear across to the other. Though his hair was graying, and he was missing a tooth, under present circumstances Andy considered him handsome. Len had been a Ranger before the Civil War and had rejoined when the force was reorganized after the reconstruction years.

Andy said, "Len, you oughtn't to've drug Bethel half-way across Texas."

"But ain't you glad I did?"

"Seein' her is better medicine than anything the doctor has given me." Andy warmed to Bethel's smile. Her dress wrinkled and her long brown hair in a tangle from the long trip, she had never looked so beautiful.

Len said, "Sergeant Ryker sent me to make sure you wasn't just layin' down on the job. I tried to tell Bethel it was too hard a trip for her, but you've tied yourself to a stubborn woman."

Andy squeezed her hand. "I've found that out."

Len's face went serious. "I'm supposed to try and pick up Bannister's trail."

"It'll be cold by now. Anyway, if it wasn't for him, I'd be layin' dead somewhere out yonder."

"But he shot you, didn't he?"

"It wasn't him." Andy explained about Ches and Speck. "Bannister stopped them from finishin' the job. Then he took me to a cow camp for help."

"You may be givin' him too much credit. He did that

for hisself. He knew that if you died, he'd be blamed for it. He'd be charged with two killin's instead of one."

"Whatever his reasons, he did it. I don't feel right about huntin' him down."

"That choice ain't up to me or you. Maybe a judge'll see fit to give him some slack."

Andy knew Len was right. And if any Ranger could find Bannister, Len was the one. He was like a grassburr that refused to be shaken off.

Bethel said, "It won't be your worry, Andy. As soon as the doctor says you can travel, I'm putting you in the buggy and taking you home."

"We can't go off and leave my horse and packmule."

"We can tie them on behind."

Len said, "It's better this way. The sergeant had rather you was home. Doctors and boardin' houses cost money."

Andy was not surprised. He was not even certain the state would pay him for the days his wound had kept him off duty. The money dispensers in Austin could be arbitrary, especially when expenditures did not bring them some political benefit.

Len said, "I brought my own horse, but I'll take your packmule. Tell me where Bannister was the last time you seen him."

They made the trip home in slow and easy stages, camping before sundown each day to allow Andy more time to rest. Bethel seemed to enjoy cooking in camp, and Andy enjoyed lying on a blanket, watching her. However, he felt wrung out by the time they reached the little frame house at the edge of Fort McKavett, near the banks of the San Saba River. Bethel had to help him unharness the buggy horse. His shoulder was board-stiff and painful. He had limited use of his arm. "I'd better report in," he said as Bethel supported him to the door.

Sternly she said, "You'll do no such thing. I'll send one of the town boys to camp with a message. If the sergeant wants to see you, he can come here. The state of Texas doesn't own you. I do."

At another time he might have argued, and might even have won, but he was too tired and weak to put up much of a case. He said, "You could get me fired."

"We might be better off." Tears glistened in her eyes. "Look at you, all shot up. Next time, instead of bringing you home to get well, I might be bringing you home to bury."

"This kind of thing doesn't happen often."

"Once more may be enough. Tell me the thought of facing another gun doesn't make you feel cold."

It did, but he would not admit it. He could see they were dangerously close to an argument. "We'll talk about it tomorrow. We're both tired now."

"I'll feel the same tomorrow, and the day after that. You don't have to be a Ranger. We could get by somehow."

He would not promise what he could not deliver. "When it's time."

Sergeant Ryker knocked on the door as Andy was finishing his after-supper coffee. Bethel invited him in, giving him no chance to speak before she declared, "He's only been home two weeks. He's a long way from being well."

Removing his hat, Ryker gave Andy a quick and critical study. "You've got your color back. Think you can sit on a horse?"

Andy said, "I already have, a little, just to see if I could."

Bethel protested, "He needs more time."

Ryker said, "Austin is ridin' us about expenses. If you stay off duty much longer they'll make us discharge you."

Andy nodded. "Been expectin' that. I guess I'm strong enough to stand horse guard." Most Rangers disliked being assigned to loose-herd company horses on grass. They considered it monotonous, even demeaning. A day on horse guard could feel like a week. From Andy's viewpoint, however, it was preferable to losing his job.

Ryker said, "Maybe someday a gang of outlaws will stage a raid on Austin, and the money changers will realize how much they need the Rangers." One difficulty was that most incidents requiring Ranger attention occurred far away from the state capitol, so the lawmakers were only dimly aware of them, if at all.

Andy asked, "Heard anything from Len Tanner?"

"Got a couple of wires. He lost Bannister's trail."

"If Len can't find Bannister, nobody can." Andy could not say he was sorry. Bannister could have left him to die but had risked capture to help him. Such a man deserved to be forgiven for killing a horse thief.

The sergeant said, "We're not givin' up. There's more than one way to sack a cat."

"How?"

"Bannister's been livin' in Junction with his wife. It stands to reason that he'll sooner or later come back, or at least try to let her know where he's at."

Andy glanced at Bethel. "I sure would, if I was him."

"The sheriff down there has been watchin' her mail. He hasn't reported anything so far. Of course, Bannister might be cagy enough to send word by somebody instead of writin' a letter."

Andy was thinking faster than Ryker was talking. He said, "She might try to join up with him."

The sergeant nodded. "I'd like for you to go down to Junction and keep an eye on her. If she leaves, you follow her."

Bethel frowned.

The sergeant said, "You might be there a while. It'd give you a chance to be useful while you finish healin' up."

Bethel cried, "Andy, no."

Andy touched her hand. "I want to keep my job."

"Then let me go with you."

Andy glanced at Ryker. The sergeant said, "That'd be contrary to regulations. If Bannister's woman made a move, you might have to go without takin' time to say good-bye."

Bethel's shoulders drooped.

Ryker spoke softly. "I know how you feel, girl. Many's the time I've had to ride away and leave my wife. Andy can wait till tomorrow before he goes off."

Andy said, "Thanks, Sergeant." He watched through the open door as Ryker rode away. Then he turned back into Bethel's arms.

"We've got tonight," he said.

Before arriving in Junction, Andy took off his badge to make himself less conspicuous. The sheriff guided him toward a modest frame house with peeling paint once white but now a soft shade of gray. He said, "She putters around with the flowers by the porch and goes to the store most mornin's. Otherwise, she doesn't show herself much. I've got the postmaster watchin' to see if she gets any mail. She hasn't had a letter since Bannister left."

Andy frowned, thinking of Bethel. "Seems like a man would want to let his wife know somethin'."

The sheriff shrugged. "I would, and you would, but everybody ain't like us. There's some men that don't know how to appreciate a good woman."

"How do you know she's a good woman?"

"People around here like her, other than some of the womenfolks. You know how women can be about judgin' other women, especially one that's good-lookin'."

Andy said, "And this one is good-lookin'?"

The sheriff continued, "She is, but she doesn't go in for paint and powder and such. She's pretty much of a mystery."

"Did you know Bannister?"

"Some. Makes his livin' handlin' horses. He'll be gone for weeks at a time, then come in with a big string to sell. We never know where they come from, but he's appeared to be honest enough, considerin' his occupation. An honest horse trader is one who never cheats his neighbors. He goes somewhere else to do that."

"You don't suppose he deals in stolen horses?"

"Possible, but I never got notices on any of them. I've had no cause to suspicion him."

Andy studied the house, wishing the woman would come outside so he could get a look at her. "How did he come to shoot a man?"

"Somebody stole a roan horse from him. One day Cletus Slocum rode into town on that roan, bold as all get-out.

Bannister challenged him, and Cletus took out a-runnin'. Bannister ran him down. Willy Pegg swore that he saw Bannister kill Cletus in cold blood."

"Do you believe him?"

"That lyin' weasel? No, everybody knows he's a lackey of the Slocum family. But it don't matter what I believe. On his testimony I had to swear out a warrant."

"What do you know about the Slocums?"

"They're a hard lot. They come out of the brush down on the South Llano. Folks around there have lost cattle, sheep, even goats and hogs. There ain't nothin' too low for the Slocums to steal. But knowin' it and provin' it are two different things."

Andy said, "Sounds like Bannister might've done the community a service."

"There's plenty that think so, but if anybody besides Pegg saw the shootin', they haven't come forward. Afraid to, I guess. The Slocums are a bad bunch to get on the wrong side of. They was raised on catclaw brush, alkali water, and rotgut whiskey."

Andy frowned. "Are *you* scared of them?"

The sheriff considered. "A little, to tell you the truth, but that don't keep me from tryin' to do my job. Ordinarily Junction is a decent town, as towns go. That Slocum bunch dances to different music than most of us."

Andy knew he might stand here the rest of the day without a glimpse of Mrs. Bannister. He said, "I need a place where I can watch without bein' noticeable."

The sheriff pointed with his chin. "I've got a shed yonder. Side door faces this way. You can sit in there out of sight but have a good view of the Bannister house."

"Good."

"I don't think you need to watch her all day. She keeps a horse and buggy at the wagon yard. I doubt she'd go anywhere without them. And the postmaster will alert us if she gets any mail."

Andy saw the sheriff's logic. He recognized a slim chance that Bannister himself would come back. If he did, he would almost surely use the cover of darkness. And if his wife left town, she would also likely do so in the dark. He said, "I'll rest in the daytime and keep watch durin' the night." His shoulder remained stiff and more than a little sore, though not enough to keep him from his assignment.

The sheriff said, "Good idea. Come with me and I'll buy you a drink. I need it whether you do or not."

"Just one. I'm on duty."

"Rangers are always on duty. The beauty of bein' a sheriff is that nobody can fire me except the voters."

The saloon was built of square-cut stones, the walls double thick. A painting of a Longhorn steer graced a slab of wood over the door. "Nothin' much fancy in here," the sheriff said, "but the beer is good honest German brew. What the world needs is more honest beer. And more honest men, German and otherwise."

He stepped inside and stopped abruptly, gazing at four men who sat at a table near the back of the room. He elbowed Andy and said, "There's the three Slocum brothers, Vince and Judd and Finis. The other, with the chubby face, is Willy Pegg. Around here they call him Never-Sweat."

"What does he do for a livin'?"

"Hangs around people like the Slocums, pickin' up whatever drops off of their table. Got a wife who takes in washin'."

Andy was conscious that the four men were staring at him. He took a place at the bar alongside the sheriff, waiting to see if the Slocums made any sort of move.

One did, after a time. He pushed away from the table and approached the sheriff, limping a little. He was a large man with dark stubble that needed shaving, and black eyes that cut like a sharp blade. He declared, "Hey, Sheriff, you ain't goin' to find Bannister in here."

The lawman shook his head. "Nor anywhere else, looks like. It seems he just plain evaporated."

"You ought to be out lookin' for him instead of wastin' time in town."

"Finis, you know my jurisdiction stops at the county line."

Slocum turned toward Andy. The intensity of his eyes raised a tingle along Andy's spine, the kind that came when he heard a snake's rattle. Slocum demanded, "Who the hell are you?" as if he had every right to know.

The sheriff said quickly, "He's a cousin of mine, lookin' for a ranch job. Not often I get to see my kin anymore."

Slocum made no effort to hide his disbelief. "You're a liar. He looks like the law to me. I can smell them every time."

The sheriff said, "He's just a cowboy out of work."

Andy admitted nothing. It usually paid to keep one or two cards up his sleeve.

Slocum pointed a thick finger in the sheriff's face. "You'd better find Bannister before we do, or there won't be enough left of him to feed a buzzard. I'll bet that woman of his could tell us where he's at."

The sheriff's voice reflected a flash of anger. "Don't you even think about botherin' Mrs. Bannister. Folks around here would cut you into little pieces and feed you to the catfish."

Slocum did not yield. "You better find him."

"Nice feller," Andy muttered when Slocum had retreated to his table.

The sheriff replied, "Every word he says, you can write in your Bible. He means it. Those Slocums remember every slight and insult that was ever sent their way, and they've evened the score for most of them."

Andy stabled his horse at the wagon yard with a lean and hungry-looking man who introduced himself only as Spence and who reminded him of Len Tanner. At the sheriff's suggestion, he began taking his meals at a nearby small boarding house. The proprietress was a middle-aged German woman who spoke limited English and showed no curiosity about Andy's business. Her eyes brightened with interest only when she counted the coins Andy placed in her hand. Her silence suited Andy better than her cooking, but he could not expect everyone to cook as well as Bethel.

His first full day, he saw Mrs. Bannister leave her house with a basket in her hand and walk up the street to a store. When she returned, she carried groceries. Andy checked his pocket watch. A little after nine in the morning. A slat bonnet covered most of her features. He noted, however, that she was slender—some would say skinny—and walked proud and straight as if she had a ramrod tied to her back. He considered her attitude defiant, as if she silently dared anyone to call her husband a murderer.

He admired loyalty, whether misplaced or not. He felt guilty as a burglar for spying on her.

He dozed through the day, waking occasionally to look toward the Bannister house. He saw no activity there. At dark he set a chair just inside the door and settled down for the night watch. Lamplight shone in her windows until nine o'clock, then winked out. The night passed without incident. He suspected he was wasting his and the Rangers' time here, but at least his shoulder was having a chance to heal, and he was still on the payroll. His main concern was that this assignment kept him away from Bethel.

Next morning, hoping for a closer look at the woman, he walked to the store before nine o'clock and sat on a bench near the front. He began whittling a stick, hoping she would pay little attention to an idler. Every town seemed to have a few of the spit-and-whittle persuasion.

She was later than yesterday. He began to think she might not appear. Finally she did, carrying the basket. He managed a quick glance at her face. It startled him. She was beautiful. His male reaction brought a rush of self-recrimination. A married man had no business letting his mind drift in that direction.

Presently she came out of the store, the basket on her arm. He concentrated his attention on his whittling, hoping she would not realize he was watching. His gaze followed her as she walked back down the dirt street.

He became conscious that the husky grocer had stepped outside and stood beside him. The sheriff had told Andy his name was Addison Giles. The grocer wiped his large hands on a canvas apron and said, "Fine-looking woman, don't you think?"

"I wasn't payin' much attention."

"I saw you watching her." Giles was a stout man of about forty who probably could toss flour barrels around without straining himself. His voice coarsened. "I hope you're not thinking about taking advantage of her situation."

Andy used his most innocent voice. "I'm a stranger here. I don't know the lady's situation."

"That's Donley Bannister's wife. He's on the run, accused of murder. Most people feel like he got a raw deal. He had to leave Geneva here by herself."

"I'm sorry to hear it."

The grocer's face was somber. "Don't get the notion that she's helpless, though. She's got friends who'd make short work of the Slocum brothers or anybody else that tried to do her harm. Any stranger who drifts into town, we want to be sure the Slocums didn't send for him. Do you know them?"

"The sheriff pointed them out to me."

Mention of the lawman brought a grunt from the grocer. "What business have you got with the sheriff?"

"Kinfolks. He said he might find me a job."

The grocer grunted again. "Whatever Geneva Bannister does or doesn't do is nobody's business but her own. I hope I've made myself understood."

"You've made it mighty clear."

Giles left him and went back into the store. Andy arose, closing his knife and tossing away what remained of the stick. Geneva Bannister was no longer in sight. He returned to the sheriff's shed and lay down on the cot, hoping to sleep a while. He kept seeing the woman's face, the features fine, the eyes a dark brown, almost black.

He knew that if he were Donley Bannister, he would do

whatever was necessary to get back with her. Even kill, if it came to that.

Andy had been in town a week without seeing anything that aroused his suspicion. More and more he felt he was wasting his time and the state's money. The sleep he managed during daytime did not make up for what he lost at night, watching the Bannister house. What he was doing made him feel like a spy. He took no pride in it. His only consolation was a letter from Bethel, sent to him at the sheriff's office. It had been written the day after he left. In it she told how much she already missed him.

He thought often about the time he would be able to leave the Ranger service and build a house for Bethel on his hill-country land. There they could dwell in peace without duty constantly interrupting their lives. But they would have to eat, and his place was not large enough to provide a living. He wondered how many more Donley Bannisters he would have to trail before he could make the break.

This assignment was made even more unpleasant by the nagging realization that Bannister had in all likelihood saved his life. It was not Andy's place to ask questions or pass judgment, however. Once he did his part, the matter was out of his hands. He could tell himself he was not responsible. That sounded simple, but he could not turn off his feelings as he would blow out a lamp.

He was at the livery barn, brushing his horse, when Finis Slocum appeared unexpectedly. He gave Andy a suspicious looking-over and declared, "You're the feller I saw with the sheriff a week ago. How come you're still around here?"

Andy made a guess at Slocum's weight and decided the

man had him bested by thirty or forty pounds. Andy would probably be badly outmatched in a fistfight. *If it comes to that,* he thought, *I'd best just shoot him.*

He said, "Still tryin' to find me a ranch job."

"Jobs are scarce around here. You'd be better off in a bigger town, like San Antonio. Lots of ranchers go there to do business."

"I like these hills."

"People that hang around with sheriffs can get awful unpopular. I already don't like you very much."

"I'm sorry. I try to get along with everybody."

Slocum gave Andy a long frown, plainly trying to figure him out. He started to move away but turned back. "You been hearin' much talk while you been here?"

"Some. Mostly about how everybody needs a good rain."

Slocum shook his head and left, dissatisfied. Andy had a disturbing feeling that the man might figure him out sooner or later. Even more bothersome was the possibility that Geneva Bannister might do so as well.

He sensed one morning that something had changed. The woman made her usual trip to the store, carrying her basket. When she emerged her face was flushed with excitement. Grocer Giles stepped out onto the porch to remind her that she had forgotten her basket. She quickly returned for it, then started toward her house, her step lighter than Andy had seen it before. Shortly afterward, the grocer walked down to the wagon yard. The liveryman Spence met him at the door, and they went inside together, out of sight and hearing.

Andy waited a while, then went to the wagon yard. His black horse was in an open corral with several others. The horse stood still while Andy brushed him.

The liveryman stepped out of the barn and observed Andy for a minute. He said, "You're shinin' him up like you're fixin' to leave us."

Andy said, "Can't leave till I find a job."

Spence let his suspicion show. "Some people around here say you may already have one. With the Rangers, maybe?"

Andy swallowed. Had everybody figured it out? "Why the Rangers?"

The liveryman glared. "Because you've been spyin' on folks that deserve to be let alone."

Andy found it difficult to nap during the rest of the day. He had a strong premonition that something was about to happen. He had learned to trust his hunches. At dusk, though feeling a little sleepy, he began his steady watch on the Bannister house. About nine o'clock, as usual, the lamplight winked out. After a few hours he began to think he had let his imagination run away with him. He found himself dozing off.

He was brought suddenly awake by hoofbeats and the whispering sound of thin iron rims cutting tracks in the soft street. Blinking, he made out the form of a buggy stopped in front of the Bannister house. A portly man stepped down. Though Andy could not see him clearly, he guessed him to be the grocer Giles. He heard a muffled knock on the door and saw lamplight in the window. A woman came out onto the porch, bearing a bundle. The man took it from her and placed it in the buggy while she went back into the house to bring out something more.

That was all Andy needed to see. He trotted to the

wagon yard to saddle his horse. He was tying his pack on
a little mule when a man spoke behind him. "The middle
of the night is an odd time to be goin' somewhere." Turning
half around, he saw stable keeper Spence.

"I got a job," Andy said.

"After midnight? You owe me a board bill on that horse
and mule."

Andy paid him. He noticed, with no surprise, that Geneva Bannister's buckboard was not in its accustomed
place. Her buggy horse was gone, too. The stable keeper
said, "You're fixin' to follow Miz Bannister, ain't you? I
hope you ain't goin' to arrest her."

Andy had realized he had not fooled everybody in regard to his mission here. He said, "I've got no reason to.
As far as I know, bein' married to a fugitive is not a crime."

"She's got a right to go anywhere she wants to, ain't she,
without bein' bothered?"

"I don't intend to bother her."

"You figure she'll be goin' to Donley."

Andy had no argument against that. He did not attempt
one.

Spence shrugged. "I can't stop you, but I ain't wishin'
you no luck. Donley always gave me lots of business.
He used to keep his horses in my pens till he got them
sold."

"He ought to've been slower on the trigger."

"Cletus Slocum would've killed him."

Andy held the black horse to a walk as he moved into
the street, the packmule following. A small cloud had
drifted overhead, covering the moon. He could see little
past the horse's ears except vague shapes. Stopping short

of the Bannister house, he heard the faint sound of buggy wheels and the tread of a horse moving in a fast trot. The buggy was going northwestward. That fit with the direction of Donley Bannister's flight. Andy found the pace that would keep him within hearing and followed the sound. In a while the clouds drifted on. Moonlight allowed him to see the buggy moving along a well-traveled road that meandered around a rocky hill. He dropped back farther so Geneva Bannister would not see him.

He thought once he heard someone coming behind him. He stopped and listened, holding his breath. A deer burst out of a thicket and bounded away. Satisfied, Andy lightly touched spurs to the horse's ribs and moved on. The buggy maintained a steady pace except when it encountered rough ground. The dark hours dragged by. As color began to show in the east, Andy pulled back farther, knowing Mrs. Bannister would see him if she happened to look behind her.

A while after sunup the buggy stopped at a small creek. Andy pulled in amid some live-oak trees to hide. He watched the driver dismount, stretch, and remove a bundle from behind the seat. His jaw dropped. This was not Geneva Bannister. This was a man, short, heavyset, and he was alone. The grocer!

"I'll be damned!" Andy exclaimed. He felt a flush of anger, first at the people who had fooled him, then at himself for allowing them to do it. He realized that Addison Giles had been a decoy, luring him away so Geneva Bannister could make her escape in some other direction. Andy had never been close enough to see the difference.

When his initial anger was vented, he rode toward the buggy. He saw no reason to conceal himself.

The grocer smiled as Andy approached him. He said,

"Welcome. I was just about to fix me some breakfast. Would you join me?"

"I'd rather jail you."

"For what? Can't a man take Sunday off and go fishing?"

Andy was not sure it was Sunday, but that made no difference anyway. "What're you doin' with Mrs. Bannister's buggy?"

"She was kind enough to lend it to me. I promised I'd bring her some fish."

Andy looked in the buggy. "Where's your fishin' pole?"

Giles feigned surprise. "By George, I forgot to bring it."

Andy gradually saw humor in the situation, though it was painful. "Looks to me like you caught the fish you were really after."

The grocer smiled again. "One of them. The others are coming behind you."

Turning, Andy saw three Slocum brothers and Willy Pegg pushing their horses into a long trot. Finis Slocum's face was contorted with anger as he reined up just short of the buggy. Glaring at Giles, he said, "Smart son of a bitch, ain't you?"

The grocer did not change expression. "Smarter than some."

Finis's gaze searched in all directions. "Where's she at?"

Giles said calmly, "There's just me and the Ranger here."

Finis jerked his thumb at Pegg. "Go look around."

Pegg made a wide circle and returned. "Ain't nobody else here."

Finis cast a smoldering gaze at Giles, then concentrated on Andy. He cursed until he was hoarse. "We'll find her yet, and then we'll find him. As for you sons of bitches, people that poke their noses into other people's business sometimes get their noses broke." Jerking his head, he said to his brothers, "Come on. We've been dealt one off of the bottom." The three and Pegg turned their horses around and started back toward town, quarreling, the brothers blaming one another. Pegg hung back a little, out of the line of fire.

Andy said, "They thought the same as me, that they were followin' Mrs. Bannister."

"No, I believe they were following you. They thought *you* were following Geneva. Help me get a fire started and we'll fix some breakfast. Unless you've lost your appetite."

Andy brought himself to grin. "Nothin' wrong with my appetite. Just lost a bit of my reputation."

He gathered wood while Giles sliced bacon from a slab and placed it in a skillet, then poured ground coffee into a pot. "I don't get to enjoy this outdoor life near often enough," he said. "Running a store sure ties a man down."

Andy had made many a meal on an outdoor fire, and missed many a meal for lack of the fixings. He saw no romance in it. "I like it better when I can put my legs under a table," he said. "Especially when my wife does the cookin'."

Giles pointed a fork toward the buggy. "You'll find some tin plates in yonder."

Andy lifted the edge of a tarp. He found a carpetbag and several boxes and bundles. The buggy was too well provisioned for a one-day fishing trip, but he decided against saying anything about it. He sensed that all was not as Giles claimed it to be. He saw a saddle, a blanket, and a bridle beneath the tarp. Surely Giles did not plan to ride off on the buggy horse.

Afraid his face might betray what he was thinking, he kept his back toward Giles for a long moment. When he turned, he said, "I'd like nothin' better than to stay with you for the day. I've never done much fishin'."

Giles blinked, and for just a moment Andy saw concern. Andy added, "But I'd better go back and send a report to my sergeant. I'm afraid I'll get dressed down for lettin' Mrs. Bannister slip through my fingers."

Giles's look of relief confirmed Andy's suspicion. The grocer said, "A man shouldn't feel disgraced just because a woman fools him. It happens all the time. My wife, for instance . . ."

Andy sipped coffee and ate bacon and cold biscuits, probably leftovers from last night's supper at the Giles house. The pudgy grocer talked on a wide range of subjects—business, the weather, politics—but carefully avoided what was foremost on both men's minds. Finished, Andy pushed to his feet and said, "There's no use puttin' it off any longer. I'll go in and take my medicine."

Giles extended his hand. "I hope there aren't any hard feelings."

Andy accepted the handshake. "You did what you thought was right, and I did what I was told to."

Andy mounted the black and rode southward until a bend in the trail took him around a heavy live-oak thicket. He worked his way inside it and dismounted, tying the horse. The mule followed, as it had been trained to do. Andy moved afoot to the edge of the motte where he had a clear-enough view of the creek crossing and Giles's buggy. There he found a seat on a fallen dead limb and waited.

3

Geneva Bannister stood beside her horse at the edge of a live-oak clump, watching Addison Giles and the buggy some three hundred yards up the creek. She asked stableman Spence, "Do you see a sign of anybody else?"

"Nope. Just Giles, waitin' where he's supposed to."

"We can't be too careful. It's not only the Slocums we have to worry about. There's that man you say is a Ranger."

"I accused him, and he didn't deny it."

"I've known for several days that he was watching me."

"But we fooled him—and the Slocums too."

Geneva was not so certain. "My husband is a horse trader. He says it's always the ones you underestimate that will beat you on a deal. Let's wait a while longer before we ride down there."

They had waited in the dark past midnight until both the Ranger and the Slocums left town, following the buggy. Then they saddled two horses from the stable and took a roundabout course to reach this rendezvous point. They had arrived in time to see first the Ranger, then the Slocums, ride up to the buggy. The Ranger had remained the longest but had finally turned back toward town.

Spence said, "I'll bet the Slocums were mad enough to bite theirselves when they found they'd followed Giles. By now they've probably figured out that he baited them to clear the way for you."

"I just hope the Slocums don't do him any harm. Addison is one of the kindest men I know."

"Don't you worry about him. Even with his gray hair,

he can wrestle an ox to the ground. You could worry about *me,* though." Spence was spindly and would probably snap in two like a dry stick.

"I worry about both of you."

Her concern was genuine. She realized that Giles and Spence were putting themselves at risk by helping her get away. She suspected both were in love with her, or at least felt a physical attraction. Giles was married to a woman who complained a lot. Spence was a bachelor. She suffered pangs of conscience about taking advantage of them, but both had offered of their own will. Her eagerness to rejoin Donley overrode her sense of guilt.

She said, "I think it's all right to ride down there now."

"Whatever you say."

She sensed reluctance. Spence had grabbed at this chance to enjoy her company, offering protection should anything go wrong. Shortly she would leave him and Giles and go on alone.

Giles had a cup of coffee and a broad smile waiting for her as they rode in. He said, "Looks like everything worked out. They all probably figured you lit out for Fort Worth and points east."

"I hope so," she said.

"Got some bacon here, and a few of last night's biscuits if you'd like to eat before you go on."

"I'll eat them while I travel."

Spence removed her sidesaddle from the horse she had been riding and stowed it in the buggy. He took out Giles's saddle and put it on the horse.

She felt like kissing both men out of gratitude but feared it might stir up futile feelings that were already too near the surface. Spence's eyes were as sad as if he had just buried one of his kin. "You're good friends," she said. "I can't thank you enough." She shook hands, and Giles helped her up onto the seat. She said, "I promise, Donley and I will be back when the time is right."

Spence said, "I might just shoot them Slocums myself."

She knew he was speaking rashly, in the spirit of the moment. Neither he nor Giles was likely to do anything that extreme, though she suspected the husky Giles would be the wrong man for the Slocums to hem up in a corner.

She saw a long stretch of gravel the creek had deposited during overflows. She put the buggy on it to minimize tracks. She stayed on the gravel as long as it lasted, a couple of hundred yards, then angled back on the trail northwestward toward Fort McKavett.

Looking behind her, she saw that both men were still watching. Ever since her teens, she had been aware that men were drawn to her, that she could manipulate them with a smile, a half promise not really meant. At times that invigorating power had served her well. Yet it could also bring troublesome consequences when men took it to mean more than she intended. She had taken pains not to misuse it here, but Giles and Spence had needed no persuasion. In fact, this ploy had been Giles's idea.

She thought about the Ranger and the embarrassment he must be feeling. He had been young and good-looking. For no good reason she could think of, she had caught herself wondering if he was married. She had quickly curbed the thought. She had a man already. Donley Bannister had remained heavy on her mind ever since he had left town ahead of the vengeful Slocums. She had waited for him to kiss her good-bye. It still stung her that he had not.

She remembered in the early days of their marriage that

his passion had been strong, but with time it had ebbed while hers remained warm. With Donley, the horses came first. They were where his true passion lay.

The winding road was by turns rocky and rough, skirting rugged limestone hills, then smoothing awhile as it meandered around live-oak mottes and scattered cedars in the valleys. Now and then her passing set deer bounding away, their white tails flashing. She flushed a flock of wild turkeys, which soared off into a thicket and settled on the limbs.

She met an occasional traveler. She wished she could avoid them, but she knew she would arouse more suspicion by attempting evasion than by simply meeting them head-on. It might strike them as unusual, seeing a woman traveling alone, but by the time they reported it in Junction she would be miles farther on. Her tracks would be obliterated by the many who would travel this way after her.

She saw three horsemen coming south along the wagon trail. As they approached she took them to be cowboys. They were singing, which told her they had probably spent too long in a Fort McKavett saloon. The singing stopped as the three pulled out of the road and stared. Geneva's heartbeat picked up a little. She looked quickly behind her, hoping some traveler might be coming from that direction to help her in case of trouble. She saw no one.

A rifle lay beneath the buggy seat. She resisted an urge to reach down for it. She had long recognized the necessity for guns but had almost rather pick up a snake than handle one. After Donley's shooting of Cletus Slocum, she had even less liking for them.

One of the cowboys removed his hat and made a broad gesture of welcome. He was young, with just a hint of soft whiskers. "Ma'am," he said in a youthful voice much too loud, "why don't you get down and tarry a spell with us? Better yet, why don't I join you in the buggy? Me and you will go a ways up the trail together and leave these two drunks behind."

He reached out as if to touch her. One of his companions, suddenly sober, took his arm and pulled him back. He declared, "You damned idiot, can't you tell a lady when you see one? This could get you horsewhipped. Even shot."

"I was just funnin' with her."

"There ain't nobody laughin'." The sober one touched fingers to the brim of his hat. "Sorry, ma'am. He ain't usually like this. He's just a big old kid, and it's the whiskey talkin'. If you feel like he's insulted you, we'll take the double of a rope to him. He'll know better next time."

Though Geneva's heart still raced, she gathered composure enough to say, "Never mind. When he's sober, tell him he's lucky my husband didn't see this. You'd be picking him up in pieces."

"First waterhole we come to, we'll throw him in it. He'll sober up fast."

"Just don't drown him."

She set the horse into a trot to quickly put the cowboys behind her. Looking back, she could see that the older pair were giving the other a severe talking-to. He was taking it with his head down.

She realized she had been in no danger, at least not from the single cowboy. Had the other two been equally reckless, she might have had to take up the rifle. She could, even if she did not like it. She had reluctantly learned the use of it as a girl. She was a crack shot.

The incident pointed up the hazards faced by a woman traveling a long distance alone. To justify this risk, Donley had better be damned glad to see her, she thought. In point of fact, his letter—written in someone else's hand— had indicated where he had gone, but it had warned her not to follow after him. She had decided to do it anyway.

The third day, the trail led into the village of Fort Mc-Kavett on the San Saba River. Though she wished she could pass through without anyone seeing her, she needed supplies for the trip ahead. From here she would travel northwestward to Fort Concho and, finally, the rolling plains many days farther on.

McKavett had been a military post before the war. The original army structures had been converted to civilian use or cannibalized for newer buildings. She was aware that a Ranger camp existed near here. She wondered if the Ranger who had followed her buggy from Junction had come from this post.

She intended her visit to be short so she could avoid excessive scrutiny. She stopped in front of a stone building whose sign proclaimed *Groc. & Sundry Merch.* She deflected a curious merchant's questions with a story she had made up along the way about she and her husband breaking out a new farm. She bought enough goods to last several days, about all the buggy had room for, then crossed the river at a shallow ford. The San Saba was broad and clear, its banks shaded by towering native pecan trees. She resisted a temptation to stop there and rest.

Downriver, the merchant told her, Spanish padres long

ago had built a mission but were slaughtered by hostile Indians, the buildings destroyed. The last Comanche raid had torn through this part of the hill country barely more than a decade ago. As a small girl in Erath County she had hidden beneath a bed while her mother held a rifle ready in case Indians prowling outside took a notion they wanted more than horses. The memory sent a chill along her back, though she knew she need not worry about Indians anymore, not here.

She had always marveled at her mother's courage and wondered if she could match it should the need arise.

She had never camped by herself before this trip, but she had no dread of it. Because the cowboys had been a reminder of her vulnerability, she pulled the buggy a hundred yards off the trail and stopped behind a live-oak motte that would hide her from anyone passing by. She hobbled the horse, then scooped out a small fire pit and lined its perimeter with limestone rocks. She prepared a small supper, washing it down with boiled black coffee that left grounds stuck in her teeth. She wished for a tent to shield her from the damp that carried a hint of rain.

She pulled up dry grass and made a crude mat on which to spread her blankets. She wrapped herself in them and listened to the sounds of the night. She wished Donley were lying with her. She had missed him. Though he presented a rough exterior to most people, she knew it was a defensive posture meant to gain advantage over those who might challenge him. He occasionally spoke roughly to her, too, but in the privacy of their bedroom he had sometimes been tender and loving. She wished he could have been that way more often.

She awakened at daylight, built a new fire and started

the coffee. She fried bacon and two eggs she had bought in Fort McKavett. Traveling had given her a strong appetite. She put her belongings back in the buggy and poured leftover coffee on the flickering coals, then kicked sand over the pit to smother them.

Darkening clouds threatened rain, but none fell until late afternoon. The wind blew it in beneath the buggy's top. Wrapping a blanket around her shoulders in an effort to stay dry, she began looking for shelter. She saw a low goat shed, but a couple of dozen goats were huddled beneath it. She did not care to share the night with them.

She was about to despair of finding a dry place when about dusk she spotted a house two hundred yards from the trail. She found a dim wagon trace and turned onto it, winding past live-oak trees and junipers. The house was plain, the sort of nailed-together box-and-strip structure common to this developing land. It had once had a coat of paint but was in need of another. In back were a barn and an open shed and several pens built of upright live-oak branches. Seeing no sign of anyone outside, she pulled up in front of the house and shouted, "Anybody home?"

She thought for a minute that no one would answer, but the door opened slowly. A man peered out, showing only his face at first, then pulling the door all the way back. "Yes, ma'am," he said. "Let me help you down from there."

Friendly-eyed, he was approaching middle age. A bristly stubble darkened his face, for he had not shaved in two or three days.

She said, "I'd be obliged for a chance to get out of the rain."

"You've found it," he said, smiling, raising both hands to support her as she climbed down from the buggy. "You go right on inside. I'll put away the horse and buggy while you move up close to the cook stove and get dry."

Geneva had not seen a woman, though there were curtains on the two front windows. "Sure your wife won't mind?"

"I'm a widower," he said.

"I'm sorry." Geneva paused, considering the potential complications of being in the house with a man she never saw before.

He seemed to read her thoughts. "Don't you worry, ma'am. I can see that you're a lady, and I've always tried to be a gentleman. Even if I ain't had much trainin' for it." He lifted the tarp that covered her belongings. "Need me to bring any of this in?"

"Just the carpetbag," she said.

The dampness had given her a chill. She spread the wet blanket across the backs of two wooden chairs and stood in front of the stove, shivering a little, holding her hands near the source of the heat.

In a few minutes the man returned, casting off a woolen poncho from his shoulders. "Got your horse and buggy took care of," he said. "Are you gettin' dried out all right?"

"I'm fine, Mr. . . ." She had not heard his name.

"Nathan," he said. "Jess Nathan."

"I'm Geneva Bannister." She said it before she thought better. If Nathan had heard of Donley Bannister, he might put two and two together.

She looked around the spartan room, which had a cast-iron cookstove, a plain wooden table and four chairs, an open cabinet for kitchen utensils, and little else. A closed door indicated a bedroom, probably just large enough for a bed and perhaps a chest of drawers.

He apologized, "If I'd known a lady was comin', I'd've cleaned the place up a little." He felt his chin. "And shaved."

"Everything looks fine, Mr. Nathan. The main thing is that it is warm and dry."

"It's gettin' late for you to go any farther. You're welcome to spend the night here."

Geneva involuntarily glanced toward the bedroom door. "Thank you, but there's a problem."

"No problem at all. You'll have the bed. I'll sleep in the barn. I've got a cot out there for when company stops by."

"Just the same, don't you think people might talk?"

"I've been hurt by horses and run over by a wagon, and I've been in a couple of foolish fistfights that didn't do me any good. But talk has never hurt me. Besides, the only way anybody'll find out is if you tell them. I won't."

"You're a kind man, Mr. Nathan."

"Just tryin' to remember my upbringin'. I was about to start some supper when you came. I'll bet you're hungry."

"I am. Show me where everything is, and I'll fix the supper."

"It's a deal. I don't often get to eat a meal cooked by a woman."

She sensed that Nathan was a lonely man, living here by himself. The window curtains told her a woman had once lived here too, but they were faded and beginning to fray.

Trying to make conversation, she said, "I saw a field out yonder, and some cattle."

"I've got the startin' of a nice little ranch. It'll be bigger someday. Losin' my wife took the heart out of me for a while, but I've got myself back on the road now."

"You need to find a good woman."

"I suppose, but women like Martha don't come along often—women willin' to scrape by on a hardscrabble place like this and take it on faith that things'll get better."

"There may be more of them than you think. A lot of women would be glad to have a husband who's settled down, knowing every day where he is, knowing that come night he'll be home where he belongs."

Nathan was silent awhile, deep in thought, perhaps reviewing old memories. He said finally, "It always seems like the best ones have been taken already. I'll bet you're married."

"Yes, I am."

"Happy?"

"I suppose." She was not sure exactly what *happiness* meant. It had to be more than simply settling for occasional shining moments that never lasted long enough. She said, "The coffee has come to a boil, if you're ready for it."

After supper she washed the plates and utensils in a large tin pan. Nathan dried them on a towel that once had been a flour sack and placed them on open shelves. It occurred to her that Donley had rarely helped her in the kitchen. Finished, they sat at the cleared table and talked. Actually, Nathan did most of the talking. He told of coming to Texas from Missouri after the war, bringing with him his childhood sweetheart, living on little more than beans and cornbread while he sharecropped cotton on worn-out ground. Gradually he had saved enough to buy a section of land here in the Concho River country. There had been two children, but neither had lived past the first year. Martha had gradually pined away and died just as their fortunes seemed at last to be on the rise.

He asked questions, but Geneva was wary about telling too much, especially regarding her life with Donley. It had had its high points, but it also had its lows. Donley was reckless, ever ready to gamble on the long chance. She never knew if he was going to bring home a bag of silver or simply an empty sack.

As sleepiness tugged at her eyelids, she looked toward the bedroom door, wondering if Nathan meant what he said about sleeping in the barn. True to his word, Nathan lighted a lantern and gathered up a couple of blankets. He said, "There's a bar for the front door, if that'll ease your mind. But I promise you won't need it."

"I'm sure I'll be fine, Mr. Nathan."

She lighted a lamp and carried it into the bedroom, which was as small as she had expected. One window faced toward the barn. She blew out the lamp before she undressed.

She lay awake a long time, thinking about Donley, wondering if he would really be pleased to see her despite sending her a message to stay put. She found herself comparing him to Nathan. Her impression of the rancher was that a promise made was a promise kept. He had probably never had as much money in his hands at one time as Donley occasionally did when he made a good trade on a string of horses, or when the cards favored him in a high-stakes game. Donley's trouble was that he could never hold on to it. It came easily and went the same way.

Her last thoughts before sleep carried her away were of Nathan. She felt conflicted between gratification that he had not taken advantage of her, and disappointment that he had not even tried.

She had not barred the front door.

4

Andy was pleased to see that Geneva Bannister's buggy remained on the trail toward Fort McKavett. He had half expected her to go around, avoiding the town and any report that might find its way back to the Slocums. She probably also knew of the nearby Ranger encampment. For whatever reason, though, she went into the little settlement. He saw her stop at a store.

That would occupy her a while, he thought, time enough for him to steal a few minutes with Bethel. He should also report in to Sergeant Ryker, but that would take away from the little time he could be with his wife. Instead, he would send Ryker a note.

Nearing the door of his and Bethel's house, he shouted. The dog came running, scattering chickens that were pecking around the yard. As Andy dismounted, Bethel rushed to him, her skirt flaring, spooking the horse and packmule. He had to make a quick grab for the reins. He said, "Don't you know not to scare a horse that way?"

She threw her arms around him. "Two weeks gone, and the first thing you do is fuss at me."

She smothered his attempt to answer by pressing her lips against his and saying from the corner of her mouth, "Hush up and kiss me." She was a little thing, the top of her head barely coming up to his top shirt button, but she had surprising strength when she embraced him.

Breaking free, he said, "I haven't got long. I'm trailin' a woman."

Her eyebrows went up. "A woman?"

"Not one you need to worry about. She must be over thirty years old."

"What do you want with an old woman?"

"We don't want her, we want her husband. If things work out, she'll lead me to him."

"If she's an old married woman, I guess it's all right." Bethel laughed. "Come in the house."

"I don't have much time."

She kissed him again and gave him a coquettish smile. "Then let's not waste it standing out here where all the neighbors can watch us." She stopped in the doorway and waited while he tied the horse. The mule would stay close.

Inside, she closed the door behind them and fell into his arms.

By the time he came back outside an hour or so later, the black horse stood hipshot and appeared to be half asleep. The mule had strayed off a little way, grazing. Andy said, "Mrs. Bannister could already be pretty far along on the trail to Fort Concho. I stayed some longer than I intended to."

Bethel clung to his arm as he walked toward the horse. Her face was flushed, her eyes shining. She squeezed his arm and smiled. "Do you wish you hadn't?"

"No, except that you keep makin' it harder and harder for me to leave."

"All part of the plan. Maybe someday I'll convince you not to leave at all."

"The way I feel right now, I could ride over to the Ranger camp and tell Sergeant Ryker that I'm quittin'."

"Why don't you?"

"Because despite what they say, newlyweds can't live on love alone."

She said, "I think we could, for a while."

Andy awakened at first light, wondering if he smelled like a goat. Unable to find another suitable shelter away from house and barn, he had made a cold camp beneath a low-roofed shed, sharing space with twenty or so spotted goats. He had followed Geneva Bannister at a respectful distance and saw her turn the buggy toward a plain little ranch house. Hunched up beneath a yellow slicker, rain running off the brim of his hat, he had watched her go inside. Shortly afterward a man came out and took the horse and buggy to a shed. It was obvious she intended to spend the night there.

He had little hope that the man was Donley Bannister. It seemed unlikely that he would come back so soon and be this near to the scene of the shooting, but Andy had learned that fugitives could be unpredictable. He remembered one who had robbed the same bank a second time within a week, dodging posses still out hunting him for the first offense.

He waited for darkness before riding closer. Leaving his horse and packmule tied, he walked to a side window and cautiously looked inside. Geneva sat at a table, in earnest conversation with a man wearing the plain clothes of a rancher or farmer. Andy did not recognize him, but he knew this was not Donley Bannister.

Perhaps he was kin of Geneva or Donley, or he might be simply a stranger with whom Geneva had sought shelter on a rainy night. If that was the case, Andy thought, Donley had better be broad-minded about his wife. Even a tolerant man might scratch his head over this situation. There did not appear to be another woman in the house.

Somewhat later, from beneath the goat shed, Andy saw the man carry blankets to the barn. He did not return to the house. Though it was none of Andy's business one way or the other, he felt a measure of relief.

Damp, chilled, Andy did not sleep much. He kept thinking about Bethel. He had much rather have spent the night with her. Instead, he had to settle for the goats and the shed's accumulated odors.

Next morning the man milked a Jersey cow and carried the milk to the house. He sat the bucket on the porch and knocked on the door. Geneva opened it, smiling. The man touched the brim of his hat in response. Smoke rose from the chimney, reminding Andy that after spending the night in a cold camp, he was not going to have breakfast for a while, if at all. At least it was no longer raining.

After an hour or so, the man ventured out and hooked Geneva's horse to the buggy. Andy kept low. He watched the man help Geneva up onto the seat, then take off his hat as she extended her hand to him, holding for a long moment. She set off to rejoin the trail that would continue taking her toward the Conchos. Andy waited until she was three hundred yards along before he caught up his animals and rode down to the house. He knew she would move far ahead of him, but he could catch up.

The man was at the barn, saddling a horse. He looked up in surprise at Andy's approach. "Howdy," he said affably. "All of a sudden I'm gettin' a lot of company. Somethin' I can do for you?"

Andy said, "You can tell me about the lady who just left here."

"Mrs. Bannister? Ain't much to tell. I never met her before yesterday evenin'. How come you to ask?"

Andy showed his badge. "I'm a Ranger. Name's Andy Pickard."

"Mine's Jess Nathan." A worried look came into the man's eyes. "Is she in trouble?"

"She's not, but her husband is. Did she tell you about him?"

"She called herself Mrs., so I knew she was married. I didn't think it was my place to ask personal questions. I did get a feelin' that everything ain't just right."

"Did she say where she's goin'?"

"No. I figured if she wanted me to know she'd tell me, and she didn't." Nathan frowned. "Look, Ranger, she struck me as bein' a real nice lady. I wouldn't want to see her hurt."

"I'm afraid that's already happened. There's not much me and you can do about it. You're sure she didn't mention where she's headed?"

"She didn't. And to be truthful, I don't believe I'd tell you if she had. Like I said, she's a nice lady. I wouldn't want to add to whatever problems she's already got."

Andy sensed that Nathan had become mildly infatuated with Geneva Bannister. He had suspected she had the same effect on Addison Giles and the liveryman Spence. He would bet that Nathan had not slept well last night, lying in the barn and thinking about the woman sleeping in his bed.

He said, "Maybe you'll feel different if I tell you the whole of it."

Nathan appeared dubious, but he said, "Come on down to the house. I suspect you haven't had any breakfast."

"Nor much of a supper yesterday. I stayed all night under your goat shed."

"I slept in the barn. You could've joined me."

"I didn't want to tip my hand too early."

Nathan fried bacon and eggs and listened without comment while Andy told him what he knew about the trouble between Donley Bannister and the Slocums. While Andy wolfed down the breakfast, Nathan said, "I know about the Slocums, a little. They've made a couple of sashays up into this country, carryin' off cattle. Even stole sheep one time. A man has got to be low to steal sheep."

Andy said, "That's their reputation."

"But if you're followin' Mrs. Bannister to try and find her husband, who can say that the Slocums ain't doin' the same thing?"

"They tried at first. She got them decoyed away on a wild-goose chase."

"But she didn't shake you off."

"She almost did. She's a sharp lady."

"But like you say, a lady."

Andy finished his eggs. "It'd be better for her and her husband if I find him and bring him back to stand trial. The talk around town is that no jury there would convict him. The only thing the folks blame him for is that he didn't kill the other Slocums too. But if he doesn't come back and get cleared, he'll stay on the run and drag her along with him."

Nathan considered. "I didn't lie to you. All she said was that she still had a long ways to go. She didn't tell me where."

"Clean out of Texas, maybe."

"Maybe. She was headed north. There's a lot of country between here and the Canada line."

Andy grimaced. "I doubt that the money counters in Austin would pay my expenses to go as far as Canada."

"I wish I could go along and help you. I can see where it'd be a favor to her in the long run. But I've got my livestock to take care of, and a crop that'll need weedin'."

"I started by myself. I'll go on by myself. But much obliged for the thought. I wish I could stay and get better acquainted."

"She's got an hour or so start on you."

"That buggy'll leave deep tracks in the mud."

Putting his horse into an easy lope, Andy caught up. He held back just out of sight, occasionally moving close enough to be sure she had not changed direction. A rider came along, heading south, leading four horses tied head-to-tail. Geneva stopped him. They talked for a minute, and he pointed northwestward.

As the horseman approached him, Andy raised his hand in greeting. "Howdy," he said. "I'm tryin' to catch up to a lady in a buggy."

The rider hesitated. Andy pulled his jacket open to reveal his badge.

The rider said, "I met her. She wanted to be sure she was still on the right trail to Fort Concho. I told her she was."

Andy started to ride on.

The rider asked, "Is the lady married?"

"I'm afraid she is."

"Seems like the best ones always are. I guess I'll have to keep lookin'."

"Good luck," Andy said, and put the black horse into a

trot. The little packmule followed as if it were tied to the horse's tail.

Fort Concho had been built at the confluence of three rivers. Its original mission had been to protect travelers from Indians on the San Antonio–El Paso road. Now Indian hostilities had ended except for Apache raids far to the west. The fort seemed to be marking time, awaiting closure. It was still home to the Tenth Cavalry Buffalo Soldiers, however, and was a vital source of revenue for the fledgling town of Santa Angela on the north bank of the Concho River. Though the citizens by and large had a strong prejudice against black soldiers, that prejudice did not extend to the money they spent.

Because it was late afternoon, Andy felt it likely that Geneva would spend the night in town before traveling on. He discounted the possibility that she might meet Donley here. This was only about a hundred miles from the scene of the shooting. Every sheriff within two hundred miles probably had his description.

Andy's first move was to visit the post and dispatch a wire to headquarters. He wrote it in longhand, wishing he had taken school more seriously when he had the chance.

I wish to report that I have arrivved at Fort Concho. Am keeping Mrs. Bannister in site. No sine yet of her husband. Will follo unless orderd otherwize.

He was surprised that the telegraph operator was black. He had heard that most buffalo soldiers were illiterate, a result of their upbringing in slavery. The trooper read the scribbling and smiled. He said, "Be all right with you if I correct the spelling?"

"Go ahead," Andy said. "I didn't know there was anything wrong with it."

The wire was sent. The operator asked, "Do you want to wait and see if there is any answer?"

"I'll be back and check with you before I leave town."

He crossed the river and presented himself to the sheriff, as was customary. He briefly explained his mission. The sheriff, a middle-aged man of solid build, removed a smoking cigar from his mouth and asked, "Need any help?"

"I believe I've got it under control. I expect I'll be movin' on in the mornin'."

"Where are you stayin', in case a message comes for you?"

"At the wagon yard. The only place cheaper is the riverbank. My horse and packmule have earned some grain."

He remembered the wagon yard from a previous visit. Looking over the animals in an outdoor pen, he recognized Geneva's buggy horse. He visited with the hostler while he unsaddled his black and removed the pack from the mule. He pointed toward the buggy horse. "Nice-lookin' animal," he said. "Reckon it's for sale?"

The hostler shrugged. "Not as I know of. It belongs to a lady who came in a while ago." He nodded toward Geneva's buggy, parked beside the barn.

"Reckon where she's stayin'? I might decide to ask her about the horse."

"I told her Mrs. Tankersley's hotel is a nice place."

"Are you sure that's where she went?"

"I watched her all the way. Pretty women like that don't come in bunches."

Andy would like to rent a hotel room too, but Ranger budgets did not provide for luxury. He would sleep on a cot in the wagon yard. At least that would be off the ground.

The hostler warned, "You may have a hard time sleepin' tonight. The soldiers got paid today, and they'll be noisy. It's a caution how quick they can drink up thirteen dollars."

"Even us Rangers get paid more than that." Andy immediately wished he had not spoken. He had put his badge in his pocket, not intending to noise it around that he was a Ranger.

The hostler quickly put things together. "Then you ain't really interested in that horse. You're interested in the woman. Did she kill somebody?"

"She didn't do anything except maybe marry the wrong man. I'm hopin' she'll lead me to him."

"If you shoot him, she'll make a fine-lookin' widow. Every bachelor in the country will be after her. And some that ain't bachelors."

"I don't figure to shoot him. I'm supposed to bring him in so a jury can find him innocent and turn him loose. Then he won't have to be on the run anymore."

"If he's innocent, I don't see no reason to try him in the first place. It's a waste of the taxpayers' money, and I'm a taxpayer."

"Naturally it's wasteful. It's the government."

Andy walked down Chadbourne Street and found a café. He splurged on a two-bit meal. While he sat finishing his last cup of coffee, two black soldiers paused at the door and looked in. The proprietor gave them a threatening frown, and they moved on.

The man said, "I'll be glad when they shut down the fort and all those dark-complected Ethiopians are gone."

Andy did not speak his thoughts, but it seemed likely

that some of the town might shut down when that happened. He remembered something old Preacher Webb had told him years ago: the worst punishment God could inflict on the world would be to give people everything they wished for.

Returning to the wagon yard, he took his blanket roll and spread it on a steel cot. The hostler came and said, "I hope you're not a smoker. A careless cowboy come near burnin' this place down a while back."

"A man is entitled to only so many vices. I don't waste mine on tobacco."

Tired, Andy quickly dropped off to sleep. Sometime later he was awakened by boisterous shouting and celebratory gunshots. He raised up on one elbow but could see little in the darkness. A lantern burning near the open barn door showed him nothing. He tried to settle back down to sleep but kept being jarred by the noise. Occasional shots continued to be fired. After one, he sensed that the tenor of the shouting changed. It turned angry. Footsteps indicated that men were running. Somewhere a window was smashed, and another.

Hell of a place to get any sleep, he thought, and turned over for another try. He had managed to doze off when someone shook his shoulder. "Ranger, wake up. The sheriff says he needs you."

In the darkness he could not see the young man's face. He asked, "What's the trouble?"

"Somebody shot one of them darkey troopers, and now there's hell to pay. The soldiers are swarmin' across the river lookin' for the man that done it. If they don't find him, just about anybody else will do."

Pulling on his boots, Andy asked, "Where's the sheriff now?"

"At the jailhouse. He's locked up the man that pulled the trigger, but he may not be able to keep him. He needs all the help he can get."

Andy put on his holster belt. He said, "This sure isn't the way I intended to spend the night. I wasn't plannin' on havin' to shoot anybody."

"You never know what you may have to do around here come payday."

Andy did not count the soldiers who clustered in front of the jail. To do so would probably scare him. Many were armed with rifles and pistols. Others carried driftwood clubs picked up along the river. They shouted furiously at the sheriff and another man, evidently a deputy, standing in front of the door. The sheriff held a shotgun close to his chest. The deputy had a rifle.

Andy saw a pathway open up between the members of the mob. He rushed through it, the young man following. Someone grabbed at him, but he jerked loose and joined the sheriff and deputy at the door. Soldiers grappled with the young man and prevented him from getting that far. The sheriff raised one hand, calling for quiet. It was slow in coming, but most of the shouting died down.

"You soldiers," he said, "I'm callin' on you to go back across the river. There's been killin' done, but the man that did it is behind bars. He'll stand trial accordin' to Texas law."

A soldier with sergeant's stripes shouted, "And get turned loose, like they always do?"

"That'll be up to a jury."

"A white jury," the sergeant declared. "You think they'd ever convict a white man for killin' one of us?"

The sheriff shouted, "I don't want to shoot anybody. But I would do it to protect my prisoner."

The crowd surged forward. The sheriff tried to swing the shotgun into line, but someone struck him on the head with a heavy club. He went down. Hard-hit, the deputy went to his knees too. Andy reached for the sergeant who had shouted loudest. He grabbed him by the collar and shoved the muzzle of his pistol against the man's neck. "Now you-all back away," he ordered. "I don't want to kill anybody, but I've got my finger on the trigger. If anybody jostles me, this pistol will go off."

The sergeant yelled, "Don't nobody jostle him."

The troopers moved back a little. Andy found himself looking into the muzzles of a dozen or more guns. His heart hammered. Any one of them could kill him in an instant. He tried to hold his voice steady, but it quavered. He said, "If anybody shoots me, I'll pull this trigger as I go down."

He had found over the years that the ones who shouted loudest were usually the first to cave in. The sergeant begged the others, "Back away. He'll blow my head clean off."

An angry buzz showed the troopers were still in a mood to fight, but their comrade's plea stayed their hands.

Andy seized the moment. "Everybody ease back. No use in anybody else gettin' bloodied up. Payday is supposed to be a time to celebrate, not to get yourselves killed."

A soldier demanded, "You guarantee that the prisoner will pay?"

Andy knew the realities. "I guarantee he'll be tried. I can't promise you anything beyond that."

"Then he'll go free. They always go free. A soldier's life ain't worth six bits in this town. Not if'n he's black."

Andy kept his grip on the sergeant's collar but lowered the muzzle an inch. It appeared to him that the mob's anger had peaked. The men had had their confrontation, and several had had their say. Gradually they began fading back into the darkness. A few loitered a short distance away, watching, muttering empty threats.

Andy told the sergeant, "I'm puttin' you in jail for the night."

"What for? All I done was talk."

"Sometimes talk can do more damage than a gun."

The rioters had released the young man who had summoned Andy. He knelt beside the sheriff and said, "Looks to me like he's out cold. The deputy don't look good either."

Andy said, "Help me get them inside, then you better run and fetch a doctor. I'll lock the door."

The sergeant voluntarily helped carry the two lawmen into the jail and place them on cell cots. He asked, "You really goin' to lock me up?"

Andy nodded. "That way your friends won't come back and burn the jailhouse down." He frowned. "You've got to realize that what you-all did here tonight was wrong."

"As wrong as shootin' a soldier in cold blood? We was just tryin' to get justice. There ain't no other way we'll see it around here."

Andy recognized the futility of arguing, for the sergeant was right. "I know. Maybe someday things will be different."

"Someday. That's what they always tell us when they

want us to stand back and be quiet. It'll be better some-day."

"I wish it was otherwise, but it isn't. Probably won't be till we've been dead and buried for a hundred years."

Two men were locked in separate cells. One appeared to be a cowboy overloaded on whiskey. Andy assumed the other was the man who killed the soldier. After taking a sidearm from the sergeant, he pointed him into an empty cell and asked, "For the record, what's your name?"

"Joshua Hamlin. *Sergeant* Joshua Hamlin. When you write it down in the book, don't forget the *sergeant*. I been a long time gettin' that far."

The sheriff was stirring a little. He mumbled incoherently, vigorously moving his hands as if he were fighting. Blood had trickled down the side of his head and into his collar. Andy found a water pitcher and wash pan. Using a wet towel, he wiped away as much blood as he could. It continued to ooze slowly.

The deputy had raised up. He sat on the edge of his cot, holding his head with both hands. He let out a sharp oath when Andy inspected his wound. He wheezed, "What did they hit me with, a sledgehammer?" He opened his eyes wide, evidently having trouble focusing. "They didn't get the prisoner, did they?"

"No, he's still safe in his cell. I'd like to go in there and stomp the clabber out of him for the trouble he's caused."

"I'll do it myself when I get my feet under me. How's the sheriff? I saw him go down before I did."

"He took a bad lick. I've sent for a doctor."

Andy heard a knock on the door, then the young man's voice. "Ranger? It's us—me and the doc."

He unlocked the door and pointed the doctor toward the sheriff. He said, "He took a mean blow to the head. Hasn't come around yet."

The doctor set his black bag on the floor beside the cot and bent over the mumbling lawman. "I'll see what I can do."

Andy wandered back for his first good look at the prisoner accused of the killing. The register showed his name to be Ephraim Burnsides. That seemed too high-sounding to be real. Probably made up, he thought. The culprit looked like a road tramp. Eyes defiant, he smelled of whiskey but appeared cold sober. A close call like tonight's should sober up anybody, Andy thought.

The prisoner regarded Andy with apprehension. He demanded, "Who the hell are you?"

"A man who's tryin' awful hard not to go in there and beat out what little brains you've got. Do you have any idea the hell you've stirred up?"

"I don't let no darkey get uppity with me. He sassed me, so I shot him, like any self-respectin' white man would do. I don't see anything wrong with that."

"You got the sheriff and his deputy both hurt tryin' to protect you."

"That's their job. It's what they get paid for." The prisoner stood up and gripped the bars. "How long they goin' to keep me in here?"

"I've got a good mind to turn you loose right now and set you on the street. I wonder how long it'd take for the soldiers to rip off both your arms and beat you to death with them."

Fear flickered in Burnsides's eyes, then evaporated

quickly. He knew as well as Andy did that such a thing could not be allowed to happen. He said, "You're responsible for takin' care of me."

"Not me. I'm just passin' through. The local law is responsible, and it's layin' out yonder helpless on account of you." He placed a hand on the cell door. "Now, do you want me to turn you loose?"

The prisoner retreated to the back of his cell. "Go to hell," he said.

The doctor's face was grim. He told Andy, "Neither man will be able to do much for a while. I understand you are a Ranger."

"I am."

"Then you'll have to take over here, at least for now."

"But I've got another job to do."

The doctor shook his head. "Right now this town is sitting on a ton of black powder. It's just waiting for a spark. For the moment that is more important than your assignment, whatever it may be."

Andy saw his point, but he knew also that several roads led out of Santa Angela. He could only guess which Geneva Bannister might select while he was tied up here, guarding a prisoner who did not deserve all this attention. He nodded toward the young man. "What about him?"

"He is not an officer. He is the sheriff's nephew. I am sorry, Ranger, but you have inherited the responsibility, like it or not."

Andy swore in frustration. He was at a fork in the road. Both roads called to him, but it was painfully clear which was the most urgent.

"You're right," he said in regret. "I've got no choice but to stay."

From time to time during the night, he stepped outside to look and listen. The town had gone quiet, deceptively peaceful. He sensed that it slept fitfully at best. Sleepy-eyed, he watched the first bright rays of sunshine break in the east and hoped the long dark hours had cooled tempers on both sides of the river.

Andy unlocked the cowboy's cell. He asked, "You got someplace to go?"

"Back to the ranch. Done spent all my money."

"Then you'd better get started. If the trouble comes back, you don't want to be caught in the middle of it."

"Much obliged. I was in a cold sweat last night, thinkin' they might bust in here and not know which of us to lynch." The cowboy picked up his belongings but paused at the door. "I don't reckon you could lend me five?"

"Git before I change my mind."

"Next time I may take my business to a different town." The cowboy disappeared down the street.

The sheriff struggled to his feet to relieve himself. He seemed disoriented, lost. The deputy was more stable but said he had the worst headache of his life. He was seeing double. He said, "I hope you'll stay a while, Ranger. I couldn't blow a hole in the wall with a double-barreled shotgun, and the sheriff is worse off than I am."

"I don't see where I've got a choice. I'll stay as long as I'm needed."

He badly wanted to go to the wagon yard and watch for Geneva to move, but he dared not leave the jail while the prisoner remained in it.

At mid-morning an attorney showed up, wearing a black swallowtail coat and an officious expression. He said, "I have here a court order for the release of Ephraim Burnsides."

Andy had expected this. His opinion about most criminal lawyers was that they were well-named. He answered that the sheriff was incapacitated and unable to acknowledge the order. "You'll have to wait till he's in better shape. That may be a couple of days."

The attorney argued, "What is your capacity here?"

"I'm a Texas Ranger, passin' through on an assignment. I've got no authority to let your man go."

"On the contrary, because you seem to be the only officer here in possession of his faculties, I contend that you do have the authority. I demand that you release Mr. Burnsides. Otherwise I shall have no choice but to bring the judge and force you into compliance."

Andy's stomach soured at the prospect of releasing the prisoner. He said, "His life will be dirt cheap once he walks out into the street."

"It is the responsibility of the law to protect him."

"The *local* law. Look at them. They're in no shape to help anybody."

"There should be no problem from the soldiers. The commanding officer has ordered all military personnel restricted to the post."

"Let me see your warrant."

The paper showed that bail had been paid in the amount of one hundred dollars. Andy said, "That's not much of a price to place on a soldier's life."

"A *black* soldier," the attorney pointed out. "From time to time those people have to be reminded of their proper place."

Grudgingly Andy signed the release order. He fumbled through two rings of keys before he found one that fitted the lock. Burnsides showed no gratitude. He growled, "Good thing you didn't hit me last night, Ranger. You'd be takin' my place in that cell."

"Get out of here before I hit you anyway. I was in the middle of a job, and you've probably blown it to hell." To the lawyer Andy said, "You'd better collect your fee right now. If your client has got any sense, he'll clear out of town and never come back."

"But that would forfeit his bail."

"A hundred dollars? That's not much of a price to put on a life, white man or black." Andy reconsidered. "In his case, it may be too much. Half that would be about right."

Burnsides said, "I need a drink. A bunch of drinks." He jerked his head, and the lawyer followed him.

Andy felt an emptiness, seeing Burnsides walk out into the open sunshine. As the rioters had predicted, he was escaping justice. It was a foregone conclusion that even if he went to trial, a white jury would acquit him. It was the tenor of the times.

Andy approached the black sergeant's cell. "Do you think you've simmered down enough that I can afford to let you go?"

Hamlin looked toward Burnsides's cage. "You turned him aloose."

"I had to. His lawyer served me with a court order. But he'll stand trial."

"He'll go free, like they always do."

"I can't argue with that. But I'm offerin' you a chance to leave if you want to take it. Or you can stay in here."

"That cot is way too hard for my achin' bones. I'll go."

The soldier picked up his belongings, which amounted mainly to eleven dollars, a large pocketknife, and the army pistol. Andy asked him, "Where did you come from, Sergeant?"

"Mississippi. I was born a slave, but we got emancipated when I was still too young to move cotton bales. By and by the army come along lookin' for some of us to be soldiers. Said it was our chance to be somebody." His face twisted. "Bein' somebody don't mean some lowdown white trash can't kill us any time they take the notion."

Andy said, "You'd best head straight to the post. I'd hate to see you back in here."

"I'd hate to *be* back in here." In a minute Hamlin was out of sight.

The sheriff was asleep again, his head wrapped in a white bandage. The deputy sat in a horsehide chair, eyes pinched in pain.

Andy said, "Since we don't have a prisoner to worry about, I need to walk over to the wagon yard and check up on things."

The deputy said, "Take your time. We ain't goin' nowhere."

As Andy had feared, Geneva had left town soon after daylight. The hostler offered no information about the direction she had taken. She could have chosen the west, which would take her to the Pecos River and beyond. But she might run into Apache trouble there. She could have gone east, toward Fort Worth, or she could have traveled northward, toward the cross timbers and the rolling plains. He decided to take his horse out a while and try to pick up her tracks. At least when he left here he might have some inkling about her direction.

He picked the western road, traveling it for a time without seeing tracks he could be sure were left by the buggy. He circled around to the north road. Again, if her tracks had been there, later travelers had obliterated them. He had no more success on the trail east. He started westward back toward town, frustrated. He would have to stop at Fort Concho and send a wire to headquarters. He hoped his superiors would understand that the situation had been taken out of his control.

At the edge of town he saw a horseman moving toward him at a steady lope. Andy discerned that he wore a soldier's uniform. Close up, he recognized the sergeant who had spent the night in jail. Hamlin rode a conventional stock saddle, not army issue. His brown horse had a brand, but it was not the army's U.S. Andy thought it likely that the mount was stolen.

He called, "Hold up a minute. I thought you were goin' back to the fort."

Without replying, Hamlin brushed past and galloped eastward. Andy started to follow and challenge him again but decided against it. If the sergeant was deserting, that was the army's business. Andy had trouble enough on his hands trying to keep up with Geneva Bannister.

He rode first to the post to send the wire. The same black soldier read Andy's message with a quizzical look in his eyes. "Still want me to fix the spelling?"

"Suit yourself. They pay me for ridin', not writin'."

The telegrapher tapped out the message on his key. He looked up and said, "Aren't you ever going to let Sergeant Hamlin out of jail?"

"I turned him loose several hours ago."

"He's never reported back in. Some of the boys are

afraid he's in trouble in that hog wallow across the river. Come dark, they may go looking for him."

"They'll have to look farther than Santa Angela," Andy said. "I saw him a while ago, ridin' like the devil was on his tail."

The telegrapher registered surprise. "It's not like Sarge to desert. You sure there wasn't somebody after him?"

"Nothin' was chasin' him but his shadow. It was havin' a hard time keepin' up."

The hostler met Andy as he dismounted at the stable door. His face flushed with excitement, he said, "I'm glad you got back. There's big trouble down the street."

Andy had seen no commotion at the fort. "Trouble?"

"That Burnsides, the one who shot the trooper yesterday. He got in a quarrel with a black soldier. Don't know who drawed first, but Burnsides took a bullet square in the brisket."

"Kill him?"

"He never took another breath."

"Sergeant Hamlin!" Andy declared. He remounted and moved down the street at a run.

He found a small crowd clustered around a body on the sidewalk. The deputy was there, his head bandaged from the previous night's ruckus. He looked up at Andy and nodded painfully. "Glad to see you, Ranger. We've got a messy situation here."

"So I heard." Andy dropped the reins and stepped up for a closer look. Burnsides was slumped there, soaked in blood.

The deputy said, "People say a soldier came up on him and started callin' him names. Burnsides drew a gun, but he was drunk and missed. The soldier was sober and hit what he aimed at. He grabbed a horse from a hitchin' post and took to the tulies."

Andy said, "It was Sergeant Hamlin, the one we had in jail."

"How do you know?"

"Because I met him on the east road. He was cuttin' a hole in the wind."

"Why didn't you stop him?"

"I didn't know about this. Chasin' deserters is the army's job."

"It's my job now." The deputy looked anxiously at the men in the crowd. "I'll need a posse."

Andy said, "Are you sure you're fit to ride?"

"No, but I'm better off than the sheriff is. I'll wire the peace officers around us to be on the lookout. Then I'll take some men and hit the trail."

"In that case, I'll be gettin' on about my business, if it's not too late." Andy doubted that the deputy's posse would catch Hamlin. More than likely, officers in another county miles away would intercept him. Meanwhile, innocent blacks were likely to suffer the painful consequences of mistaken identity.

He returned to the wagon yard to pick up his belongings and the packmule. The hostler seemed to be wrestling with a dilemma. He said, "I don't generally poke my nose into other people's business, and I didn't mean to tell you this. But you said it would be a favor to the lady if you took her husband back to stand trial. Maybe this'll help you a little. She asked me how far it is to Colorado City."

"Thanks." Andy paid him a dollar extra and struck off on the road north. His shoulder ached, but he pushed his mount into a lope. He had a lot of miles to make up.

5

Geneva Bannister looked back occasionally, watching for any sign of pursuit. She had been nagged by a persistent feeling that someone was behind her, but she had seen nothing. The Ranger who had kept her under surveillance in Junction had not fooled her for long. She was sure she had shaken him off just as she had shaken off the Slocums. She did not intend to let anyone use her to get to her husband.

The long trip had given her plenty of time to think about Donley. She had loved him, or she would not have married him. Over time, however, she had found reason to question her choice. Usually when he left he did not tell her where he was going or how long he would be gone. From the first he had been vague about his business, making her wonder if he had good reason to avoid explanations. When he returned he usually brought back a string of horses for sale. He always gave her money enough for food and other necessities. She could not complain that he was a poor provider, though he would have been a better one had he stayed away from poker tables.

She wondered about other things. After the initial honeymoon glow of their marriage, his passion had cooled. She did not believe he was finding pleasure in other women during his travels. In most respects he had a Puritan sense of right and wrong. Several times she had heard him express disapproval of men who cheated, whether at cards or with women. He had even less respect for women who strayed from the narrow way.

She found herself thinking now and then about the rancher, Jess Nathan. He seemed stable, tied to his land and his memories. She wished Donley were more like him.

The stableman had said it would probably take her three days to reach Colorado City—four, if she wanted to be easy on the buggy horse. She decided not to push. It was still a long way to where Donley's letter had indicated he had gone. She did not want the horse to give out.

Unlike the night she had sought shelter at Nathan's place, the sky was cloudless, offering no hint of rain. As she had done most nights on the trail, she pulled off a short distance at dusk and stopped behind a cluster of trees that should hide her from anyone passing by. She fed the horse a bit of grain, then staked him to graze at the end of a long rope. She built a small fire and began to prepare a simple supper.

She had finished eating and was sipping coffee when she was startled by the sound of something moving through the grass. Setting the cup down, she fetched her rifle and waited with her back to the buggy. A horseman appeared around the trees and paused, looking first at the dwindling fire, then at her. Fear leaped into his eyes at the sight of the rifle pointed at him.

Quickly raising his hands, he stammered, "Ma'am, please don't shoot. I don't mean you no harm." He was black, and he wore an army uniform.

She asked, "What do you want?"

"I smelled the smoke of your fire and thought maybe I might find somethin' to eat. I'm powerful hungry."

Her strongest impulse was to drive him away, for she was afraid. Yet, she could sympathize with his hunger. Keeping the rifle trained on him, she said, "I didn't fix much, and I ate it myself. There is some bread I bought in town, and you can fry some bacon."

"I'd be mighty obliged, ma'am. My name's Joshua Hamlin. Don't be afeered of me. I'll eat, then be on my way." He dismounted, dropping the reins. The horse stood still.

She kept her distance while the soldier sliced bacon and dropped it into a skillet. She had been aware of trouble in Santa Angela but had not known the particulars beyond the fact that troopers from the fort had created a riot of sorts. The town had quieted down by the time she left soon after daylight. She suspected that this soldier had something to do with the trouble. He was probably running away.

The firelight revealed something she had not noticed. She said, "You have a stain on your uniform. Is that blood?"

He kept his head down, not looking her squarely in the eyes. "I'm afraid so, ma'am. I was in a fight."

"Is that your blood, or his?"

"His, ma'am."

She had a sudden hunch. "You've killed a man."

"He wasn't no man, hardly. But I expect there's folks huntin' me."

The soldier looked up. Geneva stepped backward, bumping against the buggy. She gripped the rifle harder and said, "Don't you come any closer."

The soldier said, "He killed one of my men. I knowed the law wasn't goin' to do nothin' about it. He needed killin', but I didn't set out to do it. I just figured to cuss him out real good. Then he drawed a gun, and I had to protect myself."

Needed killing. That was what Donley had said about Cletus Slocum. Geneva shivered, remembering.

The soldier said, "After I done it, I took out to the east, then cut back north. I reckon I shook them loose because I ain't seen nobody comin' up behind me."

That was similar to the tactic she had used to throw the Slocums and the Ranger off her trail. She said, "It's likely they've wired every sheriff around here. They'll be watching for that uniform."

"I ain't had a chance to swap for somethin' else."

She considered before offering, "I have a few of my husband's clothes in the buggy. See what you can find." She stepped away, giving him room. Almost immediately she wondered why she was aiding a fugitive. It was contrary to her normal inclinations. Perhaps it was because his situation seemed similar to Donley's.

The sergeant took a shirt and a pair of trousers. He was smaller than Conley, so they would hang loose on him. Even so, they would be less conspicuous than the uniform. He said, "Once again, ma'am, I'm obliged."

"Just take them and go." She let the rifle barrel sag a little, but she could raise it again in a second. "You'd better not stay on the trail. They'll be watching it."

"I've been hidin' durin' daylight and travelin' by night."

"Do you have anywhere to go?"

"Nowhere special, just someplace a long ways from here." The sergeant rolled the fresh clothes and tucked them under one arm. Mounting his horse, he said, "There's one more favor I wish you'd do for me, ma'am. If somebody was to ask, you might neglect to remember that you seen me." He rode away at a trot and was quickly lost in the dusk.

Geneva listened to the hoofbeats until they faded beyond hearing. Only then did she place the rifle back in the buggy. She was still trembling. In girlhood she had heard frightful stories about black men brutalizing white women. She had dismissed most of them as exaggerations, a hold-over of old anxieties about slave rebellions. The soldier's sudden appearance had brought them rushing back, arous-ing old fears. Yet, the man had made no threatening move toward her. He had seemed as frightened of her as she was of him.

He had admitted to a killing. If the person killed was white, the soldier stood a poor chance of living long enough to go to trial. His remaining time was likely to be short, and the end terrible. Despite the fright he had given her, she felt sympathy for him.

She was up the next morning before full daylight, mov-ing sluggishly, her eyes itching from lack of sleep. She had relived the previous evening a hundred times, occasionally slipping off into a nightmarish half sleep, dreaming of a shouting mob placing a rope around the soldier's neck and hanging him from a tree. Only, sometimes the victim was not the soldier—he was transformed into Donley Bannister.

Late in the morning half a dozen horsemen approached her from the north. As they pulled up beside the buggy, she saw a deputy's badge on one man's shirt. He touched fingers to the brim of his hat and said, "Pardon, ma'am, but we're lookin' for a man."

Geneva hoped nothing in her expression gave her away. "As you can see, sir, I am traveling alone."

"We got a wire to be on the lookout for a darkey soldier from Fort Concho. Seen anybody like that?"

"I can't say that I have." She consoled herself that it was not exactly a lie, just an evasive answer.

"There's a good chance he's ridin' north from Santa Angela. If so, he's probably still south of us." His voice darkened with concern. "You oughtn't to be travelin' alone, ma'am, with a murderer on the loose."

"A murderer! Who was killed?"

"A nobody who called himself Burnsides. We ran him out of our town a while back. But he was white, and a darkey shot him down while he was drunk. We can't let a thing like that just go by."

"I suppose not."

"If you're nervous, ma'am, I'll get one of these men here to ride along with you. Just in case."

"Thank you, but I have a rifle with me, and a pistol. I don't see that I have anything to worry about."

"Be on the lookout, then. No tellin' what a desperate man like that might do. Especially a darkey."

The posse continued south on what Geneva knew was a wild-goose chase. The lawman had indicated that the victim had been a man of no account. The soldier had told her as much too. She felt better about aiding him in his flight. Perhaps kind strangers had helped Donley in the same way. She would like to think so.

Donley had told her of a business acquaintance in Colorado City who owed him money. She needed it, for the trip had lightened the weight of her purse. Moreover, the buggy horse was wearing down from the steady pace all the way up from Junction. A couple of days' rest would be good for the horse as well as for her.

The western march of railroad building crews had prompted the birth of the town. Almost overnight, it had become a busy supply center as well as a cattle shipping point for a broad area of western Texas. Its buildings still looked new, the paint fresh. The lumber that had gone unpainted had not yet darkened from time and weather. She crossed the railroad tracks and picked out a likely-looking general store. Stopping in front, she started to climb down. A well-dressed man stepped up and extended his arms, offering to help her. She took him to be a banker or a lawyer. No one else wore clothes like these. Not many could afford to.

"That's kind of you, sir," she said. "Traveling alone, I have not had much help the last few days."

"You've been traveling alone?" The man looked shocked. "Madam, has nobody warned you that a black murderer is on the loose? He is being hunted in a dozen counties. Rumor is that he has killed two or three white men and forced himself on a couple of helpless country women."

She found it remarkable how quickly fear could create rumors far worse than the reality.

The man said, "They made a bad mistake sending those blacks out here to watch over us. It's they who need watching, not us. Anyway, you had better stay here in town till the killer is caught and disposed of."

Disposed of. The words gave her a chill. It sounded as if he were a mad dog to be dispatched without ceremony and dragged off somewhere for the buzzards to feed upon.

She changed the subject. "Do you know a man named Luther Fleet?"

The man frowned. "Fleet? Yes, but I can't imagine what a lady like yourself would want with him."

"My husband told me he owes us money."

"He owes money to many people. I would not wager a nickel on your chance of collecting. But be that as it may, he lives in a nondescript shack south of the railroad tracks.

You'll be able to recognize it by a belligerent bulldog he keeps chained at the front to ward off people who might want to do him injury. Those, I must say, are numerous."

The description took her aback. If Fleet were that disreputable, she did not understand why Donley would have done business with him. She asked, "What does he do for a living?"

"That, madam, is a question many have asked. Except for gambling, at which he exhibits some limited skill, he has no visible means of support." He tipped his hat. "You have my best wishes."

A little shaken, she contemplated moving on through town without bothering to see Fleet. But she needed supplies to continue her trip. The sergeant had almost finished the bacon, and she was short on flour, sugar, and coffee. She was unsure how far it might be to another town if she maintained her northerly direction. In the store she paid the merchant for the goods she bought, then counted the money that remained from what Donley had left for her. It was not much.

Like it or not, she needed to find Fleet.

The balding merchant, who reminded her a little of Addison Giles, loaded her purchases into the buggy. He said, "I assume your husband is waiting for you."

She said, "Yes, but farther on."

The merchant frowned as the other man had. "This is not a good time for a lady to travel alone."

"You're thinking about the fugitive soldier? The chances are that he is nowhere around."

"Then again, he could be watching us this very minute. Were I you, I would stay in town until he's caught. You can find good accommodations at Mrs. Kelly's boarding house, across the street and down yonder a way."

"I'll consider it. Thank you for your concern." She knew she could not afford to stay in the boarding house unless Fleet paid up.

The merchant gave her a lift into the buggy. She drove to the corner, turned and crossed back over the tracks. She followed a dirt street past a couple of low-order saloons and through what she easily recognized as a small red-light district. Two hundred yards beyond was an unpainted shack. Behind it stood a barn built mostly with used lumber, and a set of wooden corrals that held several horses. A bulldog waddled out from the shade of a narrow porch and strained against a chain, snarling as if it meant to do murder. Geneva had to pull hard on the reins to prevent the buggy horse from turning away.

She stopped in front of the house but did not climb down. She saw no way to reach the front door without passing too close to the dog. Soon she heard a man's voice from inside, "Dog, shut up out there!"

The dog did not let up. A pudgy, unshaven man came to the door and stood in his socks, his shirt unbuttoned most of the way down, the tail of it hanging out. Obviously the commotion had awakened him from a nap. "Damn you, dog, I'll take a whip to you if you don't quit that noise." He turned his attention to Geneva. "Who the hell are you, and what the hell do you want here?"

She was tempted to retort, *Nothing that you have*. But she could not turn away so abruptly. She needed the money. She said, "I'm Geneva Bannister."

"Never heard of no Geneva."

"Donley Bannister is my husband."

"Oh, Donley. Well, he ain't here. Ain't been here in a while."

"I know. I'm on my way to meet him."

"I don't see where that has anything to do with me."

"He said you owe him money. I need it."

Fleet scowled. "Who don't? Well, get down and come in. We'll talk about it."

Geneva nodded toward the dog. "Not till you tie him up short."

The dog continued a low growling. Fleet said, "Hush up, or I'll take a quirt to you." The dog quieted but watched Geneva with distrust. Fleet wrapped the chain around a post several times, shortening the dog's range of movement. To Geneva he said, "Now you can get down."

He did not offer to help her.

Though the dog could no longer reach her, she gave it a wide berth. She found the inside of the house as spartan as the outside. Newspapers had been pasted to the walls to serve as a cheap form of wallpaper, the house's only insulation. A half-empty whiskey bottle stood on a plain kitchen table.

"Drink?" Fleet offered.

The thought of drinking with him repulsed her. "No, thank you."

"Hope you don't mind if I take one. My stomach goes sour when I get woke up too fast from my nap." He uncorked the bottle and took two long swallows.

She said, "The money, Mr. Fleet."

"The money." He blinked as if he had already forgotten. "Well, now, that raises somethin' of a problem. I ain't got that much."

"How much do you have?"

"Just enough to start me in a game tonight. There's a couple of outfits in town to ship cattle. Their cowboys'll be ripe for the pickin'. I'll pay you in the mornin'."

"I do not intend to spend the night in this town."

"I don't see where you got any choice. I said I'll pay you in the mornin'."

"But I'm broke, almost. I can't afford a boarding house."

"You can stay here."

Her face warmed. "With you? Not on your life."

"Savin' it for your husband, are you? Well, you don't need to worry about sharin' the bed. I'll be playin' poker most of the night. When I come back, I'll sleep in the shed."

Geneva wanted to forget the money and rush out of this house, out of this town. But she could not get far with the little money she had left.

Fleet took the decision from her hands. He said, "Whatever you want for tonight, you better bring it in now. I'll put your buggy under the shed and throw your horse into a pen with mine."

She brought in two blankets, her purse with the pistol in it, and her rifle.

Fleet noticed. "You figure on huntin' bear? I don't think you'll find any in this house."

Crisply she said, "You never know what kind of animal might come prowling around."

He was grumbling as he drove her buggy to a low shed. She took the pistol from her purse and checked to be sure it was fully loaded. That evening she cooked supper, never letting herself stray far from the purse.

Fleet drank much of the remaining whiskey, his flabby face reddening and his eyes watering. He loosened up and began to talk. "Old Donley, he's a good judge of horseflesh. Him and me, we've made a right smart of money tradin' together. He knows where to get them for nothin' and where to sell them high. And he savvies how to steer clear of the sheriffs, too."

Geneva had suspected that Donley's horse business had a side that would not stand much daylight, but she had kept telling herself that her imagination was running wild. She tried not to hear everything Fleet was saying.

He slurred his words. "It's a long ways from Indian Territory down to that Junction country. Them Indians got more horses than they need, since they ain't goin' out on the warpath anymore. Fifty here, seventy there, they don't hardly miss them. And even if they do, the army won't let them off of the reservation to try and bring them back."

"You're telling me that you and Donley steal horses?"

"*Steal* is a strong word. After all, how else do you reckon them Indians got ahold of them in the first place?" Fleet gave Geneva a long, lustful study. "I can see why he picked you. He's always had an eye for good-lookin' horses. Women and horses ain't that much different. There's few things prettier than a slick, young mare."

Curtly she said, "I am not a mare, Mr. Fleet."

"But slick and young. I wonder how long it took him to unhook your buttons the first time."

Geneva felt warmth rising in her face. "You've said enough, Mr. Fleet. I thought you were going to a poker game tonight."

She wondered how he could expect to play successfully after putting away so much whiskey. But by the time he prepared to leave the house, his hands steadied, and he walked a straight line. Flexing his fingers, he said, "Whiskey sharpens me up. You watch, I'll trim those cowboys tonight. I'll take hide, hair, and all."

After he was gone, she checked the front door to see if she could secure it. There was no lock, nor was there a way to bar it. The best she could do was to brace a chair beneath the porcelain doorknob. She did the same for the back door.

She was tired, but she could not bring herself to lie in his bed. She spread her own blankets on the floor. She lay awake and fully dressed, listening to the sound of a train passing through town, to a piano playing somewhere down the dirt street, to boisterous laughing and whooping. Once she heard a couple of men talking loudly, approaching the house. The bulldog's chain snapped loudly as the animal ran to the end of it, giving the passersby a warning.

A man said, "That dog's lookin' for raw meat. This ain't the right house anyhow." The voices trailed away.

Geneva considered giving up and leaving before Fleet came home. She would have to go out the back door to avoid the bulldog. She could hitch her horse to the buggy and be a few miles north of here before sunup. But the purse contained little more than the pistol. She took it out for reassurance, knowing she might have to show it to convince Fleet to pay what he owed. She managed finally to fall into a restless half sleep, still hearing noises from outside, a night train passing.

She came suddenly and fully awake when she heard Fleet's voice. "Move aside, dog. I'm comin' in." Heavy boots tromped onto the porch. He pushed against the door. The chair held for a moment, then slid away and fell over with a clatter. A match flared. Swaying, Fleet lighted a lamp and held up a handful of bills.

"Told you, by God. I cleaned them boys to a fare-thee-well."

Geneva rose quickly to her feet, clutching the purse. "You were going to sleep in the shed."

"Changed my mind. You been lookin' down your nose at me like you was special and I was dirt. Now we'll find out which is the better man, me or Donley Bannister."

He lunged toward her as she dropped the purse and brought up the pistol. He grabbed her with strong arms, pinning her against him and forcing her back. She managed to place the muzzle against his leg as he pushed her onto the bed and fell on top of her. She jerked the trigger.

He screamed in pain and rolled away, his eyes wide with surprise. "You bitch! You shot me."

On her feet, she pointed the pistol at his groin. "I'll do it again if you don't leave."

He fell to the floor, crying, gripping his upper leg with both hands. "My God, I'm bleedin' to death."

"You will if you don't go and find some help."

Whimpering, he dragged himself to the door on hands and knees, leaving a trail of blood. He picked up the chair and used it to support the wounded leg as he dragged himself out onto the porch, then to the ground. Perhaps because of the blood smell, the dog attacked. It dug its teeth into Fleet's leg and clung until it reached the end of the chain. Fleet was yelping as he dragged himself up the street.

Daylight was three or four hours away, but for Geneva the night was over. She grabbed up what belonged to her, including the wad of bills Fleet had brought. She did not take time to count them, for this was no time to quibble over small matters. She hitched her horse to the buggy and crossed the tracks at a brisk trot. The business houses were dark, the streets quiet except for a few noisy cowboys weaving their way toward the shipping pens where their chuck wagons were camped. The moon was dull but yielded enough light that the trail north was easy enough to see.

She doubted that her husband and Luther Fleet would ever trade horses together again. And for a while, at least, Fleet would have little interest in ladies' buttons.

6

Andy had become acquainted with Colorado City during the long days he had spent there, being treated for the wound two stray outlaws had inflicted upon him. Geneva Bannister had a long head start, but he traveled faster on horseback than she could in the buggy on the road north-westward from Santa Angela. A posse riding south in search of the fugitive soldier had told him about meeting a lady traveling alone. He came within sight of her early on the third day and trailed well behind.

He shortened the distance as she approached Colorado City. He thought it conceivable, though unlikely, that she might meet her husband here. He watched her stop at a general store and talk briefly with a well-dressed man who definitely was not Bannister. Then she returned to the south side of the railroad tracks and pulled up in front of a plain shack that suggested something less than prosperity.

Presently she unloaded some of her belongings. A man bulkier than Donley took her buggy and horse to a shed. Perhaps he was a relative, or at least a family friend.

Watching him from a distance, Andy realized he had seen him before. His name was Fleet, and his disposition was sour. At the sheriff's suggestion, Andy had asked him about Bannister. Perhaps it made sense that Geneva Bannister was paying him a visit inasmuch as he knew her husband.

Confident that she would not travel on for a while, Andy crossed the tracks and rode to the courthouse. The sheriff greeted him with a handshake that could crush walnuts. "Thought you had a gutful of this town already. How's the shoulder?"

"Pert near healed. Still aches a little now and again."

"Comes from sleepin' on the ground too much. You ought to have a decent bed at night."

"Hard to manage when you're trailin' somebody. Besides, Indians say sleepin' on the ground is the healthiest way. They claim that healin' powers rise up from mother earth."

"So, who are you after this time?"

"It's still Donley Bannister. I don't suppose he's been back?"

"We haven't seen or heard of him. Right now everybody's huntin' for a soldier out of Fort Concho. Killed a man, they say."

"So I heard, but my job's to look for Bannister." Andy told about trailing Bannister's wife up from Junction. He described the shack he had seen her enter.

The sheriff's eyebrows lifted. "Sounds like Luther Fleet's place. When Bannister was here, before I found out he was wanted, Fleet and him visited the whiskey joints and gamblin' tables. Fleet played pattycake with the ladies while Bannister just played poker."

"Bannister didn't pay attention to the women?"

"A man can have strict morals about one thing but not about another."

Andy thought Geneva Bannister would probably be pleased to hear about this side of her husband's character, if she didn't already know.

The sheriff said, "Tonight you can sleep on a soft bed over at my house."

"Thanks, but I've got to keep an eye on Mrs. Bannister. I almost lost her at Santa Angela on account of the soldier trouble. I don't want to chance losin' her again."

The sheriff shrugged. "You might not get much sleep. Some cow outfits are in town. The only people who'll get much rest tonight are over in the cemetery."

"Sounds like Santa Angela after payday at the fort."

"You can't blame the boys for cuttin' loose. They don't often get to the big city."

The town had a long way to go before it could live up to the *city* part of its name, Andy thought. It was slim pickings compared to San Antonio, Fort Worth, or even Austin. But it must look like cowboy heaven compared to a ranch bunkhouse or lonely line camp.

He saw no reason to hurry, so he took time to drop in at the boarding house where Dr. Coleman had placed him for observation. Mrs. Kelly, the landlady, met him at the door, flour on her hands. She rubbed most of it into an embroidered apron tied around her ample middle, then gave him a brisk hug. Delighted at his recovery, the landlady asked about Bethel and Len Tanner. She told him in no uncertain terms that he was going nowhere until she fed him the best supper he had enjoyed since bidding farewell to his young wife. He did not object.

She said, "A drummer moved out yesterday, so your old room happens to be empty. You'll sleep in a soft bed tonight."

He had to tell her, as he had told the sheriff, that duty prevented his accepting the offer. He said, "Maybe when this job is done I'll come back here and sleep for a week." He knew that was unlikely.

"Be sure and bring Bethel. I declare, I don't see how you can keep going off and leaving that girl behind. There ought to be something better for you than being a Ranger."

"There is, when I can afford it."

After supper he rode back across the tracks to be sure Geneva's buggy was still in the shed where Fleet had placed it. A little farther on he found a vacant shack from where he could watch the Fleet house without being obvious. As darkness settled in, he saw Fleet leave the house and stride toward a saloon south of the railroad. Horses were tied in front, indicating that several cowboys were already there.

Sidestepping a growling bulldog, Andy peered through a side window into Fleet's house. He saw Geneva block the front and back doors by wedging chairs beneath the door knobs. Then she spread blankets on the floor. That surprised him, for he could see what appeared to be a perfectly good bed. At least this indicated that she would not be going anywhere tonight. He decided to watch Fleet instead. The man might know Bannister's whereabouts. With enough whiskey in his belly, perhaps he could be induced to share that knowledge.

Hopeful that Fleet would not remember him, Andy followed the man to the saloon. He entered, plunging into an invisible wall of noise. Laughing, singing, clinking bottles and glasses together, many of the cowboys appeared to have made an early start on the evening. Andy ordered a beer at the bar and watched Fleet seat himself at a poker table, a small roll of bills in his hand. The bartender carried a full bottle and a glass, setting them on the table beside him. Three cowboys approached Fleet. One said, "You won everything I had the last time I was in town. I want a chance to win it back."

Andy thought of a spider welcoming a fly into its web. Smiling cordially, Fleet said, "Welcome, cowboy, take a seat. All of you take a seat. This is your chance, because I'm feelin' unlucky tonight."

Andy took his beer to a table in a dark corner away from the several lamps and sat down to watch. From time to time he touched the glass to his lips but swallowed little. The level of whiskey in Fleet's bottle went down and down. In spite of that, the cowboys' money inexorably moved toward the gambler's side of the table. Andy knew within reason that Fleet was cheating, but at the distance he could not see how he was manipulating the cards. The other players were too deep into their whiskey to realize it.

Two men came through the door and paused to look around. Andy recognized the chuck wagon cook and the kid who had brought him to town after his wounding. Andy pulled his hat brim down and lowered his head, but he was too late. They walked toward him.

The kid said loudly, "Howdy, Ranger. Looks like you healed up all right."

Andy made a sign for quiet. In a low voice he said, "I

don't want everybody here to know I'm a Ranger. Just call me Andy."

The kid said eagerly, "You fixin' to arrest somebody? I want to watch you do it." Frowning, Cookie nudged the cowboy with his elbow.

Andy said, "Just watchin' a feller, is all." Motioning for the two to sit, he beckoned the bartender. "Bring them whatever they want."

The bartender demanded, "What about you? You've done nursed one beer for two hours."

Andy did not want to attract attention. "Bring me a fresh one." When the bartender turned away, Andy poured the remaining warm beer down a knothole in the pine floor.

The wagon cook licked his lips. "That's an awful waste."

"I need to stay sober."

Cookie turned to the kid. "That goes for you, too. We've got to herd these cowboys back to camp after a while. Otherwise they'll scatter like a bunch of Old Mexico steers."

The kid made no attempt to conceal his curiosity as he stared at Andy. "You ain't given up bein' a Ranger, even after gettin' shot? Next time, you're liable to end up with six foot of dirt in your face."

The cook said, "You've got no place to talk, tryin' to be a cowboy. If some bad bronc don't stomp your brains out, some wild cow will run her horn through your belly and out the tail of your shirt."

The men who sat in on Fleet's game dropped out one by one, their money gone. One groused, "You told us you felt unlucky. I'd hate to play you when you didn't."

The cook said, "Kid, it's time to haze them toward camp." Gradually the two managed to shepherd the cowboys out the door.

Fleet stuffed a large handful of bills into his pocket and told the bartender, "Look out there and be sure they're all gone. I wouldn't want them gettin' a notion to take it back."

The bartender stepped outside, then back in. He said, "All clear. Looks like you had a good night."

"It ain't over yet. I got somethin' even better waitin' at the house."

"Anybody I know?"

"Naw, she holds her nose too high for the likes of me and you. But I'll bring her down off of her high horse."

An ugly picture flashed in Andy's mind, sparking anger. Whatever she was or was not, Geneva did not deserve this. He realized that to intervene would tip his hand. She would know at once why he was here. Still, he could not simply stand back while Fleet carried out his intentions. He would do whatever he had to.

The bartender glared at him as he walked out the door. Andy had occupied space for perhaps three hours without adding enough to the till to pay rent on the table. He trailed fifty yards behind the staggering Fleet. Fleet cursed the dog and stomped up onto the porch. He pushed against the door. It resisted until he put his shoulder to it and forced it to give way.

Andy heard Geneva's voice raised in alarm and the sounds of a scuffle. Drawing his pistol, he sprinted up to the porch, ignoring the dog that nipped at his heels. As he was about to rush through the door, he heard a shot and Fleet's high-pitched scream. Fleet staggered to the door, squalling in pain. Andy realized that he need not show himself to Geneva after all. He jumped down from the porch and flattened himself against the side of the house as Geneva slammed the door behind Fleet.

The gambler stumbled across the narrow porch and down to the ground, trying to support himself with a chair. The bulldog attacked him. Fleet's cries ascended to a higher pitch.

Andy could only guess how badly the man was hurt. Fleet turned loose of the chair and began dragging himself on hands and knees, whimpering. Andy had come to help Geneva but now needed to help Fleet instead. He took the man's left arm over his shoulder. He said, "I see a light in that house yonder. Maybe they can give you some help, or send for it."

He helped Fleet onto the small porch and hammered his fist against the door. "Somebody! Got a hurt man out here."

Through the door's oval glass he saw the bobbing of a lamp being carried from somewhere in the back of the house. An angry-eyed woman in a low-cut nightgown opened the door and shoved the lamp into Andy's face. "We're closed for the night," she declared. "Go somewhere and sleep it off."

She was into her thirties, Andy guessed, with a hard mouth and too much color in her cheeks. He said, "This man's been shot."

She blinked. "Luther Fleet. Can't say I'm surprised. But what did you bring him here for? Look at him, bleedin' all over my clean porch."

"And apt to die here if we don't get it stopped."

The woman said, "Wait till I get an old blanket. I don't want blood all over the livin' room floor."

Andy said, "Grit your teeth, Fleet. Looks like the milk of human kindness has turned to clabber."

The woman brought a blanket, doubled it and spread it on the floor. "Lay him there."

Andy saw that the wound was in Fleet's leg, a long way from his heart. It could be dangerous, however. He could bleed to death, or he might even die from shock. Andy told himself he should muster some sympathy, but he regretted only that Geneva had not shot him a lot higher up.

He said, "Bring me some clean rags if you've got them. Towels would be better."

The bleeding slowed under the pressure of his hands and the towels. Andy said, "Fleet, I oughtn't to help you at all. I want you to tell me about Donley Bannister."

Fleet's face twisted in pain. He rasped, "Donley who? Don't know no Donley."

Andy squeezed the wounded leg. Fleet yelped like a kicked dog. Andy said, "Think a little harder. Maybe it'll come to you."

Fleet trembled, cold sweat glistening in his face.

Andy said, "For what you tried to do to that woman, I ought to let you lay here and die."

"Oh, God, no. You've got to help me."

"Only if you help *me*. Where can I find Donley Bannister?"

"I don't know, honest to God. All I know is that she's on her way to see him. Somewheres north, where he gets his horses. That's all she told me."

A man emerged from a back room, tucking his shirttail in. He was buckling his belt as he sneaked out the back door. An overweight young woman with tousled hair appeared from the same room, trying to close a flimsy housecoat. Wide-eyed, she bent over the bleeding man, then rushed out the front door to throw up. When she returned, the other woman said, "Flora, get some clothes on and go bring Dr. Coleman. I don't want this man to die here. It'd give the place a bad name."

Andy wondered what kind of name it already had.

The woman asked him, "How come I get the notion that you're some sort of a law?"

"You're right. I'm a Ranger."

"You must not be much of a shot, hittin' him in the leg."

Andy saw no reason to tell her the truth. He said, "I don't get to practice as much as I ought to."

The doctor came, grumbling about being rousted in the wee hours of the morning. He looked at Andy in surprise. "Ranger, I wouldn't expect to find you in a place like this. How's the shoulder?"

"A lot better than this man's leg."

The doctor knelt, setting his black bag on the floor. "Luther Fleet! I wondered when somebody was going to catch you drawing the wrong card."

Fleet whined, "She tried to kill me. Please, don't let me die."

Coleman said, "I'll do all I can. I know several people who would like to have a chance at you. I would not want to deprive them of that pleasure." He spent some time cleaning and dressing the wounds.

The woman said, "Doc, I want you to get him out of here."

Finishing up, Coleman said, "If I'm not mistaken, Fleet lives in that shack just down the road."

The woman nodded. "Him and that mean bulldog. A bullet in the brisket would be good for both of them."

The doctor said, "Andy, let's carry him out to my rig and take him home."

Andy had managed all the way from Junction to prevent Geneva's seeing him. He suggested, "What about the boardin' house, where somebody can look after him?"

Coleman shook his head. "This is one customer Mrs. Kelly would not make welcome. I do not wish to arouse her anger."

Andy beckoned the doctor out onto the porch and quietly explained his dilemma. He said, "I can help lift him into your rig, and help get him down. But I can't let Mrs. Bannister see me."

Coleman nodded. "Being a Ranger puts you into some unsavory situations, doesn't it."

"When you're huntin' a criminal, you don't look for him in the church house."

With both Andy and the doctor supporting him, Fleet whimpered all the way from the doctor's buggy to his porch. "Damned woman," he complained, "I owe her for this."

Andy said, "That's one debt you'd better forget about. Next time she's liable to shoot you in the heart."

The doctor said, "That would require a good shot, for it would be a small target indeed."

The bulldog threatened but backed away when Fleet cursed it. On the porch, Andy freed Fleet's arm and said, "He's yours, Doc."

The doctor said, "I can handle him the rest of the way." He pushed the door open and helped Fleet inside. He deposited the wounded man on the bed, then lighted a lamp. Andy backed away into the darkness.

Coleman returned to the porch. He said, "You were worried for no cause. There is no woman here."

Andy swore under his breath and hurried into the house

to see for himself. "She didn't waste much time gettin' away," he said.

Fleet whined, "I had three hundred dollars on the table. Robbed me, she did."

Andy said, "Like you robbed those cowboys tonight?"

Fleet cursed. "If I ever run into her again, she'll be sorry she ever saw me."

Andy said, "I'm sure she already is."

A partial moon showed him the way to the shed. He was not surprised that Geneva's horse and buggy were gone. He retrieved his horse and packmule from where he had left them staked. As he rode by Fleet's house, the doctor hailed him from the porch. Rolling down his sleeves, he said, "You are a peace officer. It is your place to give the sheriff a full report."

"I need to follow Mrs. Bannister."

"You won't be able to pick up buggy tracks in the dark."

Reluctantly Andy said, "I guess you're right." If he started now, in the dark, he might indeed take the wrong road, for several wagon trails led out of town in a more or less northerly direction. If he waited, other buggies or wagons might leave similar tracks. He would be unable to tell them apart. Still, protocol had to be considered. He would report to the sheriff, hoping he could find the right trail afterward. He seated himself on the courthouse steps. There fatigue caught up to him, and he fell asleep. He awakened to find the sun was up. He went to the restaurant and ate breakfast, watching through the window for the lawman to appear.

The sheriff arrived at his office after eight o'clock. Andy told him what had happened. He said, "She shot him in self-defense. I was fixin' to go in there and stop him, but she beat me to it."

The sheriff said, "I've been hopin' somebody would put Fleet out of my misery for a while. Too bad she left the job half done."

Andy laboriously scribbled a message on a sheet of paper. "I'd be much obliged if you'd wire this to Fort McKavett. They'll want to know where I'm at and where I'm headed."

"I'll take care of it."

"I hope Sergeant Ryker sends word to Bethel. I'd write her a letter, but God knows when she'd get it. Or if." He had rather dig a ditch than write a letter. Even to compose a brief message to headquarters was as slow as pouring molasses in January.

The sheriff asked, "How much farther do you think you'll have to go?"

Andy shrugged. "I've got my orders. I'll go wherever it takes."

7

In her rush to get away from Fleet's house and escape the town, Geneva had no time to reflect on what she had done or give way to anxiety. When the town was behind her, however, the pent-up fear and anger burst loose in a torrent of emotion. Stopping the horse, she shook uncontrollably, a rush of tears burning her eyes. She leaned out over the side of the buggy and vomited. She covered her face with her hands and cried as she had not cried in years. She vented her hatred of the man who had tried to attack her, then yielded to a suppressed resentment against Donley. Because of him, she was forced to endure this long, sometimes frightening trip alone. Because of him, she had fallen vulnerable to the likes of Luther Fleet. Now, for all she knew, she would be regarded as a fugitive from the law, just as her husband was. She could not be sure Fleet would survive the loss of blood.

She became aware of a lighted lantern coming toward her, bobbing in rhythm with footsteps. Instinctively she reached for the rifle. The lantern stopped moving. Its yellowish light showed her a middle-aged man with a derby hat and a paunch. He asked, "Are you all right, ma'am?"

She had trouble finding her voice. "I'm fine."

"I heard you cry out. I thought you might be hurt."

She could not see past him in the darkness. She asked, "Where did you come from?"

"Chuck wagon camp, right over yonder. I'm the cook, about to start fixin' breakfast."

"Up early, aren't you?"

"The cook always gets up early. Fact is, though, I just got back to camp an hour ago. I had to herd a bunch of cowboys in from town. There wasn't much point in goin' to bed, so I didn't."

"I'm sorry I disturbed you. I'll be moving on."

"You're out awful early yourself, ma'am. Seems to me you might be in some kind of trouble. Anything I can do to help you?"

She found his voice to be kindly, but she did not know if she could trust him. After tonight's experience, it might not be easy for a while to trust any man. She said, "It's my own problem. I'll work it out."

"Anyway, you look like you've been through a bad time. A cup of good, strong coffee might make you feel better. And I'll be fixin' breakfast before long."

The thought was tempting. Coffee might give her strength. "You're very kind."

"Swing that buggy off of the trail and follow me. It's just a little ways."

She saw the glow of a campfire, which laid a soft light on a wagon with chuck box attached.

The cook said, "Better stop here. You wouldn't want to run over any sleepin' cowboys, though there was a time tonight that I would've been tickled to do it myself." He helped her down from the buggy. He removed a wash pan from a three-legged stool and motioned for her to sit. "Hope you don't mind drinkin' out of a tin cup. I washed them all clean last night. Some of these cowboys don't care about such things, but I do." He grabbed the coffeepot by the fire and poured her a cup.

"Anything's fine," she said. The first taste burned her lips. She blew on the cup to cool it. Her hands still trembled.

The cook said, "I ain't pryin'. You don't have to tell me your troubles if you don't want to, but sometimes it's good to talk about what bothers you. It lets somebody else help you carry the load."

She said, "I shot a man tonight."

The cook looked startled. "Kill him?"

"I don't think so, but I should have. I just hit him in the leg."

The cook nodded. "I expect he had it comin'. Who is he?"

"His name is Luther Fleet."

She saw recognition in the arch of the cook's eyebrow.

"I know him. Gambler. Thief. In bad need of a neck stretchin'. You sure you didn't kill him?"

"He dragged himself away from there, squealing like a pig caught under a fence. He tried . . ." She stopped, ashamed to bring out the words.

The cook seemed to sense the rest of it. "You should've stayed and told the sheriff. He'd find a way to finish where you left off and make it look like Fleet started the fight."

"There's a good reason I didn't want to see the sheriff. I'm on my way to join my husband, and there are people who would like to know where he is. They tried a while to trail me."

"Are you sure they're not still behind you?"

"I've watched, but I've seen no sign."

"Has your husband got a name?"

She nodded. "Donley Bannister."

The cook grunted. "I remember him. He came by our camp some time ago. Went on, then came back and left a wounded Ranger with us."

Geneva gasped. "He shot a Ranger?"

"No, he said somebody else done it. He just happened to be there. Like as not, he saved the Ranger's life. Not everybody would've done it in his situation. We gathered that he was on the dodge."

Geneva pondered the irony. Donley had saved a Ranger, yet other Rangers were looking for him. Life could be hard to figure.

The cook said, "You'll feel better after a good breakfast. I'll get it started."

Geneva was concerned about letting more people see her. "I'd best be on my way."

"Don't you worry about any of these boys talkin'. Most

of them will be so hung over they won't remember you was here. The rest, well, they know I'd bend a pot hook over their heads if they told anybody whichaway you went."

Geneva looked toward the eastern sky. She saw no sign yet of sunrise. "Just a quick bite, then I'll be gone."

The cook busied himself with getting breakfast, greasing two Dutch ovens and molding balls of dough, fitting them into place. He heated gobs of lard in a deep iron skillet and dropped in strips of steak rolled in flour. He said, "It don't vary much from day to day, but neither does cow work." He frowned in thought. "Some of these boys have got a powerful grudge against Luther Fleet for cheatin' them at cards. Addin' what he done to you, I think the wagon boss'd allow them time today to pay the gentleman a visit."

Geneva was not prepared for that. "Surely you wouldn't lynch him."

"Nothin' that drastic. We'd just tickle him with the business end of a quirt and convince him that there's taller cotton someplace else."

She could see rough justice in the suggestion. "I wouldn't want you winding up in jail."

"The sheriff'd do this himself if the law didn't hold him back."

The cowboys were slow about emerging from their bedrolls, many groaning and belaboring the shortcomings of Colorado City whiskey. Geneva finished her breakfast before most got their feet under them. She told the cook, "I'm obliged for the breakfast, and the comforting words."

He gave her a lift into the buggy. "A pleasure, ma'am. And don't you worry about any of us talkin' out of school. We never saw nor heard of you."

First daylight was beginning to break in the east as she

left the camp and took the trail northward. Some of her faith in men had been restored.

Andy was still in the sheriff's office when the madam rushed in, short of breath and face flushed with excitement. "Sheriff," she said, "you better get yourself down to Luther Fleet's house. The way he's hollerin', they must be killin' him."

"Who?" the sheriff demanded.

"A bunch of cowboys. Must be seven or eight."

"Did you actually see them doin' anything to him?"

"No, but I heard him squallin' like a baby."

Winking at Andy, the sheriff lighted a cigar. "Reckon we ought to go down there and do somethin' about it?"

"Soon as I finish my coffee." Andy refilled his cup from a pot on the lawman's round-bellied wood heater. "He cleaned out a bunch of the boys' pockets last night. They've probably sobered up and realized he cheated them."

"We'll need to go down there after a while and talk to them. More coffee?"

"I just got a full cup."

The madam stared at them in exasperation. "I risk life and limb runnin' up here to tell you, and you're not goin' to do anything?"

The sheriff said, "We'll get around to it."

She said, "I've done my part. They can hang his hide on the barn door for all I care. And yours too."

After she left, the sheriff said, "I reckon we'd better get down there before the boys carry things too far. I'd hate to have to feed them all at the county's expense."

Andy was concerned about the time he was losing here while Geneva was on the move, but he feared the sheriff might need help. They rode together in the sheriff's buggy, across the tracks, then west along a well-beaten trail past the house where Andy had taken Fleet after Geneva shot him. Half a dozen horses stood around Fleet's shack. Several cowboys came out and caught up their mounts. Andy saw a derby hat and recognized the wagon cook among them.

Cookie headed off any potentially incriminating questions. "Sheriff," he said, "you better go see about Luther Fleet. Looks like he's done somethin' to himself."

"Like what?"

"Best we can tell, he was whippin' himself with a quirt, like them penitentes over in New Mexico."

The sheriff asked without much show of interest, "Is he dead?"

"No, he's still breathin'. Keeps sayin' somethin' about God. Is it all right with you if we ride on? We need to get back on the job before the boss fires us."

"You-all go ahead," the sheriff said. "Me and the Ranger can take care of it from here."

"*Muchas gracias.*" The cook frowned. "Bad enough him cheatin' the boys, but it was a lot worse what he tried to do to that woman."

The sheriff asked, "What woman?"

The cook caught himself. "One we heard talk about."

The cowboys rode away. Andy said, "The only way they could've heard about it was from Mrs. Bannister herself. She must've gone by their camp."

"It's north of town, just a little ways out."

Andy nodded with satisfaction. "Then I ought not to have much trouble pickin' up her trail."

The cowboys had shortened the leash so that the bull-dog could do nothing more than threaten. Entering the shack, Andy and the sheriff found Fleet sitting on the edge of his bed. His shirt was off, his long underwear pulled down to his waist. He looked up bleary-eyed, having trouble focusing on them. He whined, "For God's sake, don't whip me no more."

The sheriff said, "It's me, and a Ranger. We came to see if you're still alive."

"Not by much."

Fleet's back and shoulders were raw, laced with quirt cuts long and deep, seeping blood.

The sheriff said, "You thinkin' about filin' charges?" He made it sound more like a warning than a question.

"If I did, I doubt I'd live to testify."

"Probably not." The sheriff's tone was matter-of-fact. "It seems to me that you've worn out any welcome you ever had here. Was I you, I'd hunt for a place where the water runs free and the sun always shines. Somewhere a long way from this town."

Fleet grunted. "Soon as I heal up enough to travel. Between gettin' shot and then bein' worked over with a quirt, I'm gettin' damned tired of this place."

The sheriff poked a finger at him. "If you ever come here again, you'd better just be passin' through on the train, and you'd better not get off."

Fleet hunched his shoulders and grimaced in pain. "I can't think of nothin' that would bring me back. But you've got to give me time to sell out."

"I'll give you till Saturday. If you can't ride a horse by then, you can buy a ticket on the train."

"You're a hard man, even for a sheriff."

"If I was a hard man, I wouldn't have waited for a woman to shoot you. I'd've done it myself."

Walking away from the shack, Andy said, "I hope you won't do anything to the cowboys."

"Why should I? They said he quirted himself. It'd be his word against theirs. Justice don't always move in a straight line, but it generally finds its way."

Andy said, "Sheriff, I like the way you think."

"I don't see any other way of thinkin'. What's right is right, and sometimes what's wrong is right, too."

Riding north, Andy found the cowboys breaking camp. The cook and the kid were loading pots and Dutch ovens into the wagon, behind the chuck box. The cook said, "We'd offer you coffee, Ranger, but we just poured out what was left."

"Much obliged all the same, but I need to move on. I don't suppose you'd tell me if you've seen a woman pass this way in a buggy."

The cook looked Andy squarely in the eyes. "I don't suppose we would."

Andy nodded. He took that answer to be as good as if the cook had said yes. He said, "Don't work too hard," and rode on. He had no trouble finding and following the narrow tracks of the buggy.

The trail led him close to the dugout where he had been shot, but he had no interest in seeing that place again. He passed it by. So far as he could remember, it was a long way north to a town of any consequence. From here on for several days he would see little but a thin scattering of ranches, established in the wake of the buffalo slaughter. There had been some hide camps in the past, but those would be gone now. Instead of gathering buffalo hides, men with no better work to do were gathering buffalo bones to be shipped to Europe for the making of bone china.

Remembering the great shaggy herds he had seen as a boy, living among the Comanches who had captured him, he gave way to a fleeting melancholy for so much that had been lost.

At times the wagon road threatened to disappear, and with it, trace of the buggy. It was easy to imagine how the land had looked before, for it had changed but little. Cattle grazed now where the buffalo had been, but the landscape remained as he remembered it from boyhood, crisscrossed by narrow old trails beaten out by cloven hooves over uncounted generations. The Indians had survived here on what nature provided, little affected by distant events. The white man, living with and for his cattle, depended upon distant markets and took his chances upon prices set by others, hundreds and even thousands of miles away.

Andy had the feeling that he could even yet throw off most trappings of the white man's civilization and survive. That would not happen, however. For Bethel's sake, he had taken on responsibilities that would forever limit his personal choices. He might at times mourn the trading of complete freedom for a shared life, but he had resigned himself to it. He had chosen his path and could no longer change it.

He caught a hint of wood smoke. It was so quickly gone that he thought at first he had imagined it. When it came again, it was stronger. Somewhere off the trail, a campfire burned. His immediate thought was that he had overtaken Geneva Bannister. He reined up, his gaze carefully searching for the source of the smoke. At length he found it, ahead and off to the right. So far, her buggy tracks had not left the wagon trail. This must be someone else, for a couple of traveling hours remained in the day. She had not been in the habit of stopping early.

Warily, remembering the incident in the dugout, he checked his rifle, then his pistol. He kept to the lower ground of the rolling terrain, hoping to see before being seen. He was surprised by the sudden appearance of a man on horseback. The rider was no less startled. He froze for a moment. Andy recognized him as Comanche and raised his hand. The Indian lifted a rifle, then lowered it partway.

Andy had had little occasion to use Plains sign language in recent years, but what he needed came back to him. He indicated that he meant no harm and asked permission to come into camp. The surprised Indian hesitated, then signaled a reluctant welcome without lowering the rifle further. Approaching him, Andy reached back into memory for half forgotten words. They came haltingly.

"I am a traveler, like yourself," he said. The Indian wore no war paint. Andy guessed that he was a member of a small hunting party, off the reservation in violation of federal rules. Small groups now and then returned to old hunting grounds despite government prohibitions. Such forays were hazardous. Any whites they encountered were likely to assume they had hostile intentions and shoot them on sight.

The Indian's eyes narrowed in distrust. "How is it that you speak like one of us? You are Tejano."

"I was raised among the People. The Tejanos took me away from them."

"Did Father Washington send you to force us back?"

"I am with the government of Texas, not of Washington. I did not know you were here."

Sharply the Indian said, "This was our land. The Tejanos took it from us."

"I know." Andy also knew that the Comanches had taken it from the Apaches. He did not know who the Apaches took it from. "You are in danger here if anyone sees you."

"But there is hunger where the government wants us to live. We came here to find buffalo. All we find is bones."

"The buffalo are gone."

"Surely not all of them. There were so many."

"I have not seen one in years. I am sorry, Uncle, but they are truly gone. Only their bones are left." Andy saw sorrow in the man's face and felt sorrow of his own.

The hunter said, "I am tired of searching. You are welcome to come with me to camp."

Andy had never forgotten the contentment he had found in his brief boyhood years with the People. He felt a yearning to be in that company again, at least for a few hours. Wherever Geneva was, she would soon be stopping for the night. He could find her tomorrow. "It would give me pleasure."

The modest camp was well hidden in a hollow where its fires were unlikely to be seen unless someone came directly upon them. It consisted of a few buffalo-hide tepees smaller than those used in long-term camps.

Andy was the subject of intense scrutiny and some open expressions of hostility until he spoke in the Comanche language. As he explained the circumstances that had caused him to spend several of his boyhood years among the People, he sensed a positive change in the listeners' feelings toward him. He said, "If I had known you were here, I would have brought meat into camp." He had seen several antelope scattered to graze, watching him with curiosity, then flashing white rumps as they turned and fled. They would run a short distance, then stop to see if he was following. Finally they would cut in front of him and disappear over a hill.

An elder said, "We have antelope, but we had hoped for buffalo."

Andy could only express condolences. He smoked with them and listened to their unhappy talk about life on the reservation. They spoke longingly of better times when buffalo had been plentiful, before soldiers and government agents ruled their lives.

At length Andy asked, "Did anyone see a white woman traveling alone?"

The elder said, "We saw her. We did not allow her to see us."

"That is good," Andy said. "She might have shot at you." With Luther Fleet she had demonstrated her ability to use a gun.

"We feared she would bring the soldiers. Is she your woman?"

"No. I follow her because I need to find her husband. He has killed a man."

"The People kill our enemies, but we do not kill our brothers. The white man kills whoever stands in his way."

"Most don't. Those who do must accept punishment. It is my work to find them and bring them in."

"You are like a soldier, but you do not wear the blue."

"I am not a soldier. I am a Ranger." The old horseback warriors knew the Rangers from bitter encounters and shedding of blood by both sides.

The elder's face hardened. "Many times I have fought them. How can you be of the People, yet be one of those?"

"All things change. Now the People and the whites are friends."

"Only if we do what they tell us, and stay where they put us. It is a hard thing to live under the *teibo*'s rule and call him friend." He spoke of the whiskey peddlers, bringing with them degradation and despair. He spoke of horse thieves who raided the remudas and drove away the best of the People's mounts.

Andy shared antelope stew with the Comanches. These were not of any band he had known, though they recognized a few names he asked about. He was careful not to mention anyone he knew to have died. There was a taboo against speaking names of the dead.

He took a chance and asked about Steals the Ponies, who had been like a brother to him. The elder's eyes were clouded with sadness. "He lives, but he is sick of spirit. He has lost the one who was his wife. His son does not follow the old ways. He talks of going to the government school and becoming like the white man. It is hard for a boy to become a man now. He has no enemies to fight, no buffalo to hunt. They have taken all that from us. They are trying to make us all women."

Andy could only nod, for he had no argument to counter what the elder said. Someday, he thought, he should take time off and go to the reservation, to seek out Steals the Ponies and whatever others remained of those he had known. But it would not be a happy reunion. It would be more like a funeral.

As night fell and the fires died down, the Indians repaired to their tepees. They did not post a guard. Andy had long recognized this as a regrettable weakness that on occasion had brought disaster to them at the hands of their enemies. He rolled out his blanket and slept in the open. Once in the night he thought he heard a stirring of hooves. It did not happen again. He decided it had been caused by a couple of the Indian horses, staked beside their masters' tepees.

As first light spread across the rolling plains, he saw horsemen surrounding the camp. One glance told him they were soldiers, waiting for the Comanches to arise. That happened quickly as alarm swept like a whirlwind through the camp. Andy pulled on his boots and hat and walked out toward the nearest men. Several rifles were pointed at him.

"No need to shoot," he said, raising his hands. "I'm white."

A lieutenant pulled in front of the others, stopping just short of where Andy stood. "What are you doing with these Indians?"

"I happened across them late yesterday. I stayed the night with them."

"Man, don't you realize how dangerous that was? You are lucky you still have your hair."

"There's nothin' dangerous about these people. They're just hungry and huntin' for meat. They don't get enough on the reservation."

"How do you know?"

"They told me."

The lieutenant made no attempt to hide his suspicion. "*Told* you? How could you understand their language?"

"I lived with them when I was a boy."

"And you just happened across them? You weren't waiting here to sell them whiskey?"

"I wouldn't do that for all the money in Texas. Whiskey has been their ruination."

"We'd best take you back with us to the fort. You can plead your case to a higher authority than me."

Andy said, "I'm a Texas Ranger on official business." He took the hidden badge from his shirt pocket. "My name is Andy Pickard."

"I thought Rangers were supposed to shoot Indians on sight, not camp with them."

"That was a long time ago. Things are different now."

"Not all that much. What is your business here?"

"I've been trailin' a woman whose husband is a fugitive. I hope she'll lead me to him."

"What do these Indians have to do with it?"

"We just happened to cross paths."

"Then you will have no objections if we take them back to the reservation where they belong?"

"Objections? Hell yes, I've got objections, but I have no authority to do anything about it. I just hope you'll treat them decent. Try to look at the situation through their eyes."

The officer looked as if his stomach ached. "I have to look at it every day. Frankly, I don't like it any better than you do, but I am just a shavetail. The powers that be do not listen to second lieutenants." He gave a signal to the soldiers to start gathering the Indians. He asked, "Who is this man you're looking for?"

"His name is Donley Bannister. He killed a man down in Junction."

The lieutenant frowned. "Bannister? I know that name. As a matter of fact, we've been looking for him too. He's part of a horse-stealing ring that operates on the reservations and up into Kansas."

Somehow that was not a big surprise to Andy. "Down south he's known as a horse trader, but not as a thief."

"Where do you think he gets the horses to trade?" The lieutenant watched as the Indians finished gathering their scant belongings and mounting their horses. "By the way, we've been advised to watch out for a black soldier who murdered a man at Santa Angela. The authorities believe he came up this way. By any chance have you come across such a man?"

"I was at Santa Angela when it happened. I haven't seen him since."

"We'd like to find him before some lynch mob does."

"The outcome will be the same, won't it?"

"Hanging? Yes, but the army will do it with some civility."

Civility. Andy shook his head. No matter who did it, there would be no civility about it.

Flanked by the soldiers, the Indians began to move. Andy saddled his horse and rode up beside the elder. "I am sorry, Uncle."

Sadness dulled the old Comanche's eyes. "Nothing is like we knew it before. This land is no longer home. The reservation is not home. For the People there is no home anywhere."

Andy wished he could say something to bring comfort, but any such words would sound hollow and false. It was not in him to lie to this old man.

The elder said, "This is no life for one who has hunted

his own meat and fought his own battles. This is a slow death, and we die without pride."

Watching the Indians move east with the soldiers, Andy allowed scenes and sounds from his boyhood to drift through his mind. For a few moments he lived in the past before the distant bawling of a cow jarred him back to the reality of now. His throat swelled in grief for what had been but would never be again.

He turned away and rode west, hoping to come across the tracks of Geneva's buggy.

8

Andy's black horse was wearing down. So was Andy, but he was not yet ready to give up the search, though it had begun to appear a lost effort. He hoped to find a ranch where he might borrow, trade, or buy a fresh mount. The little packmule showed no signs of giving out, but a rest would be helpful for it too.

He had been seeing cattle, most bearing the look of longhorns brought up out of South Texas. Many ranches on the lower and high plains were being stocked with cow herds from the brush country below San Antonio. Some, showing English blood, were coming down from Colorado now that the buffalo slaughter had opened the range for cattle operations and the Indian troubles were over. He thought this was a likely-looking region for a ranch, but he already had his sights set on land far to the south, in the hill country.

He saw a wooden windmill tower and reined in that

direction. He found that it served what appeared to be a ranch headquarters. A box-and-strip house stood surrounded by scrub oak trees common to the cross timbers area. Beyond it stretched a long building which he took to be a bunkhouse. Barn, sheds, and corrals were set off at a respectable distance. A ranch wife would want her house to be well away from the outdoor facilities' flies and dust.

Three men were in a corral, breaking a young horse. Andy rode up to the fence and watched a cowboy hold the bronc by the ears while another swung into the saddle and pulled his hat down tight. The bronc pitched out across the corral. The rider lost one stirrup, which flopped about wildly as the horse jumped. The cowboy took a firm hold on the saddlehorn and managed to keep his seat. Sweating, the bronc circled the corral several times, gradually slowing as it went around. Finally it stopped, heaving for breath. The cowboy dismounted and quickly stepped away to avoid being pawed.

Only then did the three notice Andy. An older man with a salt-and-pepper beard walked toward the fence, acknowledging him with a neutral nod neither friendly nor unfriendly. "Howdy. I don't believe I know you."

"Name's Andy Pickard. Are you the boss?"

"No, she's up at the house, fixin' dinner. Will I do? My name's Ben Danforth."

Andy dismounted and shook hands through the fence. "I'm a Texas Ranger. My horse is about ridden down. I was hopin' I might be able to swap for a fresh one."

The rancher nodded. "It can be done, but I wish you'd come yesterday. You'd've had more to pick from. Thieves ran off a bunch of our horses last night. Some of my boys are out now, scoutin' around and hopin' to find them."

"Do you have a lot of trouble with horse thieves?"

"They're worse than heel flies. They steal cattle, too, but they seem to like horses the best. They can get away with them faster." His eyes took on a hopeful look. "By chance are you on their trail?"

"I've been followin' a woman, hopin' she'd lead me to her husband. I don't know for sure that he's a thief, but he's wanted on a murder charge."

"Has he got a name?"

"Donley Bannister."

"Then you're lookin' for a horse thief. Every rancher around here knows his name, but not many have seen his face. Most of us would walk ten miles barefooted to see him hang."

Andy took a minute to digest that. He had heard from the army lieutenant that Bannister stole horses, so he was not exactly surprised. It disappointed him, nevertheless. He wondered if Geneva Bannister knew about this part of her husband's life. Though he would like to think she didn't, she would have to be naïve not to harbor some suspicions.

The three finished working with the bronc and turned it into a pen, where it went immediately to a wooden water trough serviced by the windmill. Danforth said, "That'll do till after dinner, boys." He turned to Andy. "Come on up to the house with me. The wife'll be ringin' the noon bell pretty soon."

He walked out of the corral and made a long study of Andy's horse. "Pretty good-lookin' animal," he said. "I don't know if we've got anything that'd be a fair swap for you. Tell you what: I'll make you a trade with the agreement that you can always trade back once your horse has rested up and taken on some feed."

Andy was pleased. "That's more than fair." They shook hands.

Mrs. Danforth was a plump little woman with her graying hair rolled up in a bun and a smudge of white flour across her nose. She bustled around her simple kitchen with the energy of a bumblebee. She said, "Glad to have you, Ranger. We don't see much law around here except what our menfolks handle for themselves. I don't guess people back east would approve of how they enforce the law, but if they don't do it, it doesn't get done."

Danforth said, "There are times when we have to make a quick judgment and strike while the iron is hot. The law and the courts are too slow and too far away. If we don't take care of things ourselves, the lawless element runs over us."

Andy frowned. "You're talkin' about vigilantes."

"Call them what you want to, but sometimes they're the only law enforcement we've got."

Andy had seen examples of quick justice without benefit of a judge. It went against his grain, yet he could see the Danforths' viewpoint. A situation always looked different to a victim than to an outside observer who had experienced no pain.

Danforth said, "I don't suppose you've run into a rancher named J. Farrell Vanderpool?"

"I don't believe I have."

"Once we get some of these northern counties organized, he'll probably be elected a judge. He's already pronounced sentence on several renegades, and no pettifoggin' lawyers got a chance to muddy the waters."

Andy thought of an old legal adage: there is no appeal from the graveyard.

The cowboys came to the house, spurs jingling and boots clumping heavily on the porch. They paused outside to wash their hands and faces and comb their hair. This was not a bunkhouse cook shack. It was a woman's kitchen, and she expected civilized behavior.

Mrs. Danforth said, "I've cooked for everybody. When are the rest of the boys coming in?"

Her husband spooned a generous amount of white gravy over his fried steak and buttered a hot biscuit. "We won't know that till they show up."

They finished the noon meal. Saying they had another bronc to ride, the two cowboys returned to the corral. Danforth seated himself in a rocking chair on the front porch and motioned for Andy to sit too. He lighted a pipe and puffed quietly a while before asking, "You been up in this part of the country much, Ranger?"

Andy had not burdened him with the story of his years among the Comanches. He said, "A long time ago."

"I can see why the Indians didn't want to give it up. If the criminal element didn't pester us like horseflies, this'd be a grand place for a rancher. Good grass, good water even if sometimes you have to dig a hole for it. Hot in the summer, maybe, and a little cold in the winter, but show me any place that's perfect."

Andy felt at ease, sitting here with Danforth. For a little while he put Donley Bannister out of his mind. He said, "I've always wanted to have a ranch someday. I will, when I've saved enough money."

"You'll need a good wife."

"Already got her. She's waitin' for me down at Fort McKavett."

"Don't let her wait too long. One day you're young and

frisky and can do anything. Next day you look in the mirror and your hair is turnin' gray. It takes you twice as long to do half of what you used to."

From the corner of his eye, Andy caught a movement. Three horsemen were coming in from the north, pushing their mounts. They circled around the corrals and stirred dust riding up to the house. Danforth pushed to his feet and walked down the steps to meet them. He asked, "Find anything?"

One of the cowboys declared excitedly, "Sure did. We found the thieves' camp hidden in a draw about seven or eight miles from here. They've rigged up a brush corral. Got a dozen or fifteen horses in it, and most of them ours."

Andy noticed how the cowboy referred to the horses as *ours,* though in reality they probably belonged to Danforth. Cowboys tended to take a proprietary interest in animals owned by whomever they worked for, caring for them as if they were their own.

Danforth knocked the ashes out of his pipe and turned to Andy. "Got time to chase some horse thieves?"

Andy said, "I'll *take* the time."

Mrs. Danforth came out onto the porch, drying her hands on a dish towel. She cautioned, "Ben, you be careful. Don't you get any of our boys hurt. No horse is worth that."

The cowboys took time to catch fresh horses from among nearly a dozen that had been placed in a corral as a protection against theft. Danforth pointed out a sorrel for Andy. "He's not the prettiest one in the pen, but he'll take you a long ways and bring you back."

Andy saddled the sorrel, then joined Danforth and his

men. The cowboy who had brought the report took the lead. They left the corrals in a trot, then moved into an easy lope as their horses warmed up. Andy felt exhilarated after the monotony and frustration of trying to follow Geneva Bannister's buggy. The jolting brought pain to his healing shoulder, but he made up his mind not to let it slow him.

The men alternated between a trot and a lope. Late in the afternoon the cowboy in the lead raised his hand. The other riders stopped and circled around him. He said, "The draw is just past that hill yonder. How do you want to handle this, Mr. Danforth?"

Danforth looked at Andy and said, "My old cavalry captain always believed in chargin' right in amongst them. Throw them off balance before they have time to think about it, he said."

Andy shrugged. "I've got no quarrel with that."

Danforth had left the corrals in a high state of enthusiasm. Now his face was grim. "We'll form a line and sweep down on them in a run. Holler like rebels. If we can stampede their horses and set the thieves afoot, they'll be easy pickin's. Keep yourselves low. I don't want to explain to Mrs. Danforth why I let one of you get killed."

They rode up on a rise. Below, a brushy draw a hundred yards wide crooked its way among the rolling hills. Andy saw campfire smoke rising from the middle of it. Beyond, he spotted a dozen or more horses standing in a crudely thrown-together corral of cut brush.

Danforth led the charge, firing a pistol and shouting like a Comanche. The cowboys struggled to keep up, yelling, firing, holding a ragged line as they plunged into the camp.

A man on a dun horse spurred out of the draw and galloped away, leaning over his saddlehorn, lashing the mount's hindquarters with a quirt. Two men seemed momentarily frozen in surprise beside the campfire. Afoot, they ran futilely toward their stampeding horses, then fired wildly at the oncoming riders. Andy concentrated on the man who was escaping. Remembering that Donley Bannister had ridden a dun, he vigorously applied spurs to the sorrel.

He soon saw that it was not going to be enough. Danforth had spoken about the sorrel's endurance but had not said anything about its speed. The dun was faster, quickly widening its lead. Andy drew the rifle from its scabbard, stopped the sorrel and stepped down. He knelt and drew a bead but missed. The range was too great.

The rider had gotten away.

Remounting, Andy returned to the camp. The stolen horses had broken through the brush barrier. Three of Danforth's cowboys were circling them, gathering them up. Danforth and the other two stood in the middle of the camp.

One man lay on the ground. He was not one of the cowboys, so Andy surmised that he was a thief. Another man stood trembling, his hands raised. In a wavering voice he was pleading, "You got us all wrong. We don't know nothin' about no stolen horses."

Sternly Danforth said, "You lie. Most of the horses penned here belong to me."

"Me and Speck, we just rode in. We don't know nothin' about them."

Speck. Hearing that name made Andy take a better look

at the man on the ground, then at the one standing. They were the two he had encountered along with Bannister in a dugout. The one called Ches had put a bullet through Andy's shoulder.

The man on the ground was unconscious. In rhythm with his heartbeat, blood pumped through a hole in his chest. It was obvious that he was dying.

Andy confronted the other man. "I know you," he said. "Your partner called you Ches. If it hadn't been for Donley Bannister, you'd have killed me."

The thief seemed startled. "You're that Ranger."

"I am. Who's the man who left here on horseback just now?"

"You ought to've recognized him. If it hadn't been for him, you wouldn't be standin' here now."

Andy's suspicion was justified. "That was Bannister?"

"Yes, damn him. He ran off and left us. I hope you get him."

"I will, sooner or later."

One of the cowboys knelt beside the fallen man. "He's dead, Mr. Danforth."

Danforth said, "The wages of sin." His eyes smoldered with threat as he gave his attention to the surviving thief. "There's bound to be a bigger and better camp someplace. You want to tell me where it is?"

Ches said, "If it was just Bannister, I would, but I ain't goin' to inform on anybody else."

Danforth grunted. "So there's more. We're dealin' with a ring of thieves."

The three cowboys had circled the stolen horses and

brought them up. Danforth looked them over with satisfaction. "Take them on back to the ranch, boys. We'll be along directly." To Andy he said, "There's a bay in that bunch that'll do you a better job than the sorrel you're ridin'. Why don't you go on with the horses? Me and a couple of my boys have got a job to do here."

Andy sensed what that was. He saw by the fear in Ches's face that he sensed it too. He said, "It'd be better if you turned him over to the local law."

"We would, if there *was* any local law. The courts are too far away, and like as not he'd be on the loose again in no time. Maybe in a few years it'll be different."

Andy could assert his authority and take the prisoner, but that would interfere with his search for Donley Bannister. At the moment, Bannister was the bigger fish.

He spurred to catch up with the cowboys driving the horses. They had traveled half a mile when two shots echoed behind him.

It was cold justice, but justice nevertheless.

9

It was obvious to Geneva that Quincy Harpe tended to his horses' welfare better than to his own. After wasting much time crisscrossing the hills in what seemed a hopeless search, she had found Harpe's place many miles away from any recognizable road. It had an extensive set of sturdy horse corrals, but the picket cabin looked like a wreck almost ready to happen. Its walls were off plumb and leaned dangerously away from the prevailing winds.

She guessed that it had originally been built as a buffalo hunters' camp without regard to permanence.

A letter from Harpe had set her off on the long search for Donley Bannister. It had assured her that her husband was in good health and hard at work. It had also said he wanted her to wait in Junction. Under no circumstances was she to follow him.

She had done so anyway. It was in her nature to obey orders only when they suited her.

A heavy lump of a man stood on the front step, a rifle in his hand, watching the approach of Geneva's buggy. His wide mouth curved downward in a hostile scowl. As she drew on the reins, he demanded, "Who the hell are you, and why have you come here?"

"I'm Geneva Bannister. I've come to join my husband."

Harpe took a step forward. His belligerence made her want to shrink from him, but stubborness allowed her no retreat. He demanded, "Didn't you get the letter?"

"I got it, but my place is beside my husband."

"Ain't no tellin' who might've followed you here."

"Nobody followed me. I've been careful."

A large-boned woman, handsome in a rough-hewn way, stepped out of the house and stood beside Harpe. Her long black hair lifted and fell carelessly in the wind. She said, "Did I hear you claim to be Donley's wife?"

"I am. Is he here?"

"No, and I don't know when he's liable to show up. Best thing for you would be to turn around and go back where you came from."

"I've come too far to go back."

"Donley said you were supposed to stay put. Didn't you read the letter I wrote for him?"

"I thought your husband wrote it."

"He can't hardly write his own name. And who ever said he's my husband?"

"I just assumed . . ."

"Things here are different than you're used to. This ain't exactly a church encampment. Well, since you've come anyway . . ." She turned on Harpe. "How come you're standin' there lookin' like a fence post? Help her down. She's probably hungry."

He protested, "She can't stay here."

"She stays if I say so, and I say so. Now, go put her buggy away. You can bring her things in later."

Harpe did as he was told, and Geneva followed the woman inside.

Geneva said, "I want to go wherever my husband is."

"God knows where he's at right now. Could be over in Indian Territory or north as far as the Nebraska line. He don't let moss grow on him." She beckoned with a sweeping hand. "Come on in, and I'll fix you somethin' to eat. You're lookin' kind of lank. We'll need to fatten you up a little before Donley gets back."

Geneva admitted, "Meals have been a little skimpy on the road."

The woman said, "My name's Emmy. Just Emmy. Used to have a last name, but after two husbands I gave up usin' it." She busied herself at a cast-iron stove. "Can't say I blame you too much for followin' after Donley, even though he told you not to. He's considerable of a man. Wisht he was mine instead of the one I've got. You must be some woman for him to slip a ring on your finger. You must've put a hex on him."

Geneva had no satisfying reply. "I didn't do anything special. We met, and things just naturally happened."

Emmy sensed Geneva's discomfort. She said, "I don't mean to be a pryin' nuisance. It's just that I've been curious about what you've got that's taken such a powerful hold on Donley. It's hard to keep a stud horse in one pasture when there's mares across the fence. Yet, I've never known him to pay attention to another woman." She shouted, "Quincy, go fetch me some more firewood. Damned if you ain't let the wood box go nearly empty."

Geneva asked, "Why does he let you order him around like that?"

"He likes my cookin'. Quincy's got no hold on me, nor me on him. We stay together because it's convenient. I do the cookin' and keep the house. He takes care of business and brings in the money. A little bit, anyway."

"What kind of business?"

"I figured you knew. Horses. They gather them here, and Donley takes them down south where nobody knows the brands. Small investment, big profit."

Geneva wondered that she felt no resentment. "You're implying that Donley's involved in stealing horses." She had accepted his easy explanation for lengthy absences, that he was traveling far to buy horses for trading. She had loyally avoided dwelling on the possibility that he was stealing them, though an inner voice had been telling her for some time that everything did not add up.

Emmy frowned. "I ain't implyin' nothin', honey—I'm tellin' it to you straight. Donley may be a Bible-quotin' Puritan on some things, but he's got no compunctions about takin' other men's horses."

Geneva asked, "Did he tell you he's wanted for killing a man?"

"Yeah. Them Slocums have operated up in this country some. All of them need killin'. If Donley hadn't done it, the law would have to sooner or later. He saved them the trouble."

"Most people back there say he was justified, that a jury would clear him. I came all this way to talk him into going home and getting it over with."

"You can't ever be sure about a jury. Trustin' in a jury is how I lost my first husband. They hung him higher than the Confederate flag."

"That's terrible."

"And after we slipped them ten dollars apiece to turn him loose. Crooks, the whole bunch of them."

Harpe tromped into the house with an armload of wood. "When're you goin' to get my dinner fixed?"

Emmy said, "I'm busy takin' care of Geneva. You'll have to finish fillin' the wood box before I cook anything for you."

Harpe walked out, grumbling to himself.

Emmy said, "Men. You've got to keep jerkin' them up short. Otherwise they get the notion that they're in charge."

Geneva ate what Emmy placed in front of her. She was not sure what it was, but she was hungry enough not to ask questions.

Emmy said, "You'd best give up any notion of huntin' for Donley. Stay here with us and wait. He'll show up sooner or later, bringin' a bunch of horses."

"Quincy may object to my being in the way."

"He objects to just about everything. Don't pay no attention to him. I don't."

"I can pay for my keep. A man named Luther Fleet was in debt to Donley. I collected it from him."

"Luther Fleet? That four-flusher is in debt to just about everybody. How did you get him to pay?"

"I shot him."

"Dead, I hope."

"I just put a bullet in his leg."

Emmy's eyes brightened with admiration. "I don't know what Donley ever did to deserve you, honey. You're welcome to stay here as long as you want to, and Quincy be damned."

"Maybe a little while, till Donley comes or we hear where he is. I'll pay my way."

"Hang onto your money. You earned it fair and square."

The cabin was cramped and uncomfortable, but it offered rest and relief to Geneva after the grinding physical demands of the long buggy trip. In a day or so she settled into Emmy's routine, helping to keep the house and cook the meals. Nights, the horses being accumulated for trading were penned to keep them from straying or being stolen by a different set of thieves. Days, Harpe let them out of the corral to graze so they would hold their flesh and strength. He rode out occasionally to prevent them from drifting too far. The rest of the time he mostly loafed around the cabin or the barn, eating and drinking, grousing about one thing or another. Very little seemed to please him.

He made no effort to hide his resentment of Geneva. Her being here relegated him to sleeping in the barn. Whatever romance he was able to wheedle from Emmy was inconvenient and on her own terms. At best, the pair's relationship was an uneasy one of grudging mutual need, not strong affection.

One day Harpe opened the corral gate, then rode up to the cabin. "Horses comin'," he shouted. "Better start fixin' dinner."

Geneva felt a sudden excitement and ran outside. "Could Donley be with them?" she asked.

Harpe shrugged indifferently. "He ain't the only one does business around here."

Geneva hurried toward the corrals. Emmy caught up with her and said, "We better move back to the cabin. We wouldn't want to spook the horses away from the gate. If it's Donley, you'll see him soon enough." She frowned. "And you'd better hope he's glad to see you. When things go against his grain, he can scare a grizzly bear to death."

That was a side of him Geneva had rarely seen, though she knew he could be provoked to extreme reaction if the offense against him was strong enough. He had shown her no remorse over shooting Cletus Slocum, though he grieved about having to shoot the crippled roan. His only other expressed regret was that he had not been able to shoot the rest of the brothers and make a clean sweep of it.

She saw one rider take a position just past the gate to haze a dozen horses through. Two more men brought up the rear, pushing the remuda. The nearest man was dark, wearing a beaded vest. He wore a broad-brimmed hat with an eagle feather in its leather band. She thought he was probably Indian.

Watching the other two through the curtain of dust, she realized that neither was Donley. One was black. The other was white, a man in his thirties, sitting ramrod straight in the saddle.

Emmy said, "I don't know the darkey. The white one's Curly Tadlock. You better watch out for him. He's as handsome as a new pair of boots and slick as owl grease with the ladies. Don't give him so much as a wink, or he'll drag you to the haystack behind the barn."

Geneva could not help smiling. "You've been there?"

"Once. I was weak, and I reckon he was desperate. Anyway, he's good-lookin'."

"What did Quincy say?"

"Quincy doesn't say anything to Curly. He knows Curly'd clean his plow. And he knows I'd crown him with a skillet if he got high-handed with me. Donley was awful mad about it, though. He's like a Holy Roller preacher when it comes to he-and-she stuff."

"I'm not interested in Tadlock, or any other man but my husband."

"Then you'd better make that plain to him right off. I'll bet a dollar Curly makes a move at you before he ever sits down to dinner. He tries every woman that ain't old and ugly."

Once the driven horses were inside the corral, the Indian led his mount through and closed the gate.

Emmy said, "We call him Chief because none of us can pronounce his real name. He's pretty handy at gatherin' up Indian horses."

"But he's an Indian himself."

"A Tonkawa. They're friendly to the whites and enemies to the other tribes. His bunch almost got wiped out a while back when the Comanches and some others made a raid on them. Slaughtered men, women, and young'uns like cattle."

Geneva shuddered. "I thought Indians just killed white people."

"There's been more Indians killed by other Indians than was ever killed by white folks. Or white folks killed by Indians, for that matter. Chief hates all tribes except his own. Takin' their horses is his way of gettin' even. He don't look at it as stealin'."

"I suppose he would call it an act of war."

"Yeah, but he don't mind takin' money for it. Indians have found out what a dollar is worth. They don't work for beads anymore."

Harpe frowned as he walked up to the Indian. "Ain't many horses for all the time you been out."

The Indian frowned back, a hard look in his eyes. "You no like, you go yourself."

Harpe held up both hands defensively. He was obviously afraid of the Indian. "No offense meant. Just noticin', is all."

Tadlock dismounted and tied his horse outside the corral. He said, "This ain't much to show for the risk. We had to outrun some awful mad Indians to get even this many."

Harpe said, "Looks like we may have to move the operation."

Tadlock said, "Country's gettin' settled up to where you can't ride ten miles anymore without somebody comin' to see what you're up to."

Harpe jerked his head toward the black man, still in the saddle and watching the horses across the fence. "Where'd you get him? You know it's risky to bring strangers here."

"He showed up where we were camped. He was lookin' for somethin' to eat, and we needed help with the horses."

Harpe looked eastward, his eyes worried. "You sure none of them Indians followed you?"

"They ran into soldiers takin' some breakouts back to the reservation. That's as far as they got."

Harpe said, "Maybe Donley will come in with a bigger string."

Tadlock said, "Not if he runs into the kind of trouble we had. Those Indians baycd after us like a pack of bloodhounds." He seemed to notice Geneva for the first time. A broad smile broke across his face, the teeth a bright white against the dusty, stubbled face. He said, "Well, now, the scenery has picked up considerable all of a sudden. Who is this beautiful lady?"

Harpe said sourly, "She's Donley's wife, and I hadn't noticed her bein' beautiful. Mostly she's been a nuisance."

"I'm surprised that Donley sent for her to come up here."

Harpe growled, "He didn't. She came on her own. A damnfool thing to do if you ask me."

"I don't believe I asked you." Tadlock removed his hat as he approached Geneva. Long, curly hair spilled down over his forehead. He said, "Ma'am, I'm known in these parts as Curly Tadlock. I'd be pleased to know your name."

She wondered if that was the name he was known by in other places. Remembering Emmy's admonition, she said coolly, "You may call mc Mrs. Bannister."

Still smiling, he said, "Why is it that the best-lookin' ones are always *Mrs.*? It's like runnin' up against a locked door. But most doors have a key, if the right man knows how to find it."

Harpe looked from one to the other in confusion. "What's this about keys? There ain't no keys around here, nor locks neither."

Tadlock said, "Some locks can't be seen, but a man of experience can find a way to open them."

Even as she mentally rejected him, Geneva was physically stirred by Tadlock's boldness. She sensed that she needed to stay as far from him as possible, but it would be difficult in close quarters. She hoped Donley would get here soon.

Emmy said, "Come on, Geneva. We need to fix dinner for the workin' men." As they walked toward the house she said, "Like I warned you, he's already made a move. Watch that you don't let that smile and slick talk get you. Your husband ain't one for sharin' what belongs to him. Somebody could get hurt."

"I won't give Tadlock any encouragement."

"He's already got that. Seein' you was enough to touch him off."

While the biscuits browned, Geneva started to set the table. Emmy stopped her. "The Indian and the darkey ain't eatin' with white folks. They'll take their dinner outside."

Geneva knew the custom but questioned it. "They've all been working together, haven't they?"

Emmy shrugged. "That's different from eatin' together. Work's one thing. Social life is somethin' else." She took the biscuits from the oven, almost dropping them as the hot pan burned her fingers. "How'd you come to meet Donley in the first place?"

"He stopped by our place in Erath County while he was on a horse-buying trip."

"Are you sure he was *buyin'* them?"

The black man finally turned so Geneva was able to see his face. Recognition gave her a light shock. This was the soldier who had ventured into camp early in her trip. Joshua Hamlin still wore the shirt and trousers she had given him to replace the uniform that would have identified him. "Mr. Hamlin."

Open-mouthed in surprise, he touched fingers to a floppy old hat he had picked up somewhere. "Ma'am," he said. "Looks like we been travelin' the same road."

Tadlock asked Geneva suspiciously, "You know him?"

"We crossed trails some days ago. I gave him something to eat."

"It's a bad habit, feedin' strays. They take to followin' you. Are you sure he didn't?"

"Nobody followed me."

Hamlin and the Indian filled their plates and carried them outside. Harpe had eaten a large breakfast, but he heaped his plate with all the food it would support. He and Tadlock hunched at the table together. Midway through the meal Harpe said, "I still don't like it, Curly, you bringin' that darkey here. First time a lawman questions him, he'll spill all he knows."

Tadlock said, "Don't worry about it. As soon as we're through with him . . ." He left the rest unspoken.

Geneva was stunned. She knew she had not been meant to hear that. Donley would not be a party to such treachery, using a man's labor, then disposing of him like a worn-out boot. But he might not get here in time to stop it.

She wondered if she should talk to Emmy about this. The woman gave no sign that she had heard, or perhaps she had but chose not to acknowledge it. Likeable though she might be, she was hardly an innocent party here.

And I won't be either if I stay long, Geneva realized. She decided to take a chance and speak to Tadlock. "You wouldn't really kill him, would you?"

He said dismissively, "The world ain't goin' to miss one burr-head. There's too many of them as it is. Besides, we can't have him talkin' about us."

"But he won't. The fact is that he's running from the law."

"How do you know?"

"He told me he killed a man."

"White?"

"As far as I know."

"All the worse. Him bein' black, they're probably lookin' high and low for him. They'd hang him, but not till he told everything he knows. Since he's goin' to die anyway, I don't see nothin' wrong with us rushin' it a little." Tadlock turned away from her, a signal that the subject was closed.

After eating, Harpe and Tadlock took a nap on the floor. The Indian and Hamlin rested a while on the porch, then went back to the corrals. There they sorted through the horses, saddling them one at a time and trying them. The Indian did much of the riding. A few pitched, but he stuck like a cocklebur. The horses gave up before he did.

Geneva watched Hamlin. He rode several horses while the Chief rested. One managed to pitch him off. He climbed back into the saddle, dismounting only when the horse had worn itself down.

Tadlock had finished his nap and was watching over the fence. He said, "That's enough, boy. We'll work them another round in the mornin'. Then we'll pay you off and let you go on your way."

Geneva shuddered.

The sergeant wiped sweat onto his shirtsleeve and walked toward the cistern beside the house. Geneva waited until she felt confident no one was paying attention, then moved close to him.

He said, "Ma'am, I sure was surprised when I seen you this mornin'. I want to thank you again for your help. I was pert near done in."

She said, "I've come to help you a little more. You've got to slip away from here the first chance you get. Travel as fast and as far from this place as you can."

The sergeant appeared startled. "They fixin' to turn me in to the law?"

"Worse than that, they intend to kill you. You've fallen into a den of thieves. They're afraid you'll tell what you know about them."

"I don't know much to tell. Mr. Tadlock promised to pay me twenty dollars to help him with his horses. Took me a while to figure out they was stolen."

"Don't sell your life for twenty dollars. Get away."

Hamlin murmured, "Yes'm. Reckon I better." He looked up, concerned. "I hope you won't get in trouble over this."

"They won't know I told you."

"God's blessin' on you, ma'am." He started to turn away, then hesitated. "Since you had a warnin' for me, I got one for you. I heard Mr. Tadlock makin' bad talk about you to that Indian. He don't mean you no good."

She nodded solemnly. "I know."

When Emmy called that supper was ready, three men responded. Emmy asked, "Where's that darkey? Didn't you tell him supper's ready?"

Harpe grumbled, "No, and I ain't goin' out after him. He ought to know when it's time to eat."

The Indian took his plate onto the porch. Harpe and Tadlock seated themselves at the table without waiting for Geneva and Emmy. Harpe demanded, "Bring that coffee over here."

Emmy said, "It's on the stove. Go get it yourself. I ain't no waitress."

Harpe mumbled under his breath and filled his cup at the stove. "Women these days have got it too easy. Not like my old mother. When Papa spoke, she jumped."

Tadlock said in a gentle voice, "Emmy, would you mind bringin' us the coffee, please?"

Emmy smiled. "I'd be tickled to."

After she poured coffee for him, Tadlock said, "There's women even talkin' about wantin' to vote. They don't know a damned thing about politics."

Harpe nodded agreement. "What with uppity women and high taxes and darkies free to do whatever they want to, the world is slidin' straight down to hell. It's harder and harder for an honest workin' man."

Geneva and Emmy exchanged glances. Emmy flung a challenge at Harpe. "What would you know about honest workin' men?"

The men finished eating. Emmy stepped out onto the porch and said, "Chief, I wisht you'd go tell that darkey to come get his supper before it's all cold. I ain't cookin' twice."

The Indian returned after a time. "Don't see him."

Harpe snickered. "Probably laid up someplace asleep. It's hard to get a decent day's work out of them people."

Tadlock's eyes showed concern. "Maybe he's run off."

Harpe blinked. "How come? You think somethin' spooked him?"

"It don't take much to spook a darkey. Chief, go take another look."

The Indian was soon back. "Horse gone. He gone."

Harpe began looking worried. "We'd better track him down."

Tadlock frowned. "It's comin' on dark. Looks like rain too. By mornin' he'll be long gone." Facing Harpe, he clenched a fist. "You sure you didn't say somethin' to scare him away?"

"I never spoke six words to him since he came here."

Both men turned toward Geneva. Trying to hide a quick rising of anxiety, she said, "When would I have had a chance to say anything?"

Emmy motioned with a cast-iron lid lifter from the stove. "Nobody had to say anything. You two had murder in your eyes, plain as if you'd wrote him a letter. Don't you be layin' the blame on Geneva."

Harpe grumbled, "Blame ain't all I'd like to lay on her."

Tadlock said sharply, "Watch your mouth. She's a lady." His voice softened as he spoke to Geneva. "You'll have to pardon Quincy for his poor upbringin'. He grew up in a cow lot."

She knew his smile was false, meant to reassure her. She saw something ugly in his eyes.

The soldier was right about him, she thought. *It's time Donley got here.*

10

Andy had spent a miserable night in the rain. He had unpacked the mule the evening before and spread his tarp between two bushes, trying to simulate a tent, but he was wet in spite of that. Now it was morning, and he shook with a chill. He had gathered dry wood before the rain started, managing to keep it fairly dry through the night while he sat cramped beneath the tarp, covering himself the best he could with a slicker. He built a fire and made coffee while he tried to warm up.

Geneva Bannister's trail had simply disappeared. Too many wagon and hoof tracks had been made after her passage, covering up those left by her buggy. He had cut a zigzag pattern back and forth, covering many miles over several days, hoping in vain to find where she had gone. He had visited several ranches and cow camps, inquiring if anyone had seen her. Now he feared the rain had obliterated whatever sign she might have left.

Somewhere to the north was an army post where he might be able to send a wire back to headquarters. He dreaded having to admit that he had spent so much time and had traveled so far on a failed search. He was aware that many Ranger missions came up dry, but those were other men's, not his.

He vaguely remembered this area from his long-ago time with the Indians, but settlement had brought wagon roads, a haphazard scattering of ranches, even a few small villages. Some he knew about, many he didn't. Landmarks were limited. To the east lay Indian Territory and its tribal reservations. To the west stretched the far-reaching Llano Estacado. He was east of the escarpment in a hilly, often sandy, thinly wooded area known as the Cross Timbers.

Geneva and Donley Bannister could be anywhere in this vast, thinly settled region. Much of it was only sketchily documented so far. Some recent maps still left it largely blank except for one word printed across it: *Comanche*. Less than a decade had passed since the horseback tribes had been driven from it.

He finished the little that passed for breakfast. The clouds were breaking off. Morning sunshine pierced them here, there, and yonder. He decided to let his bedding and tarp dry out rather than pack them wet. He spread them on bushes to give them air and sunshine. The site resembled a careless nester's camp, he thought, but who was to see it besides himself?

After a time, somebody did. Half a dozen horsemen topped over a hill to the west, paused there, then moved in his direction. His first thought was of Indians. He was not alarmed. They should give him no trouble unless they came shooting without allowing him a chance to talk. The few who ventured into this region anymore were usually harmless hunting parties, sadly doomed to failure like the one he had encountered several days ago. Occasionally they had a military escort. More often they were off the reservation illegally.

He discerned that these were white men. He knew of no one who might have reason for hostility toward him except perhaps Bannister. He raised his right hand to demonstrate friendly intentions as the riders came close. He saw no friendliness, however, in a man with a fierce black beard who pushed out a little ahead of the rest. He carried a rifle across his lap. The rider gave Andy a challenging study with bullet-gray eyes beneath heavy brows black as pitch. He demanded, "Who are you, sir? Give an accounting of yourself."

All the men were well armed. Andy could see that they were not merely ranch hands out on a cow hunt. He said, "My name is Andy Pickard, and I'm waitin' for my beddin' to dry."

"But why are you here? What is your business?"

His manner aroused a flare of defiance in Andy. "Maybe I'd better ask about yours. How come all the questions?"

The man shifted the rifle slightly toward Andy. "I am J. Farrell Vanderpool. My ranch is north of here. These men and I have been on the trail of horse thieves. In the absence of information to the contrary, we must suspect that you may be one of them."

Andy knew the name. Ben Danforth had told him about Vanderpool and his lethal campaign against thieves. He could see that these men were deadly serious. Stalling them could be hazardous. Though he had been coached to say no more than necessary about whatever mission he was on except to fellow lawmen, Andy said, "I'm a Ranger. I'm on the hunt for a fugitive." He opened his jacket to show his badge.

Most of the larger plains ranches were financed by English and Scottish investors and by Eastern banks. The man who faced him had the look of a Chicago or St. Louis banker sent out here to manage investments for speculators hoping to cash in on what was being called the beef bonanza. Vanderpool studied Andy a minute longer. "Who is the fugitive you are after? Perhaps one of us knows something of him."

"Donley Bannister. I had him in sight once, but his horse outran mine."

"We are familiar with the name."

Andy explained that he had been trailing Bannister's wife in hope she would lead him to her husband. "I lost track of her some days ago. I don't suppose any of you have come across a woman travelin' by herself in a buggy?"

Vanderpool looked to the other riders. None had anything to contribute. He said, "I am sorry. However . . ." He turned in the saddle. "Bring that boy up here."

Andy had not noticed a black rider who remained behind the others. Recognition jolted him. This was the army sergeant accused of killing a man in Santa Angela. Andy struggled to remember the name. Hamlin, that was it. Joshua Hamlin.

Vanderpool said, "We came across this boy yesterday. He said he was running away from some horse thieves who intended to kill him. He has been trying to take us to their camp, but has had trouble finding his bearings."

Andy saw that Hamlin no longer wore the uniform. His clothing hung loosely, at least a size too large. His horse was a sorrel, not the brown he had been riding when Andy had seen him making his escape.

Andy asked, "Do you remember me, soldier?"

The reluctant sergeant nodded. "Yes, sir. You're the Ranger that throwed me in jail."

Vanderpool seemed intrigued. "How is it that you know this boy?"

"He's a soldier at Fort Concho, or was. Shot a man and lit out runnin'."

Vanderpool was surprised. "I took him perhaps to be a thief, but I did not take him for a killer."

Andy said, "The man he killed had murdered a soldier. I reckon he deserved what he got." He turned back to the sergeant. "How did you come to get mixed up with horse thieves?"

Downcast, Hamlin said, "I didn't know they was, at first. They offered me twenty dollars to help them drive some horses they said they had bought. Then this lady come to me and said they figured to kill me when they didn't need me no more. They was afraid I'd talk to the law."

"What lady?"

"They called her Miz Bannister. That's all the name I heard."

Andy felt a surge of hope. "Was her husband with her?"

"No. They said he was comin' with some more horses, but I didn't see him. I lit out when nobody was watchin'."

A grim smile creased Vanderpool's face. "These thieves have been a plague to my neighbors and me for much too long. We'd welcome your company if you would like to come along and help us, Ranger."

Andy said, "I'd be tickled to."

Hamlin said, "I rode all night long. It was cloudy, so I couldn't see the stars. Come mornin', I was plumb lost. Still am."

Vanderpool told Andy, "We don't give a damn about some shooting that took place two hundred miles from here. I'd like to hold on to this boy till he finds the thieves' camp for us."

"He's yours till then. After that, he's my prisoner."

Vanderpool extended his hand. "Deal."

Andy reached back into a saddlebag and brought out a set of handcuffs. He thought better of it and put them back.

"We'll trust you, Joshua, not to try and run away. To do it would just get you shot."

The sergeant's shoulders sagged. "I shot that man in self-defense. But when everything's done, they'll hang me, won't they?"

"I can't speak for a judge and jury."

"They'll all be white. Sure they'll hang me."

Vanderpool said, "You can cross that bridge when you get there. Right now, boy, let's find those horse thieves."

Geneva walked to the window and looked toward the corrals.

Emmy said, "No use workin' yourself into a lather. Donley will show up in his own good time."

"I wish he were here now."

"Curly Tadlock's been after you again, ain't he?"

Geneva nodded. "Every chance he gets, he puts his hands on me. I pull away, but he keeps pushing."

"He always did fancy himself as God's gift to womankind. He can't understand why they don't all see him like he sees himself. Your husband'll set him straight. Curly won't admit it, but he's afraid of him."

"Then why does he keep making a try for me?"

"Because Donley's not here. Curly is one to get while the gettin's good."

Geneva thought of Luther Fleet. "I'll shoot him if I have to. Not to kill him, but to put him in his place."

"It'd be a service to womankind."

"I don't understand Donley, partnering with a man like that."

Emmy gave her a pitying look. "It's the money. Curly's good at what he does. He knows where to find horses and how to get away with them. Donley knows where and how to dispose of them for a good price. They don't like one another much, but as long as the partnership pays a profit, they'll act like they was born twins."

Tadlock and the Indian—mostly the Indian—rode the horses each day, giving special attention to those not yet well-broken. Tadlock had commented, "We don't want some farmer throwed off on his head before we get all the horses sold. It's bad for business."

Harpe had done no riding. He usually sat on the fence, making critical comments about the others' horsemanship. The three were discussing the black soldier as they came into the cabin for supper. Pouring a cup of coffee for himself, but not for Harpe or the Indian, Tadlock said, "We could've got a few more days' work out of him, ridin' those horses."

Harpe said, "I still wonder how come he left."

"No tellin'. Them people are superstitious, you know, like Indians." He caught himself. "All except the Tonks."

The Indian shrugged.

Tadlock said, "The trouble is that he's apt to fall into the hands of the law. When he does, he's liable to bring them down on us like a thunderstorm."

"Business is dryin' up around here anyhow," Harpe said. "It's time we quit this place for good."

"Soon as Donley shows up. We'll throw his horses in with these and leave here."

Emmy was disturbed. "You'd abandon this camp?"

Tadlock said, "It's been abandoned before. Look at it. Some windy day this rickety cabin'll fall in and hurt somebody."

She said, "I'll admit it ain't much, but it's all the home I've got."

Tadlock shook his head. "In our business it don't pay to get attached to one place. A change of climate from time to time can be healthy." He turned to Geneva with a sly grin. "Same thing goes for people. Sometimes it's good to change things around and have some variety. It keeps us from gettin' stale."

Geneva gave him a look of silent contempt.

They saw the dust first, and Harpe's voice trembled with nervousness. "What if it's a posse? That black boy could be fetchin' a hangin' party here."

Tadlock tried to calm him. "It's probably Donley, bringin' in a bunch of horses."

Harpe argued, "But what if it ain't?"

"Then we'll fight them off. Most posses break up pretty fast when they smell gunpowder." He calmly took his rifle from the corner where he had placed it.

Geneva's heart lifted at the thought that Donley might be coming. She would no longer have to put up with Tadlock's sleazy innuendoes, his unwelcome hands taking every opportunity to touch her as if she were a lady of the line. She opened the cabin door.

Tadlock demanded, "Where do you think you're goin'?"

"To meet my husband."

"Better be sure it's him before you run out there. If it ain't, you might take a bullet before they see that you're a woman."

She realized Tadlock was right to be cautious. She retreated to where Emmy waited near the kitchen stove.

Watching through the window, Tadlock sighed in relief. "Everything's all right. It's Donley." He walked outside, carrying the rifle.

Geneva was close behind him. She could not see Donley's face, but she recognized him by the erect way he sat on his horse, as if he owned the world. A half-grown boy helped Donley push a small gathering of horses through the gate, then stepped down inside to close it. Donley dismounted outside the corral and tied his horse to the fence. Geneva began walking toward him, then moved into an eager trot.

Donley turned, stiffening in surprise. He was too startled to respond as she threw her arms around him. He did not return her joyous kiss. Instead, he said, "Geneva, what the hell are you doin' here?"

His angry reaction took her by surprise. "I wanted to be with you. I was afraid you couldn't come back to get me."

"But I sent word that you wasn't to come. Don't you know it's dangerous up here?"

She glanced back toward Tadlock, coming along with Harpe and the Indian. "I didn't know *how* dangerous till I came."

Tadlock looked into the corral and grumbled, "Is that all the horses you could find? Hardly worth the time and trouble."

Donley bristled. "You don't know how much trouble. I was lucky to get away with these. It don't look like you got many more."

"We had to shake off half the Indian nation. What's your excuse?"

"Ranchers. They think a lot of their horses. They got Speck and Ches. Damn near got me too."

Tadlock pointed his thumb toward the boy in the corral. "Who's that? Where'd you get him?"

"Orphan boy. He's all right. He's been a help to me."

"But he's apt to have a long memory. That's dangerous."

Geneva shuddered, remembering that Tadlock and Harpe had planned to kill Hamlin when they were through with him. She feared they might decide upon the same treatment for this sandy-headed kid. He looked to be only fifteen or sixteen, too young to realize what a dangerous situation he had stumbled into.

She said, "Donley, we've got a lot to talk about."

Donley's voice was still sharp. "We damned sure do. I thought you had more sense than to follow after me. Them Slocums could've trailed you, or the law." He spotted the buggy parked beside a shed. "You came in that? It leaves tracks a blind mule could follow."

"Nobody followed me. I saw to that." His reaction stung her like a lash. She said, "I thought you'd be glad to see me."

"Somewhere else, but this is the wrong place."

"Everybody says no jury would convict you for killing Cletus Slocum. I want you to go back with me and give yourself up. A quick trial, then you won't need to run anymore."

Donley's eyes were fierce. "You must be crazy if you think that's all there is to it. Ain't you figured out yet what we've been doin' here?"

"I have, I'm sorry to say. But perhaps they don't know about it down there."

"Even if the court turned me loose, I'd have the Slocum brothers waitin' to shoot me in the back first chance they got. I doubt I could get them all."

"We wouldn't have to stay there. We could go some-where far away and make a new start."

"Doin' what? All I know is horses."

"You could settle in one place and raise them honest."

"A black horse can't change his color." Donley turned his back on her and spoke to Tadlock. "Curly, the climate around here has turned hotter than hell's hinges. We've got to quit this place."

"I already decided on that. Just been waitin' for you to come in." Tadlock's expression turned dark. "You think somebody's on your trail?"

"Nobody I've seen, but I feel it in my bones. Every time I look back over my shoulder, my hair starts to raise up. Soon as we get some dinner, we'll take all these horses and head west."

Tadlock cast another glance into the corral. "With such a piddlin' few, there won't be much money to split."

"In this kind of business there always comes a time when your luck goes cold. You pick up what chips you've got left and run like the devil was after you. Chances are that he is." Donley beckoned to the boy. "Come on, kid, let's get somethin' to eat. Don't unsaddle your horse."

Emmy was not keen about leaving. "It ain't much," she said, "but it's got four walls and a roof."

Donley said, "So's a jailhouse. Besides, what would you do here without menfolks to take care of you?"

She glanced at Harpe. "Better than I've done *with* some I could name."

Harpe growled, "Then stay here. There ain't nobody cares."

Geneva and Emmy prepared a hasty meal for the men and the boy. Geneva thought it odd that Tadlock and Harpe took theirs out to the narrow porch and ate with the Indian. They talked in low tones that did not carry back inside. Their conspiratorial manner made Geneva uneasy.

Emmy gathered the food that remained in the cabin. She put it into a cloth sack.

Donley said, "Good idea. We won't be passin' any stores for a while."

Tadlock and Harpe came back inside, the Indian moving up beside them. All three held pistols, aimed at Donley. Tadlock said, "We ain't all goin'. Us three are, and that woman of yours, but you're stayin' here."

Donley's face flushed. Instinctively he started to reach for the pistol on his hip but stayed his hand. Three muzzles were pointed at his stomach. He declared, "I always knew it, Curly. You're a damned thief."

"I learned from a good one." Tadlock nodded at Geneva. "Get over here, woman. I'm takin' you along."

Donley grabbed her arm and pulled her up against him. "Like hell you are."

Tadlock said, "Sorry it's worked out like this, but I don't want to keep lookin' back, wonderin' when you're comin' after me."

He fired. Donley staggered. He bent forward from the waist, then fell on his face. Screaming, Geneva dropped to her knees beside him. Before the shot's echo died, the panicked boy bolted out the door and ran for the corral.

Tadlock said, "Go after him, Chief. Don't let him get away."

The Indian hurried outside.

Tadlock grabbed Geneva's wrist and roughly pulled her to her feet. He said, "Donley's dead. You don't have to hold yourself back for him anymore. You're goin' with me."

Geneva tried to reach Donley's pistol. Tadlock jerked her away from it. "Come on, I ain't got time to fool around." He threw an arm around her waist and drew her toward the door. He said, "I tried bein' nice to you and got nothin'. Like it or not, you're mine now."

He shouted back over his shoulder for Harpe to pick up the grub sack. Emmy followed Harpe out the door, crying in anger and holding Donley's pistol with both hands. She called, "You turn Geneva aloose!" She fired a wild shot in Tadlock's general direction.

Tadlock shouted, "Quincy, do somethin' about that crazy woman before she hurts somebody."

Harpe swung the food sack and knocked Emmy down. He picked up the pistol she dropped and shoved it into his waistband. He said, "Just for that, you're stayin' here."

The kid was on his horse and out of the corral in a run, leaving the gate open. The Indian ran to close it before the penned horses could escape. He took one futile shot in the boy's direction.

Tadlock cursed. "Damned Tonk never could shoot straight."

The boy was quickly gone, lost from sight amid a scattering of oak timber. The Indian asked, "You want me get'm?"

Tadlock said curtly, "You couldn't catch him now. Let's saddle our horses."

In the corral, Harpe led up a horse for Geneva. "I put Emmy's sidesaddle on him," he told her. "She ain't goin' with us. I wisht you wasn't neither."

"So do I," Geneva said. Harpe gave her a boost into the saddle. She weighed her chances of doing what the boy had done. Perhaps when they were out of the corral.

Tadlock shouted, "Open the gate, Chief." He circled the horses and started them toward the opening. Geneva moved in among them. When she was clear of the gate she put her horse into a run northward, the direction the boy had taken. The wind whipped her face and tugged at her hair. She felt a momentary exhilaration as it seemed she had broken free. But she heard a horse rapidly coming up behind her. Tadlock cut in front and grabbed her reins. He jerked them out of her hand and wrapped the ends around the horn of his saddle. He brought both horses to such an abrupt stop that Geneva was hurled to the ground. She felt a sharp pain in her shoulder as she rolled.

He dismounted and pulled her to her feet. Crying in frustration, she doubled her fists and beat them against his face and chest. He slapped her so hard that her head snapped back. She thought for a moment he had broken her jaw.

Angrily he said, "You'd just as well make up your mind right now. You'll do what I say and go where I tell you. I'm not puttin' up with any more nonsense." He boosted her onto her horse, then cut two long leather strings from his saddle and bound her hands. He tied them to the horn over which her right leg was bent. Leading her horse, he cut across country and caught up to the fast-moving west-bound remuda.

Harpe scowled. "If it'd been me, I'd've given her the back of my hand and left her afoot."

Tadlock said, "Like you did Emmy?"

"You've got to keep women in their place, or they'll take over the world."

Sourly Tadlock said, "I saw how well you kept Emmy in her place. She had the Indian sign on you from the start."

"It don't bother me one bit to leave her behind. There's always a better one down the road."

Moving in a long trot, Tadlock holding her reins, Geneva had time finally to think about Donley, lying face-down on the floor. She wished she could cry for him, but she did not want Tadlock to see her tears. She wanted him to see only strength and defiance. She thought too of Emmy, left by herself with not even a horse to carry her away from that awful place.

She had to concentrate on staying in the saddle. She felt awkward and out of balance with her hands tied to the horn.

The Indian rode near the lead horses. Suddenly he turned in the saddle. He pointed and shouted excitedly. "Riders come!"

Geneva looked back. Behind them a quarter mile or less came a cluster of horsemen moving in a lope. She felt a sudden exhilaration. This must be the posse Donley had dreaded. Perhaps they would set her free.

Tadlock swore. "Hangin' party, sure as hell." He seemed torn for a moment, looking toward the driven horses in front of him, then back to the pursuit rapidly coming up behind him. Indecision did not delay him long. "Let the horses go," he shouted. "Every man for himself."

He spurred savagely, forcing Geneva's horse to keep up. The terrain was hilly and rough. The horses had to dodge their way among the oaks and scrub brush. Geneva feared she would lose her seat and be dragged, or trampled beneath the hooves.

She heard shots. The Indian stiffened, then slipped out of the saddle. He lay crumpled, not moving. His horse galloped on to join the others, the stirrups flopping.

In a panic, Harpe cried, "They got Chief!"

Tadlock urged his horse and Geneva's to more speed. She tried to work her hands free so she could jump off, but the bonds were too tight.

He warned, "I know what you're thinkin'. You'd just break both legs and maybe your head."

Harpe yelped in surprise as his horse suddenly went down. Legs flailing, it pitched its rider out into the grass. Harpe rolled, then was on his feet, yelling for Tadlock to help him.

Tadlock kept riding.

Running afoot, arms outstretched, Harpe begged, "Pick me up. For God's sake pick me up."

Tadlock ignored him. He spurred toward an oak thicket that stretched for several hundred yards.

Geneva managed a quick glance back. She saw Harpe raise his hands as the posse surrounded him. She could not hear him, but she imagined he was pleading for his life.

Tadlock said, "Maybe they'll waste a few minutes with Quincy and give us a longer lead."

Geneva protested, "He's your partner. Don't you care what happens to him?"

"I care about what happens to *me*. Quincy never toted his weight in the first place."

He plunged into the thicket. Geneva had to duck her head and bend low to keep heavy limbs from dragging her out of the saddle. Lighter ones cracked and splintered under the impact. They pulled her hair, tore at her dress, and deep-scratched her skin. Pain made her want to cry out, but she would not allow herself to show weakness to Tadlock.

They had ridden several miles, much of it through thickets

that slowed them to a walk but hid them from sight. Finally Tadlock stopped. "Got to let the horses rest," he said. "Looks like we've shook loose." He untied her hands. "Get down if you want to. Just don't get no ideas."

Geneva hurt all over. She bled in a dozen places where rough limbs had cut into her skin. Her dress was torn, leaving one shoulder bare and badly scratched. She slipped from the saddle and felt her legs give way as her feet touched the ground. She went to her hands and knees. She felt dizzy and for a bit was unable to gain her feet. Tadlock did not help her up.

He said, "We left a trail. If they've got a good tracker, they'll be comin' on."

"I don't know if I can go any farther."

"You've got a lot of travelin' left in you yet."

"Do you have any idea where you're going?"

"Someplace where it'll just be me and you. You've been with the wrong man up to now, but I'm twice the man Donley Bannister ever was. I'll make you forget you ever knew him."

"One thing I'll never forget is the way you shot him down in cold blood."

"He'd've done the same to me, soon as we didn't need one another anymore. I just did it to him first."

"Like you tried to do to that black man, and to the kid?"

"Odd about that darkey—like he knew what we had in mind for him. I always wondered if somebody warned him." He frowned at her. "You maybe?"

Pride made her straighten her shoulders. "Yes, I did it, and I'm glad."

He nodded toward their back trail. "I wouldn't be surprised none if he led that posse here. If so, it's your doin'."

"I just wish they had gotten here sooner, before you shot Donley."

"He'd likely be dead by now anyway. They'd've hung him. Me and Quincy and the Indian too. This way, he died quick. He didn't have time to think about it."

Geneva made up her mind that if the chance came, she would not give Tadlock time to think about it, either.

He pointed his thumb toward the horse. "Climb on. It's time we got movin' again. They ain't made a rope yet that fits my neck."

11

Hamlin had begun to recognize landmarks. He assured Andy and Vanderpool's possemen that they were near the thieves' camp. "I remember that lightning-struck tree yonder. I was thinkin' I was glad I wasn't there when it happened."

A rider approached from the south, his horse running hard. Andy drew on his reins and said, "He's awful anxious to get away from somethin'. He's ridin' like he's seen Indians."

Vanderpool leaned forward in the saddle. "There are worse things around here than Indians." He squinted. "He's nothing but a kid."

The boy reined up in time to keep his horse from running headlong into those of the posse. His face glistened with sweat. His eyes were alive with excitement. He blurted, "They tried to kill me back there."

Andy asked, "Who did?"

"Feller named Tadlock. He killed Mr. Bannister, and he was fixin' to kill me."

The name struck Andy hard. "Bannister? Donley Bannister?"

"Yes, sir. Shot him in the belly for no reason a'tall."

"How did you come to be with Bannister?"

"He said he'd pay me a dollar a day for helpin' him drive some horses to a camp. We hadn't much more than got there when the killin' took place."

Andy felt an unexpected regret. "You're sure Bannister is dead?"

"I seen him go down. I was next, so I left there."

Vanderpool glanced toward the sergeant and said, "That sounds very much like the soldier's story."

Andy nodded. "Hire them, then kill them before you have to pay up. That's one way to hold on to your money." He turned back to the frightened boy. "Who else was there?"

"An Indian and a man called Quincy. And two women-folks."

"Could you lead us to the place?"

The boy vigorously shook his head. "I don't want to go back there."

Vanderpool said, "Now, son, we're your friends. We won't let anybody hurt you. I'll pay you ten dollars to take us to that camp."

The boy thought it over. "Ten dollars?"

"Cash money. I have it right here in my pocket."

"Have I got to go all the way in?"

"Just show us the place."

Andy asked, "Boy, didn't you know you were dealin' with horse thieves?"

"Yes, sir, I kind of figured that's what they was. But a dollar a day . . ."

Vanderpool lost most of his fierce expression. "I hope this is a lesson to you. Running with the wrong people can get you killed. How old are you, son?"

"I ain't for sure, but I think I'll be sixteen along about Christmas. I used to know, back when Mama was alive. But she died, then Pa went off huntin' for a job and never came back. I've got nobody to ask."

"Are you looking for work?"

"That's how come I joined up with Mr. Bannister."

"When we're through here, you can go with me to my ranch. I'll start you at twenty dollars a month. I may raise that once I see what you can do."

"I can do most anything."

"Right now you can lead us to that camp."

The boy took the lead, Hamlin riding beside him and confirming the directions. Andy pulled his horse in close by Vanderpool's. He said, "You're not as fierce as I took you to be, hirin' that boy."

Vanderpool shook his head. "If nobody helps him, likely as not he will turn to thievery and become another thorn in our sides. But if he takes to honest work, he can be an asset instead of a liability."

Assets and liabilities sounded like banker talk to Andy, but he understood what Vanderpool meant.

Vanderpool said, "I can sympathize with his situation. I was an orphan boy myself, but I was fortunate. A good-hearted man befriended me. He set my eyes to the future and my feet on the road to prosperity. Perhaps I can do something for this boy before he drifts beyond salvation."

Andy could relate to that. He said, "A lot of generous people helped raise me. Some Indian, some white."

"Then you and I both know how difficult it is for an orphan boy to make it over to the green side of the hill."

The boy and the soldier stopped and waited for the rest to catch up. The boy pointed. "That's the place, that cabin down there. They had maybe twenty horses in the corral when I left. They're gone now."

Vanderpool swore. "And the thieves with them, I'd wager."

Andy said, "Just the same, we'd better ride careful goin' down there."

The posse moved their horses forward in a walk, rifles and pistols drawn and ready. The boy stayed behind for a few minutes, then became nervous about staying by himself. He spurred to catch up.

Hamlin said, "Boy, you stay behind me. If there's any shootin', you skin out like a scared rabbit."

The boy looked to Vanderpool for confirmation. Vanderpool said, "Do what he says, son. He's been in the same fix you were, and got out of it just like you did."

Andy carried his rifle across his lap. He had always felt more comfortable with a rifle than a pistol, though he was proficient with both. A rifle had more authority.

The picket cabin's roof sagged, and the front wall seemed bowed a bit. The door was open. A raw-boned woman stepped out onto the shaky porch, one hand shading her eyes. Vanderpool signaled for the posse to stop. He and Andy rode forward.

Andy spoke first. "Anybody in there with you, ma'am?"

The woman looked him over critically before she spoke. "One man. He's not in any shape to give you trouble. If you're a posse lookin' for horses, they've done left."

Andy said, "I've been lookin' for a man named Donley Bannister. The boy back yonder says he's been killed."

"Come in and see for yourself." She turned back inside.

Andy and Vanderpool glanced questioningly at each other, then dismounted and walked cautiously to the cabin. Andy carried his rifle, Vanderpool a pistol. The woman waited just inside the door. She said, "You won't need them guns. For once in his life, Donley's harmless."

Bannister sat on the edge of a sagging bed, his long underwear peeled down past his waist, his trousers around his ankles. He held a folded cloth against his groin. His pinched face bespoke pain. He squinted, trying to get a good look at Andy. "Well, I'll swun. You're that Ranger I took pity on. Thought you might've died."

Andy said, "I heard you'd been killed."

"It ain't because the son of a bitch didn't try. He shot my pocket watch all to hell. If it hadn't been for Emmy, I'd've bled to death."

Emmy said, "The bullet just went in a little ways. I dug it out, along with the innards of his watch. He's about quit bleedin'."

Andy said, "I've been huntin' all over for you, Bannister."

"It's a sorry state you've found me in. If I'd had any notion he'd shoot me, I'd've shot him first."

Vanderpool broke in. "You've got your man, Ranger. Now we want to move on and get our horses back. Are you going with us?"

Andy considered. "Bannister, it doesn't look to me like you're goin' anyplace for a while."

Bannister grimaced. "How could I? They carried off every last horse on the place." He took a deep and painful breath. "Kidnapped my wife too. I want you to bring her back."

That disturbed Andy. Trailing Geneva Bannister so far, he had taken a proprietary interest in her welfare. "We'll do what we can." To the woman he said, "Patch him up good. When we get back, he'll be needin' to ride."

Emmy said, "I want you to know that Geneva's a good woman. Much too good for the likes of Curly Tadlock to be layin' hands on her. Kill him first, then arrest him."

"You're askin' me to be judge, jury, and executioner."

"I've heard that's what Rangers do."

"It's been known to happen, but it's not supposed to." Andy followed Vanderpool out the door. He started to tell the boy to stay behind, but it occurred to him that Bannister might take the youngster's horse and escape before the posse returned. Afoot, he could not get far.

Vanderpool told the boy, "Stay with us. If there's any shootin', you drop back out of range."

"Yes, sir. I don't want to lose that job."

The trail was easy to follow. It was impossible to hide the tracks of twenty or so horses. Vanderpool spurred into a lope, the posse stringing out behind him. Andy tried to pull even with him, but he could not catch up to the vengeful rancher.

Andy saw the dust before he saw the horses. He heard Vanderpool's exultant shout: "There they go, boys. Let's get them."

The pursuers tore through brush thickets and around the rolling hills. Andy could see the horses plainly now. The thieves had abandoned them and were running for their lives.

Vanderpool pulled his horse to a sliding stop, jumped to the ground with his rifle, took deliberate aim and fired. Two hundred yards ahead, a man toppled from the saddle. The rancher remounted, shouting with enthusiasm. Following his example, one of the possemen was on the ground, kneeling with his rifle braced on his knee. He fired, and a thief's horse went down. Its rider jumped up and went running, arms outstretched. Andy could not hear his voice, but he judged that the man was begging the remaining two riders to pick him up. They did not acknowledge him. In a few moments the posse surrounded him. His hands up, he cried for mercy. Andy half expected one of the possemen to shoot him.

Vanderpool said, "Riley, you and Boyd stay here with him. We're going after the other two."

Andy had slowed but not stopped. He put his horse into a full run again. He had seen that one of the two riders was a woman. She had to be Geneva Bannister. He had also seen that her hands were tied to the saddle. The other rider was leading her horse.

He tried to level his rifle, but the muzzle danced crazily as the horse cut to one side and then the other, avoiding the scrub brush. Firing from a running horse would waste ammunition. Worse, he might hit the woman by accident.

The pair disappeared into a dense thicket. Andy was tempted to plunge in after them, but Tadlock could hide in the timber and set up an ambush. He slowed to a trot. Vanderpool and Hamlin pulled up beside him. Vanderpool said, "I hate to leave him unhung, but he could be drawing a bead on one of us right now."

Andy said, "I don't like leavin' that woman in his hands."

"She's a horse thief's wife. I doubt he can do anything to her that hasn't been done before."

"Everybody told me she's a lady."

"If so, she shows poor judgment in the company she keeps. We've got our horses back. We've killed one thief and caught another. The boys and I are going home." He nodded toward the sergeant. "What about him?"

Andy said, "He's my prisoner. So is Donley Bannister."

"They're no longer of concern to me . . . *us*. You can have both of them so long as you take them far away from here."

"That I'll do."

"We'll stop at the cabin and get something to eat before we go on. You're welcome to join us."

Andy looked toward the thicket. "What do you think, Joshua? Are you game to go in there?"

The sergeant nodded. "I owe that lady."

Nerves tingling, Andy entered the thicket where he had seen the two horses go. Though he searched diligently, he could find no tracks, no clear sign of their passage. The fugitives had broken off small tree limbs in their passage, but he realized that many more had been broken by wind and last winter's ice. He could not distinguish one cause from another.

He admitted, "We'll never trail them through this mess. Not unless you're a better tracker than I am."

Joshua said, "What we need is an Indian, but he's la-yin' out yonder dead."

Andy knew further search would be futile. He said, "We'd just as well turn back. Maybe Bannister will have some idea where they might be goin'."

Approaching the cabin, he saw that the recovered horses had been placed in a corral. The posse's mounts were tied to the fence. Andy dismounted and tied his horse outside the cabin. Inside, he found Emmy cooking at the iron stove. The captured man—name of Quincy Harpe, he was told—sat on the floor, against one wall. His expression was bleak, his eyes downcast.

Vanderpool appeared buoyant. "From now on the thieves will know they can find no safety in our part of the country. We have broken them for good."

Andy doubted that. He suspected that the ranchers would continue facing the same problems. Only the cul-prits' faces would be different.

Bannister still sat on the edge of the bed. He had pulled his underwear back up. A bulge showed where Emmy had placed a large bandage. His anxious eyes focused on Andy. "You didn't find her?"

"We lost them in the brush."

"Couldn't you follow the tracks?"

"We didn't find any."

"I could've. I wish I'd been with you."

Andy's hopes improved. "You're a tracker?"

"Damn right. How do you think I managed to find so many horses?"

Andy asked, "Do you have any idea where Tadlock might be headed?"

"I know half a dozen places he might try for. If I could

get a line on his direction, I'd have a better notion where to look for him."

"Do you think you're able to ride?"

"To get my woman away from that snake before it's too late? You bet I can ride."

Andy said, "Just don't forget that you're under arrest. If you try to escape, I'll have no choice but to shoot you."

"I'll stick to you like a cocklebur till we find Curly and my woman. After that, we'll see."

Andy looked at the sergeant. "And you, Joshua?"

"Like I told you, I owe the lady."

The meal used up most of the food from the bag Harpe had dropped when his horse was shot from under him. Emmy said with resignation, "I can't stay here by myself without any grub. The cabin is fixin' to fall down anyhow."

Bannister said, "You're a good scout, Emmy. You can take my woman's buggy, and her horse." He glanced up at Andy. "Unless you're arrestin' Emmy too."

"She's not in my fugitive book. She's free to go wherever she wants to."

Emmy nodded. "Thanks, Ranger." She looked gravely at Harpe, hunched in fear against the wall. "I guess you know that posse won't let him get to town alive."

Andy knew she was probably right. These men were in a mood for revenge against horse thieves. He was fortunate to keep Bannister from their grasp. He said, "He knew what the chances were when he chose this business."

She said, "He's a weaklin' and a coward, but he *is* a man. Somebody ought to cry over him. I reckon I'm the only one that will."

Finished eating, the possemen hitched Geneva's horse to the buggy for Emmy and gave her the little food that remained. They put Harpe on one of the recovered horses, bareback. A posseman hinted that he would not have to travel that way long.

Emmy stood beside Harpe, tears on her cheeks. She clung to his hand until the posse took him and moved out, driving the rest of the recovered horses except one left for Bannister to ride. Bannister helped her into the buggy. He kissed her hand and said, "You've got a good heart, Emmy. Give it to a man that deserves it."

"If I ever find one," she said. She flipped the reins and moved away.

Bannister climbed painfully into the saddle, biting his lower lip. His face was pinched from the effort. He said, "All right, Ranger. Show me where you lost that trail."

"You don't look fit to ride."

"I'm a long ways from dead yet."

The three rode out, Andy's packmule following. Andy showed Bannister where he had lost the fleeing Tadlock. Walking his horse back and forth in a zigzag pattern, Bannister managed after a time to find the tracks. He said, "At this point, Curly was just tryin' to get away. He hadn't settled on a direction. We'll have to follow the tracks a while before we can figure out which way he means to go."

Andy glanced at the sun, by this time low in the west. He said, "The day's gettin' short. Night'll be on us before long."

Bannister looked somber. "I expect my woman's thinkin' about that too." He grumbled in a voice too low for Andy to hear.

Andy asked, "Did you say somethin'?"

"No, just cussin' myself for all the times I could've shot him and didn't." Riding pensively, Bannister said, "My woman told me she thought a Junction jury would turn me loose."

Andy said, "That's the way everybody was talkin'. They were sayin' you acted in self-defense, and the community was better off with one less Slocum to worry about."

Bannister asked, "I suppose now you'll charge me for horse-stealin'?"

"Junction is a long way from here. Maybe if you come clear on the murder charge, they'll forget about the horses."

Wincing, Bannister pressed his hand against the bandaged wound. "Damned horses didn't come cheap. They cost me a bad bellyache and a perfectly good pocket watch."

"If it hadn't been for that watch, the slug might've gone through your gut."

"Looks like those horses have cost me my woman too."

It seemed peculiar to Andy that Bannister was not calling his wife by her name. He kept referring to her as *my woman,* as if she were a piece of property, like a horse. Andy said, "I can tell that you're hurtin'. I don't think you can ride much more till you've rested."

"I couldn't rest, thinkin' of him havin' her, doin' what he wants to with her. Damn it, I had Emmy write and tell her not to come up here in the first place."

The statement surprised Andy. He said, "When she got the letter, I took it for granted that you wanted her to join up with you. I counted on her leadin' me to you."

"I'm sorry you didn't find me sooner. Curly might have an extra hole in him now, instead of me." Bannister bent forward, pressing his hand against the bandage. He sucked a sharp breath between his teeth.

Andy said, "Any time you want to stop . . ."

"Not as long as there's light enough to see by."

Bannister lost the tracks twice. Andy wondered if he could find them again. He did, but only after losing time.

Bannister said, "At first Curly was just runnin'. Now he's takin' pains to make himself hard to follow."

Andy asked, "Do you have any idea where he's headed?"

"Not yet, but he can't go far enough to get away from me. I could've overlooked him takin' all the horses. I might even forgive him for shootin' me in the belly. But then he stole my woman. By the time he gets done with her . . . she'd be better off dead."

The tone of Bannister's voice troubled Andy. He heard no affection in it, only a strident possessiveness. Andy could not conceive of feeling that way toward Bethel.

Joshua said, "She was kind to me when I was hungry. And she gave me warnin' that Mr. Curly figured to kill me when the work was over with."

Andy noticed that Joshua deferentially used the term *mister* even in speaking of a man who had planned his murder. For himself, he would have used some of Bannister's more pungent terminology.

He said, "We'll get her back."

Bannister's expression was dark. "After Curly's finished with her? She won't be the same."

Eventually it became clear that the tracks were leading westward. Bannister leaned forward in the saddle and pointed. He said, "Now I've got a notion where he's goin'. A worn-out reprobate named Wilkes is livin' in an old buffalo hunter camp. He was of help to me sometimes in the horse business."

Andy asked, "How far to his place?"

Bannister's face creased with frustration. "Too far. There ain't no way we can get there before night."

"Dark shouldn't stop us if you know where it is."

Bannister clenched a fist. "It's a dugout. We could pass right by and not see it."

Andy said, "Maybe it won't be like you think."

"It will. I know Curly. I'll kill him if it takes the rest of my life to run him down."

Bannister's mood became increasingly desperate as the sun dropped behind low-lying clouds that indicated rain somewhere to the west. At full dark he made an anguished cry, then conceded that traveling farther would be useless. He was slow and easy in climbing down from the horse. Turning his face away to hide the pain, physical and emotional, he said bitterly, "Curly's got her at Wilkes's place by now."

Andy asked, "What kind of a man is Wilkes? Maybe he'll take up for her."

"He couldn't stand up against Curly. Even if he tried, it'd be because the nasty old fart wanted her himself."

"We'll catch up to them tomorrow."

"Tomorrow will be too late. It would've been better if he'd killed her instead of draggin' her away with him."

The bleak tone of Bannister's voice increased Andy's uneasiness. He said, "I can't imagine wishin' Bethel was dead, no matter what somebody did."

"You can't imagine it because you ain't been there. I have." Bannister poked at the little fire they started for coffee. "I never told her, but she wasn't my first wife. The other one . . . she was a pretty little thing. Made me think of pink roses. She'd never been off of the farm before. A slick lawyer come along, whisperin' pretty words in her ear. Talked her into runnin' off with him. After a while she came back, carryin' his baby and beggin' forgiveness. I tried, God knows, but every time I touched her, I'd think about her layin' with him. I wanted to strangle her. When she died birthin' the baby, it was the best thing for both of us. Otherwise, there's no tellin' what I might have done."

Bannister's words were chilling. Andy said, "But that one left of her own choosin'. This one was taken by force."

"In the long run, it all comes out the same. I don't know if I could look her in the face again."

As Andy lay down on his blanket, Joshua leaned close and said quietly, "I got a cold feelin'. I'm afraid Mr. Bannister may do somethin' awful when we find her."

The same thought had begun to haunt Andy. "It'll be up to us to keep it from happenin'."

The soldier brooded, staring into the flickering coals as the campfire burned down. Andy sensed that he was thinking ahead to what awaited him upon his return south. A legal hanging was probably the best he could hope for. A lynching was more likely.

That thought, and concern for Geneva Bannister, left Andy sleepless. He sat up, poking wood into the fire a piece at a time to keep it going. Joshua left his blanket and sat beside him. He said, "It sure is a dark night. I ain't been able to sleep none either."

Andy said, "We'll pay for it tomorrow."

"I always slept good of a night when I was a soldier. Always felt like the army would see to it that I had somethin' to eat and a place to lay my head."

Andy asked, "How'd you come to join up?"

"I was still a growin' boy when emancipation come. I got awful tired of draggin' a cotton sack. I sure didn't want to be doin' it the rest of my life. A recruiter come along and gave me a bunch of talk. Said all I had to do was put my X on a piece of paper and I'd be a soldier. I'd have plenty of money and plenty to eat. He stretched that story some, but he was right about one thing: I could make somethin' of myself in the army. Long as I wore that uniform, I wasn't just another field hand. I was special. It ain't just everybody that gets to be a sergeant, neither." His expression turned melancholy. "Now I've lost all that on account of a no-good piece of white trash that needed killin'. I wish somebody else had done it instead of me."

Andy nodded with sympathy. "I do too."

"Now it looks like the devil has got ahold of Mr. Bannister, like he taken hold of me. He may do somethin' he'll always be sorry for."

"That's why we have to make sure he doesn't get out of our sight."

12

Geneva was desperately tired, and she hurt all over from the fast, rough ride. She was not accustomed to traveling on horseback. Only the fact that her hands were tied to the saddle had kept her from falling—that and the dread of being dragged.

She said, "Can't you untie me? My wrists are bleeding."

Tadlock offered no sympathy. "You'd try to run away again. That's how come I tied you in the first place."

"Where would I go? I have no idea where we are. I'd have nothing to eat, and what money I had was left in the cabin."

"Good. Maybe now you'll do what I tell you to."

"At least let me get down and stretch my limbs. They feel paralyzed."

Reluctantly Tadlock conceded. "I reckon if anybody's still trailin' us, they're way behind." He pulled in close and untied her hands. "I'm holdin' onto your horse. Don't get any notions about runnin'."

She rubbed her wrists. They were sticky with blood and burned as if she had held them too close to a fire. It would be useless to try to get away from him now. But she would keep alert. Sooner or later she might get her chance.

Never had she seriously wished she could kill someone. She had that thought now about Tadlock. When she had first seen him, he had struck her as handsome in a rough sort of way. Now she could see only the ugliness beneath. Donley Bannister's blood was on his hands. She had no doubt about Tadlock's plans for her. The thought brought revulsion.

She said, "There are certain things a woman should be allowed to do in private."

He pointed toward a clump of brush. "Go on. I need to do the same thing. But if you're tempted to try and run, forget it. I could catch you before you took twenty steps."

"I know that. I'm not stupid."

"Then how come you got hooked up with somebody like Donley?"

"Because he's a man." She corrected herself. "Was."

"I'm a man too, a better one than him."

"Some man! You shot my husband without giving him a chance."

"I'm an old poker player. I understand odds. There's times to take an honest chance, and there's times to pull one out of your sleeve. With a man like Donley, it's always paid to hold out an ace."

She knew Donley's faults. At times he drank too much, gambled too much. Now she knew he had also been a horse thief.

But God help me, she thought, *I loved him in spite of all that.*

She straightened her dress the best she could. The brush had torn it in several places. It hung loosely off one bare shoulder. She wished she had a pin to fasten it in place.

"Feel better?" he asked when she returned to where he waited with the horses.

"Some." She stalled for time, in no hurry to get back in the saddle. She hoped someone was catching up. She asked, "Are we going anywhere in particular, or are we just wandering around?"

"It's comin' on night," he said. "We've got nothin' to eat, thanks to that damned Quincy keepin' the grub sack. Besides, it looks like it might rain. I know a feller who lives a little ways on."

"Friend of yours?" That thought brought her no comfort.

"I wouldn't call him a friend. Done business with him now and again, but I never let him get close to my money." He held the leather strings that had bound her. He said, "I won't tie you if you'll promise to behave yourself. I don't fancy havin' to chase you through the brush again."

She said, "I won't run." To herself she added, *Not yet.*

She did not see the dugout until they were almost at its door. It had been built into a hillside. A crude rock chimney protruded from the dirt-covered roof. She smelled wood smoke. Near the dugout was a well, its circular stone wall rising three feet up from the ground. A little farther away a sagging shed was topped by a tangle of brush, next to a nondescript corral of scrub oak branches and trunks.

Tadlock said, "There used to be buffalo bones scattered all over these hillsides till the bone pickers gathered them up."

Born in Texas, Geneva had seen the great buffalo herds grazing free and had been told unbelievable stories about them. She said, "It's hard to imagine all those thousands wiped out in a few short years."

"Money," Tadlock said. "Some people will do anything for money."

Like steal horses? she thought. *Or kill a partner so you can grab his share?*

Tadlock said, "It don't pay to ride up to a camp without lettin' them know. Some people shoot first and then ask who you are." He shouted, "Hello the house!"

A shaggy black dog trotted toward them, barking. It stopped short, turning halfway around and tucking its tail as if prepared to run in event of a threat.

"A coward," Tadlock said. "A lot like the man that owns it."

The wooden door opened slightly, and the muzzle of a rifle poked through. A gravelly voice called, "Who's that out there?"

"It's Curly Tadlock. You know me."

The door swung inward. A gray-whiskered man in grimy clothes cradled a rifle in his arms, his hand on the trigger guard. "Damned right I know you. You done wore out your welcome around here."

"Just a little misunderstandin', Wilkes. You goin' to let this lady wait out here with night settin' in?"

The man lowered the rifle, squinting to see better. "A lady? That changes the complexion of things. Send her in while you put your horses in the pen out yonder."

Geneva did not like this man's looks any better than she liked Tadlock's. His ragged beard had felt neither scissors nor razor in weeks and was a stranger to a comb. He looked her up and down as if he were appraising a mare. "A fine figure of a woman," he said. "Don't you know better than to run with the likes of Curly Tadlock?" She flinched as he touched a rough palm to her bare shoulder. He took her hand and examined the abrasions left by the leather strings that had bound her wrists. "It don't look like you've come of your own free will and accord."

She said, "He killed my husband, then dragged me with him."

He said, "Appears to me like you're in somethin' of a fix. But say the word and I'll blow his lamp out. He's overdue for a reckonin'."

The longer she studied him, the more uneasy she became. She sensed that Wilkes could be as bad a bargain as Tadlock. She said, "Badly as I hate him, I wouldn't want his blood on my hands."

"It wouldn't be on your hands, it'd be on mine. They've been bloodied before."

She did not doubt that. His eyes were those of a wily old coyote.

The tiny room was a boar's nest, just large enough to accommodate a small, rough fireplace, a table with one chair built from wooden crates, and an unmade bed with wide rawhide straps instead of slats. A stained canvas was stretched across the ceiling to catch dirt that might otherwise filter in from the sod-covered roof. On a grate in the fireplace, hot grease sizzled in a cast-iron skillet.

Wilkes said, "I was about to fry up some venison to go with my biscuits and beans. I hope that suits your fancy, because I ain't got much else."

"Venison will do," she said, noting that he picked up the sliced meat with dirty hands. She did not feel hungry.

He said, "Sad to say, it's been a long time since a woman set foot in this place. All I ever see is renegades like Curly. Not what you'd call the salt of the earth."

"Do any lawmen ever come around?" A bit of hope was behind the question.

"Not since I've been here. I've known people to ride by within fifty yards and not see this dugout. I don't get much company unless it's on business."

She could guess what kind that was. "Curly says you've done business with him."

"And generally wished I hadn't. He don't give nobody an edge." Wilkes frowned. "You say he killed your husband. Would I know him?"

"Donley Bannister."

"Donley!" The man's face registered surprise. "He wouldn't be an easy man to kill. Curly must've shot him in the back."

"No, but he took Donley unaware. He didn't give him a chance."

"That's Curly's way." Wilkes glanced toward the rifle he had set beside the door. "What would you give to be free of him?"

"I don't have anything to give you."

"I ain't talkin' about money."

"I don't know what you mean."

"I think you do. You're a grown woman." He gripped her bare shoulder again, harder this time.

Geneva felt ill. To trade Tadlock for Wilkes would hardly be a gain except that Wilkes might be easier to get away from. He was many years older and probably slower in his movements. She said, "That's asking too much."

"It ain't a lot. I may not be the man anymore that Donley was, but the fire ain't plumb out. I could show you a thing or two."

Geneva shrank away from him, but the room was too small for her to go far.

Wilkes said, "You keep thinkin' about it. Right now why don't you finish fryin' up that venison and fix us a pot of coffee? I'm hungry."

The fire had burned low. A small shovel leaned against the fireplace. Geneva used it to stir the coals and coax them to greater heat.

Tadlock entered the dugout, carrying his saddlebags and a blanket roll that had been tied behind the cantle of his saddle. He saw Geneva at the fireplace and said, "Hurry up with that supper, woman."

Wilkes watched him narrowly. "What you got in them saddlebags?"

"That's my business."

"I'll bet it's all the money you've cheated out of poor folks like me."

"You always had both eyes wide open. I was just faster on my feet than you were." Tadlock fetched a tin plate from a small shelf on the wall and speared the first piece of venison with the point of a knife. "Pour me a cup of that coffee," he commanded.

Geneva remembered the way Emmy had talked to Quincy Harpe. With a flare of resentment she said, "You're not crippled. Get it yourself."

Tadlock slapped her, hard. She stumbled backward, almost falling onto the bed. He said, "Now get me that coffee."

Hands shaking, she poured it. Her face was aflame.

Tadlock said, "I like spirit in a woman, but I want her to always remember who the boss is." Finishing the coffee, he said, "Wilkes, I've never seen a time when you didn't have some whiskey around. Where's it at?"

Hesitantly Wilkes reached under the bed and brought forth a bottle. He thrust it at Tadlock and said curtly, "You owe me for this. Careful you don't choke on it."

"If it's like most of the stuff you get, I probably will." Tadlock took two long swallows without stopping for breath. Grimacing, he wiped his mouth on his sleeve. "Even worse than I thought."

Wilkes reached for the bottle, but Tadlock withheld it from him and took another drink.

Wilkes brooded, watching his whiskey slowly disappear, swallow by swallow. He said, "What would you take for your woman, Curly?"

"She ain't a mare for buyin' and sellin'. Even if she was, you wouldn't have enough money to buy her with." Tadlock cut a quick glance at Geneva. "What would you want with her, anyway? You're too old for a woman like her."

"I ain't *that* old."

"Just when you thought you had her, she'd skin you and hang your hide on the door."

Wilkes's eyes narrowed. "I might decide to take her away from you."

"Big talk for a burned-out old renegade. I've got a notion to boot you halfway to the Pease River." He gave Geneva a long, hungry study. "Wilkes, this bed ain't big enough for three. You're sleepin' outside tonight."

Wilkes reacted with anger. "You eat my grub, you drink up my whiskey, and now you're takin' my bed?"

Tadlock jabbed a forefinger against Wilkes's chest. "You heard me, old man. Take your damned greasy blankets and go, unless you want me to grab you by your scruffy neck and throw you out."

Wilkes trembled with rage. "Damn you, Curly!" He grabbed the rifle from beside the door and swung around.

Tadlock was too fast for him. He grabbed the rifle and twisted it from Wilkes's hands. He opened the door and kicked Wilkes out through it. He shouted after him, "For that, you'll sleep outside tonight without any blankets." He set a bar in place against the door.

The dog set up a frenzied barking.

"Damned old fool," Tadlock said. "He's lived too long." He turned an angry gaze upon Geneva. "Did you put him up to that?"

Geneva felt as if the blood had drained from her face. "It was his own doing."

"It looks like I've got to watch you every minute. I hope you're worth it."

Wilkes was beating on the door, demanding to be let back inside. Tadlock tried to ignore him but finally cursed and gathered the blankets from the old man's bed. He opened the door and threw them outside, shouting, "Take them and go sleep under the shed."

Geneva demanded, "You're going to make him stay outside? This place belongs to him."

"It doesn't. He found this empty dugout and just squatted here. Be thankful I didn't shoot him. I may decide to do it anyway before we leave here."

She struggled to keep some semblance of composure, but she lost control. She slumped into the chair and let her tears spill in a rush.

Tadlock said, "I never saw a woman yet that didn't break down and cry at the least little thing." He studied the nearly empty bottle and said, "Look under that bed and see if he had another."

She found one and handed it to him. He opened it, letting the cork fall to the dirt floor. He dragged the chair against the door and seated himself so that she could not escape. He motioned toward the narrow bed. "Sit down there," he said. "I want to look at you a while." He tipped the bottle upward and wiped his mouth again.

Geneva's hope gradually began to rise. If Tadlock kept working on that bottle, he might drink himself unconscious. Then she could get away.

But after a while he set the bottle on the floor and moved toward her, arms outstretched, his eyes burning. Desperately she attempted to duck past him, but he caught her arm and twisted her around. He pushed her backward onto the bed and fell on her with all his weight. His breath was heavy with whiskey as he forcibly pressed his mouth against hers. She struggled until he slapped her again, harder than the last time.

"It's payday," he said.

After a long time she became aware of daylight showing through the cracks in the wooden door. He lay beside her, his eyes open, trying to focus on her face. He brought a rough hand up to caress her cheek. He said, "I told you I'm a better man than Donley ever was." Slowly he moved his hand down to her shoulder, then to her thigh.

Turning her face away, she closed her eyes, hating him, wishing him dead.

He attempted to arise, but his legs betrayed him. He sat down heavily on the edge of the bed and rubbed his forehead. "Sorriest whiskey I ever drank. It's a wonder it didn't kill Wilkes a long time ago." He jerked a thumb toward the fireplace. "What I need is black coffee. Stir them coals and get a fire started. And fry up some of that meat. My stomach feels like there's two cats fightin' in it."

He drank the first cup of coffee in several long gulps without stopping, though it was steaming hot. He wolfed down a strip of venison and demanded more. Satisfied, he appeared to be almost sober. He reached for her. She backed away, looking for something she could use to protect herself.

He said, "You can't go nowhere till I'm ready to let you. Then we'll go together."

She saw the fireplace shovel with which she had stirred the coals. Her first intention was to strike him with it. Instead, she pushed the shovel deeply into the fire, then hurled live coals and hot ash into his face.

Tadlock screamed and brought his hands up to cover his eyes. Some of the coals had gone down into his long underwear and set it to smoking. Dancing wildly around the room, he bumped into the bed, then the table, and almost fell into the fireplace. Howling like a wounded dog, he found the door and staggered outside. He cried, "My eyes! My eyes!"

Shaken, Geneva pitched the shovel away and quickly put

on the tattered dress that Tadlock had thrown on the floor.
She dropped a slab of bacon and a bag of coffee beans into
a cloth bag. Tadlock's pistol and gun belt lay across the
back of the chair. She shoved those into the sack. As an
afterthought she picked up his saddlebags. Wilkes had
speculated that they contained profit from Tadlock's sales
of horses. However much or little it might be, he owed
her that for his brutal treatment and for killing her husband.

Tadlock was at the well, his underwear smoldering. He
wailed loudly as he emptied a bucket of water over his
head. She hurried past him, pausing to drop Wilkes's rifle
down into the water, out of reach. She ran to the pen where
three horses stood waiting for feed: hers, Tadlock's, and
one she supposed belonged to the old man.

Wilkes slouched out from under the shed, rubbing his
eyes. He appeared to have slept in his clothes. He demanded, "What's Curly hollerin' about? You didn't shoot
him, did you?"

She did not answer him.

He said, "You ought to've. He'll be comin' after you."

Saddling her horse, she said, "Not for a while, he won't."
She unfastened Tadlock's rifle scabbard from his saddle,
carrying it and the rifle with her. She opened the gate and
drove the other two horses out ahead of her. She intended
to take them far enough that Tadlock would have to waste
a lot of time trying to catch them afoot.

She had no clear idea where she was going. Her intention at the moment was simply to put as much distance as
possible between herself and Tadlock. Later she would decide what to do.

She wished now that she had killed him.

13

Bannister was up and saddling his horse when dawn was still a distant promise. Andy could not see twenty feet.

Bannister said, "Come on. We're losin' daylight."

Andy said, "You can't even see yet. Let's make some coffee first."

"I can see enough. Ain't got time to waste for coffee." Bannister mounted and rode off. Andy and the sergeant saddled quickly.

Joshua said, "He's ridin' like he knows where he's headed."

"I hope when we get there that we can see the place. He talked like it'd be easy to miss."

"Might be better for Mrs. Bannister if we do miss it. I don't know which man to be the most scared of—Mr. Bannister or the man that carried her off."

As light began to spread across the hills, Andy saw a scattering of bleached buffalo bones, all that remained to show for the great slaughter of a few years ago. He thought of the Indians he had encountered earlier in their futile search for the sacred animal. Most of these buffalo had been killed for their hides and nothing more. The meat had been left to feed wolves and other prairie scavengers. Facing starvation, the People had eventually been forced to give up the struggle for freedom and drag themselves to the reservation.

Andy could see why Bannister had not wanted to risk missing the dugout in the dark. It would have been easy to miss even in daylight had Bannister not led the way. Andy saw a rock chimney first, its top extending only a couple of feet above a small hill into which the rude dwelling had been built. Next he saw the brush corral.

"No horses in the pen," Bannister said grimly. "They're already up and gone."

A black dog came from beneath a shed and began barking. A ragged old man followed warily, stopping twice to give the visitors a careful study as if ready to turn and run. He stared at Bannister in disbelief. "Donley!" he exclaimed. "Curly claimed he shot you dead."

"Wilkes, you ought to know not to believe everything he says. How long has he been gone from here?"

"He ain't gone." The old man nodded uneasily toward the cabin. "He's in yonder, ravin' out of his head. I think he's dyin'."

"And my wife?"

"She rode off after daylight and took the horses with her. I'd be gone from here myself if she hadn't left us afoot. Curly went plumb crazy after what she done to him."

Bannister demanded, "What did she do?"

"Threw fire in his face, a shovelful of coals and hot ashes. Burned him awful bad."

Bannister muttered, "Just a taste of what he's got comin' when the devil gets ahold of him." He turned toward the dugout's wooden door and shouted, "Curly, drag yourself out here."

Wilkes said, "I doubt he can do that. Last time I looked in on him, he was barely able to move. He found my old six-shooter and tried to aim it at me. I took it away from him." The pistol was in Wilkes's waistband. Andy quietly relieved him of it.

From inside, a hoarse voice called, "Who's that?"

Andy called, "Texas Ranger. Come out with your hands up."

"I can't," Tadlock answered. "You'll have to come in."

Andy shoved the door open. His jaw dropped as he saw a man lying on a crude bed, his swollen face spotted with deep and ugly pits. One eye appeared burned beyond healing, the other pinched almost shut. From the waist up, much of Tadlock's long underwear was gone, blackened remnants clinging to an angry mass of blistered skin. The dingy little room smelled of burned flesh.

Tadlock asked plaintively, "Who are you? I can't hardly see you."

Bannister approached the bed, his voice crackling with fury. "I'm Donley Bannister. You never expected to see me again, did you?"

"Donley!" Tadlock rasped. "But I thought . . ."

"Thought you killed me?" He grabbed Tadlock by his shoulders and shook him violently. "What did you do to Geneva?"

Tadlock shrieked in pain. "Nothin' to what she done to *me*. Burned me to death, pretty near."

Bannister shook him again. "Tell me what you did to her. Answer me, damn you!"

Andy pulled Bannister back from the edge of the bed and said, "Go easy. He can't tell you anything if you kill him."

Bannister's face was scarlet. "I'll kill him, all right, but he's goin' to talk first. Where is she, Curly?"

Tadlock's voice broke. "She done this to me, then she rode off."

Andy decided he had to take charge, for he saw murder

in Bannister's eyes. "Tadlock," he said, "I'm a Texas Ranger, and you're under arrest."

"Get me away from Donley. He'll kill me."

"Looks to me like he's got good reason."

"She didn't have no call to burn me alive. My God, look at my eyes."

Bannister said, "Lend me that six-shooter, Ranger. I'll finish what she started."

Andy stepped in front of Tadlock, shielding him. He told Bannister, "You've got a good chance of comin' clear for killin' Cletus Slocum, but this man is helpless. Killin' him would be plain murder."

Bannister stood fuming, his legs braced, his feet a little apart. He said, "Looks like he's near dead already. How was she, Curly? Was she worth it?"

Tadlock whimpered. "Somebody do somethin'. I can't stand this pain."

Wilkes said, "I tried to rub hog lard on him. He screamed like a baby."

Joshua was moved by Tadlock's plight. He said, "Maybe we can take him somewhere."

Wilkes said, "You wouldn't get two miles with him. He was afire when he come runnin' out of that dugout. He sucked in a lot of smoke and flame. I reckon they burned out his innards."

Tadlock coughed up blood. In spite of himself, Andy felt a grudging sympathy for Tadlock. This was a hard way for a man to meet his final reckoning.

He said, "You-all go back outside. There's no point in tormentin' this man any further."

Bannister was grim. He leaned over Tadlock and

whispered something Andy could not hear. Andy assumed it was a curse. Then Bannister walked out with Joshua and Wilkes.

Andy stood at Tadlock's bedside, staring at the ruined face, the blistered body. If this had been a wounded animal, he would not have hesitated. But a man, even a wretch like Tadlock . . .

He removed all but one cartridge from Wilkes's pistol and laid the weapon near Tadlock's head. He said, "There's just one bullet. Don't waste it."

Outside, Andy found Bannister digging a grave. He said, "I wouldn't have expected this of you."

Bannister grunted. "I want the pleasure of droppin' him in the hole and throwin' dirt in his face."

A shot sounded from inside the dugout.

Startled, Bannister demanded, "What the hell did you do?"

Andy said, "I gave him a choice."

Reluctantly he reentered the dugout, followed by Joshua and Wilkes. He had seen men die, but he had never seen what could happen when a man held a pistol to his own head and fired. He thought for a moment that he would gag.

Wilkes cursed softly. "This place ain't goin' to be fit to live in now."

Andy went back outside and found Bannister still digging, a bitter look on his face. Bannister said, "I wanted him to die slow, screamin' with every breath. You cheated me out of that."

Andy said, "At least nobody can say that Mrs. Bannister killed him. The only bloody hands are his own."

They wrapped Tadlock in his blankets and lowered him into the grave. Andy said, "I don't know much about prayin'. Anybody want to say somethin'?"

Joshua waited for someone to speak. When no one did, he removed his hat, bowed his head, and said, "Lord, there ain't none of us can say we ain't sinned in your sight, so it ain't our place to speak bad about this man. Whatever wrongs he's done, they're over with now. I hope you can see your way clear to forgive him, and I wish everybody here would too." He glanced at Bannister. "The grave makes everybody equal—saint and sinner, black man and white. Praise the Lord. Amen."

Andy said, "I've heard some high-paid preachers, but I never heard a prayer said better."

Joshua shrugged. "I've talked to the Lord a right smart lately, since I killed Mr. Burnsides."

"Does he ever answer you?"

"Every time."

Andy had checked his fugitive book but found no one in it who fitted Wilkes's description. Two prisoners were enough anyway. He handed the empty pistol to Wilkes and asked, "What are you goin' to do?"

Wilkes said, "I don't think I'll want to stay here anymore. I figure when the lady turns my horse loose, it'll drift back here for feed. Then I'll go look for a better place."

Andy turned to Bannister. "Where do you suppose your wife has gone to?"

"I imagine her first thought was to put as many miles between her and Curly as she could. After that, she might decide to go back to her old home in Erath County. That'd be southeast of here. Or she might decide to go back to

Junction. That'd be pretty near due south. We'll have to try and follow her tracks till we get a clear idea whichaway she's headed."

"You're the tracker. Go ahead."

They traveled until nearly dark before making camp. Andy arose at daybreak. He was dismayed to find that Bannister had slipped away sometime in the night, taking Andy's pistol.

Joshua gazed with worried eyes at Bannister's tracks. "I'm afraid he figures to find her before we do. You reckon he's still got notions about doin' her harm?"

"It's hard to say what's in a man's mind when he's been through as much as Bannister has. We'd better saddle up and go."

In their haste, they skipped breakfast.

After a couple of miles Geneva quit driving the horses that belonged to Tadlock and Wilkes. They followed her a hundred yards, then stopped to graze. She looked back, half expecting to see Tadlock trailing her but knowing he couldn't catch her afoot. She wondered how badly he was burned. Not badly enough to pay for the shame and humiliation he had visited upon her, she thought. She shuddered, remembering the animal violence, as if through her he was taking out all of his angers and pent-up hatreds. She still felt the hurt, the nausea, the loathing.

Despite her eagerness to get far away, she considered waiting in ambush and killing him with his own pistol when he came for his horse. The weapon was still in the sack she had brought from the dugout. She discarded the idea, knowing that to see him would probably set her to shaking so badly she could not hold him in the sights.

She looked about, trying to find her bearings. The rolling plains stretched in all directions as far as she could see, a choppy land of sand and grass, mesquite and scrub oak. Somewhere to the west lay the rugged breaks that marked the eastern edge of the higher and even more extensive staked plains, until recently the domain of Comanche and Kiowa. Surely somewhere in the midst of this far-reaching prairie must be a town where she could buy supplies, and new clothing to replace the tattered and torn remnants that barely covered her.

She would need money, and she had none of her own. She had not yet looked in Tadlock's saddlebags. She unbuckled one side and lifted the broad flap. Wilkes had been right. There *was* money, perhaps several hundred dollars. She felt a momentary lift, tempered only a little by the knowledge that Tadlock had gained it by stealing and selling other people's property. At least now it was in needier hands than his.

When she found a town, perhaps she could buy a buggy. Her body was sore from the unaccustomed horseback travel as well as from Tadlock's harsh treatment. But money was useless unless she could find a place to spend it.

She had been seeing cattle. Where there were cattle there must be a ranch, with people. And she began to feel thirsty. It stood to reason that if she followed a cattle trail it should lead to water. She chose one that appeared to have been heavily used. She gambled that the southward direction would lead her toward water rather than away from it. She hoped that cattle moving along the trail after her would eliminate her tracks and thwart any effort by Tadlock to follow her.

She came eventually to a stream angling southeastward,

as they tended to do in this part of the country. It might be a tributary to the Brazos, she thought, or one of the other major rivers that angled across Texas on their long course toward the Gulf of Mexico. At this moment it did not matter which river.

Several cows loafed on the bank, having drunk their fill and now placidly chewing their cud. A couple rose to their feet in alarm and trotted away. The rest watched her with suspicion but chose comfort over flight. She moved upstream from them and dismounted. Her horse dropped its head and began to drink. She lay on her stomach and cupped her hand in the water, sipping eagerly.

Her thirst satisfied, she considered how comforting a bath might feel. Her hands and arms were grimy from two days of travel and dust and sweat. She was eager also to rid herself of whatever physical stain Tadlock had left with her. She feared the emotional stain would remain a long time.

After unsaddling and staking the horse to graze, she removed the badly torn dress and her underclothing, then waded into the water. It was pleasantly cool but not cold. She scrubbed the garments as best she could without soap, then carried them out and spread them across a clump of brush. She reentered the stream and soaked in leisure while her clothing dried in the sun. The water relaxed her. She felt that along with the sweat and grime it carried away whatever remained of the long night with Tadlock.

Dressed, she built a small fire. She realized that she had left the dugout too hastily. She had grabbed what little food appeared handy, but she had no knife to slice the bacon, nor a pot or can for boiling coffee. She decided to ride farther in hope of finding a house or a cow camp.

Her horse, picketed on the stream bank, jerked its head around and poked its ears forward. A horseman was coming in her direction. For a panicked moment she thought of Tadlock. Reason quickly told her it was unlikely that he was this close behind her.

A small man, not much over five feet tall, rode up with a "Howdy, ma'am."

She was conscious that her remnant of a dress gave her only partial cover. The torn skirt revealed one leg up past the knee. Hunching, trying to cover both the leg and her bare shoulder, she demanded, "What do you want?"

The rider was quick to recognize her embarrassment. He discreetly looked away and said, "Didn't mean to take you by surprise. Looks like your horse might've throwed you off and dragged you. Maybe this'll make you feel more at ease." He untied a yellow slicker from behind the cantle of his saddle and handed it down to her, turning his head while she put it on.

Still not trusting him, she stammered a little. "Th-thank you. I'm sorry you had to see me in this condition."

"I didn't see a thing. I don't need the slicker right now noway. It don't look much like rain."

She guessed him to be in his forties, thin, wiry, his hair partly gray and in need of cutting. His whiskers had not felt a razor in a while. He was a long way from handsome, but his eyes were kindly. He said, "By the looks of things, you've been through a right smart of trouble. Is there any way I can help you?"

"You could tell me how to reach a town. Any town."

"There's one in every direction, but none you could get to between now and night. It ain't far to our house, though. I'd be glad to take you there."

Suspicion still lingered. "*Our* house? Who else besides you? A wife?"

"No, ma'am, just me and my brother Jock. Neither one of us has ever found a woman willin' to put up with two old Scotchmen." He seemed to sense what troubled her. "You don't need to fret about us doin' you harm. We're just a couple of stove-up cowpunchers. Been years since we done any carousin' and carryin' on. McPherson's my name, Scotty McPherson."

Geneva began to ease. Instinct told her this little man was just what he said he was. She said, "I hope you'll pardon me if I seemed rude, Mr. McPherson. You're right, I've been through so much the last couple of days that I don't know up from down."

"You'll feel better when you've had a good supper. I'll saddle your horse for you while you gather up your possibles. I don't believe I heard your name."

"It's Geneva Bannister." As an afterthought she added, "*Mrs.* Bannister."

Geneva had to keep tugging at the slicker to keep it from falling away from the leg crooked over the sidesaddle's horn. McPherson must have had a lot of talk bottled up in him for a long time, for he kept a one-sided conversation going as they rode southward. In time they cut into a wagon road that showed it was used frequently.

He said, "We see a lot of traffic on it. Somebody passes by our place every two or three days. If it's gettin' toward evenin', we invite them to stay all night. Me and Jock love company."

"Do you have many neighbors?"

"Quite a few. A couple of them ain't more than twelve

or fifteen miles away. It's a caution how this country's set-tlin' up."

"What made you and your brother decide to come here?"

"We came down from Kansas with a buffalo skinnin' outfit. When the hide trade dried up, we put our money into cows. Our old daddy always taught us to be of a savin' nature. With hard work and the Lord's help, we're pretty well fixed now."

Geneva expected to be greeted by a barking dog, but their arrival was announced by a screeching peacock instead.

McPherson said, "Don't pay any attention to old Loud-mouth. He's our watchdog, but he doesn't bite."

The house was not large. It was built of lumber, box-and-strip style, with a porch facing east, away from the afternoon sun. A little distance in the back were a barn, also of lumber, a low shed, and a set of cattle pens. Chickens pecked around the yard. A milk cow stood waiting at a corral gate.

McPherson said, "We've got just about anything we'd ever need—milk, fresh eggs, a few hogs so we can put up plenty of salt pork. Even got a little garden. Ain't nothin' beats fresh tomatoes."

With two old bachelors living alone, Geneva expected to see the kind of boar's nest that Wilkes's dugout had been. She was pleasantly surprised to find the homestead neat and well-kept, as if there was a place for everything, and everything was in its place.

A man came out of the house with a milk bucket in his hand. Seeing the riders approaching, he stopped and stared. He was not much taller than Scotty McPherson. The resemblance in their faces told Geneva that this was the brother.

Jock McPherson stared at Geneva. "Where'd you find the stray, Scotty? And why the slicker? It ain't rainin'."

"I'll tell you later. Help her down and I'll put the horses up."

Jock gently eased her to the ground. "I'm Jock. I'm a bit older than my little brother, and a sight better lookin'."

Geneva would not have said that. Like his brother, Jock had neglected the razor for some time, and a haircut would have been a considerable improvement. But crow's-feet crinkled at the edges of the same kindly blue eyes. His broad smile revealed a gold filling in one front tooth.

He said amiably, "You go on in the house and make yourself to home. I'll be in as soon as I finish milkin' the cow."

The inside of the house was as neat as the outside. The furniture was spare but utilitarian. There were only two rooms, one with a pair of cots, a bureau and a mirror. The other was kitchen and living room combined. A coffeepot sat steaming on a wood-burning range flanked by a deep wood box. Shelves lined one wall. A water bucket and a wash pan sat atop a flat cabinet. The kitchen table had only salt and pepper shakers and an empty cup from which Jock had evidently been drinking.

Geneva thought the well-kept house had one thing missing: there were no curtains on the windows. Otherwise it would be easy to believe a woman lived there.

Scotty returned before Jock did. He said, "Ma'am, we need to do somethin' about that yellow slicker, but I'd bet there's not a dress to be found in less than fifteen miles."

She said, "If I had a needle and thread, maybe I could sew this one up a little." That was a forlorn hope. The dress was beyond salvation.

He said, "Would you object to wearin' man's clothes? I'm thinkin' Jock's would be a fair fit."

It would hardly meet the demands of propriety, but neither did her present situation. "Anything would be better than this."

He went into the bedroom and opened a standing cabinet. Rummaging, he brought out a shirt and a pair of trousers. "You might try these, ma'am."

"Are you sure Jock won't mind?"

"Not a bit. They'll look better on you than they ever did on him."

He closed the door to give her privacy. She took off the slicker and the dress, then donned Jock's clothes. They fitted except that the shirt was tight. She had to strain to close the top buttons. She looked at herself in the mirror and wished she hadn't. Her hair was stringy and windblown. She borrowed a comb that lay atop the dresser and did what she could to bring about some order.

Jock had returned from the milking by the time she walked out into the other room. The two brothers looked at her, then at one another. Both grinned. Jock said, "I'll never wear them clothes again. I'll just hang them up to look at and try to remember how good they looked today."

Scotty asked, "Mrs. Bannister, are you a good cook?"

"Fair to middling, I suppose."

"Would you mind takin' charge of the stove this evenin'? We've batched here so long that we've forgotten what a woman-cooked supper tastes like."

"For all your kindness, I'd be glad to."

Scotty brought a ham from a smokehouse out in back while Jock filled the wood box and peeled potatoes. Then the two disappeared outdoors while Geneva kneaded dough for biscuits and cut several slices from the ham. Later she would make gravy from the grease.

She stepped out onto the porch and said, "Supper will be ready in a few minutes."

Both men had shaved off their whiskers. Scotty sat on a bench with a towel over his shoulders while Jock snipped away at his hair. From the looks of things, Scotty had already done the same favor for Jock, if it could be called a favor. Neither man was likely ever to earn a nickel as a barber.

Her heart warmed. These gentle brothers were as far from Curly Tadlock or Quincy Harpe or Wilkes as daylight was from darkness. They revived some of her shaken faith in men.

But she felt she should give warning. Tadlock would not hesitate to kill them if they tried to oppose him. She sat in silence while the McPhersons enthusiastically dove into her cooking. They took turns complimenting her.

Finally Scotty shoved his plate back and said, "Mrs. Bannister, I wish you could stay here forever."

"But I can't," she said. "I've got to move on." She explained about Donley, leaving out the fact that he stole horses. She told about Tadlock and his shooting Donley, then dragging her away. She did not tell all that he had done to her, but she supposed they sensed the rest of it. "I left him afoot, but I have a dread that sooner or later he'll come looking for me. If he were to find me here . . . I would not wish that kind of trouble on you gentlemen."

Jock shook his head in sympathy. "So now you're a widow lady, and there's a rattlesnake slitherin' around, lookin' to find you. Me and Scotty would be glad to shoot him for you, same as we'd shoot a mad dog. We were both dead shots back in the buffalo days."

Scotty nodded. "We've still got our old Sharps fifty. It'd blow a hole in him you could drive a wagon through."

She argued, "But he might shoot you first. I couldn't let that happen on my account."

Jock said, "At least think about it, ma'am. You could have a home here as long as you want it."

She had stated her case. She knew further argument would be of no use. She would have to leave tomorrow no matter what they said.

Scotty said, "Enough of this gloomy talk. What we need now is some music. Do you like music, ma'am?"

"I do, but I haven't heard any in a long time."

Scotty brought a fiddle down from the bedroom wall. Jock had a harmonica. They played, stomping the wooden floor in rhythm to the music. At times, the wail of the fiddle sounded almost like the bagpipes the men's father would have known. Geneva felt her heart lift. In the warm glow of their friendship, she was able for a while to push Donley and Tadlock to the back of her mind. She even sang along on a few tunes she knew.

She felt she had moved out of a nightmare and into a benevolent dream.

She protested, but they gave her the bedroom and took blankets out onto the porch. "We're used to sleepin' outdoors," Jock said. "We do it for months at a time when we go with our neighbors on roundup."

The bedroom door had no lock. For that matter, the front door did not either. That did not trouble her. She instinctively trusted these men. They gave her a comfortable feeling of safety.

Hating to leave, Geneva stayed longer than she intended the next morning. Breakfast was a slow, drawn-out affair at the kitchen table. At length she asked the brothers, "Don't you intend to go out to work this morning?"

Scotty smiled. "Those cows don't need to see us every day. They take care of themselves pretty good."

Jock said, "It's hard to strike up a good conversation with a cow."

Geneva sensed that they were stalling to keep her as long as they could. She felt flattered, but she could not put down a rising concern that Tadlock might be coming. "I have enjoyed your hospitality, but I had best be moving on."

Outside, the peacock set up a loud screeching. Jock turned his head to listen. "May be somebody comin'."

Geneva's heart leaped. Jock motioned for her to keep her seat. He lifted a rifle from its place on the wall. It was as large as any she had ever seen. She guessed it was the buffalo gun Scotty had spoken of.

He said, "Don't worry. If it's Tadlock, he'll never get a chance to touch you." Jock stood in the doorway, the rifle balanced across his left arm. After a few moments he eased. "Ain't nothin' but Old Man Feeney on his way to town. It must be Saturday."

He went outside. Shortly Geneva heard him inviting the traveler in for breakfast. Feeney turned out to be somewhat older than the McPhersons, thin-shouldered, with a high-pitched voice. He said, "Can't stay but a few minutes. I ain't been on a good drunk in a long time, so I'm overdue." He added, "I sure do dread it."

That this had turned out to be a false alarm gave Geneva partial relief, but a remnant of fear still haunted her. This time it was a harmless neighbor, but the next time it could be Curly Tadlock.

She shuddered. Half an hour later, she regretfully said her good-byes to the McPherson brothers and was on her way south.

The visit with the McPherson brothers gave Geneva a happy glow that lasted a few miles, until it began to be dispelled by the repulsive memory of Curly Tadlock and the horror of seeing Donley shot down before her eyes. She resisted these images, but they came nevertheless, and with them renewed grief over her husband.

Her memory of Colorado City was darkened by her experience with Luther Fleet. In spite of that, she knew she had to pause there for supplies. Her first stop was a ladies' clothing store. The proprietress looked her over critically, for she was still wearing Jock McPherson's shirt and trousers.

Geneva said, "I need to buy a couple of dresses."

"I'll say you do." The woman shook her head as if in sympathy. "Where in the world did you get those clothes?"

"It's a long story. Just get me into something that won't scare the horses."

"Anything would be an improvement. Let me show you what I have."

Geneva walked out wearing a new dress, paid for with a little of the money from Tadlock's saddlebags. The dress was creased where it had been folded and placed on a shelf. She carried a second dress and some undergarments in a bundle beneath her arm, along with Jock's things.

She went then to a livery stable. The stableman gave his first attention to her horse rather than to her. She said, "Would you know where I might buy a buggy and a buggy horse?"

"You've come to the very place," he said, perking up at the prospect of a sale. "I don't have a new buggy, but I've got one here that seldom got out of the barn except to carry an old lady to church. You can't hardly tell it was ever used."

He showed her the buggy. She had no difficulty in seeing that it had been used, though it appeared to be sturdy enough. She had to haggle with him over the price but settled on a figure. At last she could get out of the saddle and ride more comfortably the two hundred or so miles down to Junction.

He said, "I've got a good buggy horse here. I might make an even swap for that saddle horse you've been ridin'."

Geneva had already decided against selling or trading the horse. She reasoned that by all odds it was probably stolen. She had no right to sell it. She intended when she got out of town and out of sight to turn it loose. Perhaps it would return to wherever it had been stolen from. At any rate it would no longer be on her hands and her conscience.

The buggy horse was a brown, none too young but probably serviceable enough. After settling on a price, the liveryman told her, "I forgot to mention that this horse leans a little to the lazy side. You'll need to pop him with the whip now and again. Horses will take advantage of you if you let them."

"So do some people," Geneva said.

She stopped next at a general store. The balding merchant studied her closely, then said, "I remember you from a while back. You were on your way to meet your husband. I suppose you found him?"

Tight-lipped, she said, "Yes, I did." She did not feel like confiding any more information. Thinking about it brought pain.

He said, "I remember because it was about the same time that some lady put a bullet into a gambler named Fleet." His eyebrows lifted in an unspoken question.

She did not intend to admit anything. "Did it kill him?"

"Sad to say, it didn't. But he'll have to be careful who he cheats from now on. He can't outrun them anymore."

"This lady . . . are the authorities looking for her?"

"If they are, it's to give her a medal. A bunch of people were at the railroad station to watch the sheriff put Fleet on a westbound train. They cheered his leavin'."

Geneva felt some relief in the knowledge that Fleet had not died, though at the time she had wished him dead. At least she did not have a murder charge hanging over her.

She asked, "Do you know a couple of brothers named McPherson?"

"Sure do. Nice fellers, but I can't rightly call them customers. A customer is supposed to spend some money. A merchant will starve to death waitin' on those two."

She handed him a bundle containing Jock's clothes. "Would you set this back somewhere and give it to Jock McPherson the next time he comes? Tell him Geneva said thanks."

Loading the groceries into her buggy, the storekeeper asked, "Whichaway are you headin' now?"

It was conceivable that Tadlock might come along and ask the storekeeper the same question. She told him, "East, toward Fort Worth."

"It'd be a lot easier trip if you took the train. Faster too."

"I'm in no hurry."

But she was. She had the horse moving in a trot as she crossed the railroad tracks. She tried not to look up the dirt street toward Fleet's shack but could not help herself.

She was still glad she had shot him, but glad also that he had not died.

14

Andy knew the two brothers were lying to him about Geneva. Following what they hoped were tracks of Geneva's horse, he and Joshua had come upon the McPherson place at midday. They found the pair in their house, having their noon meal.

"I'm Jock McPherson," one said, answering Andy's knock on the door facing. "You-all are welcome to have dinner with me and my brother Scotty." He gave Joshua a quick study as if having to make a decision. "Both of you."

Andy reasoned that they had cooked just enough for themselves. He declined the invitation. "We need to be travelin' on. We just want to know if you've seen a woman pass by here on horseback—a woman alone."

Suspicion came into McPherson's eyes. His brother

appeared beside him in the doorway and said, "What's this about a woman?"

Jock said, "He wants to know if we've seen one. We ain't, have we?"

The second brother said, "We're two old bachelors. Do you think if we'd seen a woman that we'd've let her get away?" He stepped back inside for a moment, reappearing with a big buffalo rifle in his hands. He demanded, "Would your name be Tadlock?"

That dispelled any doubt Andy might have had about Geneva passing this way. "Tadlock is dead. My name is Pickard. I'm a Ranger. I'm tryin' to find the lady before her husband does."

"Her husband? We thought he got killed."

"She thinks so too. We're tryin' to catch up to her and let her know she may be in some danger."

"Who from, if Tadlock is dead?"

"From her husband."

Jock said, "That doesn't make sense."

"Not to me or you, but we're afraid he's not thinkin' like normal people. He took a crazy notion that she might be better off dead after what Tadlock did to her. We need to catch up to her before he does."

The two brothers stepped back inside and conversed quietly. Returning to the porch, Jock said, "We'll take you at your word."

Scotty McPherson said, "If it'll be of help to you, Ranger, she was headed from here to Colorado City. Past that, she didn't say, and we didn't ask her."

Jock offered, "We'd be glad to go along and help you find her."

"That won't be necessary, but thanks just the same." Andy started to turn away but paused to say, "She must've made a real impression on you-all."

"That she did. Find her, Ranger, and keep her safe."

Andy stopped just north of Colorado City. He said, "We'll need to pick up some grub. The mule's pack is almost empty."

Joshua said, "I don't dast go into town. They'd grab me for sure."

Andy recognized the risk but saw no safe alternative. As a black, Joshua was likely to arouse less suspicion by riding through boldly with Andy than if he were seen circling the town by himself. He said, "Nobody knows you here except by description. If anybody asks, I'll tell them you're a new cook for the Ranger company."

"I can't even boil potatoes."

"We won't have to give them a demonstration."

Reluctantly Joshua rode into town at Andy's side. The few people they passed on the street gave them no more than a moment's notice. Stopping at a store, Andy said, "You'd better go in with me. You'd draw too much notice waitin' out here by yourself."

Nervously Joshua took his place behind Andy and walked into the store, taking off his hat. He was careful to show the deference expected of his people so nobody would pay him undue attention. The storekeeper, paunchy and balding, laid out the items Andy asked for and added their prices on a piece of butcher paper.

Andy took pains to speak to Joshua like a boss to a servant: "Go open the pack and put these things in it while I settle up the bill."

"Yes, sir," Joshua replied quietly, bowing in the traditional manner carried over from slave time.

Andy glanced at the three other people in the store. All seemed to accept without question the boss-servant relationship he and Joshua presented.

The proprietor recognized Andy. He said, "Ranger, aren't you? As I remember it, you spent some time at Mrs. Kelly's boardin' house, recuperatin' from a bullet wound."

"Yes, I did."

"I suppose that boy is a prisoner?"

"No, I picked him up to cook for my company." Andy considered before he asked, "I don't suppose you've seen a strange lady travelin' through alone? A right nice-lookin' lady?"

"As a matter of fact, I loaded her buggy with groceries."

So Geneva had acquired another buggy. That should mean her trail would be easier to follow, Andy thought.

The storekeeper said, "I remembered her because she'd been here before."

"Did she say what her name was?"

The man thought about it. "I believe she said it was Bannister. If she ever told me her given name, I've forgotten."

"Did she say where she was goin'?"

"Said she figured to head east, toward Fort Worth, but she didn't. A customer told me he met her on the road south. He was taken by her good looks."

Andy understood why she would have lied about her plans. He told the storekeeper, "If anybody asks you, you never saw her, and you've got no idea whichaway she went."

"Does that mean somebody is after her?"

"There's a good chance somebody is."

"I'm deaf, dumb, and blind," the storekeeper said.

As Andy walked out, Joshua was re-tying the mule's pack. Uneasy, Joshua said, "Did he ask you anything more about me?"

"No, I think my first answer satisfied him."

They rode on through town, crossing the tracks. Andy glanced up the dirt street toward the house where Geneva had shot Luther Fleet in the leg. He smiled, mentally revisiting that long night and its aftermath. No jury would have convicted her, he thought.

They cleared the town, but Andy could see that Joshua was troubled. He tried to calm him. "We got away with it that time."

Joshua shook his head. "But Santa Angela lays ahead of us. The closer we get, the more I feel like Daniel goin' into the lion's den. The army'll be lookin' to catch me for desertion, and the law'll be wantin' me on account of Mr. Burnsides."

"We could circle west of town and pick up the trail farther south."

Joshua thought about it. "Everybody is the same color in the dark. Maybe we'll be lucky and get to town in the nighttime. But what if Mr. Bannister gets to his missus before we do?"

"We're travelin' as fast as we can without breakin' down the horses. I don't see how he could be movin' any faster."

"Except he got a head start on us."

They were within twenty miles of Santa Angela when they unexpectedly encountered an army patrol—a white lieutenant and six black troopers. Andy and Joshua had no chance to pull off the trail and avoid them. As the patrol advanced, Andy said, "I'll do the talkin'. You just try to look like you don't understand what it's all about."

Joshua appeared ill. "I know a couple of them men, and they know me. I'm as good as dead."

The lieutenant raised a hand, signaling the men behind him to stop. His expression was severe as he rode a few steps farther. He focused his attention mostly on Joshua. He said, "We are on the lookout for a deserter. Your servant fits his description."

Andy noted that the officer automatically assumed Joshua to be a servant. It would not occur to the lieutenant that a black person might be independent and not be in some way responsible to a white. Trying to present a poker face, Andy said, "I'd bet every man you've got with you would match the same description. They all look pretty much alike to me."

The lieutenant said, "The fugitive is also wanted by civilian law enforcement here on a charge of murder."

"Then it couldn't be this boy. I can't even get him to wring a chicken's neck. Besides, him and me just came down from the plains. Ain't likely he could've been up there and killed somebody down here all at the same time."

The lieutenant signaled for his troopers to pull up even with him. "Some of you know Sergeant Hamlin. Is this he?"

Andy held his breath. Joshua somehow managed to sit stone still, staring at the soldiers, awaiting their answer.

After a long silence one said, "It ain't him, sir. The sergeant is a younger man than this'n."

The lieutenant seemed convinced, if disappointed. He gave Andy a curt nod. "Very well, you may be on your way."

Andy and Joshua rode a hundred yards before either spoke or looked back. Both were sweating. Joshua said, "They knowed, all right. They just wouldn't peach on me."

"He said the sergeant is a younger man."

"I've aged considerable in the last few days."

Darkness fell as they followed the North Concho down to the outer reaches of the village. Andy said, "Looks like we timed it right. We'll ride through the edge of town where they haven't got any streetlamps. Nobody'll pay us any attention."

Joshua tilted his hat down low and dropped his chin. Andy said, "Make like we're just a couple of cowboys ridin' through." Despite his show of confidence, his nerves were as taut as a fiddle string.

They crossed the Concho on a bridge and cut around to the east of the fort. A sentry challenged them. "Halt! Who goes there?"

Andy's mouth went dry, but he managed to say, "Me."

The sentry stepped closer, so Andy could see him better. The soldier said, "That's no answer. Who are you?"

"John Smith. Me and my hired hand are on our way down to help on the Bismark farm." Andy had heard about the farm. It furnished foodstuffs and horse and mule feed to the army. He added, "If you want anything to eat next winter, you'd better let us pass. Weeds are takin' the corn crop."

"I won't be here next winter. I'm fixin' to get my discharge. But go ahead on before the corporal sees you. He likes to bedevil civilians."

They camped south of the fort and were on their way again by the time the sun was up. To the southeast lay Fort McKavett, where the Ranger company was stationed and where Bethel waited alone for his return. The thought of passing by without seeing her brought sadness to Andy. But he remembered that he had stayed overlong the last time. Moreover, the fewer people who saw Joshua, the better. They would skirt around McKavett, then cut back into the road to Junction.

Just as they reached the point where Andy had decided to leave the trail, they came upon a slow-moving wagon, carrying a farmer and his wife. Andy hailed them. "Pardon me, folks. I'm a Ranger."

Defensively the man said, "I ain't done nothin'."

"I never thought you did. Are you goin' in to Fort McKavett?"

The farmer said, "Yep, we're about to run out of flour and beans, among other things." He gave Joshua a quick study. "Is this boy your prisoner?"

"No, he's my helper."

"Thought you might've caught the boy everybody's been lookin' for, the one that did the killin' over in Santa Angela awhile back. The way they talk, there's some that've already got a rope stretched and ready for him."

Andy hoped his face did not reveal his uneasiness. He dared not look at Joshua. He said, "I'm on a different case. Since you're headed for McKavett, would you mind takin' a couple of notes there for me? One's for my wife, the other for the Ranger camp. The storekeeper'll see that they get to where they belong."

The farmer looked at his wife. She nodded. He said, "I don't reckon we're in any hurry."

On blank pages torn from the back of his fugitive book, Andy scrawled a note to Sergeant Ryker, informing him that he hoped to intercept Donley Bannister at Junction.

The other note told Bethel that the mission was taking longer than expected, but he hoped it would end soon and he could return to her. He thought about adding *I love you,* but he suspected the farmer, his wife, the storekeeper, and no telling how many others would read it before Bethel did. Anyway, she should know by now. Once they were married, a man ought not to have to keep telling his wife that he loved her.

The farmer placed the folded notes in his shirt pocket. He said, "We're all keepin' an eye out for that soldier boy. They say some of the sportin' crowd has put up a reward for him. It was one of them that he killed."

When the wagon rolled on, Andy turned to Joshua. "You're too popular around here. I ought to've sent you packin' when we were still up north, and pretended like I never saw you. Come night, you'd better slip away."

"That'd cause trouble for you, wouldn't it?"

"I could truthfully say nobody ever told me officially that you're a wanted man. All I've heard about you has been hearsay. They can't convict a man on hearsay."

"They're liable to try."

"By then you can be long gone. There's a lot of black folks in the East Texas cotton country. You could lose yourself amongst them till the law has given up on you. Then you could go just about anywhere."

"I'd like to go back to where I was before these troubles. I liked bein' a sergeant. The army's one place where a black man can make somethin' of hisself. That's all ruined for me now."

"I wish it was otherwise, but that's how the world is. Maybe someday it'll be different."

"Someday I'll be dead. I'm livin' *now.*" Joshua paused. "I reckon I'll stay till we know the lady is safe."

Dusk caught Geneva between Fort Concho and Fort Mc-Kavett. Clouds were restless and darkening in the east, suggesting the possibility of a storm. She did not relish the prospect of camping in the rain. She had thought often about rancher Jess Nathan and the hospitality he had shown when she was traveling northward. She had been thinking of him again today, knowing this trail led by his ranch. Her heart lifted as she recognized his place off to the side of the road.

A faint wagon trail led past his barn on its way to the frame house. She pulled onto it. As she passed a goat shed, she saw Nathan by the barn, feeding grain to his chickens. He lifted a hand in greeting and tossed away what remained of the grain. Wiping his dusty palms on his trouser legs, he walked briskly out to meet her.

"Mrs. Bannister," he said, a broad smile creasing his weathered face. "Welcome to a poor man's castle."

She said, "It looks like a castle to me after the nights I've spent camping beside the road. Do you think you could find room for a visitor who wants to keep out of the rain?"

"The house is yours. Go on over. I'll put up your horse and buggy." He took a closer look. "Different horse, isn't it?"

"Different everything." She removed a small bag from the buggy. "Different me too, I'm afraid. But it's a long story."

"I've got all evenin' to listen to it."

His smile gave her more comfort than she had felt since she had left the McPherson brothers' place. It went against her nature to impose on the kindness of people she did not know, but with Nathan it seemed different. Like the McPhersons, he plainly welcomed her company. Her leaning upon him for help did not seem an imposition, at least not a burdensome one. She knew he was pleased to see her.

She carried her bag to the house. Inside, she saw that it was not as neat as the McPhersons', though it was not the boar's nest that Wilkes's dugout had been. It was evident that Nathan regarded the outdoors as his province. The house was primarily a convenience for eating and sleeping out of the weather. What it needed—what Nathan needed—was a woman, she thought.

Maybe this *woman*. She considered the idea but pushed it aside. Donley was too recently dead for her to entertain any such whimsical notions.

Nathan's noon dishes sat in a dry pan, unwashed. She could imagine his rushing through the meal so he could get back out to tend the livestock or his small field. Such niceties as washing dishes could wait for nightfall. She started a fire in the cookstove and set a pan of water on it to heat. She found a broom and began sweeping the floor.

Nathan came in, saw her at work, and said, "You don't need to be doin' that. I'll take care of it in my own time. You're a guest."

"I like to earn my keep." She swept the small accumulation of dirt out the door. "I take it you haven't had supper yet. I'll fix it."

Nathan grinned. "Lady, I wish I could hire you to stay here all the time. But I don't suppose your husband would take kindly to that."

Geneva's face fell. Nathan sobered quickly. He apologized: "I'm sorry if I said somethin' wrong. I meant it as a compliment."

With a catch in her throat, she said, "You couldn't have known. Donley is dead. Murdered."

Nathan mouthed the word *murdered* but did not say it aloud. "That's too bad." His voice was subdued. "Do you know who did it?"

"A man named Curly Tadlock. I'm afraid he's after me now."

"Why would he be after you?"

Geneva did not know how to answer him, but her silence seemed to tell him enough. He nodded gravely and said, "He won't get you if I can do anything about it. Do you have an idea where he is now?"

She shook her head. "I haven't seen him, but I've had this feeling, this tingling at the back of my neck. I'm being followed."

Nathan's voice hardened. "If he follows you here, he'll wish he hadn't." His gaze went to a rifle hanging on pegs beside the door.

She said, "I'm on my way back to Junction. The sheriff will watch out for me, and I have friends there."

"You've got a friend here too."

Unconsciously she touched his hand, then quickly pulled back. "This is my trouble. I don't want to draw you into it."

"You already have, just tellin' me about it."

They fell silent while she cooked supper. They ate quietly, most of the time avoiding looking at each other. Nathan finally broke the silence. "I'm sorry about your husband. I can imagine the shock that must've been for you, havin' it happen all of a sudden. With my wife, she was sick a little while. At least I had some time to get used to the idea before she died."

"His death wasn't the only shock I had." She looked at the floor. "I found out he was a horse thief."

Nathan took a minute to absorb that. "I'm sorry. You deserve better."

Geneva sat, hands clasped around a cold coffee cup, and told Nathan what had happened since she left here. She did not describe Tadlock's assault, but smoldering anger in his eyes told her that he sensed what she left out.

He said, "Too bad you stopped at throwin' coals in his face. You ought to've emptied a gun into him."

"I thought about that later. At the time, I just had to get away from there."

As before, he gave her his bed. Instead of sleeping in the barn, however, he carried blankets out onto the porch. He said, "Tadlock might sneak past me at the barn, but he won't get by me on the porch."

For the first time since leaving the McPhersons, she felt comfortable and safe. She did not drift easily into sleep, however. She lay thinking of Donley and trying to remember happy times, but instead she relived the pain and terror Curly Tadlock had forced upon her. Finally, for refuge from the dark memories, she thought of Nathan sleeping peacefully just outside the door. She imagined how her life might have been had she married him instead of Donley. It might not have offered much excitement, but it would not have been lonely. She would always have known where her husband was and when he would be home. She wished Nathan could have come into her life earlier. She might well have made a different choice.

She became aware of raindrops beating against the window. She realized that the slightest wind would blow rain onto the porch where Nathan lay. She arose and lighted a lamp in the kitchen, then threw a wrap around her shoulders and opened the front door. She asked, "Aren't you getting wet out there?"

From beneath a blanket he admitted, "A little."

"Come in here where it's dry."

"I'm in my underwear."

"We're grown people."

He gathered his blankets and brought them inside, covering himself with them. Geneva stoked the coals in the stove and added extra wood. She said, "You're shivering. Come over here where you can get warm."

He put on his trousers, kept dry beneath the blankets. He said, "I'm much obliged."

"Nothing to be obliged for. It's your house."

He said, "It's not the first time I ever slept in the rain. I've seen a lot worse than this one."

"It's enough to give you a chill. I'll fix some coffee."

She was keenly aware of his gaze following her while she ground the coffee and put the pot on the stove. She was pleasantly warmed by his attention.

He said, "Seein' you here in the kitchen takes me back. It reminds me how lonesome this place can be."

"Haven't you ever thought about getting married again?"

"Thought about it, but never done anything about it. I get shy around most womenfolks. Even you, a little."

"There's no need to be shy with me. I've never hurt a man in my life. Well, maybe one or two."

"I'm sure they deserved it. You're a good woman, Geneva."

She brought him a cup of coffee, then dragged a chair up close to his. She felt strongly drawn as she stared at him. He was not handsome in the way Donley was. Time and hardship had cut lines in his face, and she saw loneliness in his eyes. But he had a determined chin that told her he still had a lot of fight in him. Life might have beaten him down some, but it had not defeated him.

She noticed a badly skinned knuckle and took his hand. "You should have done something about this. How did it happen?"

"Tryin' to shut a gate on a cow that didn't want me to stop her. She won." He shrugged it off. "This kind of thing happens all the time when you deal with animals. I don't pay much attention to it."

She let her fingers run slowly over the knuckles, the palm. "They're rough," she said. "They've seen a lot of hard work."

"The Good Book says, by the sweat of thy brow . . ."

"They're honest hands. I like them."

He squeezed her fingers gently. She squeezed back, not wanting to let go.

She awakened at first light and heard Nathan putting wood in the stove and starting a fresh pot of coffee. As she entered the kitchen, he went outside to look around. He returned to say, "I don't see anything amiss. I'll be back as soon as I've done the milkin'."

"I'll have breakfast ready."

He picked up his rifle from beside the door and carried it with him.

At breakfast, they exchanged glances but little conversation. There was much Geneva wanted to say, though she could not bring out the words. She felt that Nathan was struggling with the same problem. She wished she could feel the strength of his arms around her, but she held back, as she knew he was holding back.

She said, "While I clean up the kitchen, would you mind hitching my horse to the buggy?"

Nathan frowned. "Are you sure you want to go?"

"It's best. The sooner I leave, the sooner I can get to the sheriff in Junction."

"This county has a sheriff too."

"But the one in Junction knows me." She remembered the young Ranger who had watched her before she began her journey. "And there is other law around there if he needs help."

Putting away the breakfast utensils, she heard him bringing up the buggy. She saw that a saddled horse was tied on behind. As Nathan came into the house, she asked, "Why the extra horse?"

He said, "I'm goin' with you."

"There's no reason for you to do that."

"There's plenty of reason. I wouldn't want Tadlock to catch you out on the road by yourself."

"I've traveled alone for days."

"You aren't alone now, and you won't be from here on."

She worried. "He would kill you without giving you a chance."

"Not if I see him first."

Geneva was torn between gratitude toward Nathan and fear that he would not be a match for Tadlock. She said, "You're a rancher. What do you know about gun-fighting?"

"Enough. I lied about my age and went into the

Confederate army durin' the last of the war. I learned to do what I had to, like it or not."

"Even to risking your life for me?"

Nathan hesitated. "You've just lost your husband. It's way too soon for me to be sayin' this, but you're a widow, and I'm a widower. After a suitable time . . ." He left it there.

She felt tears warm in her eyes. "I'm all mixed up inside. So much has happened to me. As you said, we can talk about it, after a suitable time . . ."

Nathan gathered up a blanket, some groceries, and a rifle. He climbed into the buggy and took the reins. Geneva tilted her head to look into his face. It was somber.

Someday, she thought, when a proper time had passed . . .

15

Andy did not worry much about following the buggy tracks, for he was sure now where she was going. He noted at one point that Geneva pulled off the main trail and went up to a ranch house he remembered from the trip north. The rancher's name, as he recalled, had been Nathan. Geneva had spent the night in the house while Nathan had slept in the barn. From that, Andy had concluded that Geneva was a lady, and Nathan was a gentleman.

A nighttime rain had compromised the tracks leading to the house, but mud had preserved those leading southward away from it. They told him the buggy had been beneath the shed during the storm. He guessed that Geneva had probably spent the night here again. The condition of the drying mud indicated that the tracks had been made as recently as this morning.

He rode up to the front of the house and shouted, "Anybody home?"

He was not surprised that no one answered. A responsible rancher should be somewhere out on his land at this time of day, not lazing around the house.

He told Joshua, "We've made up a lot of time. Maybe we can catch her before dark."

After a while he noticed something that intrigued him. He said, "See anything about the buggy horse's tracks?"

Joshua said, "Can't say as I do."

"It looks like a second horse is followin' the buggy."

"Mr. Bannister, you think? Maybe he's got between her and us."

Andy saw concern in Joshua's eyes. He knew it reflected his own. Searching for another explanation, he suggested, "It might be there's a horse tied behind the buggy."

"How could that be?"

"That rancher Nathan. I suspected he was taken some with Geneva Bannister the last time. Maybe he's decided to go along and protect her."

"But they think Mr. Tadlock is trailin' her. If Mr. Bannister catches them, they won't be expectin' him to give them any trouble. They'll let their guard down."

"He's apt to figure the worst if he finds her with Nathan."

"Then we'd better lope up."

They put the horses into an easy gallop. At the top of each hill Andy hoped to see the buggy ahead, but again and again he was disappointed. He and Joshua alternated between a lope and a trot, trying to cover distance, yet spare the horses. Finally, toward dusk, he saw a dark form a mile or so ahead. He asked, "What does that look like to you?"

Joshua squinted. "Either a buggy or a wagon. I hope it's the right one."

Closing, Andy saw that it was indeed a buggy. As he had guessed, a horse was tied behind it. He said, "We'd better slow down and announce ourselves before we get too near. I don't know how good a shot Nathan is, but Mrs. Bannister has proven she knows how to handle a gun."

They were more than two hundred yards out when he saw a man jump from the buggy, then help a woman down. He slowed his horse to a walk and motioned for Joshua to trail a little way behind him. A hundred yards out, he shouted, "We're comin' in peaceful."

Joshua said, "That man has got a rifle."

"I saw it. Raise your hands so they can see we mean no harm."

They were within twenty yards before Nathan stepped out from behind the buggy. He lowered the rifle to arm's length. He said, "We couldn't tell who you were." He frowned, his eyes narrowed. "Seems to me I remember you. Ranger, aren't you?"

"Yes. Andy Pickard's my name."

"Last time I saw you, you were trailin' Mrs. Bannister."

"Still am, or was. I see I finally caught up with her."

"She's done nothin' wrong. You've got no call to badger her now."

Geneva came out from the protection of the buggy and gave Andy a long study. She said, "I remember you from

Junction. You trailed me when I left. I thought I lost you a long time ago."

"You did, off and on. I always managed to pick up your tracks sooner or later."

"There's no need now. My husband is dead."

Andy had been trying to think of a gentle way to tell her but had not come up with any that suited him. He decided the best course was to come right out with it, point-blank. He said, "I've got news for you, Mrs. Bannister. Before I tell you, you'd better grab ahold of that buggy and hang on tight. Your husband is not dead."

She shook as if he had struck her. "But Curly Tadlock shot him. I saw him fall."

"His pocket watch took the slug. He was stunned, but he came around after a while."

Geneva swayed. Nathan put an arm around her shoulder and steadied her. She murmured a few incomprehensible words, then said, "Curly dragged me away so quickly, I didn't know. I thought he was dead."

"He's not, but Tadlock is."

She gasped. "Curly is dead?"

"Stone cold. Shot himself in the head."

"Then I've done all this running for nothing."

"Not for nothin'. You may still be in danger. Last time we saw your husband, he was talkin' wild. He might have it in mind to kill you."

Her face seemed to lose color. "Kill me? Why?"

Andy explained as best he could, though he could not quite understand it himself. "He said after what happened, it might be better if you were dead."

The news seemed to strike Nathan almost as hard as it

struck Geneva. He removed his arm from her shoulder and said, "I'm sorry. You don't deserve this."

She said, "Maybe you'd best go back. There's no reason to get yourself involved in this."

"I'm not leavin' you."

Andy considered their words to one another and the expressions in their faces. He needed no explanation. He said, "We won't make Junction tonight. We'd best find a decent place to camp."

Geneva's pulse raced as they descended the last long limestone hill before entering the outskirts of Junction. She wished for the comforting presence of Nathan beside her, but since breaking camp he had been on his horse, riding beside the Ranger. He had avoided looking her in the eyes. He had entertained a dream, only to see it shattered by the fact that Donley was still alive. She had lost a dream as well.

Joshua trailed behind the buggy as a rear guard. Once when Geneva thought Andy and Nathan were beyond hearing, she summoned Joshua to pull up beside her. She said quietly, "There's enough brush here to hide a herd of elephants. You could disappear in the blink of an eye."

"Yes'm." Joshua's voice was solemn. "Reckon I could."

"Then why don't you? You know what'll happen if you're arrested. They'll send you back to Santa Angela to stand trial . . . if you even live that long."

"If a man's vow ain't worth nothin', then he ain't either. I made a vow to Mr. Andy that I'd stick till we seen this thing through. The minute it's done, I'm gone."

"You may not get the chance."

"That's up to the good Lord. He freed Joshua from the lion's den."

"I believe that was Daniel. Joshua fought the battle of Jericho."

"That's all right too. My name's Joshua."

They heard the sound of a horse, galloping. Andy warned, "Get down from the buggy, Mrs. Bannister, till we see who this is. Anything happens, run for the brush." He drew his rifle and stepped down. Joshua and Nathan followed his lead.

The rider slowed his horse and yelled, "I'm friendly."

Relieved, Andy broke into a smile. "Everybody take it easy. It's just Len Tanner. He's an old Ranger."

Tall, lean, hungry-looking, Len Tanner stopped his horse and bent forward to pat its shoulder. "I was afraid I wouldn't catch you-all. I had to lope up a right smart."

Andy strode forward to grip Len's hand. "Did Sergeant Ryker send you?"

"He got your note. Said I'd better come and help because you've got a nasty habit of gettin' yourself shot. Headquarters is tired of payin' your doctor bills."

"You've been shot before too."

"Seldom ever. One advantage of bein' skinny is that I don't make much of a target. You-all got anything to eat?"

Andy turned to Geneva. "Would you get him a can of tomatoes or somethin', please? Otherwise he'll complain all the way in to town."

If not that, Len would talk about something else. His jaw was not often at rest except when he was asleep, and not always then.

Andy had to ask, "Have you seen Bethel?"

"Why? Do you think she's gone and left you? She ought

to, the way you keep ridin' off and leavin' *her*. If she was mine, I'd set her up on a shelf over the fireplace and just look at her all the time. Or put her in my pocket and carry her with me."

"I wish I could."

Andy and Len trailed far enough behind the buggy that Geneva would not hear their conversation. Andy explained what had happened and what he feared might when they reached Junction.

Len wanted to know about Joshua. He said, "I figured him for that Fort Concho fugitive soon as I took sight of him. How'd you manage to catch him?"

"I didn't." Andy told him all of it.

Len seemed dubious. "You mean he's come all this way with you and not once tried to get away?"

"I haven't even put him under arrest. I've had no official word that he's a wanted man."

"What're you goin' to do about him?"

"I don't know yet."

Troubled, Len said, "You could get yourself in hot water all the way to your chin."

"I've been there before."

Andy took the lead going into Junction. It was a small ranching town, its mostly lumber and stone houses scattered along the North Llano River. Nearing Geneva's frame home, he stopped and told her, "There's a chance he's got here ahead of us. I'll walk through the house and make sure he's not there. You stay out here with Nathan and Joshua."

Len went around to the back in case Bannister should slip out that way.

Nathan dismounted. He said to Geneva, "Might be better if you get down and stand behind me on this side of the buggy." He helped her to the ground and held to her arm. He said, "Nobody's goin' to hurt you if I can help it."

"I know." She leaned against his shoulder, borrowing from his strength.

She noticed two men seated on the edge of a porch across the dirt street and two houses down from her own. Recognition brought a surge of apprehension. She said, "One of them is Vince Slocum. The other is Willy Pegg. Where the Slocums go, Pegg follows like a lost puppy."

Nathan said, "Your husband shot a Slocum, didn't he?"

"Cletus. Vince and Judd are worse than Cletus was, and Finis is the worst of the lot. They must be watching for Donley."

"Did they threaten you in any way after he left here?"

"They knew I had friends who wouldn't tolerate them hurting me. They just watched everything I did, and tried to trail me when I left. I'm sure they expected me to lead them to Donley."

"I almost wish you had." Nathan immediately apologized. "That was an awful thing for me to say. It's just that I can't help hatin' your husband a little. He put you in a bad fix."

Tight-lipped, she said, "It's better if neither of us says anything more. I'm afraid we may have said too much already."

Andy emerged from the house. He said, "I went all the way through it. The bed's been slept in, and the kitchen's been used, but I didn't see Bannister."

Geneva did not have to guess. She said, "Donley's already been here. That's why the Slocums are hovering around like buzzards. They're waiting for him to show himself."

Andy said, "Buzzards just watch for somethin' to die naturally. The Slocums are lookin' for a chance to kill somebody."

Len returned from behind the house, pistol in his hand. Judd Slocum walked ahead of him, his hands raised. Len said, "He was watchin' the rear door. I figured he wasn't up to any good."

Andy said, "Neither are the others." He strode up to them, his rifle across his arm. "I'm puttin' you-all under arrest."

"What for?" Vince demanded. "We ain't done nothin'. We're just sittin' here."

"Is this your house?"

Vince glanced at the two men who flanked him. "Nope."

"Did you ask anybody's permission to sit there?"

"Never saw no need."

"Then you're under arrest for trespassin'. Throw your guns back onto that porch and step out here into the street."

Grumbling, the two brothers and Pegg complied.

Andy said, "There's one of you missin'. Where's Finis?"

"Ain't seen him," Vince said, giving the other two a sharp look that told them to keep quiet.

With these three neutralized, Andy decided one Slocum should not be too much to handle. He told Geneva, "I think it's safe for you to go in the house. If we see your husband coming, we'll stop him before he can reach you."

She cautioned, "I don't want him hurt."

Nathan argued, "But if he intends harm to you . . ."

"He *is* still my husband."

* * *

With heartbeat quickening, Geneva stepped up onto the porch, then through the door into the house. She paused, looking around, remembering. Life with Donley Bannister had not been easy. True, there had been good times here when he was at home, but there had been painfully lonely times during periods when he would be gone. Some of his absences were so long that she began to wonder if something had happened to him, or if he might even have abandoned her. His homecomings had brought her brief joy, increasingly tempered by the realization that soon he would be gone again to Lord knew where.

Now, to her regret, she knew where he had been going and what he had been doing. Some things it would have been better not to know.

She smelled tobacco smoke. The Ranger had not been smoking. The scent told her that Bannister had been here, and not long ago. She looked into the bedroom they had shared, often for too short a time. She had made the bed before she left. Now the blankets had been thrown back carelessly. She walked into the kitchen. A dirty plate sat on the table, an empty cup beside it. She felt faint warmth from the stove and found a cooling coffeepot on top. It had not been long since Bannister had cooked and eaten a meal here.

She felt a prickling sensation at the back of her neck. She heard the creak of hinges and froze, a chill traveling down her spine. For a moment she was afraid to turn around. When she did, she saw a pantry door slowly opening. Donley Bannister stepped out into the kitchen.

A startled cry lodged in her throat.

He rushed forward and covered her mouth with a big, rough hand. He said, "Don't holler. They might come in here shootin'." He lowered his hand, and she gasped for breath. He said, "Yes, It's me. I'm alive. It'll take a better man than Curly to kill me. He wasn't no man at all." He brought his hands up to her cheeks. She shrank back, fearing he was about to choke her. Instead, he kissed her, warmly.

She gasped for breath. "They told me . . ." She could not finish.

"That I figured on killin' you?" He leaned back and stared at her, his face remorseful. He said, "I was like a wild man at first. I told myself I had to kill Curly, and I had to kill the woman he ruined, like I'd shoot a crippled horse. But when I saw him layin' in his own blood like a sheep-killin' dog, I realized what a worthless piece of nothin' he was."

He bent forward and kissed her again. "You're a beautiful woman, Geneva. Nothin' Curly did could change that. I kept closin' my eyes and seein' your face. I knew I could never hurt you. But I got to worryin' that the Slocums might. I had to get back home and see that they didn't."

She tried to speak but had difficulty controlling her voice. Tears burned her eyes. "They must've known you were here."

He said, "I tried not to let anybody see me come in last night, but somebody did. When I got up this mornin' I saw the Slocums, bidin' their time. They didn't have the guts to rush the house, but they knew sooner or later I'd have to come out."

Geneva strained to speak. "There are two Rangers. They'll protect you and take you to the sheriff."

"It's a good ways to the jailhouse. All a Slocum needs is one lucky shot."

"Perhaps you should never have come home."

"I had to. I had to see you again even if it meant takin' a stand against the whole Slocum family."

A shadow came up behind Bannister. She recognized the young Ranger's voice: "Back off, Bannister. I don't want to shoot you."

Geneva said, "It's all right. He's not going to hurt me."

Jess Nathan rushed into the house. He demanded, "Geneva, are you all right?" Anxiously he placed both hands on her shoulders.

She said, "I'm fine." She looked quickly at Bannister, knowing he had to have noticed.

Gravely the Ranger asked Bannister, "Are you sure you've gotten over those notions you had?"

Bannister said, "I didn't have them very long. Look at her. She's still as pretty as she ever was. I could no more kill her than I could cut off my arms and legs. She's part of me."

In spite of what he was saying, she knew she was not the same woman as before. She never would be again.

Bannister asked, "Geneva, do you think we can ever get back to where we were?"

She could not give him the positive answer he wanted. She said, "We can try."

Bannister turned to Nathan. He asked, "Are you a Ranger too?"

Nathan said, "No, just a friend."

"Right now I need all the friends I can get."

"I'm not sure I'm your friend, but I'm hers."

* * *

Bannister grimaced and turned his attention to Andy. "Think you can get me to the sheriff's office without the Slocums shootin' me?"

"We're sittin' on all of thcm but Finis. We don't know where he's at."

"Finis, eh? Could I keep my pistol till we get there?"

Andy shook his head. "I'm afraid not. It would bust hell out of forty-'leven regulations." He reached out to receive the weapon.

Bannister shrugged. "I never thought I'd be glad for a Ranger escort. When do you want to start?"

Andy said, "I don't see anything wrong with right now." He frowned. "I looked through the house before I let her come in. Where were you hidin'?"

Bannister pointed with his thumb. "The pantry."

"I never saw it, but I'll never miss another one."

Bannister said, "You told me everybody thinks I'll be acquitted for shootin' Cletus Slocum."

"That seems to've been the general opinion around here."

"What about the horse business?"

Andy cast a glance at Geneva as he thought about it. "You didn't steal any around here, did you?"

Bannister said, "Even a bird knows to keep its nest clean." He extended his hands. "Goin' to handcuff me?"

"I don't see that as necessary." Andy went to the door for a careful look outside. He said, "Wish I knew where Finis was."

Bannister said, "He's hidin' somewhere. Probably hopin' for a clear shot."

Andy grunted. "That does cloud the picture." He stepped

out onto the porch and beckoned for Bannister to follow. "Stay close behind me."

"He wouldn't mind shootin' you to get to me."

"He may think about it some. Everybody knows you don't live long when you kill a Ranger."

Len's face fell as Bannister walked out onto the porch. "He was in the house with his wife all that time? He could've killed her."

Andy said, "But he didn't."

Bannister and the two Slocum brothers exchanged heated glances. Vince hissed, "You better be thinkin' about your last words, Donley, because you ain't got much time."

Andy said impatiently, "I want you Slocums to walk two paces ahead of us. You'd better hope your brother Finis doesn't try anything, because one of you might get in the way of a bullet."

Vince protested, "You've got no right to treat us thisaway."

Andy said, "Sue me." He turned to say to Geneva, "Stay in the house till it's over."

She started to argue. "But . . ."

Nathan said urgently, "Please, Geneva. Do what he says."

Bannister cut a glance toward Nathan but said nothing.

Geneva retreated to the porch and stood at the door, watching.

Joshua was unarmed. Because of his fugitive status, Andy thought it best to leave him that way. He said, "You stay behind us. Walk alongside Bannister."

Len said, "I was afraid you were fixin' to give him a gun."

"I considered it." Andy said to the Slocums and Pegg, "Now, you three, start walkin' toward the jailhouse." He poked Vince in the back with the muzzle of his rifle to emphasize that he was serious.

Vince grumbled, "Damned high-handed Rangers, you think you're the kings of the world. We've got a right to even the score with Donley. An eye for an eye, that's what the book says."

Andy retorted, "Somebody must've told you that. I'll bet you never read it yourself."

"Our old daddy taught us to not let any man walk over us."

"Everybody has told me it was a fair fight."

"Everybody wasn't there."

They reached the end of the block. Andy said, "Now stop." The street took a slight turn to the right. He doubted that anyone purposely laid the town out like that. This was probably the way the original wagon trail came in, so the trail gradually became a street as houses went up along its length.

Andy said, "Len, I don't like the looks of it. How about you goin' ahead of us and watchin' out for boogers?"

"Just what I was about to suggest."

Andy was in a heightened state of alert, his gaze searching along the street for sign of ambush. He saw Len pause and give serious study to a white church with a bell tower extending well above its roof. Anyone waiting in its top would have a wide-open view of the street. After a minute Len continued up the street almost to the courthouse. He turned and started back, giving Andy a come-on signal.

Andy said, "We're goin' ahead. You Slocums stick close together."

They had gone only a short way when something struck the bell and made it clang. The two Slocums and Pegg suddenly cut to the left and broke into a run, leaving Andy and the others in the open.

Instinctively Andy swung the rifle in their direction, then realized he had no reason to fire on them. He also realized that the striking of the bell had been a prearranged signal. He turned quickly, bringing the rifle's muzzle back toward the bell tower. He saw a movement there. Before he could draw a bead, he saw a flash and felt a sharp burn along his extended right arm. The arm went numb. The rifle fell from his hands.

A second shot came from the tower, its echo lost amid pistol fire from Len and Nathan. Joshua dropped to one knee and picked up Andy's fallen rifle. He fired once. The man in the tower fell backward against the bell, causing it to ring. Joshua fired a second time. Andy caught a glimpse of a bloodied face before the man fell inside the tower, out of sight.

Nathan said, "Good shootin'. You must've been some soldier."

Joshua said, "The army gave me a sharpshooter medal."

The Slocums stopped running. Vince turned and shook his fist, crying, "Murder! Everybody come see. It's murder!"

Len fired, the bullet kicking up dust near Vince's feet. Vince set out running again. Judd Slocum raced after him. Pegg knelt in the street, sobbing in helpless fright, begging that nobody shoot him.

Len said, "I can catch them if you think I ought to."

Andy said, "It was Finis did the shootin'. The others will get theirs one of these days." He grasped his burning arm. Blood trickled warm between his fingers.

Andy turned and saw for the first time that Bannister was on the ground. He asked urgently, "Are you all right?"

Bannister grunted and raised up partway to his knees. His face was going sallow. "Hell, no. That damned Finis got me square in the gut. And no pocket watch this time." Blood spilled around the hand he held pressed against his stomach.

Andy said, "We'll get you to a doctor."

Bannister wheezed, "Better call a preacher instead. There ain't no doctor goin' to fix a hole this big."

Townspeople were starting to converge from all directions. Bannister tried to hold a sitting position but could not. He sank to the ground on his back. Voice fading, he asked, "Where's Geneva?"

Geneva came running up the dirt street and pushed her way through the gathering crowd. Trembling, she dropped to her knees beside Bannister and took his limp hand.

He seemed to have trouble seeing her. He whispered, "Geneva, I'm sorry."

She cried, "I'm sorry, too. I wish you hadn't come home."

"Had to. Had to see you." He struggled for breath. "Don't cry over me. I lied to you. I shot Cletus Slocum like Pegg said. Never gave him a chance." His eyes dulled. His breathing slowed, then stopped.

Geneva wept. Nathan waited a little, then gently helped her to her feet. "I'll walk you home," he said.

She whispered, "I wish you would."

"I'll take you to my place if you'd like."

"Sometime. Not yet a while."

Andy watched them as they walked away, Nathan's arm around her shoulder. He closed Bannister's eyes and placed the man's hat over his face. He stood up, gripping the burning arm.

Len said, "I swear, you got yourself bloodied again."

"I've had a dog bite me worse. I wish you and Joshua would go over to the church tower and make sure about Finis." He looked around. "Where *is* Joshua?"

Len had a false innocent look that usually gave him away. "Well, I'll swun. After the shootin' stopped, he must've took it in his head to leave. I'll go lookin' for him in a day or two, when I get time. Right now I've got to get you patched up and take you back to Bethel."

Bethel. Andy spoke the name aloud. It was like music.

Len said, "I'll turn in the report on this. I'll say you shot Finis. No use stirrin' up a lot of questions about how that soldier boy came to be here."

Andy nodded. "That's best." A white lie, well considered, could sometimes serve justice better than the raw truth.

Len complained, "Bethel's goin' to be real peeved with me, lettin' you get shot again after I promised I'd look after you. I swear, boy, you're an awful burden to us."

Andy and Len rode toward the frame house at the edge of Fort McKavett. Len had talked all the way up from Junction, his subjects ranging from the changing weather ("It seems to get hotter nowadays than it used to") to horses ("Seems to me they was better in the old days before so much mustang was bred out of them") to Geneva Bannister's future.

Len said, "She's a mighty good-lookin' widow. Maybe I ought to go callin' on her myself, after a respectable time."

Andy thought about Jess Nathan. "I suspect her future is already taken care of."

Len shrugged. "My skirt-chasin' days are over with anyhow. I'm too set in my ways. Any woman I married would probably wind up shootin' me, and no jury would convict her."

"What'll you do when you get too old for Rangerin'?"

"By that time you and Bethel will have a houseful of kids. I'll take my pension, settle down next to your place, and help you-all raise them."

"You've got no guarantee that they'll ever give you a pension."

"Then I'll just bum off of you. I don't eat much." Len reined up. "This is far enough. I don't need another lecture from Bethel about me lettin' you get yourself hurt. I'll tell the sergeant not to look for you today. Right now you'd best report to a higher authority."

"Are you sure you won't stay? She'll probably fix us a good dinner."

"Like I said, I don't eat much. There's times when two are just right, and three are one too many." He rode off in the direction of the Ranger camp.

Bethel walked out onto the little porch, excitedly waving her hand. Andy put his horse into a trot and was glad Len had ridden on.

TEXAS
STANDOFF

A NOVEL OF
THE TEXAS RANGERS

1

Andy Pickard had often considered leaving the Texas Rangers. His young wife, Bethel, had been urging him to take up the more stable life of a stockman, or even a storekeeper—anything that would keep him close to home. Now he almost wished he had given in to her, for his sergeant had assigned him to hunt down a lowly sneak thief. Not only that, but he was sending a stranger with Andy in the search.

It seemed a waste of two Rangers' time to trail after the likes of Jasper Biggs when murderers and horse thieves roamed the land. But Sergeant Ryker had wearied of hearing complaints about the man's petty larceny. He said, "We need to slam the cell door on this chicken-stealin' tramp. I'm sendin' Logan Daggett with you. Do you know him?"

"Never met him," Andy said without enthusiasm, "but I've heard of him. I reckon everybody has."

Daggett had a long record with the Rangers, not all of it positive. Stories indicated that he had a short fuse and was given to sudden violence. He considered consequences later, if at all.

By contrast, Andy liked to think things through before jumping into deep water, weighing the costs against the gain. After giving most of his youth to Ranger service, he felt he was due a little extra consideration. He said, "It'd suit me better to ride with somebody I know, like Len Tanner."

His comment appeared to annoy the sergeant. He was used to a quick "Yes, sir," when he gave an order. "I've sent Tanner off on another job. Daggett just got into camp last night, so he's available."

Andy said, "They say he's too quick to go on the fight."

Ryker's narrowed eyes hinted at sarcasm. "And *you've* sometimes been a little slow about it. I figure you should be a good team, makin' up for each other's weaknesses."

In Andy's view, Jasper Biggs was a two-bit night-prowling scavenger. He said, "This looks like a job for some deputy sheriff to do in his spare time. It shouldn't take two of us. I could handle it by myself, easy."

"If you could locate him. But he's at home down in those Llano River oak and cedar thickets. Logan is a good tracker, and I've seen that you're not."

Andy admitted, "There's things I do better."

"Most of Logan's service has been up on the plains. Lately he got into an unpleasant incident at Tascosa. Took a bullet in his leg. They transferred him down here so he wouldn't take another in the back."

An unpleasant incident. That did not bode well, Andy thought. He wondered what Daggett had done, but he would not ask. "Which of us will be in charge?"

"He's older than you, and been a Ranger longer. But I hope you'll gee-haw together so that the question of command won't come up."

Andy thought of Bethel. This might be the time to quit, as she had long wanted. She would fret about him the whole time he was gone. Anyway, this seemed too piddling a mission for someone with his record of service. Maybe it was a sign that they were gradually edging him out. The state's money counters were always trying to cut expenses.

Ryker recognized Andy's reluctance. He said, "This'll give your bride a chance to rest. She probably gets more sleep when she has her bed to herself."

Andy's face warmed. What went on between him and Bethel was personal. They had bought a modest parcel of land on the Guadalupe River near Kerrville, and she had been pressing him to build a house on it so they could be together all the time. But he wanted to give her something better than a one-room shack. He wanted a livestock operation large enough to provide her a comfortable living. He was managing to bank some of his Ranger wages and an occasional reward, but the process of accumulation was slower than he liked.

He doubted there would be much, if any, reward for Biggs. The man's crimes were more nuisance than hardship for his victims, though Ryker said he had recently been discovered burglarizing a farmhouse at night. He had struck the owner with a chunk of stove wood before escaping into the dark.

"It's the first time I've heard of him resortin' to violence," the sergeant said. "It may mean he's gone a little crazy. Hermits like him are usually halfway down that hill anyhow. We've got to bring him in before he hurts somebody real bad."

That put a different complexion on the situation. Andy had assumed Biggs was simply lazy, though he probably worked harder at his minor thievery than if he had a conventional job, and gained less for his efforts. Even other men of the outlaw stripe looked down on him for his limited ambition.

Andy was headquartered in a company tent camp on the San Saba River near Fort McKavett. He spent his off time, limited though it was, with Bethel in a small frame house he rented at the edge of the village. She heard his horse and came out to stand on the front step, a wisp of a woman still in her mid-twenties. The wind tugged gently at her brown hair and ruffled the apron tied around her narrow waist. Looking at her after an absence took his breath away. Leaving her was always difficult.

She had developed an uncanny knack of reading his mind. With a slight tone of impatience she asked, "How long will you be gone this time?"

That was a question he could seldom answer with certainty. Some assignments were short. Others dragged on and on. He said, "No longer than I have to. I'd be obliged for somethin' to eat before I report back to camp." He paused, striving for his most persuasive voice. "No tellin' when I'll get another meal that's half as good as what you fix."

Despite herself, she allowed a tiny smile to escape. She still reacted warmly to compliments. "Tie up your horse, and I'll see what scraps I can find in the kitchen." She tiptoed, inviting a kiss.

While bustling about the small iron stove, she asked, "Who are they sending you after this time? Is he somebody I should worry about?"

He said, "He's a grubby, low-life thief who lives like a coyote down in the thickets. They claim he's too much of a coward to be dangerous."

"They say it's the cowards you have to watch the most. They come at you when you're not looking."

He said, "I always watch out for myself." He started to add that it was not in his plan for her to become a widow, but he left the thought unspoken. It might cause her to worry more, knowing that such a notion had even crossed his mind.

She baked biscuits, fried a thick slice of ham, and heated beans left over from yesterday. He could hardly take his eyes from her while she worked. Mentally he cursed Biggs for causing him to leave. But if not for Biggs, he would be going out to hunt for someone else. The desk-bound accountants in Austin could not abide seeing a Ranger idle.

Finished eating, he carried his plate and utensils to a tin pan on top of the cabinet. There, not entirely by accident, he bumped against Bethel as she put away the leftover biscuits. He folded his arms around her tiny waist. "I don't want to go," he said.

She smiled. "Then stay a while. Tell them your horse broke the bridle reins and ran away."

"He's too well trained. He never does that."

"I could run him off."

"He'd come right back."

Mischief sparkled in her eyes. "Then just lie to them a little."

He tightened his hold and kissed her. "I can do that."

Andy rode back into Ranger camp in time for supper. He found Ryker waiting, standing beside a dark-skinned, muscular man whose full mustache was mostly dark but speckled with gray. Logan Daggett stood half a head taller than Andy, and broader across the shoulders.

Ryker asked, "Did you leave her happy?"

Andy said, "I tried to."

Ryker introduced him to Daggett, then said, "Andy's got him a young wife. It's hard to juggle Ranger duty with a new marriage. You're not married, are you?"

Daggett answered solemnly, "Was once." It was clear that he did not intend to expand on that statement, and Ryker did not press the question.

Daggett asked Andy, "This man Biggs, do you know him?"

"Saw him one time, is all."

Biggs had been picked up in a Ranger sweep through the oak and cedar thickets along the Llano River and its tributaries. Like a little fish tossed back into the water, he was accorded scant notice compared to men whose names were written in the Rangers' fugitive books for serious breaches of the law. He was released with a strong suggestion that he henceforth seek honest employment, and in some distant state. He had not, of course.

Andy said, "The last I heard, he was livin' in the brush." The thickets were a haven for men who sought solitude.

Daggett said, "I hate that brushy country. Always makes me feel closed in. I like the open plains, where a man don't feel like he's bein' smothered to death."

As they saddled fresh horses, Andy noticed that Daggett had a pronounced limp. The Ranger swore under his breath as he put his weight on the right leg and lifted his left foot to the stirrup. The wound was still giving him pain.

Andy asked him, "Are you sure you're up to the ride?"

Daggett reacted negatively to the question. He said, "Never show them any weakness, or they'll come and get you."

They set out southeastward on a wagon road that led toward the town of Junction on the Llano River. A Ranger packmule followed as it had been trained to do. Daggett hardly spoke. Andy wondered what was going on behind those hooded eyes, but Daggett gave him no clue. Andy introduced him to the Kimble County sheriff. The lawman was mildly amused by their mission. He said, "Biggs is just a triflin' no-account footpad. I'm surprised they'd waste your time with him."

Andy said, "A chigger bite is triflin', too, but after a while it itches to where you've got to scratch it."

Daggett said grimly, "A little bug needs squashin' same as a big one."

The sheriff said, "There's not a chicken roost or a smokehouse in three counties that's safe from Biggs. They tell me he's got several places back in the brush where he holes up. He changes dens oftener than he changes clothes."

Daggett declared, "Even a coyote leaves tracks."

"Most people figure Biggs's petty pilferin' is a normal cost of livin' in these hills, like property taxes. I just had a complaint from a goat rancher down close to Pegleg Crossin'. You might start from there."

Andy said, "Biggs is stealin' goats now? Sounds like he's comin' up in the world."

"He takes a kid goat now and then to eat. Mostly he lives off of the land. There's hogs runnin' free in the thickets, and wild turkeys and such. He'll break into a store occasionally. One thing he never steals is soap. Last time I had him in jail, it took two days to air out the place."

Andy glanced at Daggett. "Sounds like we just have to follow our noses."

Daggett gave no hint of a smile.

The sheriff drew a rough map of the roads and trails he knew about but cautioned, "Some people who live down there are careful not to invite company. If they have to cross a road, they'll stop and wipe out their tracks. Was I you, I'd watch my back."

Andy said, "Sounds like the whole bunch deserve to be in jail."

Daggett added, "Or dead."

The sheriff frowned. "Maybe so, but we have to respect people's rights. We can't allow the law to be worse than the outlaw."

Daggett said, "An outlaw ought to not have any rights."

A buildup of clouds suggested rain. Though experience told Andy that was unlikely, he did not want to camp in the open. He asked the sheriff, "Be all right if we sleep in the jail tonight? The Austin money counters hate to pay for a cot in the wagon yard, much less for a room in a hotel."

"Sure, if you don't mind wakin' up with a sore back. Pick whatever cell you want. One bed is about as hard as another."

The jail held two prisoners. Daggett gave each of them a critical study through the bars. "What're they in for?" he asked.

The sheriff shrugged. "Nothin' serious. They took on too much brave-maker last night. They're still too red-eyed to be turned loose. They might get run over by a freight wagon or somethin'."

Daggett said without sympathy, "A man ought to have better control of himself."

The sheriff's admonition about the hard bed proved to be no exaggeration. Andy awakened with an ache in his shoulders. He worked his arms until the tension eased.

If Daggett felt any pain, he accepted it stoically, without conversation. He walked in circles a few minutes until his leg gained stability and his limp became less severe.

A deputy brought breakfast for the two Rangers and the prisoners, who seemed more than ready to put something in their stomachs besides cheap whiskey. The sheriff watched Andy finish his coffee. He asked, "Are you-all sure you wouldn't like for me to send a deputy with you, one who knows the country?"

Andy said, "Thanks, but I've been in those thickets before. I don't think Biggs will be much of a problem, once we find him."

"That's the catch . . . findin' him."

Andy doubted that they would be lucky enough simply to stumble upon a man who had a dozen hiding places. They would have to ask questions of people who had no reason to want to help a peace officer, and try to read more into their words than they intended to let slip.

Daggett finished his breakfast quickly and headed toward the door without saying anything. Andy still had eggs on his plate, but he said reluctantly, "I'm comin'." He held on to a biscuit as they went out to retrieve their horses. It irritated him to be rushed unnecessarily. Five minutes one way or the other was unlikely to make much difference. But he gathered that patience was not one of Daggett's strong points.

Making it into a bit of a contest, he saddled up in a hurry. He was determined to be on horseback before Daggett. The sheriff's deputy tied a pack on their little Mexican mule, which followed dutifully as the Rangers rode out through the open corral gate. It had been trained well.

Daggett said, "Since you've been in the thickets before, I'll let you lead the way."

Let me? Andy bristled at the older man's assumption of authority. He tried not to let his resentment show. They had to work together.

Late in the morning they stopped at the small ranch of a man who had never shown up on the fugitive lists and had always been cooperative with law enforcement officers, up to a point. The rancher wore no gun, which in itself said something about his effort to maintain neutrality. He said, "Jasper Biggs? No, ain't seen him lately, but I missed a ham out of my smokehouse a few nights ago. I figure he's been around. Lost a layin' hen, too, right off of the nest."

Andy asked, "Are you sure it wasn't a coyote that got the chicken?"

"Not unless a coyote has learned to wear boots."

"Do you know whichaway he went?"

"I made it a point not to follow his tracks. I figure a chicken or a ham now and again are a cheap price to pay for peace with my neighbors. Even a lunkhead like Jasper has got a few friends."

Daggett's voice was critical. "If enough honest people would speak up on the side of the law, things would change."

The rancher said, "Maybe, but I wouldn't want to stand on a platform wavin' the flag and find that I was out there all by myself. A man could get hurt."

The rancher invited the Rangers to stay for dinner. Seeing that Daggett wanted to move on, Andy perversely said, "We'd be tickled to break bread with you." Unlike Daggett, he took no offense over the rancher's attitude. He understood the man's thinking.

After the meal, the rancher picked his teeth while he

watched Andy tighten his cinch. He said, "I can't afford to tell you Rangers anything straight out, but if I was to give you advice, I'd tell you to travel east. You won't have the afternoon sun in your eyes."

"Much obliged," Andy said. The rancher had just told him more than he had expected to hear. "That's just where we'd intended to go."

Andy assumed that any tracks Biggs left would have disappeared by now. He was not tracker enough to have followed them anyway. But Daggett looked around for a minute and announced, "He went off yonderway." He pointed eastward.

"Are you sure?"

"His trail is plain enough. Can't you see it?"

Andy did not want to admit that he had not, and still couldn't. But Sergeant Ryker had mentioned that Daggett was a good tracker. Maybe he would be useful enough to offset his dour manner.

Andy said, "I'll bet his hideout is somewhere around here. I doubt he'd walk far to steal one chicken."

Daggett shook his head. "You can't be sure with people like that. They think different from us normal folks."

The trail faded out, leaving Daggett frustrated and discussing Biggs's antecedents under his breath. The Rangers came after a while to a wagon road and a ramshackle country store, half hidden by live-oak timber. Andy knew the place. The structure was of rough-sawed lumber, never painted. Cedar bark still clung to a hitching post in front. One saddled horse stood switching flies. A couple more horses lazed in a corral out back, shaded by a large oak.

Andy sensed that he and Daggett had been seen before they dismounted and tied their mounts. The little packmule had followed without need of a lead rope and drew up close to Andy's horse. Instinctively Andy felt for the badge he customarily wore. It was inside his shirt pocket. He had thought it prudent not to flash it around among strangers in this environment. If Daggett had a badge, Andy had not seen it. Rangers still had to provide their own, so no two were exactly alike.

A bearded man came outside, gave the Rangers a quick nod, and untied his horse. He was gone before Andy had time for a good look at him. His furtive manner suggested that he might be found in the fugitive book. But that would wait for another time. He was not Jasper Biggs.

The proprietor was a lanky, middle-aged man with a scar beneath one eye and two or three days' growth of salt-and-pepper whiskers. He wiped his hands on a faded flour-sack apron and said, "My name's Smith, and I run this place. How can I serve you gentlemen?" He waved his hand toward a plain pine bar at one end of the dark room. Bottles, lined in a row, were reflected in a cracked mirror on the wall.

Andy said, "I would've bet that your name would be Smith." It probably had not always been. "Nothin' to drink, thanks. We might take a small slab of bacon if you've got any for sale."

"Anything I've got here is for sale. Anything at all."

A girl showed herself at a door that led into a room in the back. She asked, "Did you call for me, Mr. Smith?"

The storekeeper said, "Ain't you done with the washin' yet, Annylee? You'd better get it hung out on the line if you want it to dry before dark." He turned back to Andy, "Seems to me I've seen you before. Ranger, ain't you?"

Andy was mildly surprised that the man remembered,

but most people on the shady side of the law had a memory for peace officers' faces. Through a dirty window he could see the girl hanging a tablecloth on a thin rope line. He realized that the cloth was a signal to all comers that lawmen were on the premises. He said, "You've got good recall."

"It pays in this part of the country. Every time one of you fellers comes around, business falls off faster than Annylee's drawers. Lookin' for somebody?"

"Jasper Biggs."

"Jasper? What's he done bad enough to interest the Rangers?"

"Just stayed around too long. Is he a customer of yours?"

The storekeeper's brow wrinkled. It was hard to tell whether he was frowning or enjoying a bitter joke of his own. "Customers come in the daylight, and they pay cash. Jasper comes when everybody's asleep. He seldom pays for anything except an occasional tussle with Annylee when he can steal the money someplace."

"Looks to me like you'd be glad to have him gone."

"So would most other people. But givin' him up to the law . . . that's inethical." The merchant turned toward a counter. "Was you really wantin' that bacon, or was you just passin' the time of day while you look around?"

"We don't really need it."

"I didn't figure you did. Lawmen drop in on me every so often to nose about, and most of them don't buy a damned thing."

"Maybe you're not sellin' what we're lookin' for."

"If I did, somebody would burn this store down, with me in it. Have you-all about finished what you came here for?"

Andy could recognize an invitation to leave. He looked to Daggett, who had not said a word. "I reckon." More than likely a customer or two waited out in the brush. "You can take that tablecloth down from the line."

For the first time, Andy noticed a box at the end of the counter. It had a wooden frame and was covered with metal screen. As he moved near, he heard the unmistakable rattle of a snake. He involuntarily took a step backward.

The storekeeper said, "Everybody needs a pet around the place. That's mine. Ain't he fat?"

Hesitantly Andy stepped closer, confident the snake could not escape through the mesh. "What do you feed him?"

"Mice. There's aplenty of them around here. You can reach in and pet him if you're of a mind to."

"He might not take kindly to a stranger."

The proprietor pointed, his finger near the box. The snake lifted itself partway from its coil, its mouth open, its tongue darting. "I put a ten-dollar gold piece in that cage. It belongs to anybody with guts enough to reach in there and get it. I charge people a dollar apiece to try."

"Anybody ever do it?"

"Been a good many paid the dollar, but they always jerk their hand out as soon as the snake moves."

"Anybody ever get bit?"

"One. He eats his dinner left-handed now."

Andy and Daggett walked out to untie their horses. Daggett remarked, "Looks to me like that snake has got relatives around here, walkin' on two legs."

Andy asked, "Meanin' the storekeeper?"

"I thought I heard him rattle."

The girl stood at the back corner of the store, crooking

a finger. Andy led his horse to where she waited, anxiously watching the door. She said in a hoarse voice, "You say you're lookin' for Jasper?"

"We'd be pleased to locate him."

She pointed eastward. "He's got a little throwed-together shack out yonderway. It's in the middle of a thicket and hard to see."

"How come you're willin' to give him away?"

"I don't want to be seein' him no more. I can tolerate the other men who come around here, but Jasper smells bad."

"Mr. Smith might not like you tellin' us this."

"He won't do nothin', not as long as I'm bringin' in money." Looking at the back door again, she asked hopefully, "Reckon there's any reward for Jasper?"

"Not that I know of."

"I just thought . . . well, it'll be nice to be rid of him." She quickly disappeared into the back of the store.

Daggett said, "The storekeeper *is* a rattlesnake, usin' a girl like that. I've got half a mind to go back in there and whittle on him."

"He's not the man they sent us for."

"He'd be no man at all when I got through with him."

Finding Biggs's hiding place sounded simple, but it was not. Andy and Daggett rode a tiring switchback pattern through the brush for two days without finding anything more than sharp thorns and biting insects. He thought Biggs must have hide like leather to maneuver around in this tangle of hostile growth, especially afoot. Nobody remembered that he ever had a horse.

They camped near a small spring where water bubbled from between layers of moss-covered limestone. Daggett built a fire while Andy unpacked the mule. He surprised Andy by saying, "Ain't much like home, is it?"

Andy shrugged. "It's a livin'."

"A man can make a better livin' bein' a sheriff. In some counties, even bein' a deputy."

"It costs money to run for election. Anyway, my home county has already got a good sheriff, name of Rusty Shannon. I couldn't go back and run against him. He's the best friend I've got."

"If I had my life to live over, I'd be somethin' besides a Ranger. Long days on horseback, poor food or none at all. As often as not, when you finally catch your man, a slick-talkin' lawyer gets him turned loose. You wake up one mornin' achin' all over and realize that half of what you've done with your life has gone for nothin'. Makes you wish you'd shot all the sons of bitches when you had the chance."

It was the longest declaration Andy had heard Daggett make. He considered a reply but did not offer one. He had heard some of the same argument from Bethel. Still, he could not concede that much of his life's work had been for naught. He had helped put some bad men behind bars or under the ground, and the country was the better for it.

Daggett rubbed the wounded leg, his face creased with pain.

Andy said, "Maybe you got back on it too soon. They ought to've let you rest longer."

"I can stand just about anything except bein' idle. It gives a man too much time to think. I was ready and rarin' to get back to work." Daggett poured the first cup of coffee for himself and sat back to savor it. He said, "Sergeant Ryker tells me you've got a pretty young wife. You ought

to be with her tonight instead of out here in the middle of
nothin' with a shaggy old misfit like me."

Andy said, "You're not shaggy." He realized it would
have been better to have said nothing at all. Tired, he rolled
up in his blanket soon after they finished their meager supper. The soothing sound of spring water tumbling down
the rocky creek bank helped him drift off to sleep.

A curse awakened him as first daylight erased the stars.
In long underwear and barefoot, Daggett surveyed the
scattered contents of the mule's pack. He said grittily,
"We've been robbed. Somebody got off with our bacon,
our coffee, and our sugar."

Andy had not heard a thing all night. He blinked, trying to absorb what Daggett was saying. He glanced around
worriedly until he saw that the horses and the mule remained where they had been picketed. He asked, "You
reckon it was Biggs?"

"A bigger thief would've took the horses too. Camp
cookin' is bad enough, but to have to eat it without coffee
to wash it down, or sugar to sweeten it . . ." Daggett cursed
Biggs's father, his mother, and all his brothers and sisters,
if he had any.

Andy offered, "Maybe he left some tracks."

"I already found them. Let's break camp and get on his
trail. Maybe we can catch him before he uses up all the
coffee."

Andy could sometimes see the tracks, but in the main he
relied on Daggett's keen eyes to lead them. The horsemen
moved in a ragged pattern through the thickets of cedar
and oak and several types of scrub brush. After a couple
of hours of starting, stopping, backtracking, they stirred a
hawk from its nest. It flew up and began circling overhead,

screeching a warning that they were encroaching on its territory.

Andy said, "She's probably hatchin' some eggs."

Daggett asked, "Ever been hungry enough to eat a hawk egg?"

Andy shook his head. "Not as I remember."

"I have. I was better off hungry."

Shortly Daggett raised his hand, signaling to stop. He pointed silently at a small, crude structure constructed of tree branches, the top covered by a dirty, stained canvas. Part shack, part tent, a miserable excuse for shelter, it was well hidden within a thicket. Andy saw a shallow fire pit ringed with rocks, dark with ash and charred remnants of wood. Approaching carefully, he found a skillet lying upon still-warm coals. Two strips of bacon were burned to tiny curls of black.

Andy whispered, "Looks like he left in a hurry."

"That damned hawk."

"Biggs is afoot. He ought not to be hard to catch."

Daggett seemed enlivened by the near encounter. He dismounted and peered inside the shack. "Gone. You circle to the left. I'll go to the right. Don't take any chances. If he shows fight, shoot him."

Andy might shoot a murderer, or even a horse thief, but not a man whose bite was more like a mosquito's than a snake's. "In the leg, maybe."

"Don't give him a better chance than he would give you."

Andy made his circle and met Daggett on the far side. The older Ranger's questioning eyes told Andy that he had not seen anything either. Daggett said, "I found one solitary track."

Andy said, "He must've lit out like a rabbit, or holed up

like one. He could be layin' out there watchin' us right now." The thought made him uneasy, though he knew within reason that Biggs was unlikely to fight unless cornered. Andy had not heard of his ever firing on anyone.

Daggett said, "Right now I'd give my right arm for some coffee. Let's ride back to his den."

"Hadn't we ought to go right after him?"

"He's on foot. If we can find a trail, we'll catch up to him. If we can't . . . he'll turn up someplace. He left his grub behind. He'll be hungry again before long."

Andy put up no more argument. "I'm a little hungry myself."

He looked inside the tiny shelter. It was barely large enough to accommodate one man and his meager belongings. Dirty blankets lay ruffled on a pad of dry grass. Andy did not touch them. He suspected that they contained fleas. Coyotes always had them, so it stood to reason that a man who lived like a coyote would have them too. He said, "I've seen dogs that wouldn't live in a place like this."

"If Biggs was normal, he wouldn't either. But none of them outlaws are normal. They all got a twisted brain."

"Any ideas?"

Daggett grunted. "You said you're hungry. I am, too, so we'll fix somethin' to eat. It's our own grub."

They found little food. Biggs had used up most of it. As for coffee, only a few beans remained. Grumbling about the waste, Daggett led out, searching the ground for sign. He picked up the trail easily at first, for Biggs had left in too much of a hurry to cover his tracks. But after a time Daggett drew up in frustration. "How can somebody so dumb be so damned smart?"

Andy said, "Sometimes nature shorts us one way but

makes up for it someplace else. At least we've got a notion of his general direction."

They rode slowly, watching for some indication of Biggs's passage. Dusk caught them still empty-handed.

Regretfully, Daggett said, "Let's turn back and make camp on that creek we just crossed."

Andy had nothing better to offer. They would have water, if nothing else. He said, "I'm beginnin' to think we've been sent on a fool's errand."

Daggett said, "Maybe not. Catch a man while he's still a small crook and lock him away for good. He'll never get to be a big one."

"But they *will* let him out. You know how it is with lawyers."

Shadows from the firelight cut deep furrows in Daggett's face. "There's no appeal from the graveyard."

"There couldn't be much satisfaction in shootin' a miserable thief like Biggs."

"You'd be surprised."

Andy was awakened by a shot. He threw his blanket aside and reached for his pistol. Then he saw Daggett limping into camp, carrying a shotgun and holding a wild turkey at arm's length.

"Breakfast," Daggett said.

The bird had been been shot in the head. "Fancy shootin'," Andy said.

Daggett shrugged. "I cheated. I shot it off of the roost."

They slow-cooked the turkey on two spits above the coals. Andy tore into his half as soon as it was done. "Tastes good."

"Needs salt," Daggett replied. "I reckon we'd better go

back to Smith's store and get some more supplies. That Biggs damn near cleaned us out."

Evidently they were seen before they got there, for a tablecloth was already flapping on the line as they rode up. Daggett noted it without comment. Andy felt of it. "Dry," he said. "Probably dry when they hung it out here."

Daggett grunted. "If honest folks would work together like the outlaws do, this would be a better country."

It took a moment for Andy's eyes to adjust to the dark interior of the cramped and crowded store. It smelled of whiskey and leather and kerosene. He saw proprietor Smith slouched in a wooden chair, a bandaged leg stretched out straight, the foot resting upon a pillow atop a three-legged milking stool. Annylee stood beside him, her hand on his shoulder. Smith shouted angrily, "About time you damned Rangers got here! You always show up when nobody wants you, but you're never around when somebody needs you."

Andy said, "You didn't exactly roll out a red carpet for us the last time."

He saw that the lid of the snake box was open, the box empty.

The storekeeper cursed. "That damned Biggs. Snuck in here durin' the night and got my gold piece."

Andy asked, "In spite of the snake?"

"He dumped the snake out, grabbed the coin and ran. Now the rattler's loose somewhere in the store and madder than all hell."

Andy could not suppress a smile. "Looks like he might've taken some of that anger out on you."

"It ain't a bit funny. My leg's swole up bigger than a mesquite stump."

Daggett offered no sympathy. He said, "We've got to have some groceries."

Smith growled, "You'll have to get them for yourself. I can't walk, and I ain't lettin' Annylee risk gettin' snakebit reachin' into them cabinets. She's got to take care of me."

Andy suspected that she had been carrying most of the workload around here for a long time. He said, "Maybe now you'll be more inclined to tell us which way Biggs went."

"Annylee can show you. I'll tell you one thing: if you catch up to him, you won't find him settin' down. He won't be settin' down for a long time."

"How come?"

"I let him have a dose of buckshot where it would do the most good. He squalled like a panther."

Andy said, "You could've killed him."

"I doubt anybody would've cried. Except him."

Andy and Daggett gathered what they needed. Annylee added up the bill. Andy had to correct her on the total. He was not a fast reader, but he had an aptitude with figures. She watched while they put the groceries on the mule. She lifted her foot and placed it on a fence rail, causing her skirt to slide back and expose part of her leg. She suggested, "If you fellers ain't in a big hurry, I don't expect that Mr. Smith needs me for a while."

Andy grinned at her boldness. "All we need is for you to show us which way Biggs went when he left here."

She took them to a set of footprints that led eastward into the brush. She said, "If anybody was to ask, me and Mr. Smith didn't tell you nothin'."

Daggett gave her a look that surprised Andy. It seemed to suggest pity. The big Ranger brought a large silver coin from his pocket and handed it to her. He said, "We wouldn't want the day to be a total loss to you."

She smiled. "Thanks. I'm savin' my money. Someday when I have enough, I'm goin' to leave here and go to some big city, like maybe San Antonio. I'll bet the livin' is easy there."

For her, Andy suspected, life would never be easy anywhere.

Riding away, Daggett looked back once. Regretfully he said, "It appears to me that the country's goin' downhill like a runaway train. People have got no morals anymore."

"They were already sayin' that back in Bible times."

"There was avengin' angels in those days, ready to smite the transgressors. What this country needs is some avengin' angels."

"Do you know any?"

"They'll come, when the time is right. Who knows? Maybe we're them." Daggett went quiet, focusing his attention on Biggs's tracks.

They almost missed seeing the makeshift shelter. It was given away only by yellowed leaves where a few tree branches had been broken off in an effort to hide the entrance. Daggett drew his rifle and stepped down behind his horse. Andy followed his example.

Daggett shouted, "Jasper Biggs! Texas Rangers! Come out with your hands up."

The answer was more plaintive wail than discernible words. Daggett repeated his order.

A weak voice replied from within the shelter, "I can't move. I'm dyin'."

Daggett and Andy exchanged glances. Daggett said quietly, "Be ready to shoot if he as much as wiggles."

Daggett bent at the waist and rushed through the narrow opening. Andy was one step behind him, hands tightly gripping his rifle.

Biggs lay facedown on a dirty blanket, a rail-thin man in clothes too large for him. The back of his shirt and the seat of his filthy trousers were spotted with blood and buckshot holes. Andy was instantly aware of a dank odor and knew it came from Biggs himself. The Junction sheriff had mentioned his aversion to soap.

Daggett said, "High price to pay for a ten-dollar gold piece."

Biggs turned his face upward. Ragged whiskers failed to hide his sunken cheeks and his rheumy gray eyes. He whimpered, "I think that old miser killed me. I feel like that buckshot has worked plumb through to my heart."

Andy said, "From the looks of your britches, that's not where most of it went. We'd better get your shirt off and your pants down."

Panic came into Biggs's voice. "What you fixin' to do?"

Andy said, "If it's as bad as it looks from here, we've got to dig all that shot out of you. Else it may go into blood poisonin', or even gangrene."

"You goin' to use a knife?"

"We've got nothin' else."

Biggs began to weep. He cried out in pain as Andy helped remove his shirt and pull down his long underwear and trousers. "Oh, God, I think I'm about to die."

The corners of the tall Ranger's mustache lifted in pleasure. He said, "The wages of sin."

Andy said, "He must've got some distance away before the shot hit him. They don't look to've gone very deep."

"Deep enough to kill him if they don't come out." Daggett winked. "But we'll do our best to save you, Jasper."

Andy fetched water and washed Biggs's back and rump of dried blood so he and Daggett could see more clearly what they were doing. Daggett said, "You hold him down while I pick a while. He's apt to flounce around a right smart." He took out his pocketknife.

Andy suggested, "Might be a good idea to sterilize that blade in a fire first."

"Good idea. You start one. Now, Jasper, you just lay real still and get yourself ready. This is goin' to hurt like hell. I hope you're man enough to take it."

Biggs moaned and prayed that God would let him die quickly.

Each tiny probe of the blade point prompted a whimper. Most of the shot popped out easily. Daggett wiped sweat onto his sleeve and said, "Here, Andy, you finish it. All this blood is makin' me sick at my stomach." Actually, little fresh blood appeared. The damage was near the surface, and minor.

Daggett said, "Jasper, if you live, and if you ever get out of jail, I hope you'll remember this and repent your heathen ways. Get yourself an honest job and enjoy the untroubled sleep of a righteous man."

Checking to be certain he had missed no buckshot, Andy said, "He's not goin' to ride a horse for a while."

Daggett said, "Hear that, Jasper? You may never ride again, or maybe even walk. You may have to spend the rest of your days standin' up or layin' on your stomach. Mighty poor way for a man to finish out his time, but you brought it on yourself."

Biggs's thin shoulders heaved with silent weeping.

Outside, Daggett asked Andy, "Know a ranch around here where we can borrow a wagon?"

"I think so." Andy frowned. "You spread it on pretty thick."

"Meant to. A jury is liable to take pity on such a sorry-lookin' specimen and let him get away light. The more scared he was and the more he hurt, the better he'll remember this day when he thinks about liftin' his hand to mischief again."

"I used to know an old preacher named Webb. He'd say you've got a devious mind."

"I believe in due punishment, even if I have to deal it out myself."

Andy sat on the rumbling wagon, holding the reins, his horse tied behind. Daggett was on horseback. They were nearing the outskirts of Junction when a horseman shouted and galloped up from behind. He was a large man, about the match of Daggett. Eyes ablaze with hostility, he demanded, "What've you done to my brother?"

Andy saw little physical resemblance between this big man and Jasper Biggs except that both had squinty eyes. He had always distrusted squinty-eyed people. Irritated, he said, "We've done nothin' but pick a pound of buckshot out of him. Now we're haulin' him to jail."

"Who shot him? You?"

"Not us." Andy did not elaborate, though he doubted it would be hard for the man to find out. Likely as not, the storekeeper was bragging about it to everybody who would listen.

The brother said, "He don't belong in jail. He was always kind of simple. He don't know right from wrong."

"He needs to learn. Maybe some jail time will teach him."

"No jail. You're fixin' to turn that wagon around. I'm takin' him home where I can watch over him."

Andy saw danger in the brother's eyes. He said, "You haven't watched over him very good up to now."

"Just the same, I'm takin' him."

The man's hand dropped to the butt of the weapon on his hip, but Daggett was faster. The Ranger swung the barrel of his pistol at the man's head. The stranger's hat sailed away as he slumped in the saddle, then slid off. He lay in a quivering heap on the ground.

Daggett said, "The conversation was gettin' tedious."

Biggs whined, "You son of a bitch, you could've killed my brother."

"That I could. Might yet if he don't lay still."

Andy's heart raced. He said to Daggett, "You really would, wouldn't you?"

Daggett's face was grim. "I never draw a gun without I'm prepared to use it." He looked down into the bed of the wagon. "Do you hear me, Jasper?"

Biggs only grunted.

Andy said, "*I* heard you. I don't know what to think about it."

"No thinkin' needed. Just know that I'm serious. Now you'd better catch and tie his horse. He'll be lookin' for it when he wakes up."

2

They carried the prisoner to the Junction sheriff, who seemed none too thrilled at the present delivered by wagon to the door of his jail. He said, "Couldn't you find some excuse to shoot him? The last time I had him in here, I had to burn sulphur to fumigate the place."

Andy said, "He's clean. We dumped him in the Llano River before we brought him in. Now, if you'll write us a receipt for him . . ."

Riding back toward Fort McKavett, Andy said, "I don't think Jasper's brother would really have shot one of us."

Daggett said, "Then again, he might. A man draws a gun on you, you'd better figure he means it." His voice became accusatory. "I do believe you felt sorry for that two-bit night crawler."

"I did, a little."

"A soft heart can be a liability when you're wearin' a badge. Someday you'll find your head tellin' you to do one thing but your conscience tellin' you to do another. While you're arguin' with yourself, you can get killed."

"Is that what happened to your leg?"

Daggett's face creased as he remembered. "I gave them every chance to surrender. Instead, they shot me. There's nothin' like the sight of your own blood to clear your mind."

"So you shot them?"

"It was the sensible thing to do."

* * *

Fort McKavett was no longer a military outpost. Many of its original buildings had been converted to civilian purposes. Others stood in ruins, their roofs and windows cannibalized for reuse elsewhere. Riding into the village at the edge of the San Saba River, Andy asked Daggett, "Mind if we stop off at the house before we go on into camp? I want to let Bethel know I'm back."

Daggett gave him a questioning look. "This face of mine scares dogs and little kids. She'll say I'm an example of what happens to a man who stays in the Rangers too long."

Andy would admit that Daggett looked the worse for wear, but he did not intend to remain a Ranger as long as Daggett had. He said, "On the other hand, she can see that you're still alive in spite of it all."

"Only because of some people's poor marksmanship."

A little brown dog met them. Chickens fluttered and clucked in protest as the two riders disturbed their hunt for seeds and insects. Bethel stepped out onto the little porch to see what had stirred them up.

"Andy!" she shouted, trying to look displeased but unable to control a joyful smile. "I thought you'd left me for another woman."

"I've thought about it," Andy said, "but I haven't found another one as good-lookin'."

She cocked her head to one side. "Are you bringing home any new wounds that I'll have to take care of?"

"Nary a one. There wasn't a shot fired."

Instead of coming to him as she sometimes did, she waited for him to go to her. She stared at Daggett, a question in her eyes. Andy supposed she felt shy in the presence of the stranger. He said, "This is Logan Daggett. He's been transferred to our company."

He tried in vain to read her reaction. Bethel was accomplished at concealing her opinions when she wanted to.

Daggett lifted his hat. "Ma'am." His hard features seemed to soften as he gave her a long study. He appeared to want to say something more, but nothing came.

She said, "It's nice to meet you, Mr. Daggett. Won't you come into the house? I'll fix some coffee."

Still staring at her, Daggett seemed to drift away into a moment of solemn reverie. Bestirring himself, he said, "That'd please me, ma'am, but it's gettin' late in the day. I'd best go in and report to the sergeant. Pickard, why don't you stay the night here and report in time for mornin' roll call?"

Andy was surprised by Daggett's show of generosity. "You sure you don't mind?"

Daggett turned back to Bethel. "A young lady like this needs a lot of lookin' after. I doubt you're livin' up to the job."

"She doesn't complain."

She said, "Oh yes I do, a lot."

Daggett turned away. The packmule seemed confused but followed Daggett's horse.

Andy dismounted and took Bethel into his arms.

She said, "I guess you caught your man?"

"There wasn't much to it, once we found him."

She turned and looked in the direction Daggett had taken. "How was Mr. Daggett to work with?"

"He didn't load me down with a lot of idle talk, like Len Tanner would've. He can ride for miles and not say a word."

"His eyes bother me, like something dark is hidden behind them."

"He's been through some hard times. He didn't tell me much, and I didn't ask him."

"Is that the way you'll look after being a Ranger a few more years?"

"I'll quit before it comes to that."

She frowned. "I wonder if you'll ever quit." She turned toward the door. "I'll get supper started. Or are you anxious to get back to camp?"

"Like Daggett said, camp can wait till mornin'."

Sergeant Ryker looked up from the table that served as a desk in the headquarters tent. He nodded as Andy walked in to report. He asked, "Had breakfast?"

"Yes, sir, before I left the house."

"A better one than mine, I'd wager. Daggett told me how you-all got your man. It took you longer than I expected."

"Jasper didn't leave a lot of tracks. Even Daggett had trouble followin' them."

Ryker unfolded himself from behind the table and walked outside, looking around as if to assure himself that no one else was within earshot. "I want the truth, with no holdin' back. What is your opinion of Logan Daggett?"

Andy disliked being pinned down to a judgment of a fellow officer. He said, "He's a good tracker."

"I already knew that. What about his attitude? Is he a complainer?"

Daggett had made a couple of negative remarks about the Ranger service, specifically the holders of the purse strings, but nothing stronger than Andy himself had said on occasion. "No, sir, he was determined to finish what we set out to do. As far as I could tell, that was the only thing on his mind."

"How did he treat the prisoner?"

"He took pleasure in pickin' buckshot out of Jasper's butt, and listenin' to Jasper howl. Fact is, I enjoyed it myself after the chase he put us through."

Ryker mulled over what Andy had told him. "Takin' everything into consideration, do you like him?"

Andy wished he had not been asked that question. He said, "I'm still tryin' to make up my mind."

"How would you feel if I was to send you off on another assignment with him?"

"I'd rather go with Len Tanner."

"Tanner's off runnin' down a horse thief."

"Whatever you say, then. You're the sergeant." Andy wondered how long he might be away this time.

Ryker said, "Daggett's good at enforcin' the law, but he's got a reputation for goin' off like a shotgun from time to time. You could be a stable influence."

"I'm supposed to keep the lid on him?"

Ryker nodded. "But don't look at this as a command. Consider it a challenge."

Andy could not see much difference.

Ryker said, "You know Central Texas, don't you?"

"I've spent time there."

"A sheriff friend of mine is sittin' on a keg of gunpowder. There's been vigilance committee activity and some shootin's. I'm volunteerin' you and Daggett to go help him put an end to the troubles."

"Any idea what's behind it all?"

"It started with folks accusin' one another of stealin' cattle and horses. I'm more inclined to think it's really about who's goin' to run that part of the country. There's nothin' like local politics to cause a fight. If I had my way, I'd put all the politicians on a boat at Galveston, sail it out into the Gulf, and sink it."

"Feelin' that way, how have you managed to keep bein' a sergeant?"

"By knowin' when to talk and when to bite my tongue."

Andy kissed Bethel in the house. He felt awkward about doing it outside with Daggett watching. Daggett waited with the packmule, outfitted with enough grub to last more than a week. After that, they would have to buy more, but with a stern admonition to keep the cost down to the lowest possible figure. The headquarters office in Austin was suffering through one of its frequent spasms of acute frugality.

Bethel clung to his hand. "They didn't give us much time," she said.

"Ryker has promised me a few days off when we finish this job," Andy told her. "I promise, we'll camp together in the hills. We'll even stake out the ground where we'll build the house and the barn and corrals someday."

"Someday never seems to get any closer."

"While I'm gone, you could go back home and visit your brother Farley and his wife and the little one. It's been a long time."

"But I want to be here when you get back."

"Think about it anyway."

"Write to me as soon as you get things sized up and have some idea how long you may be gone."

"You know I don't write very good."

"I've found that out. But try."

He kissed her once more, then walked briskly through the door. The early morning sun hit him squarely in the eyes. It made tears start. "Ready?" he asked Daggett.

"Always ready." Daggett tipped his hat to Bethel as she came out onto the porch. "I'll bring him home soon as I can, ma'am."

"But in one piece, please. Seems like half the time when he comes home he has a new bullet hole in him."

"It's the low class of criminals we have to deal with. Maybe someday we'll have a better sort." Daggett set off into a long trot, taking the lead. Andy followed, turning in the saddle to wave at Bethel. She watched, but she did not wave back. Her hands were clasped in front of her.

When they were well away from the house, Daggett slowed and let Andy catch up. Frowning, he said in a critical voice, "Maybe you don't know what a good thing you've got. A pretty little miss like that don't deserve to be left cryin' while you ride away to the devil knows where."

Defensively Andy said, "She wasn't cryin'."

"She was cryin' inside. Every time you leave, she wonders if the next time she sees you will be at your buryin'."

"Before we married, I warned her what it'd be like."

"It's one thing for her to hear it. It's another to live with it."

Andy was irritated by Daggett's lecturing. "How do you know so much about a woman's feelin's?"

"I had a woman once, a lot like yours. God, what I'd give to go back and do right by her this time."

"Can't you?"

"Too late." Daggett's eyes were bleak. He spurred his horse. "Come on, we've got a far piece ahead of us."

* * *

The trail at one point climbed up a layered limestone hill, strewn with loose rocks that could slip and cripple a horse. It followed along the top of a long hogback ridge. Andy could see for miles off either side across broad expanses of live oak trees and cedars, hackberries and other mixed timber, which in the far distance melded into a thin blue haze.

Daggett said, "It's a lot different from the plains. Are you sure we haven't strayed out of Texas?"

Andy said, "I think I'd know if we had. The air would feel different."

"The Central Texas hills won't be this big or this rocky, will they?"

Andy said, "Not quite. The Comanches stole me when I was a boy and kept me for a long time. They used to come down into this country to hunt, all the way from the Canadian River breaks."

Daggett said, "The sergeant told me about your time with the Indians. As far as I'm concerned, the Indians can have this part of the country."

Though settlers in recent years had thinned out the game, Andy and Daggett had frequently seen deer bound away into the sanctuary of heavy thickets. To Andy, they were a pleasant sight.

He said, "Bethel and me have bought us a piece of land in the Kerrville country. It's got good grass and water, and game."

"You ought to be there now instead of wanderin' the country like a gypsy. You're workin' on other people's problems when you ought to be takin' care of your own."

"You've been at this longer than I have. Why haven't you quit?"

"Been at it so long that it's easier to stay than to leave and start somethin' new. But you're young enough for just anything you set your mind to. Your wife talked like she's patched up some bullet holes in you."

"Several, but not all at one time."

"You're liable to get one she can't patch. Widow's black wouldn't look good on her."

"Bethel's little, but she's a strong woman."

Daggett gave Andy a silent look that called him a fool.

They took their time, making about thirty miles a day, sparing their horses and the little Mexican packmule. Andy remembered the various counties: Mason, Kimble, San Saba, Lampasas . . .

Working his way down from a hill into a broad valley, he saw a man on horseback herding sheep toward a corral of cedar stakes tied so closely together that a rabbit might not wiggle through. A dog trotted alongside him, wagging its tail and acting pleased with itself as if it were doing the whole job alone.

Andy said, "We'd just as well start introducin' ourselves to the folks."

Daggett frowned. "If we have to shoot any of them, knowin' them might make it harder on your conscience."

"I'm hopin' we won't have to do that."

"Sometimes you've got to shoot a few people before you can make things peaceful."

The dog barked at the two riders and the packmule until its owner bade it to hush. It took a cautious stance behind the stockman's horse, poised to run away at its first perception of threat.

Andy tried to present a pleasant smile. "Howdy. Are we on the right road to town?"

The sheepman was middle-aged, his stomach flat as a slab of bacon. A black pipe extended beyond several days' growth of bristly gray whiskers. He considered a moment before he answered, carefully sizing up the visitors. He said, "There are better ones, but this'll get you there."

Andy said, "I'm Andy Pickard. This here is Logan Daggett. We'll be glad to help you take the sheep the rest of the way in."

"The dog and me, we've been doing it a long time. But you're welcome to ride along with us to the house. Stay the night if you're of a mind to."

Andy said, "That'd be kind of you."

"My pleasure. We don't get much company out here. Most people regard me as a crazy old sheepherder and stay away. My name's August Hawkins."

Andy had encountered many sheepmen in his travels. As a rule he had found them to be smarter than those who criticized them, and better off financially. Sheep tended to be more profitable than cattle. Hawkins's manner of speaking indicated that he had education.

He said, "I let them spread out to graze in the daytime, but I pen them at night. There are lots of four-legged varmints around here."

"What about two-legged ones?"

"They'd rather steal cattle and horses. Sheep move too slowly. They can get a thief caught." He stared at Andy, then at Daggett. "I'm trying to decide whether you two are laws or outlaws. Sometimes the difference is hard to see."

"We're Rangers," Andy said. "We've been told there's trouble in this part of the country."

"I stay out here with my sheep. I try to keep far away from trouble that doesn't concern me."

It was the same eyes-averted attitude that Andy had observed in the Llano River thickets. He said, "Anything you might tell us wouldn't go any farther than me and Daggett."

"It won't even go that far. I have nothing to tell you." A ewe strayed away from the others, nibbling at low weeds. The dog paid no attention until the sheepman pointed a finger and shouted, "Dog, wake up and go bring her back!"

The dog sprinted out and nipped at the ewe. She ran to the others, not stopping until she had plunged in to the middle of the flock.

Andy said, "Hasn't the dog got a name?"

"If I called him what he deserves, he would probably bite me." Hawkins whistled the dog back to its place at his side. "I hope you don't mind goat meat for supper."

"Goat?"

"I don't eat my sheep. I keep them for the wool. Goat tastes quite good when it's prepared properly. My little old wife knows a dozen ways to cook it."

Andy said, "Sounds fine."

The sheepman turned to Daggett. "So far you haven't said a word."

The comment caught Daggett off guard. "All I know I learned by listenin' while others talked."

The corral gate was open. The sheep knew the routine, filing through in good order. Several lambs spooked at the shadow of the gate's crossbar and leaped over it. Andy dismounted to close the gate, built solid so no predator could work its way through. Hawkins pointed to another pen. "You can turn your horses and the mule loose in there with mine. I'll fork out some hay."

A milk cow stood outside another pen, her calf eagerly awaiting her on the inside. Hawkins said, "I'll milk first, then we'll have supper."

He led them to a log cabin. Smoke was rising from its chimney, and Andy caught the pleasant aroma of freshly baked bread.

Hawkins asked, "Does either of you speak Spanish? My wife Serafina doesn't know much English."

Andy had a smattering of it, though not enough for a deep discussion about philosophy. Daggett said he knew only *manos arriba* and *adiós,* hands up and good-bye.

Mrs. Hawkins was a busy, dark-faced little woman who might not weigh a hundred pounds. She smiled and chattered so rapidly that Andy could pick out only a word here and there. But he understood the food she placed on the table.

Hawkins said, "I hired her after my first wife died. She was a widow woman, washing clothes and cleaning other people's houses. It didn't look right, her living out here with me, so I married her. After all, I'm a churchgoing man. I go every month or two."

Andy asked, "Any children?"

"Grown and gone in four different directions. I have grandchildren I've never seen and likely never will. So it's just Serafina and me, the dog and the sheep. And this little piece of land."

After the meal, the three men sat on the porch, enjoying the cool of early evening. Hawkins puffed on the old black pipe. He said, "I suppose Sheriff Seymour sent for you. I'm surprised he'd ask for Ranger help."

Andy said, "He didn't. We got a letter from somebody who didn't sign his name."

"Didn't sign? That's not surprising. Pete Seymour has a bull by the tail. That job has made him touchy as an old bear. You'll need to handle him gently."

Andy glanced at Daggett before saying, "We try to handle everybody gently."

Hawkins said, "It got quiet around here for a while, but things have commenced happening again. A man was murdered last week."

Andy straightened. "We didn't know about that."

"A rancher by the name of Callender. Somebody ambushed him in the door of his barn."

"Any idea why?" Andy asked.

"Just a suspicion. He must've known something that somebody was afraid he'd tell."

Daggett said grimly, "Sounds to me like the work of a mob."

"Around here they are known as the regulators." The sheepman paused to take a couple of draws on his pipe. "To begin with, we have old family enmities that should have been resolved long ago. On top of that we are up against changing times. New people come into the country, crowding the ones already here. I stay out of it. I bought my place free and clear, but much of the land still belongs to the state. Anyone can use it if he has the nerve to take and hold it."

Andy said, "Things'll be a lot more peaceful when the land is all bought up. Then there'll be legal property lines."

Daggett broke his silence. "But folks'll start puttin' up wire fences, and there won't be open land anymore." That thought appeared to depress him.

Hawkins said, "I plan to put a fence around mine. Already have the wire and posts ordered. It'll keep other people's cattle out and leave more grass for my sheep."

Daggett said, "You may have a fight over it. I've seen it happen up in the Panhandle."

Hawkins argued, "If the land belongs to me, free and clear, no one else has any say-so."

Daggett shook his head. "If one owner fences his land, others'll follow. Then the free range will be gone. You'd best test the temper of your neighbors before you dig that first posthole."

Hawkins argued, "I've always gone out of my way to avoid a fight, ever since back in the sixties when I was dragged into a war that was none of my doing."

Daggett leaned forward, his voice earnest. "If I was you I'd wait and let the big operators put up their fences first. If there's to be fightin', let them do it. In the long run they always win, and you'll get a free ride."

Hawkins mused, "I never asked for a free ride during the war. Were you in that fight, Daggett?"

"I was. I learned when to stick my head up and when to keep it down. I took other people's mistakes to heart and tried not to make the same ones myself."

Hawkins's pipe had gone out. He tapped it against a post to knock the ashes from it, then refilled it with tobacco. He said, "I understand what you're saying, but I won't be letting others tell me what I can do on my own land. That's part of what the war was all about."

Andy pointed out, "The Confederacy lost."

Hawkins smiled, a ring of tobacco smoke encircling his face. "What makes you think I was a Confederate?"

Two horsemen appeared from a row of brush to the east. One wore a long beard, gray except for a few dark strands. The other was like a younger version without the whiskers. Andy guessed they were father and son.

Hawkins stood up when the two were within hailing distance. "Welcome, Mr. McIntosh. Howdy, Jake. Traveling late, aren't you?"

The old man reined up and slowly, stiffly dismounted. "Me and my boy, we've been out talkin' to neighbors." He stretched, flinching from arthritis pain. "These horses trot rougher than they used to. Must be some slippage in their breedin'."

The younger man left the saddle with an easy grace and no sign of pain. The father gave him a look of envy.

Hawkins introduced Andy and Daggett but did not mention that they were Rangers. McIntosh acknowledged them without much interest, then asked Hawkins, "Had any trouble with Old Man Teal or his boys?"

Hawkins looked surprised. "Trouble? No. They came by here with a small herd one day and asked if they could water them in my creek. I told them to go ahead. The creek bed belongs to me, but the Lord puts the water in it."

"They could've watered anywhere up or down the creek. Why do you suppose they picked your place?"

Hawkins shook his head. "It was handy, I guess. Never gave it much thought."

"They were testin' you. They were tryin' to see how far you'd let them go. Next time they won't stop with water. They'll be turnin' cattle loose on you. I heard talk in town that they've got a herd comin' up from the brush country. They'll need to put them someplace."

"I've never had any trouble with the Teals. I've left them alone, and they haven't bothered me."

McIntosh scowled. "I've known Harper Teal for years. He's an evil, greedy old man. Always was, and he's raised them boys in his own likeness. They'd steal the shroud off of a dead man."

Hawkins repeated, "They've never bothered me."

"Not yet, maybe, but mind what I've told you. All us neighbors have got to stick together. First sign of trouble, you come to us. Me and my boys'll throw in with you."

Hawkins said, "If any trouble comes, I'll go to the sheriff."

"Pete Seymour?" McIntosh scoffed. "He couldn't even protect a prisoner in his own jail."

McIntosh remounted even more slowly than he had gotten down, groaning as he settled into the saddle. "I rode too many mean broncs when I was Jake's age, and wrestled too many snuffy cattle. Now they've come back to haunt me. Be glad you're a sheepman, Hawkins. They don't fight you."

Hawkins smiled. "I have scars all over my back from rams that knocked me down and ran over me."

Andy watched the two ride away. He said, "It sounds like that letter writer knew what he was talkin' about."

Hawkins shook his head. "Old Man McIntosh has a wrong notion about the Teals. They're redheaded and bound together with barbed wire and rawhide, but they've never given me reason to be afraid of them."

"Maybe they're fixin' to."

"It's all in Old Man McIntosh's mind. He and Harper Teal have hated each other so long they probably don't even remember what started it."

Daggett said, "Once we get the lay of the land, we may have to knock some heads together."

Andy asked, "What did he mean, that the sheriff couldn't protect a prisoner?"

Hawkins said, "A year or so ago, Pete caught the leader of a ring of horse and cattle thieves. Some masked men forced their way into the jail and shot him in his cell. Caused a considerable ruckus, but it slowed down the thievery for a while. It's started up again lately."

Daggett nodded approval. "There's times when some vigilantes can help move the law along."

Hawkins said, "The prisoner was Old Harper Teal's son-in-law."

Andy said, "The Teals were part of the ring?"

"I never wanted to believe that. I like them in spite of their rough edges. And that Teal girl . . . it was hard to understand her marrying somebody like Vincent Skeen in the first place. But she was a country girl and hadn't seen much of the world. I guess his good looks and smooth talk got the best of her."

"Do you figure the McIntoshes shot him?"

"It stands to reason, they or some of their friends and kin. Skeen was a snake, and nobody blamed them much. Pete didn't break his back trying to arrest anybody." Hawkins arose. "Would you like a little drink to settle your supper?"

Andy and Daggett rolled out their blankets on the barn floor. Lying on his back, Andy said, "Hawkins seems like a good old man."

Daggett snorted. "He ain't that much older than I am. Anyway, the best old man I ever knew took a shot at me once. I haven't trusted a good old man since."

Next morning, on the way to town, Andy heard something crashing through the brush. He reined up to listen. A large brindle bull burst out of the scrub timber and onto the wagon trail in a hard run. Before Andy could shout "Look out!" it smashed into Daggett's mount and sent it tumbling. Daggett shouted in surprise, then in pain. His wounded right leg was pinned beneath the struggling horse. The bull shook itself and went running off down the trail, hooves clattering on the rocks.

A horseman broke from the brush, a rope in his hand. He pulled hard on the reins as he saw Daggett on the ground. He took a quick look at the fleeing bull, then swung from the saddle. Daggett's horse was thrashing about, trying to regain its feet. The stranger grabbed it about the neck and took a firm hold on its head. "Whoa now," he said in a quiet voice. "Be still." To Daggett he said, "Can you wiggle out from under him before I let him up?"

Daggett grimaced, straining hard. He wheezed, "See if you can raise him just a little more." Grunting, the stranger managed, and Daggett crawled backward until his leg was free. He tried to push to his feet but fell. Andy, on the ground now, caught him under the arms and dragged him far enough that the horse would not step on him in its struggle to get up.

Andy said, "I hope that leg's not broke."

Daggett's voice was laced with pain. "*You* hope? It's not yours. It's mine." He bent forward and carefully felt of the leg, starting above the knee and working down. "I think it's still in one piece." Blood seeped from a long tear in the pant's leg. "Busted that bullet wound open again just when I thought I was about to be shed of it."

With his pocketknife Andy ripped the pant's leg open to get a better look. Daggett sucked in a sharp breath and said, "That was a good pair of pants."

"You can buy another pair and bill it as groceries." Even the most honest of Rangers might use such a subterfuge to get around the state's penny-pinchers.

The stranger knelt beside Daggett and examined the reopened hole in his leg. He asked, "Got any whiskey with you?"

Daggett said, "The state don't pay for whiskey."

The stranger said, "Then we'd better bind the leg up tight anyway, to stop the bleedin'." He took out a pocket-knife and cut off part of Daggett's pant's leg. He used it for wrapping.

The first thing Andy noticed about the stranger was his size. Probably thirty-something, he was as large as Daggett, all muscle and bone. His hair was a rusty red, his jaw square, the mouth broad. A scar on his left cheek showed through several days' growth of reddish whiskers. Andy would have to rate him as one of the least handsome men he had seen in a while. Not quite ugly, perhaps, but close enough to it.

The man said, "I didn't mean to run that bull over you. I didn't even know you was there. I've been tryin' for a month to get a loop over that old rascal's horns."

Andy wondered if the stranger's horse was stout enough to handle the bull's weight on the opposite end of a rope, especially if the animal was on the fight.

The stranger said, "I was goin' to throw him down and turn him into a steer. We're ashamed to put the family brand on the sorry calves he sires."

Andy asked, "What family is that?"

"The Teals. I'm Bud Teal."

Andy remembered the name. Ethan McIntosh had had

much to say about the Teals, none of it good. Andy said, "I'm Andy Pickard. This here is Logan Daggett."

Teal said, "Seems like I've heard the name Daggett. Ranger, ain't you?"

Daggett's voice was strained. "Almost ever since I was weaned."

Teal examined Daggett's horse, feeling of its legs, running his hand along the chest, then the flanks. "He don't seem to be hurt none, just a little spooked. Let's get you on your feet and make sure you're able to stand."

Grittily Daggett said, "I can stand. I can walk. I can even ride if you and Pickard will give me a lift up."

Teal said, "I'll take you to our house. We'll get that wound cleaned and wrapped proper. Wouldn't want you to have blood poisonin' on account of me and that sorry bull."

Andy had mixed feelings about accepting Teal's offer. It was generous, and Daggett's injury needed attention. On the other hand, if the Teals turned out to be antagonists here as McIntosh charged, any favors accepted now might compromise the Rangers later.

Teal did not give Andy long to consider the dilemma. He helped Daggett into the saddle. Andy asked, "How far to the house?"

Teal said, "Just a hop, skip, and a jump. It's closer than town."

Andy decided there might be some advantage in gaining knowledge about the Teals on their home ground. He would give the McIntoshes a look-see later.

The frightened packmule had run fifty yards before stopping. Andy brought it back. He gave Daggett a quick study and asked, "Are you sure you're up to ridin'?"

"I don't see any choice. I can't stay here like this."

"You're turnin' as white as milk."

Daggett held his right leg straight, the foot out of the stirrup. He was suffering from shock, Andy realized. Shock could knock the legs out from under the strongest of men.

Teal gave Daggett a look of concern and said, "Sooner we start, the sooner we get there." He set out in the lead. Daggett rode in one wheel rut. Andy stayed even with him in the other, ready to lend a hand if he started to fall from the saddle. But Daggett seemed determined not to show weakness. He stubbornly sat straight and kept a firm hold on the reins, his jaw rigid. He avoided touching the horn, which might be taken as a sign of vulnerability.

Teal looked back with concern from time to time. He asked, "You Rangers just passin' through the country?"

Andy said, "We haven't decided."

"Did Ethan McIntosh ask for you?"

"What makes you say that?"

Teal said, "We've been expectin' him to do some such of a thing."

Andy evaded the question. He said, "We were on our way to consult with the sheriff."

"Pete Seymour?" Teal sighed. "He ought to be runnin' a ranch instead of wearin' a badge. His boots ain't big enough anymore for the job he's got."

"How so?"

Teal said, "He's gettin' old, and he can't see very good. He ain't made a move against the McIntoshes. Been a killin' lately that nobody's answered for. Been a few fistfights over one thing and another, and a drunken shootin' scrape where nobody got hurt. You can bet that if worse trouble comes, you won't need to look any farther than the McIntosh bunch."

Andy noted that Teal was saying essentially the same thing about the McIntoshes that Ethan McIntosh had said about the Teals.

Andy said, "We heard that a mob murdered your brother-in-law while he was in jail."

Teal frowned. "In our family we don't talk about him anymore. He wasn't no Teal." He moved ahead, making it clear that the subject was closed.

Andy had not seen many signs of real prosperity in these hills, and he found few at the Teals' ranch headquarters. The main house was of rough lumber, not painted. A log bunkhouse stood off to one side. The barns were built in much the same way. The corrals were of tied-together posts set upright, their bases sunk in the ground. Most of the structures were of natural materials taken close at hand. Only the main house appeared to represent a cash investment, and even it was short of ornamentation. Andy saw no gingerbread trim.

This was pretty much what his own place would look like someday when he left the Rangers and set out upon the life of a stockman, he thought. It would be spare, at least in the beginning, but it would be his—his and Bethel's.

Teal led them directly to the frame house. Dismounting, he tied his horse to a post and turned to help Andy lift Daggett down from the saddle. He said, "My sister wasn't much at pickin' a husband, but she's pretty good at fixin' up folks hurt handlin' wild cattle and rough horses. Not to say that our horses are really bad. You'd just best not go to sleep in the saddle. They'll wake you up."

The house had a generous porch that helped offset its overall plainness. Teal said, "Let's set him in the rockin' chair out here. In case there's any leakage, I expect Carrie would rather it wasn't in the house."

Andy asked, "Who's Carrie?"

"My sister. She was named Carolina, after the state where our mother came from, but everybody just calls her Carrie. None of us has ever been to Carolina."

Andy wondered if Teal's sister would look anything like him. Whatever Bud Teal had inherited from his forebears, good looks were not among them.

Blood had soaked through the rough binding, but it appeared dry. The bleeding had stopped. Andy remained on the porch with Daggett while Bud went inside. He heard voices from within the house. Shortly he saw the dark outline of a woman coming down a hallway that divided the house into two segments. Her stride was firm and determined. She came out onto the porch, a tallish woman of thirty or so, slender to the point of being skinny. She held a bottle in one hand, a bundle of white cloth in the other. She stared a moment at Andy before Bud directed her attention to Daggett.

He said, "The big feller is the one that's hurt."

Her appearance took Andy by surprise. He had expected her to be plain, even homely, like her brother. Instead, her features were pleasant, her large eyes the dark brown of coffee beans. Her hair bore a hint of red. In a country where men outnumbered women by a considerable margin, Andy wondered why somebody had not put an end to her widowhood.

Shaking her head in reproach, she untied the cut-off

pant's leg that Bud had wrapped around the wound. She asked him, "Was this the best thing you could find?"

Bud said, "In a pinch, you use what you've got."

She said, "This looks like an old gunshot wound."

Daggett did not reply, so Andy said, "It is. It just got busted open again."

She poured a cloudy-looking liquid from the bottle directly into the wound. Daggett stiffened as if she had set him afire, but through strong will he made no sound except a faint whistling as he sucked air between his teeth.

The woman said, "I'll give you one thing: most men would holler to high heaven." She glanced at her brother. "Bud did, the last time I used this stuff on him."

Bud protested, "I didn't, either."

Tears came into Daggett's eyes. He turned his head and quickly blinked them away. The woman cleaned the wound with a piece of cloth, then bound his leg. She said, "This is going to be awful sore. You won't be chasing any bulls for a few days."

"I wasn't chasin' this one," Daggett wheezed. "I was tryin' to get out of his way."

Teal told his sister, "These two men are Rangers."

Her eyebrows raised a little. She said to Daggett, "Only two of you? I thought you traveled in bunches."

Daggett was still struggling with the burn. Andy said, "Only when the trouble is big enough. We don't know yet how big it is here."

Bud said, "I'll bet Old Man McIntosh sent for you."

Andy said, "Somebody wrote us a letter but forgot to sign his name. We were on our way to see the sheriff."

Carrie's voice snapped, "The sheriff. Pete Seymour can't find his butt with both hands."

Bud took up for the lawman. "Pete's all right. It's just that people are pullin' at him from all sides. And he's gettin' a little old."

She said, "He wasn't much help when we needed him."

"He never claimed to be no Pinkerton detective."

"No," she replied sharply, "and he's sure as hell not." She picked up the bottle of disinfectant and started for the door. She stopped to tell the Rangers, "You-all are staying for supper." It was not a question; it was a command.

Andy said, "We wouldn't want to put you to any trouble."

She nodded toward Daggett. "You already have. A little more won't make any difference." She was halfway through the door when she stopped again. "In case you wonder about it, any beef you eat at our table is our own."

Andy was taken aback by her forceful attitude. He stared after her until she disappeared into the back of the house. He asked Teal, "Did we say anything to make her believe we thought otherwise?"

Teal said, "No, but lots of people have. She gets touchy as hell about it. Feels like everybody is against us."

"Are they?"

"Some, like the McIntoshes and them that follow Old Man Ethan and his boys. But we've got friends, too. Sometimes our side wins the elections, sometimes the McIntosh side does. It makes a difference who sets the taxes."

"Tax rates are supposed to be the same for everybody."

"Depends on who counts the cattle. Some count ours twice but can't find half of the McIntoshes'."

So, Andy thought, it comes down to money, as most quarrels do.

He saw movement at the barn, five horsemen riding into a corral and dismounting. Bud said, "It's Pa and the boys. They've been ridin' the line, keepin' our cattle pushed back onto our own ground."

Andy asked, "If it's state land, what difference does it make?"

"We're taxpayers. What belongs to the state belongs to us. Ain't that right?"

That was one way to look at it, Andy thought, but anyone who wanted to squat on state land could make the same argument. It left much room for disagreement and, ultimately, violence.

He found it easy to pick out the Teals. The father and the other two sons bore a close resemblance to Bud. They were sturdy, muscular men whose confident stride bespoke a certainty that they could whip the world. And like Bud, they were some of the homeliest men Andy had ever seen. The sons' hair was a darkish red, the father's a mix of red and gray. The older man spat a stream of tobacco juice, then wiped his mouth on his sleeve. His beard was streaked with dark stains. He gave his full attention to Andy and Daggett. Andy saw no welcome in his eyes.

Stopping just short of the porch, Harper Teal looked at the fresh bandage on Daggett's leg. "Who shot you?" he asked.

Bud said, "That old brindle bull ran over him."

"That bull's a stray. He don't belong to us. We've got no obligation."

"I feel like we do. It happened on our place."

The older man's eyes were sharp with criticism. "Bud, I told you to get rid of that beast."

"I was right on his tail when he ran into this Ranger. I had to stop and help, so the bull got away."

"Ranger or not, you ought to never leave a job half done." Teal's gaze cut back to Daggett. "If you're nosin' around for a payoff, like most of the badge toters I ever knew, you ain't findin' it here."

Teal's rough manner stirred Andy to defensive anger. "We don't take bribes. We'll even pay for your daughter wrappin' his leg, if you figure we owe you."

"Keep your money in your pocket. Us Teals don't take payment for small favors, and any favors we do for a Ranger are goin' to be small ones."

Daggett angrily jerked his head at Andy. "Let's be goin'. We've been here too long already."

Andy was dubious. "You're not in shape to ride."

"If I can't ride, I'll walk. If I can't walk, I'll crawl."

Bud moved between his father and Daggett. He said, "No use in you-all leavin' here mad. Pa talks rough, but he don't mean half of it. You-all stay for supper, at least. Maybe you'll feel better after you've eaten."

Andy said, "He's talkin' sense. We'll stay for supper."

Daggett flinched in response to a surge of pain. Reconsidering, he said to Bud, "As long as you-all don't expect any special favors. If we find you breakin' the law, we'll treat you the same as everybody else."

Bud assured him, "The only laws we've ever broke were those we disagreed with."

Daggett said, "I don't agree with all of them myself."

The older man's bushy eyebrows were still mostly red. They nearly joined in a frown as he said, "Bud, you invited them, so you look after them. I don't remember a time that the law ever brought me good news." He started into the house, then stopped. Muttering something about womenfolks' rules, he wiped his feet on a sack lying by the door.

Bud introduced his brothers, Cecil and Lanny. Their attitude was much like their father's. They nodded but did not offer to shake hands.

Bud said, "Daggett, you can't go around wearin' pants with one leg cut off. I'll find an extra pair for you."

Daggett said stiffly, "I'll pay you for them."

Bud turned to Andy in frustration. "I'm tryin' to act civil. What's the matter with him?"

Andy started to say but didn't, *He's thinking he might have to shoot you someday.*

3

Carrie Teal watched with silent criticism as Daggett limped to the supper table. She said, "We've got a set of crutches. Lord knows that with bad horses and salty cattle, we've needed them."

Daggett's reply was firm. "I'm not crippled. I'd feel like a fool, tryin' to manipulate a set of crutches."

"We can lend you a cane if it won't hurt your pride too much."

"I'll get by."

Her eyes flashed. "Nobody's going to beg you even if it is for your own good."

The elder Teal pulled out a chair at the head of the long

table and unceremoniously seated himself. Reaching with a fork to spear a biscuit, he said, "He's been off of the tit long enough to make up his own mind. Don't you get enough, girl, bossin' this family around? Have you got to boss strangers too?"

She said, "I worked hard to fix his leg. I don't want him to waste all that effort like some stubborn schoolboy."

Daggett was no schoolboy. He was forty if he was a day. Stubborn, though . . . Andy had seen that from the first.

Harper Teal declared, "There's a time for talkin' and a time for eatin'. Right now I want to eat." His plate was heaped with beef and beans. He dug into it as if he had a hollow leg to fill. His sons and the two cowboys followed his lead. Carrie took a seat at the foot of the table, getting up once to bring the coffeepot and refill the men's cups. Only one cowboy murmured, "Thanks." Andy said, "Much obliged, ma'am."

"You're welcome," she said, a little surprised by his manners. She probably was not used to seeing any.

Daggett picked over his food, taking a few bites without enthusiasm. His glazed eyes indicated that he was running a fever.

Carrie said, "You need to eat something and build up your strength."

"Maybe I could, if this beef came from the bull that ran over me."

Bud said, "I'll bring that old brindle down with a rifle if I have to. We've got no grass to spare for the likes of him."

The old man grunted. "You'd ought to've gone ahead and done it today. Wouldn't've hurt this Ranger to've laid there a while till you finished your job. On account of that bull, we've got these two sittin' here at our table like invited company."

Daggett flared. "We'll be gone in the mornin'. In fact . . ." He pushed himself to his feet, leaning heavily on the table. "We'll be goin' right now. Come on, Pickard."

Andy did not arise. He said, "You'd better sit back down before you fall."

Daggett limped heavily toward the door, each step painful. Andy argued, "That leg'll hurt like hell if you try to ride."

"It already hurts like hell. Come on."

Carrie and Bud caught up to Daggett on the porch. She said, "Hold up a minute. If you abuse that leg, you could lose it."

Bud said, "Pa's like an old dog with a loud growl but no teeth. I feel responsible for what happened to you."

Daggett wavered. The leg was giving him a lot of pain.

Andy said, "These folks are talkin' sense."

Daggett faced toward the barn where his and Andy's horses were enjoying some grain. It looked a mile away. Turning back to Carrie and Bud, he said, "Since you ask so nicely, we'll stay."

Bud said, "You'll like the bunkhouse. We've got plenty of room, and you won't have to listen to Pa rave. He sleeps here."

Carrie's voice softened. "I'll fetch you that cane. Maybe it'll keep you from spoiling my work."

Daggett seemed embarrassed. "I didn't intend to fly off the handle like that. I reckon it's because this thing hurts so damned bad."

Carrie brought a cane and watched as Daggett took a couple of awkward steps, trying to get a feel for it. He and Andy fell behind Bud on the way to the bunkhouse.

Carrie shouted, "Bud, if he needs anything, you come and get it! He ought not to walk any more than he has to."

Daggett muttered to Andy, "Last thing I wanted was to get us beholden to one side or the other."

Andy said, "I saw that bull in time to dodge him. Why didn't you?"

"Are you sayin' I need glasses, Pickard?"

"When are you goin' to start callin' me *Andy*?"

"When you stop bein' a pain in the ass."

Bud pointed to two empty steel cots. "Sorry we've got no corn-shuck mattresses, but it's better than layin' on the ground."

Andy said, "I'll bring in our beddin'."

Daggett sat, sighing as he straightened his hurt leg. To Bud he said, "I appreciate what you folks have done for me, but we can't play favorites. When it comes to duty, a Ranger has got no friends."

Bud said, "We ask for no favors." He frowned. "And we damned seldom get any."

The other two Teal brothers and the two cowboys drifted down to the bunkhouse after a while. Away from the old man, they spoke civilly enough to Andy and Daggett. Bud asked, "Leg feelin' any better?"

Daggett said, "If so, I can't tell it."

"I'll bring you that bull's ears, and get Carrie to fix you some mountain oysters."

Lanny was the youngest of the brothers. He resembled the others in the roughness of his features, though the freshness of youth had not yet deserted him. His brother

Cecil said, "If I read the calendar right, tomorrow's Saturday. There'll be a dance in town. You figurin' on goin' in to spark the storekeeper's daughter?"

Uncomfortably Lanny said, "Maybe. Ain't thought about it."

Cecil laughed. "You ain't thought of nothin' else for days. You know Jake McIntosh is after her too. You'd better watch that he don't beat your time."

Lanny's face reddened. Bud, the oldest, said, "Cecil, don't badger your little brother. He's of age to go courtin' if he's of a mind to."

Cecil said, "I'm just tryin' to help him see after his interests. This country ain't overrun with good-lookin' gals like Lucy."

Bud said, "Good looks don't guarantee what's inside."

Lanny stiffened. "Are you sayin' Lucy's not a good girl?"

"I don't hardly know her. I'm just sayin' you need to look farther than her blue eyes. You remember that pretty bay colt of mine? He had the roughest trot of any horse I ever rode. Kept my innards achin' all the time. Passin' him off to that horse trader was one of the smartest things I ever did."

Lanny argued, "Lucy's the nicest girl I know."

Cecil asked, "How many girls have you known?"

"I'm no green kid. I've been to town."

Bud nodded. "You came home all bruised up the last time. Some of them town boys don't like to see Teals courtin' their girls."

"I whipped two of them. I'd've been all right if a third one hadn't piled on."

Bud said, "There'll always be a third one, little brother.

We're outnumbered every time. They're liable to waylay you on your way to town."

Andy thought all the Teal brothers looked as if they could handle themselves well in a fight. They had the tight muscles and calloused, big-knuckled hands that came from hard work. Daggett said, "Maybe I'll be able to ride by tomorrow. He can go along with me and Pickard."

Andy lay on his cot, listening. He said, "It'll be just me. I'll be goin' in to talk to the sheriff. You'll stay here and try to heal up."

Daggett said, "You're forgettin' that I outrank you, so you can't tell me what to do. I'll be ready by tomorrow." He held his leg straight, resting it over the edge of the cot. The pain in his face indicated that he wouldn't be on horseback for at least two or three days.

Andy said, "That leg'll tell you. I won't have to."

Lanny said, "What would folks think, seein' a Ranger bodyguardin' me?"

Bud said, "They'd think you're the smartest man in town."

Daggett arose next morning in a bad temper. His stomach was angry because the aching wound had not allowed him much sleep. Andy had not slept much either, listening to him tossing much of the night. Daggett swung his legs off the side of the cot, then gingerly pushed to his feet. He reached for the cane and hobbled about the bunkhouse, testing the sore leg. He winced with every step but said, "It's damn near healed."

Andy said, "You can't hardly walk, much less ride. I'll have to work alone if you fiddle around and cripple yourself."

Daggett glanced about, making sure no one but Andy could hear. "How'll it look, me stayin' here with the people who may be the cause of the trouble?"

"How better to keep a watch on them?"

Daggett thought about that. "You might have a point."

Carrie stepped out onto the porch and beat an iron rod against a steel ring, signaling breakfast.

Andy offered, "I'll bring you some breakfast so you won't have to walk on that leg."

Sternly Daggett declared, "Nobody's ever had to fetch and carry for me. I'll go for myself."

Andy knew it was useless to argue. He walked slowly to keep from outpacing Daggett. The older Ranger hobbled toward the main house, stopping three times to catch his breath and let the throbbing subside. A less determined man would have given up, Andy thought.

Bud Teal walked beside them. He told Daggett, "You're the stubbornest man I ever saw except maybe for Pa. If you and him ever seriously butted heads, it'd be like two bulls tryin' to knock each other's brains out."

Andy wanted to help Daggett up the steps, but he knew he would be rebuffed in the sternest terms. Watching the Ranger struggle, he imagined he shared the pain.

Carrie greeted them at the door. She asked Daggett, "Is the leg any better?"

"Hardly feel it at all," Daggett lied.

Her expression told Andy that she knew the truth. She said, "We'll take a look at it after breakfast and wrap it fresh."

Daggett said, "You've got no call to be concerned about me. You never saw me till yesterday."

Bud said, "She's a nurse at heart. Dogie calves, stray cats, she takes care of them all."

"I sure ain't no dogie calf."

The kitchen offered the pleasant aroma of coffee, freshly baked biscuits, and fried bacon. Steam arose from a large platter of scrambled eggs on the table. Old Harper Teal was already seated in his accustomed place, eating. He said, "Hurry up, boys. We're wastin' daylight. We got work to do." He gave Daggett a swift appraisal. "I see you're on your feet. I expect you'll be wantin' to go."

Andy said, "He can't ride. I'm leavin' him here for a couple of days."

The old man did not appear pleased. Bud said, "We all agreed that it would be the best thing."

Harper said, "I didn't agree, but I reckon we can put up with him. Just don't let him get in the way of the work." He cut his gaze to Andy. "You're leavin', are you?"

Bud said, "He'll be ridin' in with Lanny. Maybe that'll keep the town boys from jumpin' all over baby brother."

The old man arched his red eyebrows and glared at his youngest son. "What're you goin' to town for? You need to stay here and tend to business."

Uneasily, Lanny said, "It's Saturday, Pa."

"Saturday, Sunday . . . one's like another. They're all workin' days around here."

Lanny's face reddened. "I promised Lucy I'd take her to the dance tonight."

Harper asked, "Who the hell is Lucy?"

Carrie broke in. "She's a nice girl in town. The store-keeper's daughter. You've seen her."

"Never did pay attention to town girls. They're spoiled

and addle-brained, flighty as a bunch of heifer yearlin's. Country girls are the best. They know how to work."

Carrie said, "Besides, I need some groceries. Lanny's going to bring them home."

The surprise in Lanny's face indicated that this was news to him, but he nodded agreement. "I'll be takin' the wagon."

The old man gave in grudgingly. "All right, but don't come home all hungover. You'll have work to do tomorrow."

Lanny said, "Tomorrow's Sunday."

Harper said harshly, "Kids! There don't none of them want to work anymore. The whole world has gone plumb to hell." He pushed up from the table. "The rest of you boys, get up from there and get your horses saddled. Mornin's half gone already." He stomped out the door, loudly clearing his throat.

Carrie watched him with a thin smile, then said, "Finish your breakfast, all of you. He'll holler whether you hurry or not."

Daggett left half of his breakfast uneaten. Leaning heavily on the cane, he went out onto the porch and sat on a bench, gingerly rubbing his leg. Carrie watched him through the kitchen window, then turned to Andy, still seated at the table. "Strange man," she said. "Doesn't talk much, does he?"

Andy shook his head. "I don't know much more about him now than I did when I met him."

"I get a feeling that a lot goes on behind his eyes, but they're like a window blind. You can't see through them."

"It might be better not to."

"I couldn't see past my husband's eyes either. I wished I had, when it was too late." She turned away and busied herself with the dishpan on the cabinet.

Andy tried what was left of his coffee, but it was cold. "I heard what happened. I'm sorry."

Her voice thinned. "He had his faults, but that was a miserable way for a man to die."

"Yes'm."

"Odd. Your Mr. Daggett took me by surprise the first time I saw him. He looks a little like Vincent. Same size and build. The eyes are different, though. There's a wildness in them, but there's sadness, too. Vincent's were just wild."

"He told me he had a wife once. He doesn't anymore."

"That might account for the sadness. Do you know what happened to her?"

"He hasn't said. And I'd rather get run over by that bull than to ask him."

"It's none of our business anyway."

Andy guessed that she would give a lot to know. He said, "He may not tell you so, but he appreciates what you did for him."

She frowned. "He could say that himself. He doesn't need you to do his talking for him."

"That's his way."

"Hardheaded. He would fit right in with the Teal family."

Lanny Teal was eating a second helping of breakfast. Andy told him, "Better hurry it up if you plan to ride to town with me."

Bud Teal grinned. "Lanny'll be ready. He's been dreamin' about that girl all night."

Lanny argued, "I still don't see where I need a Ranger to protect me."

Bud said, "You need a guardian angel, but angels are scarce in this part of the country."

Carrie took cloth and scissors and antiseptic out onto the porch where Daggett sat. She said, "Let's take a look at that leg."

"I told you it's all right." He moved the leg and grimaced. His voice softened. "But if you really want to . . ."

The wound was swollen and angry around the edges. She washed it clean, then applied antiseptic. Daggett tensed until the burning subsided. "What is that stuff?" he asked. "It feels like a white-hot brandin' iron."

She said, "If it didn't burn, it wouldn't do you any good." She bound the leg with fresh white cloth. "That's the best I can do."

Daggett said, "I don't reckon a town doctor could do any better." His face furrowed as if he dreaded what he had to say. "I'm sorry I've acted like a sore-footed badger. I'm not used to people makin' a fuss over me."

"We didn't exactly throw roses in your path, either. We Teals have been put upon by so many people, for so long, that we sometimes bristle up for no good reason. Whenever something bad happens, they decide right off that the Teals are responsible."

Andy felt emboldened to ask, "Are they?"

She almost smiled. "Now and then."

Andy saddled his horse. Lanny, wearing a clean shirt and a bow tie, drove the wagon to the front of the house. Carrie stood on the porch, watching. As Lanny started to pull away she said, "Don't lose my list. We're almost out of coffee and flour."

Andy touched fingers to the brim of his hat. "Thanks for both of us, ma'am, me and Daggett."

Riding toward town, Andy kept thinking about Carrie. He pulled in close to Lanny and said, "It's kind of your sister to look after Daggett like she has."

Lanny shrugged his broad shoulders. "She feels obliged, I guess."

"Just the same, it's kind." Andy rode in silence a while, then ventured, "She never said much about her husband."

Lanny's eyes hardened. "He's dead and buried. There's nothin' to say."

"It must've been tough on her."

"She's strong. She got over it." Lanny looked back over his shoulder as if he feared someone would overhear. "Son of a bitch was a thief and a wife beater."

Andy took a chance. "Then you ought to be grateful to the McIntoshes for takin' care of him."

Lanny grunted. "I reckon." The somber look in his face said he did not want to talk about it.

Nearing town, they passed two young horsemen who gave Lanny a hostile study but made no move against him. Once they were out of hearing, Andy said, "They looked like they didn't mean you any good. They might've jumped you if you'd been by yourself."

"I can whip two of them at a time, and they know it. I've done it before without any help."

"So I heard."

Lanny said, "When we get to town I want you to go your way, and I'll go mine. I don't want them ginks thinkin' I need Ranger protection."

Andy said, "If you decide different, I'll try to be easy to find."

In Andy's estimation, the town didn't amount to much. Biggest thing was the courthouse, with an outsized clock tower that seemed too pretentious for its setting. He counted three modest church steeples and half a dozen saloons or dramshops.

Lanny said dryly, "That's two to one in favor of whiskey over religion."

Andy said, "At least the Lord's got a toenail hold."

Lanny hauled up on the reins, stopping the wagon in front of a general store. "Here's where I get Carrie's groceries," he said.

Andy asked, "Are you sure you'll be all right by yourself?"

"Sure. I'd have come by myself if Bud had kept his mouth shut. Him and Carrie both."

Andy said, "They're just worried about you. You're their little brother."

"I'm as big as any of them."

And about as stubborn, Andy thought.

Pete Seymour, the sheriff, was middle-aged and trail-worn, his hair graying, his waist broadening. He wore black-rimmed glasses with thick lenses that made his eyes look larger than they were. He appeared annoyed when Andy walked into his office and introduced himself. He turned to a tall, lanky young man and grumbled, "Salty, I didn't send for any Rangers. Did you?"

Salty Willis was slight of build and wore clothes a size too large for him, giving him a rumpled look. Andy would have taken him for a cowboy if he had not seen the deputy's badge. "Never would've thought about it."

The sheriff said, "If I had, I'd've asked for a whole company. I don't see where one will help much."

Andy said, "There's one other." He explained about Daggett's absence. "Even two's enough to make the book-keepers holler. They'd like to disband the whole Ranger service and save the money."

The sheriff continued to frown. "Salty, you'd better go see Mason Gaines about that missin' horse. I never knew a man with so damned much to complain about." He waited until the deputy had left, then told Andy, "I wish you hadn't ridden in with that Teal boy."

"Lanny was comin' to town anyway. I thought it might prevent a fight if I rode along with him."

"It could be bad business, lookin' like you've lined up with one side against the other."

That had been Daggett's concern too. "I made it clear that we won't play favorites."

The sheriff took off his glasses and squinted at them, then put them back on. They needed cleaning. "I hate these damned things, but it's gettin' to where I can't see nothin' without them. It's hell to get old."

His eyes narrowed. "As long as you're here, I'd just as well try to get some use out of you. What did you think about the Teals?"

"None of them shot at us. I can't say the old daddy was any too friendly, though."

"Old Harper has got a grudge against Rangers. It goes back to trouble with the carpetbag police after the war."

Andy said, "But those weren't real Rangers. We've come a long way since the days of the state police."

"Harper Teal hasn't."

"What about the McIntoshes?"

"They're Yankees, come here right after the war. Old Man McIntosh once called out the state police against

Harper. Even after all these years, neither family can put the war behind them. It's like an old friend they can't say good-bye to."

"And the other folks around here?"

"Some take sides because of family ties or politics. The rest try to keep out of the way. That ain't always easy." He looked as if he had bitten into a bad-tasting pill. "Did you say Lanny Teal is stayin' in town for the dance tonight?"

Andy said, "That was his intention."

"The kid's askin' for trouble. Somebody's always itchin' to try the Teal boys on for size."

Andy suggested, "It might be a good idea if I showed up at the dance myself."

The sheriff said, "I'll be there, too. Maybe if I'm lucky I won't have to throw anybody into a cell tonight. Then I won't have to feed anybody breakfast in the mornin'."

Andy said, "We heard you lost a prisoner in that jail, a Teal brother-in-law."

Seymour frowned, the memory painful. "I got a false report of a shootin' down in the south end of the county. Come dark, several masked men rushed in and got the drop on my deputy. They didn't even bother to take the prisoner out of his cell. They poured enough lead into him to sink a boat."

"You figure it was the McIntoshes?"

"Skeen was stealin' from just about everybody. You could say that whoever killed him did the community a service. There wasn't but a few people at his funeral, and I didn't see anybody cry except his widow."

Andy said, "Too bad about her."

"I guess she still blames me, but what's done is done." Seymour took off his glasses again, wet the tip of a finger on his tongue, then rubbed the lenses. He wiped them dry with a handkerchief. "As long as you're here, you'd just as well show yourself. Visit the saloons. Set a spell on the spit-and-whittle benches. Let folks know there's a Ranger in town."

Andy stood up. "I'll start now."

The sheriff said, "One thing: you've got too friendly a face. Try to look a little mean."

Andy said, "I'll leave that to Daggett. It comes natural with him."

As Andy started toward the door, he was blocked by a middle-aged man wearing a wrinkled white suit. Seymour said, "Ranger Pickard, I want you to meet Judge Zachary."

The visitor removed a long black cigar from between a neatly brushed gray mustache and a spade beard. It was evident that he paid more attention to his beard than to his clothing. Dark eyes almost black focused on Andy, making him feel like a horse being examined by a potential buyer. "Ranger, eh? I didn't know you'd become desperate enough to send for a Ranger, Pete."

Seymour said, "I didn't send for him. He just showed up. There's another one out at the Teals'."

"The Teals? What have they done this time?"

Andy said, "Nothin' that we know of." He explained about Daggett and the brindle bull.

The judge said, "Daggett? I have heard stories about him. Not all happy stories, I am sad to say."

Andy shook his head. "They're probably way yonder exaggerated. You know how stories grow, once enough people have told them."

Seymour said, "Like the stories you hear about the Teals and the McIntoshes."

The judge said, "But there is usually an element of truth behind them. They are all contentious people. How much more peaceful the county would be if one of the families left. Even better, both of them."

Seymour said, "They're not so bad, Judge. The boys, anyway. It's those two old soreheaded daddies that need a good butt-kickin'."

"And I've given it to them the times they appeared in my court." Zachary gave Andy an intense study. "You seem an agreeable young man. How long have you been in the Ranger service?"

Andy said, "Off and on, ever since my first shave. But it's my intention to retire before long. My wife wants me to stay home."

"A commendable goal. As a lifelong bachelor, I can appreciate how difficult it must be to try to maintain a decent family life when one is always on the move."

The sheriff said, "The judge has got him a nice little ranch outside of town."

The judge said, "It is my refuge, my retreat from the daily humdrum of official duty. You must come out and visit me there sometime."

Andy said, "I'd be pleased."

"Feel free to come to my office any time you need anything from me. Warrants, that sort of thing. I have great respect for the Rangers." He glanced at Seymour. "And for county sheriffs, who too often go unappreciated and underpaid."

Andy and Seymour watched the judge leave, trailed by

cigar smoke. Seymour said, "He's a man to ride the river with. He's sharp-tongued and uses his court like a club against those who would disturb the peace, but he's held this county together for many a year."

"I'll make it a point to get better acquainted. I don't think I'd want him against me."

Seated on a wooden bench across the dirt street from the general store, Andy watched a long-legged man in a white shirt and a loose string tie approaching him. He noticed ink stains on the man's hands. Most of all he noticed the man's heavy mustache, which flared upward at the ends. Andy thought he might be able to hang a bucket from either tip.

The stranger halted and gave Andy a critical study before he said, "I understand you're a Ranger."

Andy made a small nod. "I am."

"I'm Jefferson T. Tolliver, editor of the local newspaper, *The Clarion*. Do you mind if I ask you a few questions?"

Andy was hesitant but decided this was one way to let everyone know of his presence. "I'll tell you what I know, which isn't much."

"What brings you to this neglected corner of the Texas paradise?"

"Somebody sent us a letter, askin' us to come. They didn't sign it."

Tolliver looked around to be sure no one could overhear. He said, "For good reason. They could get seriously hurt if it were known that they invited the Rangers."

"By talkin' to me now in plain daylight, aren't you afraid you might raise suspicions about yourself?"

"People are used to seeing me interview visitors to town. Have you seen enough to appraise the local situation?"

"I can see the problems. I don't know yet what to do about them."

"You are the only Ranger they sent?"

"There's one more, Logan Daggett. He got hurt along the way, so he's laid up out at the Teals' ranch."

"Daggett!" Tolliver's eyes lighted up. "I know that name. I would give my eyeteeth to write a book about him. Do you think he would consent to an interview?"

"I doubt it. I haven't seen him consent to much of anything since I've known him."

"So he is at the Teals', in the lion's den. One of the dens, at least. Do you know that Lanny Teal is across the street, loading a wagon?"

"I rode into town with him."

"I suspect that the Teals are of Appalachian fighting stock. You may have noticed that they are all redheaded. It has been only a few generations since they left the cave and gave up stone in favor of iron. The McIntosh forebears came from the Scottish highlands, and fighting is in their blood, too. It will be interesting to see which you have to shoot first, a Teal or a McIntosh."

Andy said dryly, "Either way would make a story for your paper, wouldn't it?"

"I hope I may be able to write an eyewitness account."

"And I hope to disappoint you."

A middle-aged man wearing a stained apron came out of the general store, carrying a heavy bag and dropping it into the wagon bed. A slip of a girl stood on the porch. From the distance, Andy could not tell much about her except that her hair was a light brown, and she flashed a broad smile in Lanny's direction.

Tolliver said, "That is Lucy Babcock. Lanny's been sparking her, and so has Jake McIntosh. A perfect recipe for a knockdown, drag-out fight."

Andy heard Lanny tell the storekeeper, "By loadin' up now, I can make an early start for home in the mornin'."

The girl said, "Don't forget. Come for me about seven thirty."

Lanny said, "I'll be there with bells on."

"And no drinking."

"You know I don't drink. Hardly ever. Much."

Two young men stopped near Andy and watched the scene across the street. He thought they might be the two he had seen on the trail, but he was not certain.

One said, "Look at that, would you? Lanny Teal, shinin' up to Lucy."

The other said, "What can we do about it? The last time we jumped him, he like to've broke my jaw."

"We'll tell Jake McIntosh. He's been tryin' to get under Lucy's dress for a good while."

"Yeah. We could sell tickets to that fight."

Andy had pinned his badge to his shirt so it would be conspicuous. He cleared his throat to be sure they noticed him. He made a show of taking the fugitive book out of his pocket and flipping it open.

"What are your boys' names?" he asked.

The two fell into startled silence. One finally said, "Smith. We're both named Smith." They walked briskly on down the street.

Tolliver said, "They lied to you about their names."

"I figured that."

"One is Harold Pearcy. The other is Sonny Vernon. They'd like to be bad men, but I doubt they've done anything serious enough to be in your Ranger book."

"Any kin to the McIntosh family?"

"No, but they do some work now and then for the McIntoshes. They tag along after Jake like coon dog pups."

Two men emerged from a nearby saloon door, one of them the deputy, Salty Willis. He mounted his horse and rode away. The other man cupped his hands around a lighted match and touched the flame to a carelessly rolled cigarette. He walked up to Andy and said, "I am given to understand, sir, that you are a Ranger. It would serve the community greatly if you were to knock those boys' heads together." His tone indicated that he thought Andy should already have done it.

Andy tensed a little. "I'd need a reason. You got one?"

"Nothing I can prove, but keep an eye on them. Sooner or later they'll give you reason." The cigarette appeared to bite the man's tongue. He spat out a bit of tobacco. "I suspect you are here to forestall trouble between the Teals and the McIntoshes."

Andy could not think of an appropriate reply, so he offered none.

The tall man said, "Perhaps you should back off and let the parties fight. A few funerals might clear the air."

"That's a hard way to look at it."

"It could break the stranglehold a few big people have on state land around here. Then the little people would have a better chance."

Andy argued, "They could buy it. That'd settle the matter for once and for all."

"It takes money to buy land. The poor man can't afford it."

"It won't be free forever. Texas is sellin' off pieces of it every day."

The man flicked ashes with the tip of a finger. He said, "We'll burn that bridge when we get to it." He turned and walked briskly toward Scanlon's wagon yard.

Andy looked at Tolliver, his eyes asking.

Tolliver shrugged. "Mason Gaines. The biggest blowhard and bellyacher in the county. Like so many, he wants something for nothing. But nothing comes free. One way or another, everything must be paid for."

4

Sitting beside the sheriff at the dance, Andy tapped his foot to the rhythm of a banjo and fiddle. He had heard better fiddlers, but he had heard worse too. The wooden floor creaked under the weight of dancers, some gliding with grace, some sliding awkwardly across the boards.

Seymour's feet were still. He did not seem to enjoy the music. He was here out of duty, not by choice. Andy had learned that the sheriff had been widowed for many years.

Editor Tolliver came up and stood beside Andy. He said, "There are several nice-looking ladies whose husbands are too busy drinking to pay attention to them. They'd be glad to dance with you."

"They'd change their minds when we got out on the floor."

"Do you have a wife?"

"Yes, and I wish she was here." If Andy had Bethel in his arms, it would make no difference that he danced with the grace of a wounded buffalo.

"I am a bachelor myself. Sometimes that offers advantages." Tolliver soon was whirling a young matron across the floor.

Deputy Willis was checking weapons at the door, though only a few men appeared to have brought any. So far as Andy could tell, these people were interested only in having a good time. Judge Zachary appeared in his crumpled white suit. Willis greeted him a little too warmly, as if trying to curry favor. The judge responded in a dignified but noncommittal manner.

Some men absented themselves for a while, then returned with a glow in their eyes and less sureness in their step. As they passed, Andy caught the strong aroma of whiskey.

Lanny Teal danced by him often, always with the same girl. She was a little thing, thin enough to be picked up by the wind and blown away. Her shiny brown hair, done up in curls, sparkled with tiny glass ornaments meant to imitate diamonds. Her eyes seemed to see no one except Lanny, and he appeared to be aware of no one but her.

Seymour nudged Andy and muttered, "There's a storm brewin' up."

Standing against a far wall were the two young men Andy had seen earlier on the sidewalk. They conversed with a youth he recognized as Jake McIntosh. Jake glared at Lanny and the girl, though they seemed unaware of him. They were too absorbed in each other.

The three young men walked outside together. Andy said, "Maybe they're leavin'."

Seymour said, "They've just gone for a drink. They'll come back braver than when they left."

In a while the three returned, Jake in the lead. His unsteady gait told Andy he was bent on trouble. He walked out onto the floor and gave Lanny an unfriendly slap on the shoulder.

"I'm cuttin' in," he declared. "You've danced with Lucy long enough."

Lanny bristled. "I'm the one brung her, and I'll dance with her all night if I want to."

The crowd drew away in alarm as Jake drove a fist against Lanny's jaw. Lanny's head snapped back, but he was stunned for only a moment. His right fist came up from the floor and slammed into Jake's face. Jake staggered. His two friends rushed in and began to pummel Lanny. While trying to shake them off, Lanny kept hitting Jake.

Seymour jumped to his feet. He said, "We'd better stop this before it turns into a free-for-all."

The judge stepped out onto the floor, waving his arms. "Gentlemen! Gentlemen, let's have order."

Andy saw that the crowd had mixed allegiances, some cheering for Jake, others for Lanny. He stepped between the fighters, grabbing the collars of the two who had joined the fray uninvited. He yanked them backward so hard that one stumbled and went down. The other struggled to keep his feet.

On his knees, Harold Pearcy complained, "This ain't Ranger business."

Andy jerked him to his feet. "You'll get your chance, but one at a time."

Seymour said, "Harold, Sonny, this is a private fight. Back off and wait your turn."

It was Lanny's fight, all the way. In no time Jake was curled up on the floor, his arms folded over his face to ward off Lanny's fists. He cried, "Enough. Enough." Lanny stepped back, red face glistening with sweat, one shirt-sleeve split past the elbow.

To the two young men Andy said, "Which one of you wants to be next?"

Neither appeared ready to face Lanny's fists alone. Both stood with heads down, humiliated in front of the crowd.

The judge said sternly, "You young gentlemen should be ashamed. If charges are filed against you, I promise that you will not enjoy your day in court."

Mason Gaines stepped forward, carelessly flipping a half-smoked cigarette across the dance floor. He said, "You are arresting them, aren't you, Ranger?"

Andy gripped Pearcy's collar and shook him soundly. "I was studyin' on it. But it looks like they've lost interest in fightin'."

"You said all you needed was to see them break the law."

"The boys got excited when they saw their friend gettin' his plow cleaned. I'll bet they'll know better next time."

Gaines made no secret of his disappointment. He muttered, "Maybe you'll do something when these ruffians kill somebody."

Andy wondered why Gaines displayed such an interest in these young men. He suspected they had done something in the past that irritated him. Gaines appeared to be a man easily irritated.

Andy looked to the sheriff. Seymour said, "There wasn't any real harm done except to Jake, and he asked for it. As long as they'll all leave town right now, I'll forget this happened." He shifted his attention to Lanny. "That goes for you too."

Lanny remained defiant. "I need to take Lucy home first."

"I'll see that she gets home. I want you to leave, right now. Get your wagon and travel."

He turned his attention to Jake, whose face was beginning to darken with bruises and abrasions. Resentfully Jake said, "All right, I'm goin'. The evenin's lost its flavor anyhow."

Silently Andy and Seymour followed Lanny to the wagon yard where he had left the grocery-laden wagon and his team. Scanlon, owner of the yard, said, "Leavin' already? I can still hear the music."

The sheriff said, "It took on a sour note."

The three men helped Lanny hitch up the horses and climb shakily into the wagon. Seymour's voice sounded like the messenger of doom. He said, "Go straight home, Lanny. I'll say good-bye to the girl for you."

"The dance ain't even over."

"It is for you."

Lanny said curtly, "All I done was defend myself."

Andy suppressed a grin. He thought, *A good job it was, too.*

Lanny said, "Jake didn't get half of what he's got comin' to him."

Andy asked, "How did you learn to fight like that?"

"It comes natural, bein' a Teal. With everybody pickin' on us, we get lots of practice." Lanny spoke sharply to the team and started the wagon rolling. Andy and Seymour followed afoot until satisfied that Lanny had chosen the road that would take him home.

Andy said, "The boy's got spirit."

Seymour said sharply, "I'd be better satisfied if he had less of it. It could get him killed one of these days. Him or somebody else."

Returning to the dance, they found that the crowd had diminished by half. The fight had put a chill over the festivities. Lucy was gone.

Andy said, "Looks like the trouble is over for tonight."

Seymour was not convinced. "Lanny's got two brothers and several friends. Have you ever got yourself tangled up with a feud?"

Andy's face furrowed as he remembered. "A bad one once, down on the border. The graveyards got some bigger before it broke up."

"Ever since my wife died, I've hated funerals. I do what I can to see that they don't get too numerous."

Andy accepted the sheriff's offer to sleep in an empty jail cell and save a little money. Up from his hard cot at daybreak, he ordered breakfast in a chili joint so small that a dozen customers would have been three too many. The steak was thick, however, drowned in grease-and-flour gravy and sided by a generous helping of scrambled eggs. The coffee was strong enough to walk by itself. That was the way Andy liked it.

The cook-proprietor was a stoop-shouldered man named Kennison. He was somewhere on the sunny side of sixty, his thick gray hair needing a comb, his flour-sack apron in need of soap and water. A talkative sort, he did not require much prompting before he launched into a full history of the town and much of the country around it. Andy suspected that his account might be taking a few liberties with the facts.

The cook asked, "What did you think about the fight last night?"

Andy said, "It could've led to worse."

The cook said, "Those boys are slow learners, jumpin' on Lanny Teal the way they do. He winds their clock every time they try."

"They seem to have it in for him."

"For him and all his kin. The Teals are tight with their money and have more of it than most around here. It's human nature not to like somebody who's got more money than you have."

"Wouldn't the same feelin' apply against the McIntoshes too?"

"Sure. There's lots of people who would like to get hold of their land. The Teals and the McIntoshes don't have legal title, except for a little that's on live water. They've just got six-shooter possession of the rest."

"The state will sell it out from under them sooner or later."

"They're like politicians who can't see past the next election. One day they'll turn their calendar and find there ain't another sheet."

Deputy Willis burst into the little restaurant. "Pete Seymour sent me to look for you, Ranger. Says you need to go over to the doctor's house."

Andy said, "Do you know what for?"

"Somebody brought in Lanny Teal. Looked like a herd of cattle ran over him."

Andy recognized Lanny's wagon in front of the doctor's home. The groceries bought yesterday still lay in it, badly scattered. The sheriff met Andy at the door. He said, "Take a look at what somebody brought in."

Lanny was slumped in a chair, his clothing torn, his face streaked with blood. He appeared to be in a daze, his cheekbones bruised blue and eyes swollen almost shut.

A man in farmer overalls said, "I seen the wagon and team first, standin' there in the trail. Then I found this boy layin' on the ground. Thought at first he was dead. Somebody worked him over like they meant to kill him."

The sheriff put in, "Must've been several of them. One or two couldn't have done this to him. Not him or any of the other Teals."

Lanny struggled to get up. The doctor pressed him back into the chair and said, "Be still, son. You're badly hurt." He had stripped Lanny to the waist. He washed the lacerated face and bruised body with alcohol. Lanny drew himself into a tight knot until the burning eased. The doctor applied a thick ointment to the deep scratches and open wounds.

Seymour said, "Lanny, tell us who did this."

Lanny shook his head, wincing from the burn. "Who said somebody did anything? I just fell out of the wagon."

"We know better than that. Tell us who did it."

"I pay off my own debts. I don't need no squinchy-eyed sheriff."

Annoyed, Seymour persisted, "I can lock them up and throw the key in the river."

Lanny snorted. "In jail they'd get free room and board, with nothin' to do but sleep. Damn poor punishment, the way I see it."

Andy said, "It's as much as the law allows."

"The law! Nobody by the name of Teal ever gets a fair shake from the law."

Seymour argued, "If you try to handle this yourself, you'll wind up in bad trouble."

"I've been in trouble most of my life. It don't scare me none." Lanny looked at the doctor, or tried to. "Hurry up and finish with me, Doc. I want to go home."

The doctor said, "Your eyes are swollen. I doubt that you could even see the road."

"The horses know the way."

Andy said, "I'll go with you. Otherwise that bunch might catch you travelin' alone and do this all over again."

"I'll borrow a gun. It'll be them that needs help."

"With those eyes swollen, you couldn't see well enough to shoot anybody."

"They're cowards. Maybe I can scare them to death."

"That'll be my job."

Andy drove the wagon, his horse tied on behind. Lanny sat rigidly. Each jolt of the wagon drew his mouth into a tight, thin line, but he did not complain. Old Man Teal had brought his sons up to be tough as a hickory knot.

Andy said, "We'd better stop and rest the horses a while."

Lanny offered no argument. He climbed down slowly and painfully, waving off Andy's move to help him. He said, "As long as I've got two feet under me, I'll do for myself. You can carry me when I'm in my coffin."

"That may be sooner than you think if you keep fightin' all the time."

"Us Teals never set out to aggravate anybody. All we ask for is to be left the hell alone."

About noon Andy became aware of several riders coming up behind. Spotting the wagon, they moved their horses into an easy lope. Andy drew his pistol and conspicuously held it across his lap. It did not go unnoticed.

The riders were young men. They included Pearcy and Vernon, who had jumped on Lanny at the dance. Andy did not see Jake McIntosh. He had probably gone home to nurse his bumps and bruises.

Pearcy gave Andy a hostile look. "Have you taken sides, Ranger?"

"Who would I side with? I haven't seen a halo hangin' over anybody since I've been here."

"We heard Lanny fell out of his wagon and hurt himself. We came out to see that he gets home all right."

Andy raised the pistol to be certain no one had forgotten about it. "You-all can go back to town. I've got the situation well in hand."

"We'll go along and help you."

Andy was sure they would jump him the first time they saw a chance. He said, "Now, boys, I want to be sure we understand one another. See that cow skull lyin' out yonder?" He leveled the pistol and put a bullet between the eyes. The skull shattered in a puff of dust.

Andy gave the surprised young men a moment to consider, then said, "I told you I've got the situation handled."

Pearcy growled, "An old cow skull is one thing. Shootin' a man is different."

"It is," Andy agreed. "A man is bigger, and easier to hit."

Some of the men lost interest after the shot. They were starting to turn away. Pearcy's resentful gaze followed them. Slumped in the saddle, he warned Andy, "We could get you fired. We've got friends in Austin."

Andy said, "So have I."

By this time most of the riders had pulled back. They

knew that to hurt a Ranger was dangerous business. To kill one was suicide.

Pearcy muttered about getting a Mexican *curandero* to put a curse on Lanny Teal, and on the Rangers for good measure. Andy watched him turn and follow the others toward town. He said, "I think the horses have rested enough."

The shot had taken Lanny by surprise. He said, "I'd hate to have you aim that six-shooter at me."

Andy said solemnly, "I'd hate to have to."

They reached the Teals' ranch a little before sundown. Bud, the oldest brother, came down from the porch as Andy stopped the wagon in front of the house. He frowned at Lanny. "Damn it, boy, you look like you took on the Union army and lost."

Lanny's answer was curt. "I won the first fight. If this Ranger hadn't broken it up, I'd've whipped Jake McIntosh to where he'd be in bed for a week."

"What do you mean, the *first* fight?"

"Some of his friends followed me when I started home. They came at me in a bunch."

Andy asked, "Which of Jake's friends?"

Lanny realized he had said more than he intended. He spoke quickly, "I was talkin' to Bud."

Daggett limped out onto the porch, followed by Carrie. For a moment her eyes betrayed anxiety over her battered brother. Taking a grip on her emotions, she said, "Did you bring everything I asked you to?"

Lanny said, "It's all there. Look for yourself."

She touched a bandage on Lanny's face. Her voice softened. "How does Jake McIntosh look?"

"Kind of beat up."

Harper Teal stepped onto the porch in time to hear, his reddish eyebrows meeting each other in a scowl. He said severely, "I've told you boys over and over, I disapprove of you fightin'." He moved down for a closer look at his son. "But if you can't go around it, be damned sure you win. Did you?"

Lanny loosened up and answered with pride, "Sure did. Whipped him fair and square, Pa. On the way home, they ganged up on me, but I think I put a hurt on a couple of them."

Harper nodded with satisfaction. "Always remember, never go lookin' for trouble, but if it comes, don't let nobody tread on you."

Carrie fixed an accusing gaze on Andy. "Where was the law when the McIntosh bunch was trying to beat him to death?"

Andy admitted, "Asleep, I'm afraid. After the fight at the dance, Sheriff Seymour and I made sure Lanny took the road home. We didn't think Jake was in any shape to follow him."

Angrily she turned to her father. "We've got to put a stop to this trouble, or people are going to die. Some of us, maybe."

Harper declared, "It's up to Ethan McIntosh and his brood. That damned old Yankee has got his mind set on runnin' the whole county."

She said, "Listen to yourself, throwing out the word *Yankee*. The war's been over for more than twenty years."

"Not everywhere. We're still standin' up for the little people."

Carrie braced her hands on her hips. "We're all little

people, even the McIntoshes and their kin. Compared to the big ranches, none of us amounts to a hill of beans."

"And we never will unless we fight for what's ours." The old man tromped back into the house.

Carrie stewed. "Come on in, Lanny, and let me check you over."

Lanny said, "The doctor patched me up fine."

Her voice lashed at him. "I said come in this house!"

Lanny followed her, his shoulders drooped.

Bud mused, "I pity her next husband. He'd better have a hide like that old brindle bull."

Andy asked, "Does she have any prospects?"

Bud glanced up at Daggett. "Everybody around here knows her too well. They know the red in her hair ain't just for looks." He pointed his chin toward the bunkhouse. "You'll stay all night, won't you, Ranger?"

"It's too late to go back to town."

"Don't expect too good a supper. The mood Carrie's in, she'll burn the biscuits and oversalt the beans."

Daggett had stood on the porch, leaning on his cane, observing the scene without comment. When Bud went into the house to see about his brother, Andy asked Daggett, "How's the leg?"

"Healin'. Thought you went to town to keep the peace."

"I'm afraid I didn't do a good job of it."

"Next time, knock some heads together. You'd be surprised how sensible people get when they see a little blood. Especially if it's theirs."

"You can do it yourself when you're ready to ride."

Daggett seated himself on the bench. "I kind of hate to leave. I like the cookin'."

"Or maybe the cook?"

Daggett almost smiled. "She grows on you."

At the table, Andy found the Teal family in better spirits than he might have expected in view of the beating Lanny had taken. The patriarch did not bellow at anyone. Carrie's biscuits were just right.

Harper said, "Pass me the gravy, Lanny, and tell me again how you whipped Jake McIntosh."

"Wasn't much to it, Pa. Me and Lucy was dancin' along right fine till he come in drunk, itchin' for a fight. So I gave it to him. Then a couple of Jake's friends messed in."

Carrie glanced at Andy. "What was the law doing?"

"The Ranger pulled them off of me like a pair of whimperin' pups. When Jake hollered that he'd had enough, Pickard offered to let them take me on one at a time. But they both acted like they needed to go somewhere."

Carrie looked to Andy for corroboration. He said, "That's about the size of it."

She said, "We're beholden to you."

Harper said, "Lanny could've whipped the whole bunch without help. He eats nothin' but beef, like the Lord intended when He gave us cattle. Them McIntoshes have got chickens runnin' wild all over their place. That's what makes them weak, eatin' so much chicken." He cut off a square of steak and dipped it in a gob of gravy on his plate. "The only trouble with beef is that when it's on the hoof, you've got to watch all the time that somebody don't steal it. They're always tryin'."

Andy said, "Are you accusin' the McIntoshes?"

Harper's eyes narrowed. "I will, when I find the proof."

Bud Teal had listened without comment. He said, "You know, Pa, half the people around here are convinced that *we're* doin' it."

Harper's face reddened. "Let them accuse me to my face. There ain't a man in this county that I can't whip."

"That won't convince them. They still remember Vincent Skeen."

Carrie stiffened, staring darkly at her brother across the table. She arose and quickly left the room.

Harper frowned. "That was the wrong thing to say, son."

Bud looked chagrined. "It just popped out of my mouth. But it's the truth. People ain't got over blamin' us for what he did."

Harper grimaced at the memory. "It was an awful sight for your poor sister to see."

"Yeah," Bud said, "terrible." He pushed back from the table and went outside, leaving half the food on his plate uneaten.

Lanny reached over with a fork and speared a biscuit Bud had taken but had not bitten into. He said, "No use lettin' the last biscuit go to waste."

His father gave him a critical look. Lanny said, "I've got to keep up my strength. No tellin' when Jake McIntosh may come lookin' for some more."

Harper warned, "If you see he's wearin' a gun, you better go way around him. Even Carrie can shoot straighter than you."

Andy found Bud sitting on the barn step, patching a bridle. He said, "You kind of shook up your sister."

"Didn't mean to. We tried to keep her from seein' him layin' there shot to hell, but nobody could hold her back. She'd have killed every McIntosh that came in sight that day, but we wouldn't let her have a gun."

"Now she's talkin' about makin' peace."

"She doesn't want to lose anybody else."

"Have the McIntoshes ever said anything about the jail-house killin'?"

"They don't talk about it. Neither do we." Bud accidentally punched his thumb with the awl. He flinched. "I've never understood how a sensible woman like Carrie got herself wrapped up in a son of a bitch like Skeen. The rest of us saw through him almost from the first."

Andy said, "Lanny told me he beat her."

Grimly Bud said, "Just once. She floored him with a chunk of stove wood. Hand me that leather string, would you?"

Andy knew the subject was closed.

Harper Teal stomped into the bunkhouse. It was still dark, but he thundered, "You boys get up. You're wastin' daylight."

Someone lighted a lamp. The cowboys and two of the Teal brothers crawled out from beneath their blankets. Lanny did not move. His father strode over to Lanny's cot and roughly shook the boy's shoulder. "Come on. We've got no room here for layabouts."

Lanny groaned. "I'm too stiff to move. There ain't a place on my body that don't hurt."

"Best thing for that is exercise. If you ain't off of that cot by the time I get to the door, you'll have no breakfast." Harper left without looking back.

Lanny made two unsuccessful tries to rise to his feet. He sat back on the cot, his face twisted. "What makes Pa so damned mean?"

Bud said, "Too bad you can't remember Grandpa. He was worse. They had to be tough to survive in his time. They had no easy life like we've got now."

"Easy?" Lanny gingerly pulled a shirtsleeve over a sore arm, then repeated with the other. "There's got to be a better way to make a livin'."

"But after a good day's work you go to sleep knowin' you've earned your keep."

"I've heard other people say that. Usually they're the ones who hire somebody else to do the work for them."

Harper nodded satisfaction upon seeing Lanny take a chair at the table, but he wolfed down his breakfast without comment. Finished, he pushed to his feet and said, "Carrie, you always fix too much coffee. It gives these boys an excuse to dawdle instead of gettin' out to work."

When he was gone, she said to the others, "I hope you-all set him a pace today that he can't keep up with. Bring him home walkin' on his knees."

Bud said, "I don't think it can be done. I've never seen a man who can get drunk on hard work like Pa does."

Lanny said, "The trouble is, he always wants us to be with him when he does it."

The men stood up and prepared to leave the table. Daggett turned a fierce gaze upon them. "Ain't you-all goin' to carry your stuff to the pan so the lady doesn't have to?"

Shamed, the men carried their cups, plates, and utensils to the cabinet. Daggett thanked Carrie for the meal. The other men followed suit and straggled out toward the barn. Andy pushed his chair back and arose. He said, "Thank you for the breakfast. I'll be gettin' to town."

Daggett told Carrie, "I think it's time for me to go too. It's been a real pleasure gettin' to know you, ma'am."

She frowned. "Are you sure that leg is well enough?"

"The longer I stay here, the harder it'll be to leave."

Andy was aware of a regretful look that passed between

them. He felt he had witnessed something that should have been private.

Daggett handed her the cane he had been using. "Thanks for lettin' me have the borry of it."

"It'll be here the next time you need it." She smiled. "I don't mean that I want to see you get hurt again."

"Next time I see that brindle bull, I'll let Pickard wrestle with him."

They saddled their horses. Daggett still limped. He struggled to mount up, but Andy knew better than to offer help.

Andy said, "We need a good look at the McIntosh family. I thought we might circle over to their place before we go back to town. While we're there we can give Jake a talkin'-to."

"What he needs isn't talk. A smart tap on the head with the barrel of a six-shooter would do him a world of good."

"You've been listenin' to the Teals. I expect the McIntoshes see things different."

Daggett grunted. "It complicates things when you've got to look at both sides. You're not sure who to shoot."

One of the cowboys had told Andy that to find the McIntoshes' place he had only to follow the creek. The Teals had settled on the upper part, where the springs brought it to life. The McIntoshes had come along later, taking a long stretch of the creek farther downstream. For a while Andy saw cattle bearing the Teals' T Cross brand. Then he began coming across the Bar F of the McIntosh family. After a time he heard yelling and reined his horse in that direction. He found several men herding cattle into a crude brush corral. Among them he recognized Jake and his father.

The McIntoshes saw Andy and Daggett but did not acknowledge them until the cattle were penned and the gate closed. Gray-bearded Ethan McIntosh stared hard at Andy as if trying to remember where he might have seen him before.

"I'm Andy Pickard," Andy said. "My partner and I were at the Hawkinses' place when you came by."

The old man extended his hand hesitantly, as if he might change his mind and jerk it back.

Jake said, "He's a Ranger, Papa. He was at the dance." Jake had no bandages on his face, but he showed several dark bruises and some abrasions still inflamed.

Ethan's eyes narrowed. "Were you one of them that beat my boy up so bad?"

Andy said, "No, sir. Lanny Teal did that all by himself."

"Just Lanny? That is not quite the way I heard it." Ethan cast an accusing glance at his son. Jake looked away. Ethan said, "I doubt that it is a mortal sin to improve upon the truth in a modest way. We have all done it. Look, Rangers, we have these weaned calves to brand. If we wait much longer, somebody is likely to maverick them. Somebody like those Teals."

"Go on ahead. We didn't come to disrupt your work."

Andy was not one to stand around and watch. He pitched in and helped one of the McIntosh sons to flank calves and hold them down for the branding, earmarking, and cutting. Daggett assumed responsibility for the fire that heated the irons. His sore leg would permit little more.

Ethan said, "You appear to have had experience at this."

Andy said, "Some."

"I'd think you'd want to forego your Ranger job and do something for yourself."

"My plan is to have cattle of my own when I can buy some more land."

"Buy it?" Ethan was dismissive. "There is still vacant state land to the west of here that you could use for nothing. If you don't own it, you don't have to pay taxes on it. You pay only on your cattle, and only on as many of them as you allow the assessor to see."

"The state's sellin' off land as fast as it can."

"It will never be able to sell land that has no water on it. Besides, out past the Pecos, there is more land than cattle."

"Have you ever seen it?"

"No, but I know it's there, free for the taking."

Andy frowned. "For good reason. Some of it's so sparse that a cow has to graze in a run."

Ethan asked, "Have you met Old Man Harper Teal?"

"Yes, sir."

"When Harper begins buying dry land, I will too, if only to prevent that old thief from getting what should be mine."

Andy thought about it before saying, "What makes you think he's a thief?"

"It's common knowledge. Ask anyone."

That was essentially what Andy had heard from the Teals except that they were describing the McIntoshes. The two old men had a lot more in common than they knew, he thought. He said, "If you have any proof, I'll get out a warrant."

Ethan pondered. "Not yet, but when I get it I'll shout it from the rooftops."

The cattle branded and turned out, the McIntoshes mounted their horses and started toward their headquarters. Ethan invited Andy and Daggett to go along. As they rode, the old man pointed out several varieties of grass. "It's strong and puts the pounds on them. Of course, there's brush here that cattle don't eat. I've thought it would be good for goats, if there was any market for them."

Andy said, "I've seen some white goats with long, silky hair. Owners shear them like sheep."

"I'll look into it one of these days. A man with a family needs to ring every bell he can reach. If he does not, someone else will."

In the conversation Andy found that Ethan's family consisted of a wife, three sons, a daughter named Patience, and a son-in-law named Barstow, on whom Ethan bragged at length. "He works as hard as any man I know," he said. "My daughter had her head on her shoulders when she married him."

If so, Andy thought, Ethan was luckier than Harper Teal had been with his late son-in-law.

Riding toward the ranch headquarters, Andy contrived to pull his horse beside Jake's. He asked, "How are the battle wounds?"

"The heart still pumps all right."

"I've wondered why you keep fightin' with Lanny Teal. They say he always beats you."

"Why does a man keep gettin' back on a bronc that throws him off? He hopes to wear him down."

"Lanny doesn't really want to fight you."

"What business is that of the Rangers?"

"We were sent here to try and keep things peaceful."

"Run the Teals out of the country. That'll do it."

"Funny. They said pretty much the same thing about you-all."

Jake's voice sharpened. "The day'll come when we'll have to burn them out like a wasp's nest."

Andy warned, "Do, and the Rangers will come after you."

"Sounds like you've taken sides already."

"We haven't, and we won't unless somebody forces us to."

Nearing the headquarters, Ethan said, "It is late. You Rangers are welcome to eat supper with us and stay the night."

"We'd be obliged," Andy said. Ranger protocol would have called for him to defer to Daggett, but the older Ranger might have declined the offer. Andy wanted to spend time with the McIntoshes as well as the Teals and become better acquainted with both families.

Ethan said, "In spite of anything Harper Teal may have told you, we have no tails nor horns, nor do we breathe fire. All we ask is to be able to scratch out an honest living and remain in the good graces of the Lord."

"That doesn't seem like too much to ask."

"Some people won't leave us alone, though. They accuse us of things we never did, more than likely trying to cover their own transgressions. Are we supposed to lie down and let them walk over us?"

"You're supposed to obey the law."

"That we do. You can't blame Jake if he faces off against that Teal boy once in a while. He can't be expected to stand still against Lanny Teal's provocations."

"I was at the dance. I didn't see Lanny provoke him."

"He knows Jake considers Lucy to be his girl. He took her to the dance to goad Jake into a fight."

"Has anybody asked Lucy whose girl she wants to be?"

"Jake staked his claim. That should be enough to keep everyone else away."

Andy was a bit put off by McIntosh's strong sense of family entitlement. He argued, "A woman's not like a piece of land. She's got a mind of her own."

"Not a very bright one if she chooses Lanny over Jake. Any McIntosh is worth a dozen Teals."

The McIntoshes' headquarters did not look greatly different from the Teals'. Andy saw two frame houses, one newer but smaller than the other. He assumed it was where the daughter and son-in-law lived. A bunkhouse stood halfway between the smaller house and the barn. The corrals were of upright cedar stakes, fitted closely together so no animal larger than a rabbit could work its way through. Chickens scratched around the barn. Farther away, Andy could see a hog pen. It was a more diversified operation than the Teals'.

Though the creek ran nearby, a windmill stood just behind the larger house, its wheel turning slowly. The sucker rod clanked with each stroke.

Ethan swept a wide arc with his callused hand. "It's nothing fancy like the English dukes and earls who come over here with disgraceful amounts of money, but everything you see was built piece by piece with our own hands and the sweat of our brows. A hardworking man can do well for himself."

He can if he doesn't have to pay to use the land, Andy thought. But he could foresee an end to that. It would be the end of free range people like the McIntoshes and the Teals. Changes were overtaking them whether they acknowledged it or not.

Andy asked, "What if somebody buys all this out from under you?"

"They can't. I have bought the land where the headquarters sits, and the land along the creek. I need not be concerned about the rest of it. Without water, no one else can use it."

Ethan noticed that Andy was intrigued by the windmill. He said, "It furnishes house water for drinking and cooking. With so many cattle upstream, we don't trust the creek to be clean. It's a marvel how much mud one cow can stir up. Horses are even worse."

Andy saw something more in the mill. Up to now, ranchers who staked their claims on rivers, creeks, and springs could claim by default outlying areas worthless without access to water. This had the effect of choking out latecomers who found no watered land. But in other parts of Texas, Andy had seen a trend toward drilling wells and erecting windmills that could bring up underground water where there was none on the surface. In time the free range operator would no longer be able to hold settlers at bay simply because the land was dry.

McIntosh's windmill foreshadowed his eventual defeat unless he adapted.

The son-in-law loped ahead to open the gate and hold it for the other riders to pass through. Jake joked with him. "Barstow, when are you goin' to make uncles of us? You've been married long enough to give her two babies by now."

Embarrassed, Barstow tried to string along. He said, "I'm bashful."

"When I want somethin', I jump right in," Jake said.

Jake's brother Harvey intervened. "That's how you got those bruises. You jumped in over your head."

"I'll whip him the next time. You can bet on it."

"I'll bet on it the day I see that red rooster lay eggs."

Critically Ethan said, "Jake, you should be ashamed, making crude suggestions about your own sister."

Jake shrugged. "She didn't hear it."

Ethan muttered to Andy, "I hope I can keep that boy alive till he's thirty. Perhaps by then he'll grow up."

Andy found that the McIntosh cowboys had their own cook, operating in a small kitchen at one end of the bunkhouse. The family members ate in the main house, where Ethan's gray-haired wife ruled over the kitchen with the stern authority of a top sergeant. She was assisted by her married daughter, a short, plump little woman of perhaps thirty, whose pleasant smile seemed locked in place. Andy wondered idly if she kept it while she slept.

Ethan called his wife Agatha. Like her daughter, she was short in stature, broad in the hips. Unlike her daughter, she did not smile much but issued a lot of orders. She said, "Jake McIntosh, you'll not eat at my table until you wash your face and hands and comb your hair. We may live in the country, but we do not have to be countrified."

Jake protested that soap burned the lacerations on his face. She said, "All the better. You'll know to keep your hands in your pockets the next time you're tempted to fight."

Andy soon decided he liked these people, just as he had come to like the Teals. He also realized that this was a dilemma in the making. Sooner or later he might have to act against one of the families, or both.

Leaving the McIntoshes' ranch after breakfast, he asked Daggett, "What do you say now that you've seen them all?"

Daggett frowned. "I say *damn it!*"

5

Logan Daggett sat on a bench in front of the general store, his hurt leg stretched straight. He did not arise as Andy walked up. He asked, "Where you been?"

"Around. Listenin' to talk."

"Figured out yet who to blame for the trouble?"

"Some say it's the McIntoshes. Some say it's the Teals."

"I could've told you that without talkin' to anybody."

"It's all I've got."

Daggett had been whittling on a scrap piece of pine. It was beginning to take the form of a pistol. He said self-consciously, "The blacksmith's boy has been followin' me around. I'm makin' a little somethin' for him."

This show of generosity took Andy by surprise. "We're here to keep the peace, and you're givin' him a gun?"

"I don't know how to carve him a Bible." Daggett brushed pine shavings from his legs. A small, hungry-looking dog sniffed at them and turned away disappointed. Daggett said, "I haven't seen either of those two young fightin' roosters in town."

"I hear the Teals and the McIntoshes have been busy workin' cattle."

"I hope they're workin' their own, and not somebody else's."

Andy asked, "Any reason to think otherwise?"

Daggett's voice softened. "The time I spent with the Teals gave me a chance to look them over. They don't seem like the outlaws some people say they are. Carrie told me their family history."

"Do you think she told you all of it?"

"It ain't in her to lie."

The firmness of Daggett's voice told Andy he had best tread lightly. It had occurred to him that Carrie might remind Daggett of his wife of times past. He considered before he asked, "Does she resemble somebody you used to know?"

Daggett thought about it. "Nope, not a bit."

The barking of a dog led Andy's attention to a horseman coming up the street. Tall and gaunt, he was dressed in black, like a preacher, with blankets and a war bag tied to his saddle. A rifle rested in a scabbard beneath one leg. His coat bulged over a pistol on his hip. Andy said, "Here's one I haven't seen before."

Daggett's face fell. "Oh, hell. You don't know who that is?"

"I don't think so."

"You've heard of Nelson Rodock, ain't you?"

The name was familiar to Andy, though the face was not. Rodock had a reputation as a lethal troubleshooter who usually brought a quick end to whatever problem he was hired to solve. He managed to stay within the letter if not the spirit of the law. At least he managed not to get caught.

Andy said, "He looks like he could walk into the church and preach a sermon."

Daggett shook his head. "If he did, it would be at a funeral."

Andy suggested, "Maybe he's just passin' through."

Daggett said, "He wouldn't travel around for the fun of it. He's here because somebody's paid him, or is goin' to." He jerked his head. "Come on, back me up." He limped out to intercept the rider. Andy hastened to join him.

Daggett stopped, his right hand resting near his pistol. He said, "Howdy, Rodock. It's been a while."

Rodock drew up on the reins and stared with flint-gray eyes. Recognition brought a grim smile devoid of humor or warmth. "Howdy yourself, Logan Daggett. I figured somebody sent you to glory years ago."

"You tried once. I've got the scar."

"I was having an off day. I am a better shot now."

"So I keep hearin'. They say an undertaker has gotten fat, followin' you around."

"My reputation far exceeds my record. I have not killed half as many men as some people believe. And those I *have* killed deserved it."

"You spent a couple of years as a guest of the state for tryin' to kill me."

"The time was not wasted. I learned much while I was there, for which I have you to thank."

The two men stared coldly at each other in the loudest silence Andy had experienced in a long time. At length Rodock asked, "Do you have any business with me here today?"

Daggett said, "You're not in the fugitive book. But I'd be glad to put you there if you give me any reason."

"I am much more careful than in my younger days. I intend to grow a long gray beard and die in bed." Rodock gave Andy a quick glance, but it was Daggett who held his attention. "Good day, gentlemen."

Daggett's eyes were squinted as he watched Rodock move on toward the hotel. He said, "Things were touchy enough around here before he showed up. I'd save everybody some trouble if I shot him here and now."

"But bein' a Ranger, you can't."

"Not in town, with people watchin'. But if we were out in the country with nobody around . . ."

"You'd shoot him?"

"Like a rabid dog. How else do you think a handful of Rangers managed in those bad years after the Reconstruction? We couldn't make them fear God, but we damned sure made them fear us."

Two heavily laden freight wagons lumbered up the street, cutting deep tracks in the dirt. One was loaded with spooled barbed wire, the other piled high with posts. Somberly Daggett said, "Here comes some more trouble, like Rodock wasn't enough."

Proprietor Babcock stepped out onto his store's porch. Smiling, he braced his hands on his broad hips while he watched the wagons' approach. He shouted, "It's about time you got here!"

The lead teamster pulled his mules to a stop and said, "Here's your order, Mr. Babcock."

Babcock said, "Been expecting you for a couple of days. Where have you been?"

The teamster said, "You can get only so much out of a mule."

Babcock pointed down the street. "It's too late to start for the Hawkinses' place today. Pull over by the wagon yard. You can deliver these goods to him tomorrow."

"The sooner we get away from here, the better we'll like it."

Daggett pulled a long strip of bark from a cedar post and gave it a moment's serious study. Tossing it aside, he said, "There'll be bloodstains on this wire before Hawkins gets it strung."

The teamster said, "It wouldn't be the first time. Me and Shorty got shot at over in Brown County. We tried to tell them it wasn't our wire. We just haul whatever the public pays us to."

Daggett said, "You ought to charge extra for carryin' this stuff."

"I do. This is the only hide I've got, and I place a high value on it. If I'm to risk losin' a piece of it, I expect to get paid."

Babcock's voice carried a hint of resentment. "You certainly charged enough for this job."

Daggett said, "We tried to talk Hawkins out of fencin' his land, at least till some of the bigger operators broke the ground."

Babcock appeared defensive. "It's a free country. A man has a right to do what he wants to with his own property."

Andy said, "There's been wars fought over that proposition."

Babcock flared. "Hawkins has a right to build a fence, and I have a right to sell him the wire and posts. As Rangers, it's your responsibility to uphold those rights." He retreated inside his store.

The teamsters had not moved. One said, "So you two are Rangers. Me and Shorty bleed easy. We'd be obliged if you'd stay around close. We'll even buy you both a drink."

Andy said to Daggett, "Why don't you go with them? I'll watch the wagons and see who-all takes an interest."

A great many people did. By ones and twos, they drifted down to the wagon yard once the teamsters had parked their wagons and turned the mules into a corral for a fill of grain. Andy watched Harold Pearcy and Sonny Vernon walk up. Pearcy foolishly tested a barb, then jerked his hand back. A tiny bubble of blood rose on the tip of his finger. He tried to suck it away.

Andy said, "I could've told you those barbs are as sharp as the devil's horns."

Pearcy rubbed a remnant of blood onto his trousers leg. "It was the devil that invented them."

Sonny said derisively, "Harold don't believe nothin' till he gives it a try."

Andy said, "Like jumpin' on Lanny Teal? Someday you boys'll learn there's some things you can't get away with."

Soon after Pearcy and Sonny left, Mason Gaines sauntered over to frown over the wire. He said, "I wonder if Hawkins talked to the Teals or the McIntoshes before he ordered this?"

Andy said, "I don't see any reason that he has to."

"I doubt they'll be happy about it. Once Hawkins gets his fence up—*if* he does—others will follow his example."

Andy said, "It's a free country."

"It's freer if you're big. Hawkins isn't."

Judge Zachary strolled over from the courthouse, chewing on a half-smoked cigar that had lost its fire. "I see that the rumors were correct," he said. "I am afraid this means some unpleasant days ahead."

Andy said, "I don't see any legal way somebody could stop Hawkins from buildin' his fence."

"No, but there are illegal ways. They usually end in court. Mind you, I respect August Hawkins, but he is a stubborn man. When he makes up his mind to something, he refuses to consider consequences."

"This part of the country seems to have more than its share of stubborn men."

Bud Teal was the first of his family to inspect the wire. Leaning from the saddle, he tested a barb between two fingers without cutting himself. "Wicked," he said. "I'll bet this stuff would even turn that brindle bull."

Andy said, "You haven't caught him yet?"

"Haven't seen him. Maybe he got tired of our ugly cows." He turned his attention back to the load of wire. "Hawkins is takin' a big risk with this."

"He wants to save his grass for his sheep. What's wrong with that?"

"Only that he's startin' somethin' a lot of people won't like."

"Your family for instance?"

"Lots of families." Bud reined his horse around. "I'll need to be tellin' Pa about this. I don't think he'll take kindly to it."

Jake McIntosh showed up an hour later with his father, Ethan. Jake's expression revealed nothing about his feelings. Perhaps he had none, one way or the other. Ethan was blunt, however. Fists clenched, he said loudly, "Satan's tool, it is. Any place that wire touches, the land is poisoned forever."

Andy had heard the same charge against steel plow points. He said, "It's Hawkins's own land."

"But this could spread like smallpox. The best thing is to stop the contagion before it starts."

"How do you figure on doin' that, Mr. McIntosh?"

"Even a hardheaded sheepman can be persuaded."

"You'd best not go against the law. It'd be our job to stop you."

Ethan's face twisted with indignation. "You, who've broken bread with us at our table?"

"I'd hope to break bread with you again, but we have to enforce the law. We have to protect people's property rights."

Face flushed, Ethan turned away. He said grittily, "Come on, son. We're leaving."

Jake lingered a little. He kept looking at the wire, but his mind was on something else. He asked, "Seen Lanny Teal in town lately?"

Andy said, "Not since he got waylaid on his way home from the dance."

Earnestly Jake said, "You can believe me or not, but I had no hand in that. After the fight at the dance, I was too stove up to tangle with Lanny again."

Andy said, "I'd like to believe you."

"There's been too many lies told about us McIntoshes. I'd like to move someplace where nobody ever heard of us. I'd change my name to Smith or Jones or somethin'."

Orphaned by Indians when he was a boy, Andy was sensitive to the importance of blood kin. He said, "A man shouldn't ever turn his back on family."

Jake said, "I'm proud of my family, but I hate the reputation some folks have stuck us with. We're God-fearin' people."

"Seems to me that the Teals are too."

"They'd like you to think so. It wouldn't surprise me none if they put Hawkins up to this."

Andy knew better, but it would be futile to argue the point with Jake.

The jail cell cot seemed harder than ever tonight. Dozing fitfully, Andy kept turning, trying to find a soft spot. There was none. Sleeping in the jail saved money and provided a roof for shelter, but he had not seen a drop of rain since he had been here. Shelter be damned, he thought. From now on he would sleep on a cot at the wagon yard.

He was startled fully awake by the clanging of a church bell. A bell in the middle of the night was not a call to services. He grabbed for his hat, then his trousers and boots. Still buttoning his shirt, he burst through the jail door and broke into a run. Ahead of him, men were shouting, moving toward a huge blaze near the wagon yard. Panicked horses and mules squealed and raced in circles inside the corrals.

The wagonload of fence posts was enveloped in flames.

6

One of the teamsters futilely dipped water from a trough and threw it on the fire a bucketful at a time. His efforts made no showing against the blaze. Rapidly losing ground, he gave up and stood back disconsolately to watch his wagon and its cargo go up in smoke.

Stable owner Scanlon ran excitedly back and forth, beseeching the onlookers to help save his property. Townsmen threw water on the wooden fence to prevent its loss. Others raked loose hay away from the blaze lest it catch fire and take the barn with it.

The teamster slapped at smoldering black spots on his shirt. Recognizing Andy, he said resentfully, "Kind of late showin' up, ain't you?"

"I wasn't expectin' this," Andy admitted.

"There goes half of my rollin' stock. Good freight wagons don't come cheap."

Daggett was slower getting to the scene. He still limped despite claiming that his injury had healed. He held silent. At this point there seemed to be nothing to say.

Unlike many others, Deputy Salty Willis was fully dressed. He had probably not bothered to take his clothes off when he went to sleep. He picked up a large metal container at the fence and brought it to the Rangers. He said, "Smells like coal oil."

Andy took a whiff. "That tells us how they did it. It doesn't tell us who they were."

Daggett nodded grimly. "I smell the McIntoshes behind this."

Andy asked, "Why the McIntoshes? There's lots of free range people that wouldn't be happy about Hawkins's fence. And what about the Teals?"

"Just the same, I'd bet my money on the McIntoshes."

"Don't you think you're makin' too fast a judgment?"

"Experience has taught me to play my first hunch. It generally proves out."

Sheriff Seymour came up in a trot, his shirt and trousers not yet buttoned. His boots were on the wrong feet. Breathing hard, he said, "They didn't wait long."

Andy asked, "Any suspicions?"

"I suspicion just about everybody but the old and infirm. And even some of them."

Storekeeper Babcock was trailed by his daughter. He quickly sent her home when he saw that some of the men had run to the fire in their underwear. His first comment to the Rangers was defensive. "That's Hawkins's loss, not mine. The posts belonged to him."

Andy was mildly irritated by the merchant's quick evasion of responsibility. He said, "You hadn't delivered them to him yet."

The teamster demanded, "What about my wagon? Who's responsible for that?"

Babcock was defensive. "Not me. You were paid to haul the goods, that's all. The wagon is yours."

"Was," Andy said. It and its load slumped into a smoky, smoldering heap, sending up a massive shower of sparks. The wheels lay flat on the ground.

The teamster glared at Babcock. "Nobody's paid me for the haul yet."

Babcock said, "You didn't complete it. You were supposed to deliver all the way out to the Hawkinses' place."

For a minute it appeared that the Rangers might have to break up a fight, but Babcock stopped the argument by briskly walking away.

Andy told the freighter, "Maybe you can sue whoever lit the fire. That's if we're ever able to find out who it was."

Tracks would be of no help. Too many people had added their own, hurrying to the fire, trying to fight it. Nor was the oil can likely to yield any information, for most people kept coal oil to fill lamps and lanterns, and to light stoves and fireplaces.

Andy told Daggett, "Looks to me like we're up a stump."

Daggett shook his head. "We'll keep an eye on the McIntoshes. Sooner or later one of them will make a wrong step."

Andy frowned. "She sure took ahold of you, didn't she?"

"She? Who you talkin' about?"

"Forget I said it."

"Carrie's got nothin' to do with it. I've suspicioned the McIntoshes all along."

Andy said, "We'd better get to know more about the lay of the land before we make up our minds. The first guess is wrong, often as not."

"Yours, maybe. Not mine."

Newspaper editor Tolliver was talking to the teamsters and making notes on a pad lighted by the flames.

Daggett poked Andy with his elbow and jerked his head toward a man who stood alone, watching the fire with no evident emotion. Andy recognized Rodock. He said, "Do you reckon . . ."

Daggett said, "I wouldn't be surprised."

There was no question of going back to sleep. Andy studied faces, especially those of people who seemed pleased by the conflagration. As daylight came, he found that some of the wooden spools that contained the wire were scorched. Whoever burned the posts had made an attempt against the wire as well, but the flames had consumed the coal oil, then died out.

The freighter and his helper hitched a team to the remaining wagon. He said, "I'm gettin' this load of wire off of my hands as quick as I can. Whichaway's the Hawkinses' place?"

Andy looked at Daggett. "Might be a good idea if we went with him. He could run into trouble."

"He's already had trouble," Daggett replied. "You go. I'll stay around town. If Rodock wiggles a finger, I want to see it."

Andy had breakfast, then went to the wagon yard. The freighters had already left. It did not take long to catch up to them on the road, for the wagon and its load were too heavy to make much speed.

"You were in a hurry," Andy said to the wagon's owner.

"It don't take me long to see when I'm not welcome. From now on I'm haulin' nothin' but dry goods and groceries."

"Fences are comin', like it or not."

They met a couple of travelers along the way but no one who offered any overt threat. Late in the afternoon Andy saw the Hawkinses' ranch house ahead. Starting and stopping, the wagon picked its way through a scattered band of sheep. A large wether grazed along out front. Around its neck a small bell clanged pleasantly with each step the animal took.

The teamster said, "That bell would drive me crazy, but I guess the sheep was crazy to start with. Most of them are."

Andy expected him to add "along with the men who own them," but he didn't. That was a common attitude in much of Texas.

Hawkins had half a dozen sheep in a small pen, most freshly shorn of their wool. Under a shed and on a spread-out tarp, he was shearing one with a pair of hand clippers. The wool was dusty gray on the surface, but next to the skin it was creamy white. Looking up and wiping sweat from his face onto his sleeve, Hawkins acknowledged the wagon's arrival with a nod. He finished the job and untied the sheep's legs. The animal struggled to its feet and leaped over a shadow before running out to join the others. Hawkins rolled the fleece and pushed it down into a long burlap bag before coming out through a wooden gate.

"Hello, Ranger," he greeted Andy. His extended hand

felt slick from the greasy wool. He gave the wagon a moment's attention. "There ought to be another, with the posts."

Andy gave him the news. Hawkins took it solemnly. He said, "I should have expected something like that. I came out onto the porch this morning and found a message on the wall. It was not a love letter."

Andy asked, "What did it say?"

"It said, 'No fences.' It was signed, 'the Regulators.' Had a noose drawn with it. Poor artist, but a clear message."

Andy knew of groups elsewhere calling themselves regulators. Usually they were secretive about their membership, often masked or hooded and acting under cover of darkness, enforcing their version of law and proper behavior. They might begin as vigilantes, augmenting local peace officers, but power tended to corrupt them, leading them to support private grudges and vendettas, take on political aspirations, and drive away or even kill those who might oppose them.

Andy said, "Looks to me like you've run up against a mob."

"A mob is just a gathering of people who don't have the courage to act on their own."

"But put them together, and they can hurt you."

Hawkins stared at the wagon. "A load of wire isn't worth much without posts to string it on." He said to the teamster, "How long would it take you to bring me another wagonload?"

The teamster shook his head. "Mister, I ain't haulin' no more posts. Not for you, not for nobody. Show me where to dump this wire."

Hawkins pointed. "Over there by the barn. And stack it, don't dump it." He turned back to Andy. "I'll see if Babcock can find me some more posts."

Skeptical, Andy said, "Are you sure? Might be smart to stand back a while and see how the wind blows."

Hawkins frowned. "You were too young to go to the war, but I wasn't. We fought for what we thought was right. Those on the other side were sure *they* were right. I don't think we really proved anything, but we stood up for what we believed in. That's what I'm doing now."

"But you had a whole army on your side. This time you're standin' out here all by yourself."

"I'm standing up for my rights."

Andy felt pride in the man's strong principles, but he also felt impatience. He remembered Bethel recounting a story from a book about a proud but foolish old warrior who rode into battle against a windmill, thinking it was a dragon.

The so-called regulators might indeed be a dragon.

Hawkins said, "As soon as I finish the shearing, I'll take the dog and bring in my sheep. You'll be staying the night, won't you?"

Andy thought he should, for whoever burned the wagon and left the message might return. "It's too late in the day to go back to town."

"I'll ride in with you tomorrow. I have to talk to Babcock about another load of posts."

Hawkins stuffed the final fleece into the sack. The two teamsters were unloading the spooled wire. Andy had no wish to join them at it. He said, "I'll help you bring in the sheep." That might be useful experience. Someday, when he became a rancher instead of a Ranger, he might want to keep sheep as well as cattle. Lots of hill country people seemed to prosper by owning both.

He admired the way the dog handled the sheep with little coaching. Hawkins said, "They've bred his kind in Scotland for generations. The herding instinct is part of his nature. Take him away from sheep and he'll herd hogs or chickens or whatever else he can find."

It seemed to Andy that some people were born with that herding instinct, constantly trying to control others. These nameless regulators were a case in point. Logan Daggett was another.

He asked, "What happens if a sheep fights back?"

"They never do. That's why they're called sheep." Hawkins's brow furrowed. "I'm a sheep*man*, Ranger, but I'm not a sheep."

After supper they sat a while on the porch, Hawkins smoking his pipe. They talked of weather and wool prices and other subjects but avoided what was uppermost in their minds.

Andy stretched and said, "I see the teamsters have bedded down out by the barn. I think I'll take my blanket and join them."

Hawkins pushed to his feet and tapped his pipe against a porch post. "Bring them to the house with you for breakfast. After I turn the sheep out to graze, we'll start for town."

So many things were running through Andy's mind that he could not go to sleep. He relived the burning of the posts. He kept seeing in his mind's eye the penciled warning from the regulators. He sensed that the threat was not idle. A lot of people had a stake in keeping the range open and free.

Hearing horses, he sat up and listened. He had remained in his clothes, except for his boots. He quickly put them on and strapped his gun belt around his waist. In the dim light of the moon he counted half a dozen men on horseback. As they neared, he realized that all wore hoods over their heads. One fired a pistol into the air and shouted, "Hawkins, come out here!"

The riders' attention was focused on the front of the house. They did not see Andy standing in shadow. The man brandishing the pistol shouted again for Hawkins to come out.

Andy shouted, "Hawkins, you'd better stay where you're at!"

The horsemen reacted with surprise. The one holding the pistol swung it toward Andy. Andy fired a shot that struck between the horse's feet. The frightened horse jumped. Its rider fell from the saddle, losing his hood and the pistol. On his knees, he felt around desperately, trying to find the weapon.

Andy fired again, the bullet raising dust just in front of the fallen man. He shouted, "Everybody back off! I'm a Ranger!"

He stepped up close to the man on the ground and said, "Let me get a look at you." The face was familiar. Andy had seen him hanging around a saloon in town. He had also been at the fire, watching but not joining others who attempted to snuff out the flames. He had seemed to enjoy the spectacle.

Andy held the muzzle of his pistol an inch from the man's nose and said for all the riders to hear, "You-all drop your guns so I won't be forced to kill this upstandin' citizen."

Several pistols and a rifle hit the ground. Andy knew that even if the men were unarmed, he could not long control so many still on horseback. He could not stop them if they turned and ran, so he gave them permission. "Now turn those horses around and git."

"What about our guns?" one man asked.

Andy said, "You can pick them up at the sheriff's office. I expect he'll have a few questions to ask you."

The fallen man started to arise. Andy tapped his chin gently with the pistol's muzzle. "Not you. We're goin' to have a little talk about the majesty of the law."

The riders began to pull away. The ostensible leader held back to say, "Ranger, we don't see where you have any call to mix in this. It's a community matter."

The voice was muffled by the hood the speaker wore. Andy thought he might have heard it before, but he could not be certain. He said, "It's a matter for the law when you burn up people's property and threaten their lives."

The man said, "Just the same, you tell Hawkins that if he strings any of that wire, he's liable to get hung with it."

Andy cringed at the grisly image of Hawkins strangling on a barbed wire noose. He motioned with the pistol. "Get away from here, or I'll find out how many of you I can shoot before I run out of shells."

One rider had not dropped his pistol, for he turned and fired a shot. It was not clear whether he was shooting at Andy or at the man on the ground. Andy put a bullet near the horse's feet. The animal began to pitch. The rider dropped his pistol and grabbed at the horn. He managed to stay in the saddle and ride off after the others.

The two teamsters had stood back, avoiding entanglement. Now they edged closer but kept their distance from

Andy's kneeling prisoner. The wagon owner said, "I wouldn't want to walk in your boots, Ranger. You won't know those men if you meet them on the street. One of them could step up and blow your head off."

Andy shook his head. "Every Ranger in Texas would be lookin' to kill him. A man would have to be stupid to take that chance."

"I've known a lot of stupid people in my time." The teamster waited to be sure his point had soaked in. He added, "If it's all the same to you, we'd sooner not have you ride back with us. We don't want to be anywhere close when lightnin' strikes you."

Andy smiled in spite of himself. "Fine with me. Your wagon travels too slow anyway. I would appreciate it, though, if you'd haul these guns to the sheriff."

Hawkins had come out onto the porch in his underwear. Andy asked him, "Is this man a neighbor of yours?"

Hawkins studied the face. "Bigelow, I didn't think you had the stomach for a thing like this. I thought you were all bellow and no bite."

Andy said, "It doesn't take much guts when you cover your face and ride with a mob."

Bigelow was trembling. In a breaking voice he said, "That last shot was aimed at me."

Andy asked, "What makes you think so? I figured it was aimed at me."

"They were afraid I might tell who the rest of them are. We're not supposed to get ourselves captured."

Andy said, "Then you ought to've stayed at home." He retrieved a set of handcuffs from his saddlebag and fastened Bigelow's wrist to a spoke in a wagon wheel. Bigelow complained, "Sittin' here this way makes me an easy target. And it's liable to throw a kink into my back."

Andy said, "You'd have gotten a kink in your *neck* if you'd killed Hawkins."

"We just figured to throw a scare into him, is all."

Accompanied by Hawkins, Andy reached town with his prisoner. He found Daggett before he found the sheriff. Daggett's eyes were grim as he stared at the prisoner. He said, "Why didn't you shoot him when you had the chance? There's nothin' gets a mob's attention like killin' the foremost."

"Killin' is the last resort."

"Sometimes it takes a strong dose of salts to flush the bowels."

Andy delivered the frightened prisoner to Sheriff Seymour's office in the jail. The lawman seemed not surprised. "Oscar Bigelow," he said, "I've been waitin' for you to stumble over your own feet. I always figured you for a member of Skeen's outfit, but I couldn't prove it."

Bigelow mustered up a moment's defiance. "You can't prove it now, either."

Andy said, "He won't need to. I'll file charges on you for attempted murder."

Bigelow went slack-jawed. "Murder? We didn't kill nobody."

"You fired into the house. You could've killed Hawkins or his wife. Now, if you'd like to tell who else was with you last night, I might whittle the charge down a little."

Bigelow looked at the floor. "I can't. They'd kill me."

"A few days on bread and water might change your outlook."

"I can't. I taken an oath. Anybody talks, he dies." Bigelow's voice tightened with desperation. "You won't get nothin' out of me, so you'd just as well turn me loose. I promise I'll be gone from this country before sundown."

Daggett said, "Let's sit on him a while. If he doesn't tell us what we want to know, we'll give out the word that he spilled his guts, then turn him loose. I'd bet he never gets to the county line."

Bigelow cried, "You wouldn't do that."

Daggett said, "We sure as hell would. You're no good to us if you won't talk."

Andy suspected that Daggett meant it. The idea disturbed him, but he played along. "Sounds all right to me."

Bigelow shook like a man in the throes of a bad hangover. "I just can't. You know what happened to Callender."

Seymour explained, "That's the man who was murdered a few days before you got here. I was fixin' to arrest him on suspicion when somebody shot him in the back. I figure he knew too much, and they were afraid I'd make him tell."

Bigelow said, "They gave him a day to leave the county, but he didn't want to go without his cattle. I wouldn't be that foolish."

Andy said, "You keep sayin' *they*. Who is *they?*"

"If I was to tell you, I could kiss my ass good-bye."

Daggett's face was severe. "Pickard, bein' raised with the Indians, I expect you know some ways to make him talk."

"I do, but I don't believe in usin' them."

"When you've handled as many criminals as I have, you'll change your way of thinkin'."

*   *   *

The teamsters brought the night riders' weapons to town in their wagon, dumped them at the sheriff's office, then left after a heated argument with storekeeper Babcock over who should stand the loss of the burned wagon. Babcock held firmly to his contention that he bore no responsibility for the fire, though he condescended to pay for the hauling. Thus all concerned gained some and lost some.

Babcock was reluctant to accept Hawkins's order for another load of posts, citing the trouble the first shipment had caused. Hawkins said, "I'll need several more loads of wire and posts before I can fence my place all the way around. Don't you want the business?"

The promise of additional profit brought Babcock around to Hawkins's way of thinking, though with reluctance. He insisted on payment in advance, one order at a time. He said, "You may not live to see the last load delivered."

Andy watched the sheriff inventory the captured weapons in his office. Seymour said, "I doubt anybody's goin' to claim this artillery."

Andy said, "It would be like writin' a confession."

They took Bigelow to the judge's office, but the judge was not there. A clerk said he was at his ranch. Bigelow sat handcuffed in a chair. Andy could almost smell the man's fear.

Seymour said, "Skeen's rustler gang had three or four killin's charged against them. I always suspicioned that Bigelow was one of the outfit, along with Callender, but I never had any proof. They—or somebody—has been back at it lately."

Andy said, "Bigelow talked about takin' an oath. When members have to swear an oath, it generally means the group is prepared to snuff out anybody who breaks the vow."

"What if they was to break into my jail? I wouldn't want Bigelow on my conscience, like Skeen."

Bigelow protested, "The jail is a death trap. You've got to take me someplace else."

The sheriff said, "Maybe we would, if you told us what we want to know."

Bigelow hung his head. "They'd hunt me down like a dog."

Seymour shrugged. "Then there's nothin' to do except lock you up."

Bigelow trembled. "You'd just as well shoot me now."

Daggett declared, "We're thinkin' about it." He took a firm grip on Bigelow's arm and lifted him from the chair. "I've got a sore leg, and I'm awful easy aggravated, so don't aggravate me."

Cradling a rifle across his left arm, Andy looked down the courthouse hall but saw no one. He led the way to the front door and down the steps, warily studying the light horse and wagon traffic on the dirt street. "Looks about as clear as it'll ever be," he said.

The jail and the sheriff's office were in a separate stone building adjacent to the courthouse. It was a walk of only about thirty yards in the open. They were halfway across it when a bullet struck the jail wall and ricocheted, singing. Andy swung the rifle around in reflex, searching wildly for the shooter.

A second shot brought a yelp of pain from Bigelow. The sheriff and Daggett lifted the prisoner between them and hurried him into the jail. Andy walked backward, following them and watching for rifle smoke. The shots could have come from anywhere across the street. He quickly entered the jail and closed the door.

Seymour and Daggett supported Bigelow until they could get him into a chair. The prisoner's ear was bleeding.

Seymour gave the wound a quick examination. "A couple of inches over and you'd be dead. As it is, you've just been earmarked."

Daggett offered no sympathy. He said, "A swallowfork, I'd call it."

Sobbing, Bigelow touched a hand to his ear and looked at the blood. "They want to kill me. They'll do it yet."

Fists hammered against the jail's outside door. A voice called, "Pete, let me in. It's Salty."

Seymour nodded at Andy. "My deputy. Open the door."

The lanky deputy rushed inside, carrying a rifle. Andy closed and bolted the door behind him. The deputy said, "I heard the shootin'. Anybody hurt?"

Daggett said, "Nobody that matters."

Andy studied the trembling prisoner a moment, then looked about the jail. He had not noticed before that every cell was vulnerable to a gunshot from one of the windows. An assassin would not even have to break in.

The sheriff said, "I know what you're thinkin'. That's why I put curtains over all the windows. Nobody can see in from outside."

Andy said, "Just the same, this jail would be like a shootin' gallery if somebody pulled one of those curtains down. Kerrville has got a jail that would hold a bull elephant."

Seymour put up no argument. "After dark. One of you Rangers ought to take him. The minute I cross a county line, I'm out of my jurisdiction. You know how these slick defense lawyers can use a thing like that."

Daggett said, "Every last one of them ought to be taken out and hung."

Andy said, "I'll go."

Seymour ordered his deputy to patrol the jail from outside, preventing anyone from approaching the windows.

Andy tried to sleep, but the big railroad clock seemed to try shaking itself from the wall. Each movement of the heavy pendulum sounded like the cocking of a gun. When the lamp's faint glow showed one o'clock, he arose from the cot and fetched his rifle from a rack on the wall.

The sheriff was already up and moving about. "Salty's got two horses for you out back," he said. "Ready?"

Andy nodded and fetched the keys from the sheriff's desk. He unlocked Bigelow's cell. "Come on," he said. "We got some travelin' to do."

Suspicious, Bigelow sat up on the edge of his bunk but did not move toward the door. "I want to know where we're goin'."

"Someplace where you'll be safer. Roll your pillow up in your blanket. If anybody manages a look through the window, it'll appear like you're still sleepin'."

Bigelow complied. He touched a hand to the bandage on his ear. "It burns like hell."

That sounded like a call for sympathy, but Andy could not summon any.

Daggett was on his feet. He asked, "Sure you don't want me to go with you?"

Andy said, "Three men would attract more attention than two. Besides, if somebody takes a shot at this jail, you'll be here to help catch him."

Andy handcuffed Bigelow and led him by the arm

toward the back door. He said, "Somebody blow out the lamp."

He gave his eyes time to become accustomed to the darkness, then opened the door and led Bigclow out. As Seymour had said, two horses were tied outside. He motioned for Bigelow to mount up. In barely more than a whisper he said, "If you try to run, I'll shoot you myself."

Bigelow whined, "You treat me like I'd killed somebody."

"For all I know, you may have."

The moon was but a sliver and cast little light. The shadows between the town's buildings were dark as ink. Andy held to them as much as he could. Bigelow started another complaint, but Andy cut him off. "Why don't you just holler out and tell everybody where you're at?"

Bigelow said no more. The last building was just ahead. Soon after passing that they would be among live-oak trees and cedars. He would avoid the road a while, then cut back into it when he felt they were on safe ground.

Four horsemen pushed out from behind the last building. Though the light was poor, Andy saw that they wore hoods over their heads. He tried to bring his rifle into position, but one of the riders pushed his horse into Andy's and almost jarred him out of the saddle. The man, little more than a dark shadow, shoved the muzzle of a pistol into Andy's face.

He said, "Drop the rifle. The six-shooter, too. We don't want to kill a Ranger, but we'll do it if we have to. All we're after is your prisoner."

Andy said, "You can't have him." It was a hollow statement. Though he still held the rifle, he knew he would not live long enough to bring it into play.

The rider said, "Bigelow, we don't like the company you're in."

Bigelow's voice broke. "I ain't told nobody nothin'. I ain't *goin'* to tell them nothin'. I swear."

"That's what Callender said, but we knew he'd break. He'd talk like an old widder woman."

Bigelow begged, "I won't. You know me."

"Yes, we know you." The horseman's pistol flashed fire. Bigelow doubled over, clutching at his stomach. A second shot cut off his cry.

Andy tried to bring the rifle up. A gun barrel knocked his hat off. A second blow was like an explosion in his brain. He slid from the saddle.

Through a loud roaring in his ears he heard a voice say, "Bigelow's still wigglin'."

A third shot seemed to echo for minutes. Another voice said, "Not now, he ain't."

Dogs were barking all over town. Andy heard hoofbeats receding into the night. He tried to push himself up but had no strength for it. His last thought before he sank away into darkness was that he had failed. He had lost his prisoner.

Regaining consciousness, Andy realized he was lying on a cot in the jail. He raised a hand to the place where his head throbbed most and felt a thick bandage. Blinking, he recognized the doctor leaning over him.

"Don't make any sudden moves," the physician warned. "Your brain may be like scrambled eggs after the blows you took."

Daggett's coarse voice penetrated Andy's pain. "I doubt that. There couldn't be more than a spoonful."

Andy struggled to remember what had happened. It came back to him in fragments. "They didn't let us get very far."

Daggett said, "They were layin' for you."

"But we didn't tell anybody."

"This is a tough town to keep a secret in."

Andy knew but had to ask anyway. "What about Bigelow?"

"He's about the deadest man you ever saw."

Andy felt crushed by the heavy weight of failure.

Daggett said, "The minute you found out who he was, he was a danger to the others. They figured he'd break. What they did to him and to Callender is a warnin' to anybody else who might know more than is good for him."

Andy lamented, "It'll be extra hard now to get people to talk to us."

The sheriff and his deputy came along in a while. Seymour said, "Me and Salty went over every inch of the ground out there. Never found even a cartridge shell."

Daggett asked, "What about horse tracks?"

"They're all over the place, and they all look about the same."

Daggett said, "Even if we could find the right ones, they'd probably lead us in a circle and scatter. Whoever shot Bigelow may never have left town."

Andy said, "So we have to suspect everybody we see?"

Daggett nodded. "I've been doin' that all along. As far as I know, Pickard, you're the only honest man in town besides me, and I've even got some doubts about you." A tentative smile flickered and was quickly gone.

Andy had difficulty in keeping his concentration. He said, "Soon as this headache lets up, I'm ridin' out to see

August Hawkins. I'll try to talk him into waitin' a while on his fence. The mob may not warn him anymore. They're liable to just shoot him."

Dubious, the sheriff said, "He's a hardheaded man."

"So am I, when I have to be."

Daggett said, "Yeah, or they'd have busted your skull like a watermelon."

Andy raised up a little, then dropped back onto the pillow. He felt as if a blacksmith were using his head for an anvil. "After I talk to Hawkins, I think I'll pay a visit to the Teals and the McIntoshes. They might let somethin' drop."

Daggett said, "The Teal family came to town yesterday evenin', all but the old man. They're still here. I'll go talk to them."

Andy blinked. "They were here when Bigelow was shot?"

"You're always tellin' me not to jump to conclusions. Lots of folks were in town last night."

Andy said dryly, "I suppose you'll question Carrie."

"I like to be thorough."

"Maybe I ought to go help you."

"I can handle this without help. You stay here and rest, or your brain is liable to go to clabber."

Daggett cut off discussion by walking away. The sheriff's gaze followed him out of sight. Seymour said, "Even if the Teal boys know somethin', they won't tell it."

Andy said, "Daggett knows that. It's not the boys he really wants to talk to, anyway."

The sheriff caught on. "Carrie? I'm surprised. I thought there wasn't nothin' in his veins except ice."

"There's a side to him that he doesn't show much. He's surprised me, too, once in a while."

7

By noon, Andy felt recovered enough to go outside and sit on a bench. He saw Daggett escorting Carrie into the hotel restaurant. Most people considered it the best in town, though he had visited cow camps that served better fare. Andy had seldom seen a full-blown smile on Daggett's face, but he was smiling now. So was Carrie.

There's no accounting for a woman's taste, he thought.

In a while he saw Rodock enter the restaurant. He wondered if Daggett's smile left him.

Early in the afternoon the Teal family left, Carrie and Lanny in a supply-laden wagon, the others on horseback. Daggett stood on a corner and watched until they were gone, then returned to where Andy sat.

Andy asked, "Did they tell you anything?"

Daggett shook his head. "Never got much chance to talk to the boys."

"I doubted that you would."

"Carrie said her brothers were asleep at the wagon yard when the shots were fired."

"She was with them?"

"Of course not. They wouldn't let their sister sleep in a wagon yard. They got her a room in the hotel."

"So she can't be sure they were asleep."

"They wouldn't lie to her."

It was useless for Andy to belabor the point. "I think I'll go back in and lay down a while."

"You'd just as well. I can handle anything that comes up."

Andy knew it was true, and it grated like gravel in his craw.

He was on his way to the Hawkinses' ranch soon after daylight. His head still ached and was sore to the touch. He could not pull his hat down tightly, but it was good to be up and moving. He had lain abed about as long as patience would allow.

He came upon the Hawkinses' sheep. The dog loose-herded them while they grazed, turning back any that strayed far from the flock. Andy noticed that the dog limped. The hair on one leg was matted. Evidently he had been licking an injury. Noticing small splotches of blood on several sheep, Andy felt a sense of alarm.

As he rode up to the corral, he rough-counted about thirty sheep lying dead. Hawkins bent over one, shearing its fleece with hand clippers. Hearing Andy's horse, Hawkins jumped to his feet and grabbed a rifle that leaned against a fence. With recognition came relief. "Andy, I thought one of those night riders had come back."

"It looks like you were all set to shoot somebody."

"Anyone who would kill a bunch of helpless sheep deserves to be shot."

Andy dismounted and entered the corral. Flies were already buzzing around the dead animals. Hawkins said, "I have to salvage the wool while I can." He bent back to the shearing.

Andy asked, "Anything I can do to help?"

"Just find the hood-wearing sons of bitches who did this."

Hawkins's eyes smoldered with anger as he described the attack. "They called for me to come out of the house. Said they'd burn the place down if I didn't, so I went out. The leader reminded me what happened to the fence posts and said I'd be a dead man if I tried again. I managed to haul off and hit him once in the face. One of the others clubbed me down." Hawkins rolled the fleece. "They're probably the same ones who shot up the house the other night."

"Minus one." Andy explained about Bigelow.

Hawkins took satisfaction from the news. "So now they're killing their own. If I were a member of that bunch, I'd watch my back."

"You'd best watch it anyway. They meant it when they told you to give up the fence. Next time they won't stop with your sheep."

Hawkins tied the fleece and forced it into a burlap bag. "I suppose you've come out to try and persuade me."

"That was my intention. This trouble won't last forever. Your fence can wait."

"I swore I wouldn't let them control me."

"Just for a while. Sometimes a man has to retreat so he can live to fight another day."

Andy saw reluctance in the sheepman's eyes, but Hawkins gave in. "Tell Babcock to cancel my order. One lone sheepman can't fight the mob. Or one Ranger, either."

"I promise you, we'll do our best, me and Daggett."

Jake McIntosh and his brother Ike had roped a heifer missed in the earlier branding. They had her feet tied and were heating a steel ring in a small mesquite fire when Andy happened upon them.

Jake still showed a bruise from his fight with Lanny Teal. He said, "Don't worry, Ranger. She's one of ours. Her mammy is right over yonder, carryin' our brand."

"Never thought different," Andy replied. When the ring was hot, Jake picked it up with two sticks and methodically drew a Bar F brand on the heifer's side. One of the brothers had already notched her ear.

Andy asked, "I don't suppose you've seen a stray brindle bull around here?"

Jake said, "We have. We've chased that old hellion from one end of this place to the other. I wouldn't be surprised if the Teals ran him over here to bedevil us."

"If you fenced your land, you could keep him out." Andy hoped he was planting the seed of an idea.

"Papa hates fences like he hates rattlesnakes."

"Some others do, too. I don't suppose you heard that night riders hit Hawkins's sheep last night."

Jake appeared surprised. "Did they hurt the old man?"

"No, but they killed thirty or so head."

The news left Jake troubled. "I suppose you've come over here to find out if we had anything to do with it. I swear to you, we didn't. No matter what some folks think of us, we don't go around killin' people's livestock. Not even sheep."

Andy sensed that Jake was sincere. He said, "I didn't think you-all were responsible. I just had to make sure."

Jake dropped the hot ring into the sand to cool it. "We heard about your bad luck with your prisoner. We had nothin' to do with shootin' him." He paused. "Have you talked to the Teals?"

"Daggett has. They didn't own up to anything."

"And never apt to." Jake picked up the hot ring with his fingers but quickly dropped it again. "Changin' the subject, have you seen anything of Lucy Babcock? I ain't had time to go to town."

Andy did not want to admit that he had seen Lucy hanging on to Lanny Teal's arm. "I've seen her helpin' her daddy at the store."

"Pretty as a spotted pup, isn't she?"

That was not the way Andy would have phrased it, but he said, "She is, for a fact." The little he had seen of Lucy had given him the impression that she was like an autumn leaf, swept one way, then another by whatever wind happened by.

Jake said, "I can't figure what she sees in Lanny."

"What man can ever understand a woman's mind? I don't, and I've been married a while."

"But that redheaded Lanny of all people . . . he's as ugly as a mud fence."

"He's not a bad feller when you come to know him. You could be friends if you'd get past the bad blood between your family and his."

"Damned unlikely, the way Papa and Harper-Teal feel toward each other."

Andy said, "They're two stubborn old men who've carried a grudge way too long. You're too young to remember the war, and so is Lanny."

"I have to respect Papa's feelin's. Anyway, my quarrel with Lanny is personal."

"Why don't you stand back and let Lucy make her own choice?"

"She might choose wrong. I'd feel bad about lettin' her make a mistake."

Jake untied the heifer. She jumped to her feet and pawed the ground with one forefoot, looking for somebody to fight. Jake tossed his hat at her. She flipped it over her back, then trotted away, shaking her head. Ethan McIntosh rode up with his son, Harvey. He was in the same belligerent mood as the departing heifer. He studied her a moment, then said critically, "That is not the prettiest brand I ever saw. Did I not send you to school to learn your letters?"

Jake said, "Puttin' a brand on a hairy hide ain't like writin' on a slate. The main thing is to let everybody know that heifer is ours."

McIntosh scowled. "Some don't care whether they're ours or not. We're missing a bunch down on the south side. Harvey and I are sure they have been run off." He turned upon Andy with an angry challenge. "Instead of sitting here indulging yourself in gossip, Ranger, you should be doing something about it."

Andy said, "Show me where they were at. Maybe they left enough tracks that I can follow them."

"From what I heard, you can't even take care of a prisoner."

The old man's prickly attitude got under Andy's skin, but he tried not to let it cloud his judgment. He asked, "How did you hear about it?"

"One of those infernal wagon peddlers dropped by yesterday. He sold my wife and daughter a lot of worthless doodads. It was a waste of money, but that's womankind for you. They are drawn to anything that glitters or shines."

Jake said, "Me and Ike were ridin' down on the south end yesterday. We didn't see nothin'."

Ethan's face contorted. "You wouldn't see an elephant in the kitchen unless it stepped on your foot. Someone is determined to steal us blind and push us out of this country. I see the fine hand of Harper Teal."

Andy pointed out, "The Teal place is to the north of you, not the south."

"But Mexico is not. If they drive those cattle into the South Texas brush, I had just as well scratch them out of my tally book."

Jake said, "You don't reckon Vincent Skeen has risen from the grave, do you, Papa?"

"Not likely, with the heavy load of lead he carried. But his old gang of thieves may have reunited." Ethan jerked his head at Andy. "Come on, Ranger. You, too, Jake and Ike. Get your minds on your business."

Andy wished Daggett were here. He had a keener eye for tracking. But to circle by town and pick him up would cost too much time. There was no way to know how much head start the thieves had.

Harper said, "I hope you have sufficient ammunition, Ranger."

"My cartridge belt is full."

"If we catch up to the rustlers, I want to see every one of them carry lead enough to sink him to the bottom of the deep blue sea."

"In that case, you'd better send somebody to town to fetch my partner Daggett. He prefers to shoot first and then ask questions, if he's got any."

Harper nodded. "Harvey, you go. If I sent Jake, he would stop to spark that storekeeper's daughter and forget what he went for." He jerked his head again. "Let's be gone from here."

Jake said, "But we've got no grub with us, and no blankets."

Harper's answer was fierce. "You can sleep with your saddle blanket. As for grub, you ate enough supper last night to carry you for a week. If you'd fought through the war as I did, you'd know to punch extra notches in your belt and persevere. Live off the fat of the land."

Jake still had reservations. "When you go south from here, the land gets awful skinny."

"So will we all if we let them steal everything we have." Harper started off in a stiff trot.

Jake muttered, "Papa's got a way of endin' a conversation in a hurry. Especially when it goes against his thinkin'."

Andy said, "Lots of people are like that." He thought of his Ranger partner, who had little patience for argument. Daggett took it as a matter of immutable truth that he was always right.

They reached a narrow valley where Ethan and the boys had placed a set of young cows and their calves some days earlier. Ethan said, "They would not have left here on their own volition. It's some of the best grass on the ranch, and the creek furnishes all the water they would want. The tracks indicated that they were driven south."

Andy pointed out, "That's away from the Teals' ranch."

Ethan declared, "They would not keep Bar F cattle on their own land. They had just as well go to the sheriff and sign a confession. But if old Harper is out to break us, he could pass the cattle on to accomplices to be driven out of the country."

"I don't know why you're convinced that Harper Teal is behind it."

"That old Johnny Reb hates Union men. There is little he would not do to gut me."

"I thought the war got settled at Appomattox."

"Not until every one of those old rebels is dead and

buried. Help me get the evidence and I'll bury Harper myself."

Andy glanced at Jake and Ike. Both were looking away, staying out of it.

They found a few tracks too badly windblown for certainty about the direction of travel. Andy said, "I'd say they were goin' south, but it's hard to be sure."

Ethan said, "South makes more sense than north."

Just at dusk, Andy shot a deer. That would be their supper, without salt and without coffee to wash it down. They followed the tracks until dark, losing them frequently and spending a lot of time searching.

Ethan chided his sons, "If you had been paying attention, we could have joined this trail a day sooner. By the time we catch up—if we do—our cattle will be speaking Spanish."

He had Andy and his sons up before daylight. They roasted more venison on sticks above the coals while they waited for sunup so they could see the tracks. Ethan dropped his meat on the fire but brushed away the ashes and ate it anyway. He was every inch an old soldier. He caught his sons exchanging glances of disapproval and said, "If you had gone hungry as many times as I have, little things like ashes and dirt would not bother you."

Jake replied, "We didn't say anything."

Ethan shook his head. "The younger generation! I'm afraid there is scant hope for the world."

Andy went out to check on the horses so he could grin without risking the old man's anger.

They had been underway about an hour and had proceeded only a couple of hundred yards when they saw

Daggett, Harvey, and Sheriff Seymour catching up. Ethan growled, "I don't know why they brought Seymour along. Without his glasses he couldn't even see a cow, much less her tracks."

Reining up, Daggett said, "We smelled the smoke from your campfire. It don't look like you've got very far."

Andy said, "A crow in flight would've left a better trail than this."

"It's too bad the Indians didn't teach you a lot more."

The mention of Indians aroused Ethan's curiosity. Andy had to explain that as a boy he had been stolen by Comanches and had lived among them for several years.

Ethan said, "At least the Comanches were honest thieves. They made no pretenses about their intentions . . . not like some people who go to church every Sunday. On Monday they will steal your socks without taking your boots off."

Daggett and the sheriff had brought the Ranger packmule along. Jake said, "I hope you got some coffee in that pack."

The sheriff said, "Coffee, bacon, some flour and salt."

Jake grinned. "Come the next election, you've got my vote."

Ethan cut him a glance that told him to shut up.

Daggett was not long in finding the trail of the cattle. Though he sometimes lost it, he usually found it again more quickly than Andy could. By the third day the all-meat diet had become monotonous, but the tracks were fresh. Daggett said, "You can't get but so much travel out of a cow-calf herd."

Ethan said, "Cows are the factory. If you steal enough

of them, you drive a man out of business. I am sure that is what Harper is thinking. He would love to lay his hands on my land."

Andy had given up trying to argue that the only way Ethan could protect his hold on the land would be to buy it. He hoped the three sons were more accepting of a new idea.

Daggett rode out in front, the others trailing behind to prevent compromising the trail should Daggett lose it and have to circle back to hunt for it again. Late in the day the big Ranger halted abruptly, then signaled the others to come up.

He pointed and said, "Yonder they are."

A strung-out herd of cows plodded along at a slow, foot-sore pace. Their calves, of all sizes from babies to short yearlings, struggled to keep up. Most were in the dusty drags, behind the main herd.

Andy counted four riders with them. He considered the possibility that a fifth might be somewhere ahead, marking the route.

Andy looked to Daggett. "What do you think?"

Ethan spoke up sharply. "Charge into them. Kill every man and hope Harper Teal is among them."

Andy had little concern that he would be.

Daggett said, "Mr. McIntosh's got the right notion. Slam into them hard and fast. Maybe they'll be too rattled to put up much of a show."

Andy cautioned the McIntoshes, "You know that recklessness can get somebody killed."

Ethan was not moved. He said, "If you're scared, stay back and let my boys and me handle this. These are our cattle."

Andy said, "I'm talkin' about bein' cautious. You don't want to make an easy target. And remember that it's hard to hit what you aim at from a runnin' horse."

Daggett remained in the lead, holding the riders to an easy trot as they closed the distance. They were within two hundred yards before one of the herders looked back. He shouted a warning, and two of the men quickly turned their horses around. The other, up at point, was too far ahead to hear.

The thieves fired a couple of shots, then decided escape was the best option. They spurred their horses into a hard run, sweeping past the startled point rider. He followed but could not catch up.

Waving a pistol, Ethan leaned forward and let out a furious screech as he applied his spurs. Andy thought he felt a puff of wind as the old man raced by him. Then two Rangers and four McIntoshes were in full pursuit. The sheriff trailed a little.

Ethan drew up beside the point man and fired. The rider threw up his hands and tumbled from his running horse. Looking back, Andy saw the sheriff dismount beside the fallen rider. Daggett managed to pass Ethan and pull in beside another of the thieves. The rider fired at him but missed. Daggett put a bullet into him and brought him down.

The other two fugitives managed to draw more speed from their horses and gradually widened their lead. Daggett began slowing his horse. Andy followed suit as he felt his mount tiring. The three McIntosh sons had not been able to keep up with their father. Like the Rangers, they gave up the chase.

Ethan did not stop until he realized he was far out in front all by himself, losing ground to the remaining two thieves. He reined around and came back, cursing. "We could have gotten them to the last man if you hadn't all quit."

Daggett removed his hat and wiped a sleeve across his sweating forehead. "They were outrunnin' us. You'd've been in a fix if they'd turned about and come at you out there all by yourself."

"I would not," Ethan protested. "I would have killed them both."

Andy said impatiently, "We brought down two of them, and we got your herd back." He turned to look at Ethan's sons. "Anybody hurt?"

Ike's sleeve showed a streak of blood. He said, "Just nicked me a little. It was a lucky shot."

Daggett led the way back to examine the two fallen outlaws. He spent only a moment with the first, dismissing him with a motion that said he was dead. Sheriff Seymour stood beside the one Ethan had shot in the side.

Andy dismounted but saw that this man, too, was dead. He asked, "Did he say anything?"

Seymour said, "I hoped to ask him some questions, but he just groaned a time or two and died."

Ethan drew his horse close. His eyes were wild with lingering excitement as he leaned down to look at the fallen man. "Are you sure we can't make him talk?"

Andy gritted his teeth. "It's hard to get a man to tell you much after you've killed him."

Ethan was disappointed. "Damn the man for dying too quickly!"

Daggett said gruffly, "It was you that shot him."

Ike broke the tension by saying, "Papa, our cattle are scatterin'. Let's go see about them."

Ethan and his sons rode off to gather the herd.

Andy closed the outlaw's glazed eyes. He asked the sheriff, "Do you know him?"

"Yeah. I've had to jail him for fightin'. He's agreeable when he's sober, but he's a mean drunk."

"Did you look at the other one?"

"I know him. He's finished off many a Saturday night in a cell. He's a singin' drunk."

Daggett said, "Too bad those other two got away. I don't suppose you were able to see who they were?"

The sheriff grimaced. "With these old eyes of mine? All I could do is guess."

Andy asked, "And if you were to guess?"

"I'd guess Harold Pearcy and Sonny Vernon. But don't tell Ethan. He might hunt them down and shoot them without waitin' for judge and jury."

The McIntoshes brought the cattle together. Jake caught the two loose horses and led them to where Andy and Daggett waited. He studied the outlaw's face. "I've seen that man in town."

Seymour nodded. "Did you ever happen to notice who he palled around with?"

"Never paid that much attention. When I'm in town, I've got better things to do."

They hoisted the dead man onto one of the horses and rode to where the other lay. In his pocket Andy found a crumpled letter addressed to Colley Lamkin. He scanned the letter, written to remind Lamkin that he owed the writer money.

Ethan joined them shortly and said he knew neither of the men. "I do not waste my time becoming acquainted with lowlifes." He pointed toward the herd, and his eyes brightened. "They're mostly ours, all right, but a few of Harper Teal's are in there too. That's quite a joke on Harper. He sends thieves to steal my cattle and they take some of his as well."

Andy stifled a sudden impulse. There was probably some fool law against choking an old man, no matter how much he might deserve it.

The little posse had gone through the provisions Daggett and Seymour had brought. They found a bag of coffee beans and a small slab of bacon in an outlaw's blanket roll. Andy had no compunctions against eating a dead man's food. In this case it would otherwise be left for the coyotes. To hell with the coyotes, he thought. Let them catch a rabbit.

Daggett stared over a cup of coffee at the two men tied facedown across their horses. "They won't last long if we stay with the McIntoshes and this slow herd. We'd best carry them back to town as quick as we can."

Seymour said, "They had friends among a certain element. I'm afraid shootin' them won't make any of us popular with that crowd."

Daggett replied, "We wasn't sent here to be popular. We came to bring peace and quiet. That means if you have to kill some people, you do it."

Andy said, "Maybe these two are the last."

The sheriff grunted. "I wouldn't bet a plug of tobacco on that. At least old Ethan got his cattle back. I won't have to listen to him bellyache about me bein' too old for this job."

Andy asked, "Have you ever thought about sittin' in a rockin' chair on the porch and lettin' the world handle its troubles without you?"

"I think about it all the time, but I've got nothin' to retire on. Spent most of my life protectin' other people's property but never had a chance to get my own. Damned little money, either. So here I am, wore out like an old pair of boots. My eyesight is fadin', and I've got nothin' much to show for my life. There's old Ethan McIntosh with ranch and cattle that I've helped protect for him, bitchin' because I haven't done more. You watch, he'll soon holler for me to arrest Harper Teal."

Daggett pointed out, "Don't it strike you strange that the Teals would have somebody steal their own cattle?"

"It could be a way of coverin' up."

Andy said, "Or maybe neither family is implicated. Maybe somebody *is* tryin' to break both families."

The sheriff asked, "To what purpose?"

"So when the smoke clears, they can pick up the leavin's. Mason Gaines hinted as much."

"Gaines?" Seymour rubbed his chin. "I never did cotton to that carpetbagger. Never could trust a man who was always right."

Andy said, "He could be fannin' up trouble for his own reasons. Then again, it might not be him at all."

Seymour said, "There's aplenty of free rangers that have got no love for either family. My jail ain't big enough to hold them all."

Andy said, "If we can find the right one or two, maybe that'll put the quietus on what's left."

Daggett looked at the bodies tied over two horses. "Let's lope up and get them to town before they turn ripe. We've got no shovel."

* * *

Andy attended the funeral, not to mourn but to see who-all came. Among that group, he thought, might be some of the people responsible for the troubles. The crowd did not amount to much, however. Aside from the sheriff, Deputy Willis, and the two Rangers, the gathering numbered fewer than a dozen. Even the minister was reluctant, for he had never seen the two in church and knew little to say in their behalf. Instead he preached a sermon on the wages of sin and mentioned no names.

As the attendees dispersed, Andy and the sheriff watched two county employees begin shoveling dirt into the graves. Andy asked, "Did you see anybody you suspect?"

Seymour said, "I suspect just about everybody who was here, not countin' the minister. He showed how little he knows about sin."

Editor Tolliver waited until the sheriff was gone before he approached Andy at the cemetery gate. "Might I trouble you for a few questions?" he asked.

"I don't know as I've got any answers."

"I am interested in how these two thieves came to their end."

Andy told of trailing the cattle and almost taking the culprits by surprise. "Ethan McIntosh shot the first one. Daggett got the second. We couldn't catch the others."

"Did anyone recognize the two who got away?"

Andy chose not to mention the sheriff's guess. "Never got close enough."

"And the two who were shot . . . did either of them say anything?"

"One lived a few minutes. The sheriff stopped to see about him but told us he was too far gone to talk."

"So you learned nothing about who might have been behind the taking of the cattle?"

"That's the size of it."

Tolliver's heavy mustache quivered. "Quite convenient, wouldn't you say, for anyone who might be a party to the trouble around here? The only identifiable thieves died without answering any questions."

Andy frowned. "If you're tryin' to say somethin', speak straight out."

"I hear that Ethan McIntosh has made some interesting accusations against Harper Teal."

"He's obsessed with an old grudge, and his mind is slippin'."

"I have long suspected that Sheriff Seymour has leaned more toward the Teals than the McIntoshes. He was Confederate, too. And you have only his word that the wounded outlaw said nothing. What if our esteemed sheriff did not want him to say anything?"

"Are you accusin' him?"

"Not at all. I am simply weighing the possibilities. Our sheriff is no longer young, and he faces an uncertain future. Lesser men in his position have succumbed to the temptation to profit from others' misfortunes."

"Whatever you print in your paper, you'd better be ready to back up with the evidence."

"That I shall, when and if the time comes. You may not recognize it, Pickard, but you and I are working in the same vineyard. We are both seekers after the truth."

Watching Tolliver walk back down toward town, Andy weighed the man's words. Yes, Seymour had been alone with the dying thief. If he had reason not to want the man to talk, he could easily have rushed the dying process.

Andy tried to dismiss what Tolliver had said, but the seed of doubt was germinating.

Andy and Daggett were having a late breakfast in the little hole-in-the-wall café, listening to proprietor Kennison propose solutions for the world's problems, when a rider swept by at a speed too reckless for a town street. Daggett exclaimed, "That's Carrie." He jumped up and rushed for the door. "Pay the man!" he shouted as he hurried out.

Andy dropped a handful of change on the table. It was too much, but he did not have time to wait for a count. He caught up to Daggett as Carrie jumped down from her sweat-streaked horse in front of the jail. Daggett's shout stopped her as she reached for the door. She turned, her face flushed with excitement.

The words tumbled out without allowing time for her to catch her breath. "Thank God, Logan, you're here. Our place got shot up in the wee hours this morning. We fought them off, but now Pa is on his way to the McIntoshes' ranch. He intends to have it out with Ethan McIntosh."

Daggett asked, "Are your brothers with him?"

"Yes. Somebody is going to be killed if you don't stop them."

Andy asked, "Anybody hurt?"

"One of our cowboys cut his arm on a broken window glass, is all. It was too dark for good aim, but we poured as much lead into them as they poured into us."

Daggett said, "Let's grab our horses. We'll have to ride hard to get to the McIntoshes' place first."

Andy said, "I don't think we can."

"We'll try, even if we kill two horses doin' it."

Editor Tolliver walked down the courthouse steps, attracted by Carrie's breathless manner. He said, "May I ask the occasion for all this excitement?"

Daggett said, "You tell him, Carrie. We ain't got time."

She protested, "I'm going with you."

"You've nearly killed that horse already. Best thing you can do now is to find the sheriff. Tell him what you told us, then go home."

The two Rangers hit a long trot toward the wagon yard.

8

Riding hard, Andy began hoping he and Daggett would reach the McIntoshes' ranch headquarters before the Teals. Sporadic gunfire told him they had not.

Daggett said, "Damned knotheads have already opened the ball."

Andy said, "Maybe nobody's dead yet."

He saw that the Teals were spread out afoot, taking refuge behind a wagon, behind a shed, beneath the windmill tower. Lacking clear targets, they fired at the main family house and the bunkhouse. Occasional answering shots came from the shattered windows. The invasion had taken the McIntoshes by surprise, without time to pull together in one defensive position.

Daggett did not hesitate. He held his horse to a hard trot and rode into the line of fire, waving his hat. His shout was like thunder. "Put those guns down! Stop this goddamned foolishness right now!"

Surprised by the older Ranger's audacity, Andy swallowed

hard and followed him, his spine tingling in anticipation of a bullet.

Harper Teal rose up from behind a wagon. He lifted his rifle and yelled, "Git out of the way, Daggett! You want to get shot?"

Daggett's stern voice resonated with authority. He said, "Harper Teal, you lay that rifle down." He turned toward the main house. "Ethan McIntosh, you get yourself out onto the porch. I want to talk to you. Right now!" He turned a fierce gaze back at the scattered Teal forces. "Anybody fires a shot, I'll kill him."

The combatants were so taken aback by Daggett's forceful presence that no one raised a protest. Most lowered their weapons, though they did not lay them down.

The front door opened slowly. Ethan McIntosh poked his gray head out and paused as if expecting to be shot.

Daggett said, "Come on out. There ain't nobody goin' to hurt you unless it's me. You hear that, Harper Teal? The same goes for you."

Teal did not reply, but he stepped from behind the wagon, holding his rifle at arm's length. Daggett told him to lay it on the ground.

Teal said, "First I want to see that Ethan's not heeled."

McIntosh, now farther out on the porch, raised both hands to his shoulders. "I've no weapon on me. But lest you take that as an opportunity for treachery, Harper Teal, there are more inside. They can cut out what little heart you have."

Teal put down his rifle and stepped into the open. "You Rangers have got no business here. This is a private matter."

Daggett said, "It stopped bein' private when the first

shot was fired. It's you who've got no business here, Harper. You're trespassin' on McIntosh land."

"Ask Ethan about the trespassin' he did when him and his bunch raided our place after midnight."

McIntosh looked surprised. "Us? Not a soul left this place save for my son Jake. He sneaked off to town."

Lanny Teal left his refuge behind the windmill. He shouted, "Damn you, Jake, I've told you to stay away from Lucy!"

Jake burst out onto the porch. "You go to hell, Lanny. I'll see whoever I want to, whenever I want to."

McIntosh ordered his son back into the house. "There are matters of far greater importance here than your shallow infatuation. Take up your station in case they begin shooting again."

Jake obeyed resentfully, but only after declaring, "Someday, Lanny."

Lanny replied, "How about now?"

Harper Teal glared at Lanny. "Boy, I don't know what I'll ever do with you. We've come here to set things right, and all you've got on your mind is that scatterbrained schoolgirl. I'll bet she's never scalded a hog or wrung a chicken's neck."

Red-faced, Lanny came up with no suitable reply. He muttered under his breath and looked at the ground.

Daggett said to Harper, "Ethan McIntosh swears that whoever raided your place, it wasn't him or his outfit."

Teal flushed. "If you believe that, you're a bigger fool than I thought you was. He's been tellin' folks that me and my boys are behind the cattle stealin' and other such around here. Anybody with a lick of sense knows he's a liar. That wily old scoundrel's been tryin' for years to get my scalp. He'd do better to worry about his own."

Andy said, "The fight between you two is so old, I'll bet you don't even remember what started it."

"You'd lose the bet. It was over a nice piece of creek land. Him bein' a Yankee, the carpetbag government seen to it that he got it instead of me."

"You got yourself a good ranch in spite of that."

"With Ethan workin' against me all the way. He figures if he can run me off, he can grab what's mine. But I ain't goin' noplace. I'll still be here when he leaves, or when he's lowered into the ground. Either way would suit me fine."

McIntosh had gradually moved down from the porch, scowling. "You'll have to live to be a hundred before you see either event come to pass."

Teal no longer talked to Daggett or Andy. He turned his anger directly on McIntosh. "You damned old land hog, you ain't got nothin' I want, and you ain't gettin' anything I've got. If you don't quit accusin' us or sendin' night riders to shoot up our place, I'll put a couple more holes in you than the Lord intended."

Daggett faced Teal. "Everybody's said enough. Harper, I want you to take your boys and go home. Now!"

Teal seemed torn, but after trying to stare Daggett down, he said, "All right, we'll go, but this thing ain't over. It looks to me like you've chosen who to crawl in bed with, so I'll thank you to never come back onto our place. As for Carrie, she's already had hurt enough in her life. I don't want you to ever speak to her again."

Andy started to intervene. "But it was Carrie—"

A dark look from Daggett stopped him from saying more.

Teal said, "You tell your McIntosh friends that the next time they come shootin', they'd better bring along a minister. They'll need him to preach the funerals." He made a sweeping motion with his arm. "Come on, boys. There'll be another day."

The Teals mounted up. All three of McIntosh's sons came out onto the porch, guns in their hands. The old man stood in the yard, where he and Teal had faced each other. He complained, "Is that all you Rangers are going to do? Look what they've done to my house. Look at the bullet holes."

Daggett was trying hard to keep his emotions under control. He gave the old man a look of disgust but choked down whatever he was aching to say. Andy said it for him: "Be glad there's no bullet holes in any of you. Or are there?"

Ethan said, "Not a scratch. It will be a cold day in July before the Teals ever get the upper hand over us. We'll wipe out the whole bunch someday."

Andy said, "You ought not to talk like that. People might get to thinkin' you mean it."

"Hell, I do mean it."

Andy had come to regard Ike as the most sensible of the McIntoshes. He turned to him. "Maybe you can talk to your father."

Ike was still on edge. He said, "They had no call to come down on us like they done, hollerin' and shootin'."

"Somebody raided them. They thought it was you."

Ike shook his head. "It wasn't, and that's the truth. We were all here last night except Jake, and Papa told you where he was."

"Then maybe you'd better give some thought to who it was, and the reason they did it."

Ethan declared, "It wasn't anybody but that old boar hog and his litter. He was lying through his teeth."

Andy heard the impact of a bullet on human flesh a split second before he heard the crack of a rifle somewhere out in the brush, in the direction the Teals had taken. Ethan doubled over, clutching his side and gasping for breath. Ike rushed to him.

"Papa!" Easing his father to the ground, Ike turned an anguished gaze toward Andy and Daggett. "He's been hit."

Daggett wheezed, "Damn! I didn't think Harper would do it." He dropped onto his knees beside the old man as two women came rushing from the house. He looked up at Andy. "Let's get him inside before they fire again. Let's get everybody inside."

Quickly they carried Ethan into the house and placed him on his high-backed bed. The bullet's impact had knocked the breath from him. He struggled to regain it. McIntosh's wife Agatha tore his shirt open and unbuttoned the front of his long underwear. The bullet had cut a gash across the ribs. It was bleeding.

Ike asked frantically, "Do you think it went into his lung?"

Such a wound was often fatal, if not immediately, then more slowly through pneumonia. Agatha examined the damage. "I don't think so. It appears to me that he might have a broken rib or two, but nothing he's apt to die of."

At the moment she was the calmest of the McIntoshes. She said, "The Indians couldn't kill him. Rebel bullets couldn't do it. He's not about to leave us now because I won't stand for it." She pointed to the door. "Patience and me will get him ready. Ike, don't you and the boys just stand there. Go hitch up the wagon so we can take him to the doctor."

His face grim, Daggett motioned to Andy. "Let's catch up to the Teals. We'll see if they can explain that shot."

Stepping out onto the porch, Andy said, "We don't have to catch up. Bud and Lanny are comin' back."

The two Teal brothers stopped their horses a little short of the porch. They were clearly agitated. Bud said accusingly, "I thought you Rangers were goin' to see that nobody shot at us."

"Nobody did. Not here."

"Somebody fired a shot. Lucky it didn't hit any of us."

Daggett's voice was severe. "It hit Ethan."

Bud's jaw dropped. "Ethan? I swear, Ranger, it wasn't none of our bunch done it. We figured one of the McIntoshes fired at us."

Daggett's fists were clenched. "You wouldn't lie to me, would you?"

Bud said, "Lyin' is against our religion. I'll swear on the Bible in front of all the McIntoshes."

Andy said, "Maybe another time and place. Right now the McIntoshes wouldn't believe you if you swore on a whole stack of Bibles. You'd best be goin' before they decide to take up their guns again."

Bud hesitated. "How bad is the old man hurt?"

"He'll live. But this won't improve his disposition any."

Watching them leave, Daggett muttered, "I wish I could believe them, but who else would take a shot at Ethan?"

Sheriff Seymour came along shortly. He said, "I met the Teals out yonder a ways. Is the trouble over with?"

Andy said, "For today, it looks like."

"Anybody hurt?"

"Ethan took a bullet across his ribs. They're fixin' to haul him to town. Naturally he blames the Teals. He's talkin' crazy."

"Nothin' new there. Him and Harper both talk crazy when it's about each other. Sometimes I'm tempted to go off on a long huntin' trip and let nature take its course. Things might get quiet around here afterward."

Andy said, "A graveyard is quiet, too, but who wants a big graveyard?" He considered the shot that came from the brush. He asked Seymour, "Did you see anybody besides the Teals as you rode in?"

"Nary a soul."

Andy reluctantly thought of editor Tolliver and the suspicion he had aroused about the sheriff. Seymour could have fired that shot before he showed himself. He tried to push the thought from his mind, but it would not leave him.

Daggett brooded. "There was a time when I wouldn't take a cussin' like the one I got from Harper Teal. I must be gettin' old."

Andy said, "He was mad. Maybe when he cools down, he'll see things different."

Seymour said, "Old men can be awful stubborn. I know, because I'm gettin' there myself."

Just getting there? Andy thought.

Daggett's eyes widened as a new idea struck him. "I wonder where Rodock was, him and that rifle."

Andy, Daggett, and Seymour accompanied Jake and Ike as they and the two women carried Ethan to town in a wagon. The doctor gave the old man a preliminary examination and declared, "You probably don't deserve it, Ethan, but you could live to be a hundred. After I treat your wound, it would be a good idea for you to stay around town a few days. We will want to be sure you'll not develop blood poisoning."

Ethan roared, "Stay in town? Hell no. We have no intention of throwing away good money on a hotel room. The boys and the womenfolks are taking me right back home where I belong."

The doctor said, "It is obvious that the bullet did no damage to your lungs. I am giving you my best advice."

"And at no bargain price, I'll wager. What this town needs is another doctor, a good one."

The doctor said, "It would also need patients with judgment enough to listen to him."

Agatha said, "Ethan hasn't listened to anybody but me in all these years, and not always me. Many's the time I've considered divorce, but there's my family to think of. So I just let him rant and pay no attention to him. We'll stay in town like you said, Doctor."

Movement was painful for Ethan. He indulged in heavy profanity as his sons helped him get up and out to the wagon. He complained as they placed him on spread-out blankets and was still complaining as the wagon rolled down the street toward the hotel.

Watching, the doctor commented to Andy and Daggett, "I thought you Rangers came to bring peace. I believe I have seen more bullet wounds, bruises, and abrasions since you got here than before you arrived."

Sheriff's Deputy Willis put down a whittling stick and pushed to his feet from a bench outside the saloon as Andy and Daggett approached. He said, "The sheriff asked me to keep an eye on Rodock." He jerked his thumb toward the saloon door. "He's in there."

Daggett asked, "Has he been there long?"

"Not very. He just came out of the hotel a little while ago. He headed straight for here."

"Can you say for sure that he was in the hotel all night?"

"Well, pretty certain. He was playin' poker in the saloon early in the evenin'. I got tired of watchin' him clip a couple of farmers, so I went home about ten, eleven o'clock. I figured he wasn't goin' nowhere."

"You might've figured wrong. He could've left right after you did."

Rodock was sitting alone at a table when Andy and Daggett walked in. He was playing solitaire and appeared only marginally interested in the cards. He yawned as Daggett approached him. He said, "Pull up a chair and set yourself down. You can choose the game."

Daggett remained standing. "Where have you been all day?"

"I indulged in a game of chance till the wee hours. I've spent most of the day in bed."

"Alone?"

A wry smile crossed Rodock's face. "You don't think I'd sully an innocent woman's name by using her for an alibi, do you?"

"If she was with you, she couldn't be too damned innocent."

"The fact is, there wasn't any woman. I was by myself. Is there a reason I need an alibi?"

"The Teal ranch got raided last night. Considerin' your line of work, I thought you might've left some boot tracks out there."

Rodock betrayed no reaction. Calmly he declared, "One unfortunate result from my so-called line of work is that any time something happens, people jump to the conclusion that I was involved. Why should I raid someone's ranch? What would be in it for me?"

"That's a question I'd like the answer to."

The solitaire game went against Rodock. He shuffled the cards and said, "My horse is in the wagon yard. He was there last night and has been there all day. You can ask that hay shaker, Scanlon. He'll tell you."

"Somebody could've lent you a horse."

"Do you intend to arrest me?"

"If I get some proof."

"In the meantime, I assume that you do not care to join me in a game?"

"I think we've been playin' one right along."

Rodock gave him a cold smile and began laying out the cards again. Daggett motioned for Andy to follow him outside. Andy said, "You're figurin' he could've been part of that raid on the Teals."

"Not for fun. I'm bettin' somebody paid him. Maybe Old Man McIntosh."

Andy argued, "He swore that nobody except Jake was away from his ranch last night."

"That could be the truth, as far as it goes. But the first year I went to school, I learned that two and two add up to four. Ethan vowed revenge right in front of us when we got his cows back. You heard him. He could've hired Rodock and some others to do the job for him. That way the only dirt on his hands would come from countin' out the money."

Andy could not stop thinking about the sheriff. "It could be somebody else entirely."

"It could, but right now my money's on Ethan."

"If it was Rodock, and Ethan paid him, how come he took a shot at Ethan?"

"Maybe he missed his target. He might've been shootin' at me."

"Does he hate you that much?"

"Only half as much as I hate him." Daggett lapsed into a thoughtful silence. He brushed aside some wood shavings and sat on the bench the deputy had vacated. He stared off at nothing in particular. Finally he said, "That damned Rodock. I've got half a mind to walk in there and shoot him."

"You don't know it was him. You're only guessin'."

"Even if it wasn't, he's earned a good killin' twenty times over. The old-time vigilantes had the right idea. Hang them quick and hang them high."

"You're not talkin' like a lawman."

"I'm talkin' like a lawman who's brought in more than my share of bad men, only to watch pettifoggin' lawyers and judges turn them loose. Put enough lead in one of them, and you're shed of him for good."

"The Rangers don't do it that way."

"No? Have you never seen a Ranger tell a man to run, then shoot him and claim he tried to escape?"

Andy had, a few times. The incidents had left him shaken, though he understood the frustrations that led to them. He said, "Maybe we've moved past that kind of thing. Maybe we've come into a better time."

"Not till they shut down the last jail for lack of business."

Toward sundown, Carrie Teal came up the street in a buckboard. She had a couple of carpetbags under the seat.

Spotting Daggett and Andy on a bench in front of the general store, she reined the horses toward them. Daggett arose quickly, taking off his hat and walking out to meet her. He said, "I thought you went home."

She was plainly distressed. "I did, but I couldn't stay."

"How come?"

"Pa figured out that I sent you Rangers to the McIntosh place. He raised a terrible row. My brothers took up for me, and I saw that there was about to be a fight. I had to get away."

"What do you plan to do?"

"Take a room in the hotel until he calms down."

"What if he doesn't?"

"Then I'll try to find work here in town."

"I don't think he'd stand still for that. He's liable to come roarin' in here to drag you home."

Her voice was stern. "Then there *will* be a fight."

Daggett took hold of her hands. "If you need any money . . ."

"I have a little. It wouldn't look right, taking money from you. People would talk."

"Let them talk." Daggett turned to Andy. "I'll escort her over to the hotel and see that they give her a decent room."

Andy said, "People *will* talk, sure enough."

"It'll give them somethin' to do with their idle time."

Editor Tolliver stepped out of the saloon and watched the buckboard moving away with Carrie and Daggett on the seat. He said, "It appears to me that Daggett has chosen his side."

Andy said, "Rangers don't take sides."

"Almost everybody takes sides. I thought by his reputation that Daggett was made of cast iron, but I see he has a soft spot in his armor. It will not sit well with the McIntosh faction."

"He's just tryin' to be a gentleman, that's all."

"Daggett a gentleman? That challenges credulity."

Andy was not sure he understood what Tolliver had said, but he chose not to ask. Tolliver would probably tell him at considerably more length than Andy chose to hear.

Tolliver said, "What more can you tell me about events at the Teals' and McIntoshes' places?"

Andy had told him nothing, but he knew the sheriff had. He said, "Nobody got killed." He was used to filing terse reports that wasted no words. He saw no need to give Tolliver more. The man would probably fill out the story from imagination anyway. Reading his newspaper, Andy had noticed that his writing was not handicapped by facts.

Tolliver said, "It would appear that events are building toward a violent climax. I suspect I shall soon have much to write about."

Andy began to anger. "Is that what you're hopin' for? More killin' so you can have a bigger story?"

"Most great literature is grounded in violence and tragedy. This situation could yield a book that would rank my name up there with Irving and Twain. It has Rangers, vigilantes, gunfights, everything but Indians. I might put in a few of those for extra color."

Andy had not read many books. He had never heard of Irving or Twain. "If I was you, I wouldn't start countin' the money just yet."

He did not see Daggett until he was about to bed down on his wagon yard cot. Daggett was silent as he walked into the little circle of lantern light, his mind on matters far away. Andy waited for him to say something, then asked, "Did you get Carrie settled in the hotel?"

Daggett was jarred back to reality. "Yes, and took her to supper. We had us a long talk afterward."

"Has she decided what to do?"

"She has, me and her together. What would you think about standin' up with me in the mornin' while I get married?"

"Married!" Andy blinked in surprise. "I'd think you were movin' way too fast. Are you sure you've thought this through?"

"I've thought on it a right smart. Her comin' to town just brought things to a head sooner than I expected."

"Where would you take her, and where would you live? Rangers travel around an awful lot."

"You're married."

"I don't get much time to spend with my wife."

Daggett was not moved. "Maybe I've been a Ranger long enough. Maybe it's time I find somethin' else to do. I could run a ranch for somebody, or open a store in town."

Andy could imagine Daggett on a ranch, but not running a store. He said, "Have you thought how Harper Teal will take this? You know what he said about you and Carrie, and about not settin' foot on the Teal ranch again."

"Once we're married, there won't be much he can do."

"Except maybe shoot you. He's already had one son-in-law that he hated."

"He can't hold a grudge forever."

"He's had a grudge against Ethan McIntosh ever since

the war. And what about the McIntoshes? They'll figure you've thrown in with the Teals."

"I can't help that. It's high time they put their damnfool feud aside."

"They've got too much invested in it to quit."

Andy was not convinced that Daggett realized what he was getting himself in for. He said, "You told me you were married once. What makes you think it'll work out this time if it didn't before?"

Daggett seemed to retreat back in time. His face creased, and his eyes seemed to be looking at something far away. "It would have worked the first time if I hadn't been away too much. There came a day when I was gone, and an outlaw I was huntin' for decided to hunt for *me*. He didn't find me at home, but he found my wife."

Andy guessed the rest from the savage expression on Daggett's face. "What did you do?"

"What any man would do. I hunted him down and killed him." Daggett looked away. "But it didn't bring her back to life."

9

Daggett had intended that the wedding be private, that it not be noised about. He did not consider the drawing power of his name, however. The minister was a jovial sort who loved a crowd and saw to it that the word was spread around town. By ten o'clock in the morning more people had gathered than his little church could comfortably seat. Daggett grumbled about not wanting it to turn into a spectacle.

Sheriff Seymour was there, his expression dour as he watched the McIntosh family gathering. They had remained in town until the doctor was convinced that Ethan's wound would not become life-threatening. Seymour said, "I don't see a happy face amongst the whole bunch. They're figurin' you Rangers have crawled into the blankets with the enemy."

Just one of us, Andy thought. He knew Daggett had been leaning in that direction almost from the first. He said, "I haven't taken sides, and I don't intend to."

"But if worst comes to worst, are you strong enough to stand up to a man like Daggett?"

Andy answered honestly, "I don't know."

Editor Tolliver walked from his office to the church. He wore a tailored suit. A pair of leather gloves covered the ink stains on his hands. He said jovially, "Too bad there's nobody in the McIntosh family for *you* to marry, Pickard. That would help balance the equation."

"Even if there was, I doubt that I could get my wife to agree to it."

The minister's wife sat down at the piano and began to play. Daggett looked as if he had indigestion. Andy said, "You're supposed to smile."

"I didn't figure on this bein' a show."

Andy walked up the aisle alongside Daggett, pondering the possibility that Daggett might break and run. Carrie appeared from a side room at the rear of the church. In lieu of her father, storekeeper Babcock walked with her, holding her arm. Her dress was plain, probably one she customarily wore to church. But Andy gave no thought to that. It was the woman herself who caused his jaw to drop.

He had not considered Carrie beautiful, but she was radiant now, her smile bright as sunrise. Daggett's hand shook as he grasped her fingers and the minister began the ritual.

The ceremony was mercifully short. Self-consciously Daggett kissed the bride, then hurried her out through a side door to escape the crowd. A few people shouted congratulations, and a couple offered off-color suggestions that might have prompted Daggett to turn and administer punishment had he been less eager to get away.

Turning toward the door, Andy saw Rodock. He immediately looked for a firearm. Rodock said, "Don't worry. I am not carrying. I respect the solemnity of an occasion such as this."

"I'm surprised to see you here at all."

"I like to attend weddings. They remind me not to repeat my most unfortunate mistake, marriage."

"It didn't work out?"

"My way of life was incompatible with hers. She did me the great favor of running away with a dry goods drummer. I fear that Daggett is in for a longer sentence than mine was. Unless I kill him."

"Why would you do that?"

"At the time we had our set-to many years ago, I was hired to do a job. It was strictly business, nothing personal. Unfortunately, I underestimated his instincts for self-preservation. Then it became personal."

Andy frowned. "He thinks you're here on business now."

"My business, young friend, is always confidential."

As Rodock walked away, Judge Zachary approached, smoking a black cigar. He said, "Andy, I hope you know that Rodock is a dangerous man. I would give him room if I were you."

"How do you come to know him?"

"As county judge, it is my business to keep an eye on dangerous men who come into my community. He may stand before my bench one day."

If he and Daggett don't kill each other, Andy thought.

The judge said, "I've been expecting you to drop in for a visit at my ranch some evening. I would like to hear about your years as a captive of the Indians."

"I never felt like a captive. I was just one of them."

"All the more interesting."

A small group of well-wishers surrounded the newly married couple. A nervous Daggett beckoned Andy with a subtle crooking of a finger. "Would you bring my stuff over from the wagon yard to the hotel? Me and Carrie will stay there a few days till we find somethin' a little more permanent."

"There won't be no place permanent as long as you're a Ranger. I hope you explained that to her. She's lived in one place all her life."

"It'll be a big change for both of us, but we're strong."

"Right now, you don't look like you could whip an old man with a broken arm."

"You want to try me, Pickard?"

Andy grinned. "It's too pretty a day for a fight." His grin faded as he realized that Harper Teal might come to town before the day was over, looking for his daughter. There might indeed be a fight.

He looked around for Sheriff Seymour but could not see him. The lawman had mentioned the possibility of leaving town for a long hunting trip. Right now, Andy had rather be with him wherever he was than to be waiting here for the unpredictable.

The Teals arrived in the middle of the afternoon, Harper flanked by his sons and two cowboys. Andy heard the commotion and walked out into the street to meet them. Harper reined up and faced Andy with narrowed, flinty eyes that could kill cotton at thirty paces. He demanded, "Do you know where my daughter's at? I'm here to take her home."

Andy tensed. "I don't believe she'll want to go."

"That's none of your business. She'll do what I tell her to."

"Yesterday, maybe. Things are different today."

"What do you mean, different?"

"You'll have to ask her."

"I will. Where's she at?"

Andy pointed. "The hotel. She's probably expectin' you. I was."

Harper rode around Andy. His sons and the cowboys followed but let him ride a couple of lengths ahead. Andy walked alongside Bud's horse. He said, "Your daddy is fixin' to get a surprise. I don't know how he'll take it. You'd better stay close and not let him do somethin' he'll be sorry for."

"I don't think he's ever been sorry about anything. Except maybe not shootin' Ethan McIntosh back when it was legal to kill a Yankee."

By the time Harper reached the hotel, several bystanders had fallen in behind to watch. One was Jefferson Tolliver, with the eagerness of a man awaiting a show.

Andy thought, *Whatever happens, he'll write it up twice as big as it really is.*

Harper stopped just short of the hotel steps and shouted, "Carrie! I know you're in there. Come on out. You're goin' home."

Carrie did not answer. Harper shouted again.

Andy muttered to Bud, "With all due respect, your daddy's got the manners of an Arkansas mule."

Bud took no offense. "And the stubbornness."

Carrie appeared in the doorway, a dour Daggett at her side, his arm locked with hers. He was unarmed. She said quietly, "Hello, Pa. You didn't have to arouse the whole town. You could have come in and knocked on my door like a gentleman."

"I'm gentleman enough to know that my daughter doesn't belong in a town like this. It's time you went home."

She said, "You drove me away yesterday. You said things I never thought I would hear from you."

"You sicced the Rangers onto us. I was mad."

"So was I. You're still mad, but I'm not."

Harper turned his anger on Daggett. "Ranger, I told you to stay away from my daughter. It appears like you didn't hear me."

"You were plenty loud. I heard you."

"But here you are with her, and in a hotel! I've got every right to kill you."

"You've lost any rights you had over her. Carrie and I are married."

Harper's face froze. Slowly and deliberately he dismounted. Daggett motioned for Carrie to remain where she was, then moved down the steps and faced Harper on the ground. He said, "She's still your daughter. But more than that, she's my wife."

A screeching sound escaped from Harper's throat. He brought up a hard fist and drove it into Daggett's chin. Daggett staggered backward, falling on the steps. He arose quickly, his eyes wild and dangerous. He knotted a fist and drew it back. But somehow he called up enough control to stay his hand. His voice crackled. "You're her daddy, so I'll grant you that one. But don't you try for a second."

Bud and Cecil were on the ground immediately, holding their father's arms. "Pa," Bud said, "you don't want to make a show of yourself, fightin' in the street. Besides, he can whip you."

"He'll play hell." Harper tried to shake loose, but his sons held him firmly.

Bud argued, "Daggett's a good man. It won't be like it was with Skeen."

Harper seethed. "Don't you mention that name ever again."

Andy said, "You boys had better get him home."

Harper quit struggling. He lifted his gaze to Carrie, still up on the porch. His voice dropped back to a normal level. "All right then, you've made your bed. Now lay in it. I don't ever want to see you again."

Carrie stood straight and proud. "Pa, you don't mean that."

"I never say what I don't mean."

Her face grim, Carrie folded her arms. "Then, so be it."

Harper said, "Come on, boys, let's go. I don't have a daughter no more, and you ain't got a sister." He climbed into the saddle.

Bud hung back to speak to Carrie. "Sorry, sis. Maybe he'll change his mind once he's got past his mad."

She stood firm. "How many times did you ever see him change his mind?"

Daggett climbed the steps and gently put his arms around her. "Come on back inside. We've got a lot to talk about." They disappeared inside the hotel. Andy watched the Teals ride down the street and out of town. Anger welled up inside of him over Harper's bullheadedness. It gave way after a bit to sorrow for Carrie. He wished he could say something to comfort her, but that was for Daggett to do.

He looked up to the hotel's second story. He saw Ethan McIntosh and his wife Agatha, watching from a window. They had witnessed the whole event. Likely as not, Ethan had reveled in it.

Tolliver held a stub pencil and scribbled on a pad of paper. Angrily Andy said, "Ain't you bein' awful nosy?"

Tolliver kept writing. "A newspaperman has a special dispensation to be nosy. The people deserve to know all the news."

Andy had pondered over Judge Zachary's invitation to come out to his place for a visit. Stableman Scanlon told him how to find the Zachary ranch. "It's just a couple of miles out on that trail yonder." He pointed.

The ranch was not large by Teal or McIntosh standards. The house was a small and simple frame dwelling with a little gingerbread trim around the front but little other ornamentation. The judge sat in a rocking chair on the porch. He probably had not been home long.

He bade Andy to dismount and come up on the porch

to join him. "I have some Kentucky bourbon inside if you care to indulge."

Andy declined. "I hardly ever drink anything stronger than coffee."

"I can fire up the stove and fix that."

"It's too warm for coffee. I just wanted to see this place. The sheriff has been tellin' me about it. He says you're a lucky man."

"I am. This little ranch has been a refuge to me, a real treasure."

"Doesn't it get lonely?"

"For someone else, perhaps, but not for me. No matter how tiresome the day has been, I can sit here and watch my cattle grazing. Evenings I often see deer venturing out of the thickets to browse. And listen to the birds sing! They are infinitely more pleasing than the idle chatter of so many foolish people."

Andy said, "I don't think they're always singin'. They're warnin' each other to stay away from their territory. Just like people."

"I like to think they are singing. I have always hated strife."

"Bein' a judge, I guess you've seen a lot of that."

"Far too much. There have been some who have said my court has been too strict, longer on punishment than on mercy. But sometimes it is necessary in the interest of law and order. There is right, and there is wrong. The line between them is as stark as a stone wall, but there are still those among us who do not recognize it. That is why I like this place so much. No arguments, no strife." He smiled. "Except perhaps among the birds."

Andy thought of Bethel, and how much he wanted to

give her a place like this. He mentally calculated how much he had saved in a bank in Austin. Maybe that place was closer than he thought.

He asked, "How come you never got married?"

Zachary pondered a moment. "I answered my country's call and went off to war. By the time I came back, the girl I wanted had married someone else. For a long time I shied away from likely women. Then one day I looked in the mirror, and an old man looked back at me. I realized I had waited too long. But the bachelor life has its own compensations. Were I married, I would probably have to live in town instead of here in this place of rest and solitude."

Andy had been wondering about Sheriff Seymour. He had not seen him since yesterday. He found Deputy Willis sitting in the sheriff's chair, his feet on the desk. The deputy was whittling on a stick, letting the shavings litter the floor. Willis seemed startled at the sound of footsteps, then relaxed when he saw that they were not made by the sheriff.

"Oh," he said, "it's you. I thought maybe Pete was back."

Andy asked, "Back from where?"

"A settler south of here reported losin' some stock. He couldn't be sure when they were taken. Might've been the McIntoshes, or it might've been the Teals that took them."

Andy said, "It's hard to believe either family was responsible."

"I can see how you might not want the Teals involved, now that your partner is a Teal in-law. You're lettin' your feelin's get in the way of your judgment."

"I've eaten at both families' tables and slept in their bunkhouses. Have you?"

"No, personally I've never had much use for either side.

They're too rich, and got too much land. The way I see it, everybody ought to have about the same, nobody rich and nobody poor."

"The world doesn't work that way."

"It sure as hell don't. What have you got, Ranger, besides a job and a wage? No more than me, I'll bet. I've shoved a poor man's boots under the supper table as long as I can remember. If things don't change, I'll still be doin' it when I'm an old man."

"You can't take it out on the Teals and the McIntoshes. They've got their good side, like most people."

"Billy the Kid must've had a good side, too. I'll bet he was kind to his horses." Willis cursed suddenly and jerked his right hand away from the stick. His thumb was bleeding. "Damn! I was lookin' away and cut myself." He sucked on his thumb and spat blood at a spittoon but missed. He said, "That's a lesson for both of us. When you're doin' a job, don't look away."

The sheriff had not returned by dark. Andy visited the saloons and found people still talking about the confrontation between Daggett and Harper Teal. Their conversations dried up quickly when Andy came within hearing.

Editor Tolliver was engaged in a poker game. He had the largest stack of chips on the table. He gave Andy a sly smile. "I don't suppose you have seen your partner tonight, Ranger. I suspect that he is rather busy with his new duties."

Sarcastically Andy said, "I suppose you intend to write all about it?"

"No, in regard to certain matters, silence is best. I would not wish to shock elderly ladies or confuse our youngest readers."

Andy fantasized about forcing Tolliver to eat several

copies of his newspaper, though he restrained himself from any effort to bring the dream to reality. He read the cards in Tolliver's hand and said, "I hope you don't expect to bluff your way through with two queens."

He left Tolliver red-faced and trying too late to hide his hand.

Sheriff Seymour limped into town toward noon the next day, dusty, droop-shouldered, and near exhaustion. He stopped at a horse trough and pumped fresh water into his cupped hands to drink, then removed his hat and doused his head. The water cut trails through the dust on his face.

Andy trotted to meet him as Seymour turned back toward the open street. He asked, "What's happened to you? Where's your horse?"

Seymour seated himself on the edge of the trough. "Got him shot out from under me." He scowled. "Ain't there nobody travelin' today? I never met so much as a freight wagon all the way in. I could've used a ride."

Looking tired enough to fall, he drank more water, then explained. "I was lookin' for some stolen cattle. Caught up to them south of here. There was four men drivin' them."

"Recognize any?"

"Never got close enough to be sure. I was two maybe three hundred yards away when one of them leveled a rifle at me and killed my horse. Pinned my leg under him. I managed to work my saddle gun free and take a shot at them, but I don't know if I hit anybody. I was half the night workin' my leg out from under my horse."

"Any idea whose cattle they were?"

"Never got close enough to see any brands except for one cow that dropped off and shelled out a baby. She was wearin' the McIntosh Bar F. That made me figure the Teals might've been responsible."

"Except that the Teals were in town yesterday."

Seymour shook his head. "Damn! I thought I had it all figured out."

Andy said, "I'll bet you're hungry. It's just a few steps over to the chili joint."

Seymour nodded. "Ain't eaten since breakfast yesterday. A pox on them boys."

"You say you don't know who they were?"

"Not for certain. Two of them took off arunnin'. The two who hung back and shot at me could've been Harold Pearcy and Sonny Vernon. Like I say, my eyes are none too good anymore."

While the sheriff put away two eggs and a slab of steak, Andy told him of the events he had missed. Seymour listened intently to the account of the wedding and the confrontation with Harper Teal. He said, "If I was Daggett, I'd ask Ranger headquarters to give me a different assignment, away from here. When Harper Teal gets really mad, he loses all sense of judgment. He could've shot Daggett. For that matter, he might've shot his own daughter."

"He wouldn't do anything that crazy."

"He's capable. They say in the war he killed two Yankee cannon crews, turned the cannons around, and fired them at the bluecoats. They say he got shot twice but was too stubborn to bleed."

Andy had long since learned to take war stories with a grain of salt. He said, "So you've got no idea who was stealin' the cattle?"

"If it wasn't the Teals, I haven't got the slightest notion.

I'd almost swear that Vincent Skeen had come back to life, if I hadn't seen him layin' dead in his cell."

Andy said, "Maybe it's Skeen's ghost, come back to bedevil you for lettin' a mob kill him in your jail."

Seymour snorted. "A ghost?"

"Indians believe in them. Who can say for sure that they're wrong? The Comanches were afraid of dead men's spirits. They thought they came back to do mischief."

"I don't believe in anything I can't see, and I've never seen a ghost."

"You've never seen the wind, but you've felt it. You know it's real."

"All right, you look for a ghost. I'll look for a live human bein' with no compunctions about other people's property."

Andy said, "I don't really believe in ghosts, either, but I lived with the Indians long enough to know there are things out there that we can't see or understand. Maybe one of Skeen's accomplices has taken up his idea."

"That makes more sense than some ghost spirit."

Andy nodded. "But you can't see an idea, either."

"You stayed with the Indians too long."

Andy had dropped off to sleep on a cot under the wagon yard's hay shed when someone shook his shoulder. He came awake reaching for the pistol beneath his blanket. An unfamiliar voice whispered, "Ranger, come with me."

Andy could see only a vague shape in the darkness. "Who are you?"

"Harold Pearcy. You know me. Come on, we need you."

"In the middle of the night?"

"It ain't my choice, either. I'll saddle your horse for you while you get dressed."

"I'm dressed now except for my boots, and I'll saddle my own horse. Where are we goin'?"

"To the doctor's house first. He won't come with me unless you do. Sonny Vernon needs him real bad."

Andy remembered them. The hapless pair had jumped on Lanny Teal while he was fighting with Jake McIntosh. The two had impressed Andy as potential candidates for the penitentiary. Saddling his horse, he asked, "What happened to Sonny?"

"I'll tell you about it while we travel. There's too many ears around here, and everybody don't need to know."

They rode side by side to the doctor's house. The doctor had just finished harnessing a horse to his buggy. He said, "Thanks for coming, Ranger. I could not get this young man to tell me much, and I had no intention of leaving town with him unless I had the strong arm of the law by my side."

Andy said, "I don't think either one of us ought to go anywhere till he tells us what this is about."

Reluctantly Pearcy said, "Sonny's wounded. I thought he'd get better, but he's worse. I'm afraid he's fixin' to die without he gets proper doctorin'."

Andy asked, "How did he come to get wounded?"

Pearcy hesitated. "We was drivin' cattle when somebody come chasin' up from behind us like he meant business."

Andy asked, "Who?"

"We didn't go back and ask him. There was a little shootin', and Sonny got hit. I snuck him away so nobody would see he was hurt. I didn't want the regulators comin' after him."

"Why should they?"

"Truth is, me and Sonny been ridin' with them some. They're hell on secrecy. You know what they done to Callender and Bigelow. They'd do the same to Sonny and me. I decided the best thing was to leave the country with him. But we didn't get very far."

Andy asked, "How far?"

"To that sheep outfit of Old Man Hawkins's. Him and his wife, they done what they could for Sonny, but it's not enough."

Andy suspected that Pearcy had been with the night riders who had struck the Hawkinses' place some nights earlier. He asked with sarcasm, "Are you sure you know the way in the dark?"

Pearcy was not sharp enough to catch the irony. He said, "Sure, I been there before."

Andy asked, "Which one of you killed the sheriff's horse?"

Pearcy grunted. "The sheriff? Is that who was after us?"

"It was."

"I didn't want to have no killin' hangin' over me, so I shot at his horse. We thought he might keep after us afoot, but he didn't."

"The horse pinned him down. When he got free, he had to walk all the way back to town."

"I'll bet he's mad at us."

"He is, except he doesn't know who you are. Yet."

Pearcy worried, "He'll figure it out, and the regulators will, too. Me and Sonny took those cattle for our own selves, without askin' anybody. The regulators warned us against goin' out on our own."

They reached the Hawkinses' place at daybreak, the

doctor following close in his buggy. The sheep were still in the corral where Hawkins kept them at night for safety from predators. The dog came off the porch, barking.

The front door opened a couple of inches. A man peered out cautiously, then moved onto the porch, a rifle in his hands. Hawkins said, "Andy Pickard, is that you?"

"It's me. The doctor is right behind us."

Hawkins watched the buggy come to a stop. He said, "Pearcy, you better help the doctor with his bag and anything else he may need."

Pearcy dropped the reins. Andy half expected the horse to run away, but it was trained to stand ground hitched. Andy suspected it was stolen, for Pearcy was not bright enough to school a horse.

Hawkins held the door open until the doctor and Andy entered the house. Pearcy carried the bag in, then went back outside to take the horses to the barn. Hawkins's wife was in the kitchen, poking wood into the range and setting a coffeepot on to boil. Hawkins pointed to a small bedroom. "The boy's in there, Doctor. The bullet's too deep for us to get at it. Maybe you can do better."

Sonny was unconscious. Without even feeling his forehead, Andy knew he was running a high fever.

Hawkins said, "I tried to get Pearcy to fetch you right after they got here, Doctor, but he was afraid. These boys are in over their heads."

Andy said, "They've put you at risk by comin' here. The regulators may be afraid they've told you too much."

Hawkins said, "They haven't told me a thing. I've always tried to keep to myself and avoid being entangled in any of the troubles around here. But they have landed on my doorstep nevertheless. As a Christian I could not turn these boys away. Who knows? I may be entertaining an angel unaware."

The doctor said, "Hardly an angel. But he may become one if I don't get that bullet out of him."

Andy held a lamp close while the doctor probed the wound deep in the young man's shoulder. Though still unconscious, Sonny stirred restlessly. Hawkins and Pearcy held him as still as they could. The doctor brought out the slug and pitched it to Pearcy. He dropped it as if it were a horseshoe just out of the forge. It left a smear of blood on his hand.

"Goddamn it!" he exclaimed.

Hawkins cautioned, "You boys are in too precarious a position to be using the Lord's name in vain. You may be meeting Him sooner than you think."

Pearcy asked the doctor, "How soon do you think Sonny'll be able to travel?"

"Travel?" The doctor looked at him askance. "Are you trying to kill him?"

"I'm tryin' to keep somebody else from doin' it. If they get the idea we might talk too much, they'll squash us like bugs. They've never liked us much in the first place. They just tolerated us so they could use us."

Andy said, "I don't see where you owe them anything. Tell me who they are. Me and Daggett will take care of them."

"I don't know all of them. Even if I told you about the ones I know, there'd be others. I wouldn't stand a snowball's chance in hell. For all I know, the doctor here could be one of them."

The doctor said, "If I were, that boy would already be dead."

Andy said, "If you won't tell us who they are, maybe you can at least tell us who they aren't. Were any of the McIntoshes in on that raid at the Teal ranch?"

Pearcy considered. "No, they had nothin' to do with it. But Jake McIntosh is a friend of ours. We thought he'd like it if we got a shot at Lanny Teal."

"You did that for Jake?"

"That's what friends are for. Only we never saw Lanny. Never saw anybody, really. It was too dark."

"The Teals naturally thought the McIntoshes had raided them, so they rode over to pay them back. You could've gotten Jake and some others killed."

The idea disturbed Pearcy. "Never thought of it like that."

The doctor finished bandaging Sonny's wound, then sat back and stared at the unconscious young man. "Sooner or later," he said, "someone will start looking for these two. The longer they stay here, the more they jeopardize Mr. Hawkins and his wife. The doctor in me says this boy should not be moved. The realist in me says he ought to be taken away from here as soon as possible."

Andy said, "It's plain that he can't leave on horseback. Mr. Hawkins, could you let me have the borry of your wagon?"

"Certainly. Where do you intend to take him?"

Andy thought it best to keep that information to himself. "You'll be better off not knowin'." He turned to the doctor. "When you get to town, will you tell Logan Daggett that I've taken two material witnesses to a safe place? I'll be back in a few days."

"I'll do that."

"Don't tell anybody but him. Nobody."

Sonny moaned as they carried him out and laid him atop two folded blankets in the bed of Hawkins's wagon. Andy asked Pearcy, "You know how to handle a wagon?"

"Sure. I ain't no fool."

Andy could argue with him about that, but he didn't. He said, "You can tie the horses on behind, yours and Sonny's."

Pearcy was ill at ease. "You takin' us to town? That ain't such a good idea."

"I'm takin' you where you'll be safe. You, anyhow. The shape Sonny's in, I can't guarantee that we won't have to stop and bury him."

"Sonny's my cousin. I ain't lettin' him die, not even if I have to wrestle the devil to the ground and bob off his tail."

Andy mounted his horse in the early morning light and bade good-bye to the Hawkinses and the doctor. Pearcy sat on the wagon seat, trembling, looking back toward town as if he expected pursuit.

When Andy had freed Bigelow from his cell, it was his intention to take him to a strong jail in Kerrville, beyond the regulators' home ground. He considered Kerrville now but decided instead to take the two to Fort McKavett. The town had a doctor, and the Ranger camp was nearby. The Rangers could hold Pearcy and Sonny as witnesses until they were needed.

Besides, Andy might get a chance to see Bethel.

Pearcy asked, "Where are we goin'?"

"Straight up," Andy said, "and a little to the left."

10

The wagon was built for work, not for comfort. The rough terrain shook Sonny back to consciousness. Andy told him, "Sorry, but you'll have to put up with this for a while. After a while we'll get to a better road."

Pearcy said, "You call this a road?"

It was nothing more than a wagon trail, and a poor one at that.

Andy said, "It's the best way to get us out of the county without runnin' into a bunch of nosy people."

For the fourth or fifth time, Pearcy asked, "Where we goin'?"

As before, Andy said, "You'll see when we get there." If Pearcy knew they were going to a Ranger camp, he might abandon his cousin and run. Andy hoped some time in confinement might prompt him to share what he knew.

By the time they camped for the night, Sonny was exhausted. His fever was down, however. Andy told him, "We brought a shovel, but maybe we won't have to use it after all."

Weakly Sonny asked, "Was I in that bad a shape?"

Pearcy said, "The angels were already singin'."

"All I heard was sheep."

Andy made stew from a piece of mutton Mrs. Hawkins had put in the wagon. He took it as a favorable sign that Sonny ate all Pearcy gave him. Sonny was still confused. He remembered the bullet striking him. He had patches of memory about Pearcy holding him in the saddle and taking him to a ranch house. He remembered almost nothing about his time at the Hawkinses' place or about the doctor removing the bullet. He did not understand the reason for their flight now.

Pearcy said, "Remember what happened to Callender and Bigelow? It could happen to us. Them fellers are awful afraid somebody will tell their secrets."

Sonny looked at Andy with frightened eyes. "You won't let them get to us, will you, Ranger?"

"No, I won't, but you owe me."

"We ain't got any money."

"It's not money I'm after. It's information . . . names."

Sonny glanced at Pearcy. "We can't do that. They *would* kill us."

Andy asked, "If you knew how dangerous they are, how come you to ride with them in the first place?"

Pearcy said, "We never had nothin', me and Sonny. It stuck in our craw, seein' other people have so much, and us with nothin'. We was told that if we took enough cattle from the Teals and the McIntoshes, we could end up with a piece of their land."

"I thought the McIntoshes were your friends."

"Jake is. He treats us like we're somebody. We never cared for the old man, though."

Sonny put in, "Nothin' we ever done suited that old fart. Anyway, friendship ends when there's money on the table."

Pearcy said, "Me and Sonny figured to go partners when we got some land of our own."

Andy said, "*If* you got any land. Don't you know they would squeeze you out? When you pitch a piece of meat into a bunch of dogs, the strongest will grab it all."

"Never thought of it thataway."

Andy doubted that they had thought much at all.

They had been on the trail an hour the next morning when they rode over a stretch of rising ground and suddenly came upon a horseman. Pearcy sucked in a sharp breath and said, "Oh, my God."

Andy asked, "What's the matter?"

"I know this man. I think he's a regulator."

Andy had seen him in town. It was too late now to avoid him. The man stopped his horse in one rut of the trail so that Pearcy had no choice but to pull up on the team. He gave Pearcy and Sonny a quick glance, then asked Andy, "I know these boys. Looks like you've got yourself a couple of desperate outlaws, Ranger."

Lying was not one of the things Andy did best, but he grabbed at the first idea that came to mind. "Sonny's horse fell with him and broke his shoulder. We're takin' him to his granddaddy's house till he heals up."

"Where does his granddaddy live?"

"Uvalde." That was a long way from Fort McKavett.

"Odd job for a Ranger, doin' escort service."

"I thought so myself, but an order is an order."

The man rode on. He appeared satisfied, but Andy wondered.

By the second night's camp, Sonny was strong enough that they lifted him out of the wagon and let him lie on the ground. Sitting up, leaning against Andy's saddle to eat supper, he said, "This ride has churned my innards into buttermilk."

Andy said, "The old wagon's springs are tired, like us, but we've put the worst of it behind us."

Pearcy said, "I hope we've put the regulators behind us. That bunch would hang the likes of me and Sonny without botherin' to say grace."

Pearcy almost jumped from the wagon when he saw the Ranger camp just ahead. He whirled around on the seat, his eyes wild. "What's this? What've you brought us to?"

Andy dropped his hand to the butt of his pistol to discourage Pearcy from doing something foolish. He said, "I promised I'd bring you to a safe place. I doubt there's a safer place anywhere than a Ranger camp."

"We're under arrest?"

"You've been under arrest ever since the Hawkinses' place."

Pearcy's voice quavered. "I've heard what the Rangers do to people."

"Only to people that misbehave. You ain't goin' to misbehave, are you, Pearcy?"

Pearcy lowered his head but did not answer. Andy said, "If you don't like it here, there's an easy way for you and Sonny to go free. Just give me the names I'm lookin' for."

"You know I can't do that."

"You will, when you get tired enough of this place. I hope you enjoy hard labor."

He accompanied the wagon to the sergeant's tent. Sergeant Ryker stepped out and surveyed the prisoners. He said, "Have you and Daggett already taken care of the trouble back yonder?"

Andy said, "I'm afraid not, but these two have had a hand in it. I hope I can leave them here for safekeepin'. One is goin' to need a doctor's attention."

The sergeant nodded, looking at Pearcy. "We can use a swamper to do heavy liftin' around camp. We just sent the last one off to the pen."

While a couple of Rangers took Pearcy and Sonny in hand, Andy explained briefly to the sergeant what had happened. He said, "These two boys are little fish in a lake that's too big for them."

The sergeant said, "I think we can make life miserable enough that they'll be glad to give us chapter and verse." He changed the subject. "Seen your wife?"

"Not yet. I thought I'd drop by and say howdy."

The sun was still high in the west. The sergeant said, "Your horses look tired out after the trip. Why don't you give them a day's rest before you start back?"

Andy had intended to do that anyway, but this made it official. "Sergeant, heaven must have a special place prepared just for you."

The sergeant grinned. "I'm willin' to wait." He turned his gaze toward a man approaching the tent. He said, "That's a gun salesman. Just sold me a new pistol. I'll bet he'd oblige us in puttin' on a little show for your prisoners." The sergeant went out and talked to the salesman, who smiled as he listened to Ryker's proposition. Ryker returned and said, "That buggy yonder is his. If you'll take it a little piece down the road, out of sight, we'll give your boys somethin' that'll keep them awake tonight."

Andy followed directions. In a little while he saw Sergeant Ryker and the salesman walking toward him. The sergeant paused to fire a couple of pistol shots. He shook hands with the salesman, who then climbed into the buggy.

Andy asked, "What was that all about?"

The salesman grinned. "Ryker pretended that I was a prisoner and walked me by the boys you brought in. He let them hear him say that since I wouldn't talk, I wasn't of any more use to him. Soon as we got out of their sight, he fired his pistol."

Andy whistled to himself. "I'll bet they wet their britches."

"It'll give them somethin' to chew on besides those hard biscuits. Looks to me like the Rangers could afford to hire a better cook."

In camp, Andy found Pearcy badly shaken. Pearcy declared, "He shot that man. Walked him out yonder and shot him like a dog."

Andy tried to keep a solemn face. "He wouldn't talk. There wasn't any point in lettin' him laze around and eat at the state's expense from now to Christmas."

"How long had he been here?"

"The sergeant said they brought him in yesterday."

"They didn't give him much time."

"Sergeant Ryker is not a patient man."

The sergeant walked up to Pearcy, carrying a shovel. "I want you to go out yonder and dig a grave. Three or four feet is deep enough. That feller won't be diggin' out."

Pearcy broke into a cold sweat. His eyes were desperate as he turned to Andy. "You promised that me and Sonny could go free if we told you what you want to know."

"That's what I said."

"We don't know hardly any of the regulators. We were part of a little bunch that was drivin' off cattle. They used to be members of Vincent Skeen's outfit."

"Who else is left?"

Pearcy wiped a sleeve across his sweating face. "There's just a couple that we know, Miley Burns and Ed Granger. They never did think much of me and Sonny. They just took us along when they couldn't find nobody else. And when Sonny got shot, they ran off and left us to take care of ourselves."

Andy remembered seeing Granger's name in his fugitive book. Burns might be there, too, under a different name. He asked, "Are they the ones who took Bigelow away from me and killed him?"

"I don't know. Till that happened, I never knew that Bigelow belonged to the regulators. Him or Callender either."

Andy said, "We'll want you to sign a statement about what you've told us."

Pearcy trembled. "I ain't much at writin', so you put it on paper. I'll sign it."

After Andy hugged Bethel hard enough to squeeze the breath from her lungs, she stood off at arm's length and studied him critically. "No bullet holes this time?"

"Sorry to disappoint you." He did not tell her about being clubbed unconscious when the regulators killed Bigelow. That had left only a small scar, hidden by his hair. It hurt only when he put on his hat or took it off.

She helped him unhitch the horses from the wagon and lead them to a pen. Watching him feed them, she said, "I guess you'll be going right back, as usual."

"I'm under orders to give the horses a day's rest first."

She was pleasantly surprised. "A whole day together? What will we do with so much time?"

"I suppose there's a lot of work needs doin' around here."

"A lot. But it can wait. If we've just got a day, let's don't waste it all out here with the horses."

Her arm around his waist, she led him to the house.

She made breakfast the second morning but ate little of it herself. Staying within reaching distance of him, she mused,

"I suppose it would break a dozen Ranger rules if I went with you."

"At least that many."

"What if I did it on my own, without asking you? It wouldn't be your fault then, would it?"

"You're thinkin' like a lawyer. Besides, we don't know what may happen over there. It could get dangerous. I wouldn't want you caught in the middle of it."

"There are other women in that town, aren't there? Daggett's new bride, for one."

"She was born there." He kissed her. "Best forget it. Maybe this thing will be over with before long, and I'll be back."

"They'll just send you someplace else. It'll go on this way as long as you're a Ranger."

They had been down this road many times. Andy had no fresh arguments. He said, "Can you spare some bacon, and maybe a few eggs? Eatin' gets kind of chancy on the trail."

She soon presented him a couple of sacks, both heavy, and a small basket of eggs. He said, "You must figure I'm goin' to eat a lot."

"You've got to keep up your strength for when we're together again."

He lingered with her until his conscience troubled him. This was not what the state was paying him for. He kissed her fiercely and climbed into the wagon. He said, "I'll see you as soon as I can." The team made a quick start. Andy looked back to be sure his saddle horse was still tied on behind. He saw Bethel standing with her hands clasped in front of her. She went into the house just as the trail made a bend, and he lost sight of her. He kept seeing her in his mind's eye for a long time. Someday . . .

He made better time on the return trip. He could push the team for more speed without worrying about jolting Sonny Vernon. He had time to think about the situation to which he was returning, to do some guessing about who might be involved in the trouble. He eliminated first one, then another from his list of possibles, then reconsidered and reinstated them as suspects.

Of only one thing was he nearly certain: that someone was trying to steal enough cattle from the Teals and McIntoshes to leave them in financial straits. They were also trying to manipulate the two families into a crippling fight that would leave them vulnerable to the free range advocates.

Toward dusk he found a creek and decided to camp. He unhitched the team, staking them and his saddle horse where the grass looked greenest, then started a small fire. He lifted out the sack of groceries Bethel had given him and waited for the fire to burn down to smoldering coals. He saw the horses lift their heads and look back in the direction from which they had come. Turning, he saw a woman riding sidesaddle. He recognized her on sight.

Bethel reined up and asked, "What's for supper?"

He blurted, "What in the hell are you doin' here?"

She smiled. "A woman's place is with her husband."

"Not this woman, and not this husband; not where I'm goin'."

She dismounted without help and removed her saddle. She said, "I don't suppose you have another stake rope?"

"No, but I've got a pair of hobbles. I ought to've put them on *you* this mornin'."

She led the horse to the creek and let it drink its fill, then held out her hand. "The hobbles," she said.

"I'll do it," he said stiffly. He tied the hobbles to her horse's forefeet. It would not stray far with that kind of restraint. It was likely to remain close to the other horses.

She was still smiling. "Did anybody ever tell you that your nose flares out when you get mad? It's not a handsome sight."

"You've got to go back."

"In the dark? I'd wander like a child in the wilderness. You wouldn't want that to happen to your wife."

He saw that she had him. He said, "You'll go home in the mornin'."

"Maybe. Right now, you put the coffee on and I'll see what I can fix for our supper."

He had never been able to remain angry at Bethel for long. She hummed a happy tune while she busied herself around the cook fire. As he watched her, his impatience faded. Come morning, he would put his foot down. She would have to go back. But tonight he enjoyed sharing the blankets and feeling her warmth.

Bethel asked him about the town, the trouble, about Logan Daggett. She said, "He has a severe countenance."

Andy admitted, "He doesn't smile much."

"How did he attract a woman like this Carrie Teal?"

"I ain't even figured *you* out yet. How can I understand a woman I barely know?"

Bethel speculated, "Maybe she didn't realize what it's like, being the wife of a Ranger who never gets to stay home."

Daylight brought him awake, momentarily disoriented to find Bethel lying close beside him. He listened to birds announcing the dawn and a cow somewhere, calling for a wayward calf. Gently he nudged Bethel. "Time to get up," he said. "We'll have breakfast, then I'll get you started on the road back to McKavett."

She yawned and turned aside the blanket that covered her. Wearing only a thin shift, she looked beautiful to Andy, even with her hair disheveled and sleep in her eyes. He was tempted to say there was no hurry about fixing breakfast.

She said, "How can I go back? I don't see my horse."

The hobbles lay on the ground, but her horse was gone. She said, "Now, how do you suppose he managed to get the hobbles off? That's a smart horse."

Andy felt a little of yesterday's anger rising. "Maybe he had a smart woman to help him."

"Well, there's nothing to be done about it now. He's probably halfway home."

"Not quite." Andy saw Bethel's horse a couple of hundred yards away, grazing peacefully. "I'll go fetch him while you fix breakfast."

Bethel's shoulders drooped in disappointment. "If anybody ever makes you a good offer for that horse, sell him."

By the time he returned, leading the horse at the end of a rope, Bethel seemed to have accepted the situation. At least, Andy hoped so. He said, "No tricks this time. You go on back home where you'll be safe." He knew there was a chance she would wait for him to get out of sight, then follow.

She promised, "All right. No more tricks. But you'll have to admit that it's nice to have me around."

"There's never been any question about that. But if worst

comes to worst, I don't want you gettin' caught in the cross fire."

They lingered a while after breakfast, then Andy saw Bethel on her way back to Fort McKavett. He already missed her before she was out of sight.

August Hawkins was penning his sheep as Andy pulled up in front of his house. Mrs. Hawkins came out onto the porch, speaking Spanish. Andy did not understand the words, but he understood the gestures. She was beckoning him to come inside.

Andy said, "I'll go see if Mr. Hawkins needs help with his sheep."

The dog provided all the help needed, but Andy was ill at ease in a situation where he did not understand what was being said. He shut the gate behind the sheep and told Hawkins, "I'm a little later than I figured in gettin' the wagon back to you. Got delayed some."

He explained about Bethel.

Hawkins said, "My late wife was like that. She listened politely to everything I told her, then went ahead and did what she pleased."

Andy asked, "Anything happen while I've been gone?"

Hawkins frowned. "A couple of men came by here yesterday and inquired about those two young fellows you carried away."

"What did you tell them?"

"I told them I had not seen anyone answering the descriptions they gave."

Andy said, "Did you recognize them?"

"By face. One is named Granger. If I were given to speculation, I would hazard that they were associated with your prisoners in some sort of mischief."

"I guess they were worried about what the boys might tell us."

"Did they tell you anything?"

"Sergeant Ryker is a persuasive man. Pearcy told what he knew. It wasn't much."

Hawkins frowned. "I've heard of some Ranger methods that go beyond the pale."

"The sergeant didn't hurt them. He just scared them to death."

"Your friend Daggett strikes me as someone who would do more than that."

Andy conceded, "He might. It doesn't take much to touch him off. That's why I didn't send for him to help me with Pearcy and Vernon."

"He may not be pleased that you took the full task upon yourself."

"That won't be anything new. He hasn't been pleased with much else I've done. I've found that it's best to do things my own way and ask him afterward."

At breakfast Hawkins announced that he would accompany Andy to town. "I've been waiting for the wagon so I could fetch some things from Babcock's store."

Andy said, "I'd be pleased to have the company." Exchanging talk with Hawkins along the way helped keep his mind from Bethel.

Hawkins stopped the wagon in front of Babcock's store. Andy shook his hand and thanked him for the several days' use of the wagon.

Hawkins dismissed the gratitude with a wave of his big hand. "Who knows? I may make a sheepman of you yet."

Rubbing his hands on an apron, the storekeeper stepped out onto the porch to greet Hawkins.

Andy said, "I've been gone for several days. Any excitement?"

Babcock shook his head. "Not since that set-to between Harper Teal and Ranger Daggett. The town has been so quiet that someone claimed to have seen a mountain lion sleeping in the street. I put little stock in that, of course."

Andy knew the story. The same yarn was being told about Fort Worth. He asked, "Have you seen Daggett around?"

"He's out in town somewhere. He never comes into the store except to buy some tobacco."

Andy turned, intending to take his horse to the wagon yard and turn it loose. He almost bumped into Daggett. He looked for welcome in the Ranger's eyes but saw none. Daggett declared, "You should've reported to me as soon as you got to town."

"I just now got here. Had some delay on the trip." He explained about Bethel.

Daggett frowned. "A man ought to keep a tight rein on his wife. It's his place to set the rules and hers to follow."

Andy doubted that Daggett held any such rein on Carrie.

Daggett said, "I never quite understood where you went. The doctor just told me you were takin' two prisoners to a safe place."

Andy told him about escorting Sonny and Pearcy to the Ranger camp. "Sergeant Ryker put the fear of God into Pearcy. He spilled all he knew."

"Good. Now we're gettin' somewhere."

"Not far enough. The trouble is, he just belonged to a

little bunch of cow thieves who took orders from the regulators." He related the names Pearcy had given him. "Burns and Granger were go-betweens. They never let him get close to anybody higher up."

Daggett mulled over the names. He said, "I've heard the name Ed Granger, but I can't tie a face to it."

Andy said, "If we take out Burns and Granger, that'll bust up the theft ring. But it doesn't help us deal with the regulators."

"One job at a time."

Andy was not sure he had done the right thing in sending Bethel home. He missed her, especially when he saw Daggett and Carrie together. He could not help making comparisons. He was convinced that Bethel was the prettiest of the two, though Daggett would have disagreed. Carrie was half a head the tallest and a few years the older. Bethel had grown up as the daughter of a well-to-do farmer on the lower Colorado River, though some of the farm had been lost in the bitter Reconstruction years after the war. Carrie's strong-willed family had struggled and sacrificed to build a modest ranch here in Central Texas, amid feuds and political fighting. Only a person who had nothing would consider them well-to-do. Now Carrie was estranged from her father. Bethel had lost hers years ago.

Daggett and Carrie took their meals in the hotel's dining room. Andy ate in Kennison's chili joint down the street, where the food was cheaper and just as filling, even if not so fancy. Eating in the hotel was a quick way to shrink a wallet.

Finished with his meal, Andy walked back to the hotel

and waited for Daggett. The big Ranger had not told Andy his plans, and Andy had not asked. He knew how badly Daggett disliked answering questions. Their first stop was the sheriff's office. Seymour and his deputy were both there, the sheriff taking his after-lunch nap, Deputy Willis looking at pictures in *The Police Gazette*. The sheriff opened one eye, then the other, as he heard the Rangers' boots tromping across the pine floor, their spurs jingling. Yawning, he said, "Andy, we were thinkin' about sendin' a search party out for you."

Daggett cut straight to the guts of the matter. "Do you know where we might find Miley Burns and Ed Granger?"

Seymour rubbed sleep from his eyes and put on his thick-lensed glasses. "They stay out with the owls and the coyotes. I hardly ever see them in town. What do you want them for?"

"Pickard brought back information that they're a little careless with other people's cattle."

Seymour did not seem surprised. "Granger has a squatter's shack back in the hills. He has a brother here in town. Works as a clerk at the hotel."

Daggett said, "Oh, him. I didn't connect the name. He sure don't look like a cattle rustler. He looks like a clerk."

"I don't think him and his brother see much of each other."

Andy told the sheriff, "I found out who shot the horse from under you. Like you guessed, it was Pearcy and Vernon."

The sheriff pulled out his shirttail and rubbed his glasses on it. "I suspicioned that, but I wasn't close enough to see for sure."

Andy said, "You may not've known it, but you shot Sonny in the shoulder."

"With these poor eyes of mine? It had to be the devil's own luck. Where are those boys now?"

"In a safe place. It was them—Pearcy, anyway—who told me about Burns and Granger. He was sore afraid they'd come after him to shut him up. Or the regulators would."

"What did he know about the regulators?"

"I'd better not say, not till me and Daggett have a chance to check on all of it." Though Pearcy had been able to tell him little, it might be useful to let the impression spread that he had indeed given Andy some useful information.

The sheriff's face settled into a deep frown. "In the beginnin', we needed the regulators. Things had got out of control. I looked away because they were doin' work that the law wouldn't let me do. They hung some bad men, and they ran some others out of the country when I didn't have any legal basis to do it myself. Even horsewhipped a few wife beaters and whiskey-soaks who wouldn't support their families."

Daggett nodded grimly. "I've seen it happen in other places. After a while people went to usin' the vigilantes for their own purposes. They accused innocent men they wanted to get rid of. They went to takin' whatever they wanted because folks were afraid to fight back, or even to say anything."

Seymour nodded. "That's about the way it played out."

Daggett said, "Up at Gainesville early in the war, a mob came together, supposed to be good Confederates. They got to accusin' first one man, then another, of havin' Union sympathies. Some did, I suppose, but others just had somethin' somebody wanted bad enough to bear false witness. They wound up with a mass hangin' that folks up there are still ashamed to talk about."

Seymour said, "There was a time I could've stopped it but didn't want to. Now I wouldn't even know where to start." He took a whiskey bottle from a desk drawer and silently offered it to the Rangers. They declined. He took a long swallow, then asked, "Want me to go with you after Burns and Granger?"

Daggett said, "We can handle it. It's better if you stay here in case the Teals and the McIntoshes all come to town at one time."

"You're a Teal in-law. Can't you keep that from happenin'?"

"You know what Harper Teal said to me. I don't have any more say in that family than"—he broke off as a tall man stepped through the office door—"than that newspaperman comin' yonder."

Jefferson T. Tolliver was dressed in a white suit that contrasted with the black ink stains on his fingers. His confident stride carried him up to the officers. He said, "I am preparing to go to press with this week's edition. I wonder if you gentlemen have anything of interest to tell my readers."

Andy would not have told Tolliver what time it was, but Daggett said, "We're goin' out to try and find two men. We've got it on good authority that they're cow thieves."

"On what authority, may I ask?"

"A couple of other thieves. It takes one to know one."

Outside, Andy said, "I don't see why you had to tell him that. He'll blab it all over town."

"I want him to."

"But if we don't reach Burns and Granger first, we're apt to find them shot dead or hung from a tree."

"Either way, the job gets done. The regulators would save the county the cost of a court trial."

"That's too rough for my taste."

Daggett shrugged. "Rough or not, it's justice. We're not talkin' about Sunday school teachers here; we're talkin' about a pair of cow thieves." His frown returned. "Speakin' of thieves, don't you think you were too lenient with Pearcy and Vernon?"

"I got what I wanted from them. They're not much more than a couple of kids."

"They've already set the pattern. They'll wind up decoratin' a rope or bleedin' to death through holes the Lord didn't put there. In the long run, you haven't spared them much."

"At least I've given them a chance. Maybe they'll decide to go straight."

"And maybe coyotes will quit stealin' chickens." Daggett stopped and pointed down the street. "You trot to the wagon yard and get our horses. I'm goin' over to the hotel and accidentally let the word slip that we're goin' after Burns and Granger. I'm bettin' that all we'll have to do then is to follow that clerk."

Andy saw the logic. "You've got the mind of a Comanche."

"I take that as a compliment."

11

The wait was not a long one. The hotel clerk, wearing his suit, left through a back door and trotted toward the wagon yard.

Andy asked, "What did you tell him?"

Daggett said, "Nothin' directly. I just made sure he could hear me when I told Carrie we were on our way out to find Burns and Granger. I told her I hoped we could get to them before the regulators do."

Shortly the clerk left the wagon yard through a back gate, spurring a dun horse into a brisk trot. Daggett said, "We don't want to spook him. Let him get a long head start. If we lose sight of him, we can follow his tracks."

Andy said, "You might. I wouldn't want to bet on me doin' it."

"Maybe you need to go back and live with the Indians for a while. You didn't finish your education."

They let Granger reach a distant stand of cedar before Daggett touched spurs to his horse. Andy said, "It doesn't look like he's followin' a trail. He's cuttin' across country."

"It's just as well. He won't get his tracks mixed up with somebody else's."

Andy wished for Daggett's confidence. He said, "What'll we do with them if we catch them? You know that jail isn't safe if somebody is bound and determined to get at a prisoner."

"Do you know how the Mexicans trap a mountain lion that's been into their flocks? They stake out a kid goat in an open place and wait for the lion to show up."

"So we'll use Burns and Granger for the goat?"

"Might catch us some regulators."

"The goat usually gets killed, doesn't it?"

Daggett dismissed the argument. "Two thieves. Their lives ain't worth a bucket of spit."

It became clear to Andy after a while that the beeline direction the clerk was taking would cross over land claimed by the Teal family. The man knew where he was going and was in a hurry to get there. Andy considered mentioning it to Daggett but knew it would make no difference to the older Ranger. His course was set.

The Rangers came suddenly and unexpectedly upon Bud and Lanny Teal. No one spoke for a minute, getting over their surprise. Bud broke the silence. "Daggett, what're you doin' here? Pa is just over yonder, beyond that thicket. You know what he said about you not ever comin' onto this place again."

Daggett said, "We're on Ranger business. We're followin' a man who doesn't care whose land he crosses over."

Bud nodded. "We saw a rider a little bit ago." He paused. "How's Carrie?"

"She's fine. Just fine."

"Glad to hear it. We worry about her, but Pa won't abide us even speakin' her name. Tell her we said hello."

"I'll do that."

Bud frowned. "When you catch up to that feller, do you expect any trouble? Me and Lanny will go with you if you'd like."

Andy could only imagine Harper Teal's reaction if two of his sons rode along to help Logan Daggett.

Daggett said, "Thanks, but I doubt it'll amount to much.

Just a couple of two-bit cow thieves not worth the rope it'd take to hang them."

"Do any of them answer to the name of McIntosh?"

"Sorry to disappoint you. They don't."

"I'm not disappointed, but Pa would be. He still thinks the McIntoshes are tryin' to steal us blind."

Andy said, "You don't believe that, do you?"

"Old Man Ethan is a bullheaded Yankee, but I doubt that he's a thief. Nor his boys, either."

Lanny said, "Jake is. He's been tryin' to steal my girl."

Bud said, "She's not hard to steal."

While the two Teals argued about Lucy Babcock, Daggett put his horse into a long trot to make up for lost time. Andy spurred up even with him and said, "If it wasn't for the two old men, I think the family feud would die out like a spent match."

Daggett said, "It looks to me like Ethan and Harper will live forever, unless they kill each other."

The clerk stopped occasionally, probably to give his horse a rest. The Rangers came dangerously close to riding up on him. They managed to pull into screening brush so they were not discovered. Andy said, "You might not think so, seein' him in that town suit, but he knows to take care of a horse."

"Like as not, he took to the clerk's job because it was easier than runnin' off other people's cattle. Safer, too."

"You've got to give him credit for tryin' to warn his brother."

"No credit. If he wasn't an outlaw before, this makes him one."

Late in the afternoon the Rangers rounded a chalky hill and saw a small frame house, unpainted, faded to near the

color of the ground around it. Several rough cedar-
post corrals and a small barn stretched out in the rear.
Andy could hear cattle bawling in the pens.

He said, "What would you wager that the brands aren't
theirs?"

"That would be a sucker bet."

The clerk's dun horse was tied outside the corral, alongside two others. Andy could see three men inside, among
the cattle. They seemed to be arguing.

Daggett said, "This is a good time to go among them,
while they're not lookin' our way."

By the time the men discovered they had company, the
Rangers were within pistol range. Daggett said in a gravelly voice, "Now, boys, I wisht you'd shuck any guns you've
got and pitch them into that trough yonder."

One of the men demanded, "Who the hell are you?"

Dismayed, the clerk said something Andy could not
hear. Evidently he identified the two visitors as Rangers.
One of the men seemed for a moment to toy with the idea
of fighting it out, but caution countered his instincts. He
pitched a pistol into the dry trough as ordered. The other
man had already done so. Andy assumed from a facial resemblance that he was the clerk's brother. The clerk did
not appear to be armed.

Daggett said, "I won't waste my breath tellin' you you're
all under arrest. You can see that."

"What for?" the clerk's brother demanded.

Daggett jerked his head toward the cattle, bunched in a
corner of the pen, staying as far from the men as they
could. They were range raised and not accustomed to seeing people afoot. "We've got testimony from one Harold
Pearcy that the two of you are engaged in the unlawful

takin' of cattle that belong to somebody else. The brands on these tell me that he did not lie."

Andy sensed that Daggett was toying with the men now that he had them in custody. Cat and mouse. Usually that game ended with the cat eating the mouse.

He took a quick look at the brands. They were T Crosses. Not one was the McIntoshes' Bar F. He said, "If the Teals ever catch you stealin' their cattle, they may make short work of you."

Sweating, Ed Granger said, "These strays were on our range, eatin' our grass. We just gathered them up and was fixin' to drive them back where they belong."

Daggett said, "I'd like to see you tell that yarn to a jury. They'd probably give you five years extra for bein' such a bad liar."

Granger's nervousness was infecting his partner. Burns asked, "What're you goin' to do with us?"

"Turn you over to Sheriff Seymour. He'll keep you in jail till the court convenes."

Burns argued, "A prisoner got lynched in that jail last year. The regulators never even took him out of his cell."

"How do you know it was the regulators?"

"Who else would it have been?"

"Tell us who they are and we'll arrest them before they can touch you."

Burns pleaded, "We don't know all of them. Even if we told you about the ones we know, the others would kill us for sure."

Daggett showed no sympathy. "You boys have done a poor job of choosin' friends."

It was too late in the day to take the prisoners to town. They could too easily make a break in the darkness. Andy said, "I hope there's enough grub in that shack to feed all of us."

Daggett said, "Two of us, anyway."

Resentfully Granger said, "We bought and paid for that grub with our hard-earned money."

Daggett said, "We're confiscatin' it in the name of the State of Texas. Pickard, handcuff these men to a couple of fence posts. I'll go see what I can find to eat. Catchin' cow thieves stirs up my appetite." He turned to the hotel clerk. "Can you cook?"

The clerk hung his head like a whipped dog. "Some."

"Then you come with me to the shack. I don't like to see a man's talents go to waste."

Andy counted the cattle and made a note in his fugitive book in case he was called upon to testify. He opened the gate and drove the animals out to find their way back to their home ranges or wherever else they chose to go. He led the horses into the corral, removed bridles and saddles, and put out some grain he found in the barn.

Ed Granger asked plaintively, "You goin' to leave us out here like this all night? What if it comes a rain?"

Andy had not seen rain in weeks. He said, "We'll cover you with a wagon sheet." He realized that, like Daggett, he was playing cat and mouse with the prisoners. He had not intended that. "We'll let you sleep inside if you'll behave yourselves."

Granger said, "You're not a bad sort, but I can't say as I like your partner much."

Andy replied, "Sometimes I don't either, but if I want him to know that, I'll tell him myself."

Smoke rose from the metal chimney. After a while

Daggett came out of the shack and shouted, "Supper's ready!"

Andy released the prisoners from the fence posts, then handcuffed them together to impede their mobility.

Daggett approved. "Sometimes you surprise me, Pickard."

"I learned from good teachers." He thought of Rusty Shannon and Len Tanner.

Daggett and the clerk had cooked a big supper. Ed Granger complained about the waste. Daggett said, "We'd just as well use it up. You're not comin' back here."

The two prisoners sat on the floor to eat, plates in their laps. Andy was not concerned that they would try to escape. They were having a hard time coordinating their movements enough to eat supper. Granger used his left hand, Burns his right. The hands were locked together with only a short chain between them.

The clerk was free to move around. Andy whispered to Daggett, "He didn't do anything but try to warn his brother. I have to credit him for that."

"He's got bad blood in him."

"You can't hold a man for what his kin have done. I say we ought to let him go."

"If we did, he might rouse up some friends to deliver the prisoners from us. I say we'd better hang on to him a while."

Andy argued, "A man is supposed to be considered innocent till he's proven guilty."

Daggett grunted. "What idiot said that? Everybody's guilty of somethin'."

The shack's furnishings were sparse: a small iron stove, two steel cots, the table and a couple of chairs. The stove was still too warm for comfort. Andy and Daggett hand-cuffed the pair together. The chain between them was looped around the frame of a cot. Daggett said, "You'd have a hard time draggin' that cot out the door, and a harder time tryin' to get on a horse with it. Was I you, I'd settle down and try to get a good night's sleep."

The clerk had said little. Now he protested, "They can't stretch out and get comfortable that way."

Daggett said, "They'd just as well get used to bein' un-comfortable. They're goin' to have a lot of it. Now, you lay down on that cot they're hooked to and see how quiet you can be."

"What're you goin' to charge me with?"

"We'll think of somethin'. Pickard, you take the first watch. I'll stand the last one." Daggett laid himself down on the second cot and soon was snoring peacefully. Andy pulled a chair out from the table. With his pistol in his lap, he settled down for some long, dark hours.

Daggett awakened sometime after midnight to relieve Andy. He asked, "The boys give you any trouble?"

"No, but they've been restless. I don't think they've slept much."

"Maybe by the time we get to town they'll be wore down enough to answer questions."

The handcuffed prisoners awoke with complaints about sore backs and aching shoulders. Daggett ignored them. He ordered the clerk, "Get over to that stove and stir us up some breakfast. The mornin' is half over with."

It was still dark outside.

Soon the clerk had made up a tall stack of flapjacks. Andy found a jar of syrup. Granger complained, "This syrup's got ants in it."

Daggett said, "A few ants are probably healthy for you."

Andy tried to remove as many as possible from his own breakfast, though he could not get them all. The blackstrap molasses was strong enough to overwhelm any flavor the ants might add.

Breakfast finished, Daggett sacked what foodstuffs remained and said, "Time to saddle up."

Granger grumbled, "If they kill us before you can get us to town, you'll be sorry."

"Not very," Daggett said. "Dead men are easier to transport. You don't have to watch them as close."

Granger and Burns appeared increasingly nervous. Judging that Granger would be most likely to crack first, Andy sought to add to the weight on his shoulders. He asked Daggett, "Do you know if stealin' cattle is a capital offense in this county?"

Matter-of-factly Daggett said, "Depends on the judge. I would guess Zachary to be one who favors the rope."

Burns warned his partner, "They're tryin' to scare you. Don't pay them no mind." His voice was shaky.

Granger turned on him. "Why shouldn't we talk if it saves our lives? I doubt as any of them sons of bitches would be willin' to die for us."

Saddling his horse, Burns tugged violently at the girth, buckling it too tightly for his mount's comfort. He said, "There's some things a man just doesn't do, like peach on his friends."

Granger said, "There comes a time when friendship ends and a man has to take care of himself." He turned to Andy. "Would you Rangers be willin' to make a deal?"

Andy glanced at Daggett. "What kind of a deal?"

"You just got a little rustlin' charge against us, and

there's a good chance you might not make it stick. What if we was to tell you about all the regulators we know?"

"In return for what?"

"In return for lookin' north while we ride south. We'd leave this part of the country."

"And never come back?"

"We *couldn't* come back. Our lives wouldn't be worth a Mexican *centavo* around here."

Andy asked Daggett, "What do you think?"

Daggett said, "I always like to sample the goods before I buy. Give us some names."

Face darkening, Burns said in a loud voice, "Ed, don't you give him nothin'. If you do, I'll kill you myself unless the regulators get to you first." He put his foot in the stirrup and started to swing up into the seat.

A bullet sang past him and sent splinters flying from the side of the barn. Granger exclaimed, "Goddlemighty!" His frightened horse jerked loose and left Granger down on one knee, exposed to another shot. He flattened himself on his belly.

Stunned, Andy shouted, "Everybody down!" He was already in the saddle, but he swung to the ground, drawing his rifle from its scabbard. His horse danced excitedly. Andy tried to keep it between him and the source of the first shot.

A second bullet took Burns in the chest. He gave only a grunt and collapsed like an empty sack.

Daggett found a target and fired his rifle. Andy saw leaves fly from a cedar tree. A man darted from behind it and disappeared in the cover of another. Andy and Daggett both fired at the bush. A dark figure jumped up and ran.

Shortly Andy caught a glimpse of a horseman galloping away. He took one shot but knew it was wasted.

Struggling for breath, Andy asked Daggett, "Did you recognize him?"

"Not for sure, but I smell Rodock. Him and that damned rifle."

Cautiously, aware that a second shooter could still be out there, Andy turned to examine Miley Burns. One glance told him the man was dead. He picked up Burns's hat and covered his face with it.

The clerk had kept his horse between himself and the ambushers. Now he walked over to help his brother to his feet. He asked, "Are you hit?"

Granger trembled. "No, but that bullet came so close that I could smell it." He fastened an accusing gaze on Andy. "Thought you-all were goin' to protect us. Look what they done to Miley."

Andy had no satisfactory answer. "If they want you bad enough, there's no ironclad guarantees."

Granger appeared almost ready to break down and cry. "I'm next. They'll never let you get me to town. They may get you Rangers, too."

Daggett walked out a little way, holding his rifle, searching for signs of a second man. Andy said, "We've got to try, anyway." He paused. "Unless . . ."

Granger was grasping at straws. "Unless what?"

"Unless you'd give us the names of all the regulators you know. Then maybe I could talk Daggett into lettin' you go."

"Wouldn't do any good. They'd trail me from here to the Pecos River."

"You'd need to go a lot farther than that, like maybe California. Stay put while I talk to Daggett."

Andy met Daggett just far enough out that Granger could not hear the conversation. He said, "It'll be risky, takin' him in. The regulators want him dead."

Daggett said, "It'd be a small loss."

"Gettin' those names is more important than jailin' one small-time cow thief."

"I see where you're headed, Pickard, and I don't like it."

"We can catch cow thieves any time. We were sent here to try and break up the regulators. If word got out that we have the names, I think you'd see a big cloud of dust as they left the country."

"I'd rather catch them and see them salted away in the Huntsville penitentiary. There's no punishment if you let them get away."

"They'd have to leave everything behind and start again someplace else. I'd call that punishment."

"Do it my way and they won't get to start again, not for maybe ten or twenty years. Damn it, Pickard, they're criminals. It's against my religion to let trash like this get away."

"What if you caught a little fish, then saw a chance to catch a big one? Wouldn't you take the little one off of your line?"

"But I wouldn't throw him back in the water. I'd eat him along with the big one."

Andy had sensed from the first time they met that he and Daggett would not agree on much except the weather, and perhaps not even that. He said, "Sergeant Ryker told me you have the final authority, but I'm askin' you to let me have my way about Granger. I believe it'd be a good trade."

Daggett's eyes threatened a fight. If it went that far, Andy suspected that Daggett would win. The older Ranger declared, "One of these days, Pickard, you'll turn some scoundrel loose, and he'll come back and empty a gun into your gizzard."

"That'd be my hard luck, not yours."

"And hard luck for your little wife, too." Daggett clenched a fist, then eased. "All right, tell him if he'll give us the names, we won't prosecute him."

Andy returned to the shaken Granger. He said, "I had a hard time talkin' him into it, and I don't know how long he'll stand hitched. You'd better give me the names before he changes his mind. Or before the shooter comes back."

The clerk urged, "Do it, Ed. Those regulators aren't your friends. They sent somebody to kill you."

Still trembling, Granger murmured, "There comes a time when a man has to watch out for his own skin."

Andy took the fugitive book from his pocket and turned to a blank page toward the back. Granger said, "One of them is Judge Zachary."

Andy almost dropped his pencil. "The judge? He's the last man I'd have thought of."

"He was a wheelhorse once. Now he's old and worn-out. They do what they want to and try to let him think he's still in charge. Mostly they take their orders from Scanlon, the wagon yard man."

Andy was not surprised. He had never seen Scanlon smile. He had noticed that the man was always careful in counting his change. Any mistakes made would be some-one else's.

Granger said, "Another one is the sheriff's deputy, Salty Willis. If he was left in charge of the jail while I was in it, he'd let them come in and get me."

Andy asked, "What about the sheriff himself? I always suspected he might've let them know I was takin' Bigelow to a safe place."

Granger said, "Old Pete? No, he's so honest he shines in the dark. The regulators would've killed him if they weren't afraid that'd bring you Rangers down in force. Anyway, Judge Zachary wouldn't have stood for it. They knew he'd try the whole bunch and hang them. Pete's his oldest friend."

"They could've killed the judge too."

"They need him on the bench, in case."

Andy wrote *Salty Willis* and asked, "Who else?"

Counting on his fingers, Granger began ticking off names until Andy had more than a dozen. Finally he said, "I can't think of any more. We never got to know them all. They guarded their secrets."

Andy asked, "Did they pay you to steal cattle?"

Granger said, "No, but they let us sell what we took and keep the money. They wanted each side to think the other one done it. Maybe the Teals and the McIntoshes would kill each other off. Even if they didn't, we'd eventually break both families. The regulators could pick up the pieces."

"Looks like you two were penny-ante players in a high-dollar game."

Granger said bitterly, "They'd throw us away like an old boot."

Andy had recognized a few of the names. Most were unfamiliar to him. At the bottom of the list he added a phrase: "I swear on the Bible that this testymony is true, so help me God." He said, "Sign it."

Granger asked, "Where's the Bible?"

"The thought is what counts."

Granger scrawled his name. Andy said, "Now you'd better catch your horse before Daggett changes his mind."

Granger was still dubious. "I hope you won't shoot me in the back and claim I tried to escape."

Andy said, "That's not the way Rangers do things," though he knew it had been done from time to time. The *ley de fuga* was an old custom imported from Mexico.

The clerk asked, "What about me?"

"We've got no hold on you. Go where you want to."

"I'd like to go back to town. I hope I've still got a job in the hotel."

"You don't want to go with your brother?"

"Him and me, we took different roads a long time ago."

"Fine. You can ride along with us if you want to."

The clerk shook his head. "Ridin' with you Rangers is liable to be dangerous now that you've got your list. I'd rather everybody thought I just took time off to go fishin'. That might get me fired, but it won't get me shot."

The two brothers shook hands, and the clerk rode away.

Ed Granger started to get on his horse. Daggett challenged him. "Where the hell do you think you're goin'?"

Confused and frightened, Granger said, "You-all said if I'd give you the names, you'd let me go free."

Coldly Daggett replied, "I said we wouldn't prosecute you. I didn't say we wouldn't keep you as a witness."

Andy protested, "But you made it sound like you'd turn him loose."

"It got us what we wanted from him, didn't it? He's just a miserable cow thief. All's fair in love and war, and this is war."

Feeling betrayed, Andy could see that Daggett had no intention of backing down. He said, "Are you ready to take the responsibility if somebody kills him?"

"I wouldn't have it any other way." Daggett turned toward Granger and asked, "Have you got a shovel around here someplace? You've got a man to bury."

12

Finding the ambusher's trail was no problem for Daggett. He said, "Looks like he's headed toward town. Once he gets there, we won't be able to sort out his tracks."

Andy asked, "You don't see anything special about them?"

"They look like a thousand others."

"Then they won't help us find out who he was."

"I figure it had to be Rodock, and I can figure who told him where we went. I'd like to have free use of that Deputy Willis for about ten minutes."

"Looks like he's the reason I never got Bigelow to the town limits."

"We'll get them, and everybody else on that list if they don't scatter like quail." Daggett frowned. "There's still the feud between the Teals and the McIntoshes. The job ain't done as long as that goes on."

"It's not our place to shoot two stubborn old men. That's what it may take."

All the way to town, Andy kept expecting someone to take a shot at the prisoner. Granger was slumped in his saddle, head down, as if he had already given himself up for dead. He was only slightly relieved when he saw the town ahead.

Andy said, "We've just about made it, and you're still alive."

Granger mumbled, "They'll get me all the same. That jailhouse won't stop them."

It was afternoon, and Andy was hungry. He said, "The hotel dinin' room is closed till supper, but maybe Kennison's chili joint is open."

Daggett said, "That old geezer talks till your ears hurt. He's not on the list, is he?"

"Granger didn't mention him."

"We'd better take Granger to jail first."

Andy shook his head. "And maybe leave him alone with that Deputy Willis? We'll take him with us to Kennison's. He's probably hungry, too." Andy made his voice firm enough to show that he meant to have his way. Daggett put up no argument. Andy was gratified at even a small victory over the strong-minded Ranger. There had been very few.

Noontime customers were long gone. The bewhiskered proprietor was asleep on a cot against the far wall of his small kitchen. Daggett shook him. "Wake up. You've got some hungry customers."

Kennison yawned and rubbed his eyes, trying to see clearly. "Why didn't you come and eat at noontime, like decent folks?"

"We were busy protectin' the public."

Kennison's eyes cleared enough that he recognized the visitors. "Rangers. Why didn't you say so? I can fix you anything you want as long as it's beef stew. I still got some settin' on the back of the stove. Won't take long to heat it."

Andy said, "Right now, even boiled cabbage would taste good."

Daggett said, "You don't like boiled cabbage? I always kind of favored it myself."

He would, Andy thought.

The cook noticed Granger for the first time and saw the handcuffs. "Are you feedin' him, too?"

Andy nodded. "It'll be a new experience for him, eatin' legal beef."

Kennison poked dry wood into the stove and stirred the dying embers back to life. He asked, "I know this man. What're you chargin' him with?"

Andy said, "We've got several things to choose from."

"He always had a partner when he came in here to eat."

"He won't be comin' in anymore. We buried him."

Kennison dropped a pot lid. It clattered on the stove top. "He's dead?"

Andy hesitated. He knew that whatever he told this man would be spread around town by nightfall.

Daggett declared dryly, "If he wasn't dead, we wouldn't have buried him."

Kennison moved the stew pot over onto the warmer part of the stove. "Shot tryin' to escape, I suppose?"

Daggett said, "That's as good a story as any."

Kennison ladled stew into three bowls and set it in front of the Rangers and their prisoner. He brought the blackened coffeepot and filled their cups. Instead of being critical, he seemed to take pleasure in what he believed Andy and Daggett had done. "It sure don't pay anybody to mess with the Rangers. Did he tell you anything before he died?"

Daggett said, "If he had, maybe he wouldn't be so dead."

Andy said, "We'd just as soon everybody didn't know what we've just told you. Or about us takin' Granger prisoner."

Kennison said, "The word'll get out. There's people in this town that can't keep a secret."

Andy sopped up the last of his stew with a cold biscuit. It was tasty and had the added virtue of being cheap. Daggett had already finished eating. He said, "We'd better take Granger to the sheriff."

He looked back as they left the café, Granger in tow. "Tellin' Kennison is like puttin' it on the telegraph. But maybe it'll make the right people more afraid of us."

Andy said, "Or make them shoot us from behind."

Sheriff Seymour sat in the jail office, working on the tax books. Deputy Willis was listlessly sweeping the floor, pushing the dirt just outside the door where visitors would track it right back in. Seymour stood up, looking expectantly at the prisoner. "There was supposed to be two of them."

Andy said, "We had to bury one."

"You killed him?"

"Not us. Somebody hid out in the brush and shot him."

"Too bad." Seymour took Granger by the arm and led him back to a cell. He removed the handcuffs, then locked the door. Granger looked sick at his stomach. Andy doubted that it was the fault of the beef stew.

Seymour asked, "Did you-all get anything out of him?"

Andy said, "After his partner was shot, Granger decided to give us all the names he knew."

"You got them?"

"In my pocket."

Seymour could not appear more surprised if a herd of buffalo had stampeded into the room. He glanced at Daggett for confirmation. Daggett solemnly nodded. Salty Willis looked as if Andy had kicked him in the stomach. He leaned on the broom and almost lost his balance.

Seymour asked, "Can I have a look at that list?"

Andy said, "You probably know them all." He turned to the page in the back of his fugitive list.

Seymour's mouth dropped open as he read. "Judge Zachary, for God's sake. One of the best friends I ever had." He ran his finger down the list and looked up quickly. "Salty!"

Salty Willis had slipped away.

Seymour exclaimed, "That damned whelp. And I've been tryin' to train him to take over my job when I get old."

"We'll get him," Andy promised.

Seymour said, "This list is like a wagonload of dynamite. What're you goin' to do with it?"

"Keep it safe," Andy said. "And notify company headquarters that I've got it."

"I'd as soon have a rattlesnake in my pocket. Mind if I make a copy?"

"Go ahead. It won't take long for the word to get out anyway."

Seymour copied the list onto the back of a WANTED poster. He said, "Andy, I'm worried about you carryin' this thing on you. It's like hangin' a big target around your neck."

"You've got a copy now. We can make more if we need them."

"But copies won't have Granger's signature on them. They won't carry the legal weight of the original. You could lock it in the county clerk's safe." He caught himself. "No, you can't. He's on the list."

Hearing heavy footsteps in the hall, Andy slipped the fugitive book into his pocket. He turned to see Judge Zachary stride through the office door, trailed by smoke from his black cigar. The judge said, "I didn't know you Rangers were back in town. Did you have any luck?"

Andy wondered if Willis had warned the judge. He tried to read the man's expression. "Some good, some bad. We took two prisoners, but a sharpshooter killed one of them."

"That's bad."

"The good is that we got the other one, and he gave us a list of regulators' names."

The judge's face flushed. He bit down heavily on the cigar. He asked, "Might I see that list?"

The sheriff handed him the copy he had just made. "You'll find a bunch of your friends on it. I regret to say that you'll find yourself there, too. On account of that, I'm placin' you under arrest."

The judge's face went a deeper red. "On what charge?"

"I'll have to consult the statutes. There's bound to be a law against a judge bein' part of an outfit like the regulators."

Shaken, Zachary demanded, "This so-called list, on whose word is it based?"

Andy answered, "A man named Ed Granger. He's in that cell yonder."

"Ed Granger? A common cow thief. His word would carry little weight in any fair court."

Andy asked, "How do you know he's a cow thief? Accordin' to him, you were a party to orders for him and others to take cattle from the Teals and the McIntoshes."

"I never gave such orders. The fact is that the regulators have paid little attention to me the last few years. They act on their own volition."

"Be that as it may, we've got Granger's affidavit, witnessed by Logan Daggett and me."

"An affidavit signed by a known thief? You have no case."

Andy said, "Once we round up some of your vigilante friends and get them to testify, we'll see what kind of case we've got."

The judge asked, "Where is the original list?"

Andy patted his pocket. He said, "I'm keepin' it where it'll be safe."

"You are assuming that *you* will be safe. Considering what is at stake, that may be an empty wish."

The sheriff said, "In the meantime, Judge, I'd be obliged if you'd step back to one of the cells with me."

The judge looked genuinely hurt. "I thought you were my friend."

"I am, but I'd arrest my own mother if she broke the law."

"And if your case does not stick? What of your job?"

"I'm ready to retire anyhow. But first I want to see the regulators put out of business for once and for all. Me and the Rangers will see to it that you won't get lonesome. We'll bring you some company."

"I should be allowed to post bond."

Seymour nodded. "But we'd need a judge to sign the papers. We'll have to send for one that's not under arrest."

Zachary began to wilt. "You know a prisoner was once shot in his cell here. What assurance have I that I will be safe?"

"They're more apt to try and free you than to try and kill you. It's the job of me and the Rangers to see that neither thing comes to pass."

The judge looked first at the sheriff, then at Andy and Daggett. Gravely he said, "You don't realize what you are dealing with. You could all three be dead before the sun rises." He paused, waiting for a response. Receiving none, he jerked his head at Seymour. "Very well, Pete, show me where you want me to go."

Andy heard the loud clang as the cell door slammed shut. He said to Daggett, "He's right about the list bein' shaky evidence in court."

Seymour returned, downcast. "I wish it'd been just about anybody besides Judge Zachary. He's always meant law and order around here."

Andy said, "Maybe he couldn't get the kind of law and order he wanted in court, so he turned to the regulators."

Daggett said, "Rodock didn't come here just to play cards. It's my guess the regulators have been payin' him to keep things stirred up. He was probably part of that raid on the Teals. Like as not, he was in the brush and fired the shot that creased Ethan McIntosh."

Seymour said, "When Salty spreads the word that we've

got Granger and the judge in here, the regulators are liable to come at us. And because you're carryin' the original affidavit, they'll be gunnin' for you special, Andy."

Andy had known at a subconscious level that everything was moving in this direction. Now the full cold weight of it sank in. Those men were deadly. His being a Ranger would not prevent them from killing him.

Seymour said, "I saw the county clerk in his office awhile ago. I'll go arrest him so the judge'll have somebody besides Granger to talk to."

The sheriff was back shortly, alone. He said, "His helper told me that Salty Willis stopped by and spoke to him for a minute. He left the office in a hurry."

Andy said, "Reckon he's quittin' the country, or is he roundin' up other regulators to make a fight of it?"

Seymour said, "I'd call it fifty-fifty either way."

Daggett said, "We'll lock ourselves in and stand guard here tonight in case the judge's friends try to break him out."

Andy agreed. "You'd better let Carrie know."

Daggett said, "I suppose, but I hate to make her fret."

Andy said, "She'll do that whether you tell her or not."

Seymour suggested, "You could send her away from town so she won't know what's goin' on. August Hawkins would put her up. He's got a good heart . . . for a sheepman."

Andy shook his head. "She would see through that in a minute. I'd bet she wouldn't go."

Daggett declared, "It's a woman's duty to do what her husband tells her to."

Seymour gave Daggett a sympathetic look. "You've only

been married for a few days, and to a redheaded woman. You've got some hard lessons ahead of you."

Andy saw no sign of excitement in the street. It was too early for news to have spread much. He and Daggett rode their horses to the front of the hotel and dismounted. To their surprise, Carrie sat on the veranda with her brothers Bud and Lanny. Daggett went up and self-consciously gave her a peck on the cheek.

She said, "I expected you-all to be back last night. I thought maybe you two went to Mexico."

Daggett said, "We would if we had to. Tell her, Pickard."

Andy explained while Carrie listened wide-eyed, without speaking. The clerk, Granger, stood in the doorway, listening. Evidently he had not lost his job for being absent without leave.

Daggett said, "Looks like we may be in for trouble." He shifted his gaze to Bud Teal. "What brings you Teals to town?"

Bud said, "We came to see about our sister. I did, anyway. Lanny came to see Lucy Babcock."

Lanny did not have a happy face. Andy asked, "Didn't you see her?"

Lanny didn't answer. Bud said, "He saw her. She was with somebody else, and it wasn't Jake McIntosh. There's a new man workin' in the blacksmith shop. He's better lookin' than Lanny or Jake either one, and strong enough to whip them both."

Andy had been afraid the rivalry between Lanny and Jake might touch off a potentially fatal conflict between the families. Perhaps Lucy's fickle nature had reduced that threat.

Bud asked, "What's this trouble you mentioned?"

Andy explained about the list and the fact that Judge Zachary was in jail. Bud was shaken. He said, "I always knew he didn't care much for us Teals, or the McIntoshes, either, but I felt like he was fair to us when he was on the bench."

Andy repeated what Granger had said about the regulators taking their cattle and trying to promote violence between the two families.

Lanny took the news with a sour face. "We'll tell Pa. Maybe he'll be mad enough to fight somebody besides Old Man McIntosh."

Bud shook his head. "They've butted heads too long for him to get over it that easy." He swore under his breath. "I'd've suspicioned just about anybody in town before I'd've thought of the judge. Mason Gaines, for instance. I never knew such a bellyacher, always wantin' to change things around."

Andy said, "Gaines isn't on the list. I wish he was there instead of the judge."

Bud asked, "What happens now?"

Andy said, "There's a good chance some of the regulators may try to deliver the judge. They'd like to get their hands on Granger and the original affidavit, too."

Bud said, "I'll help you-all stand guard tonight. What's more, I'll send Lanny out to the ranch to bring in the boys. Pa, too, if he'll come."

Andy said, "It's not your fight."

"That mob has been waitin' like buzzards to pick over the leavin's after us Teals and McIntoshes kill one another. Damn right it's our fight." He turned to Daggett. "Has she told you yet? She wrote the letter that brought you Rangers here."

Daggett was taken by surprise. He asked Carrie, "Why?"

She clutched his arm. "Because I was afraid some of our family would get killed if things went on like they were. I thought the Rangers could put a stop to the trouble. I didn't sign the letter because I knew Pa would raise hell."

Daggett said, "You were sure right about that."

Bud ordered Lanny, "Go fetch the boys, and don't stop to stay hello to Lucy."

Lanny shook his head. "I've got nothin' to say to her." He trotted to where his horse was tied.

Bud spotted a Bar F cowboy at the blacksmith shop. He said, "I'll go tell him what you told me. The McIntosh boys ought to be interested."

Carrie held tightly to Daggett's arm. She asked, "What makes you think they might try to free the judge tonight? If I were a regulator and thought my secret was out, I'd be busy getting away. I wouldn't have time to worry about what happens to the judge."

Daggett said, "Most of them have got cattle and other property they wouldn't want to leave."

Andy said, "Besides, they've held the whip hand around here too long to give up easy. The judge and his court have helped them hold on to that power."

Bud returned after his conversation with the Bar F cowboy. Carrie asked him, "Do you think Pa would really come, after all the hard things he's said?"

Bud said, "He wouldn't admit it, but he's been like a lost kid without you around the place."

She leaned against Daggett. "He has to get used to it.

I'm a married woman now. I'll go where my husband goes."

Bud nodded. "That's the way it ought to be. If Pa can't see it, that's his hard luck. I think you picked a good man this—" He broke off short, though Andy knew he was about to say "this time." He sensed that Carrie realized it, too. Unlike before, it seemed not to upset her.

Daggett took her in his arms and said, "We'd better be gettin' back to the jailhouse. We don't want to leave the sheriff all by himself."

Carrie asked, "What do you want me to do?"

"If anything starts, keep away from the windows. Hunker down behind a stove or somethin' else solid. And don't worry."

"Don't worry? Logan Daggett, sometimes you say the dumbest damn things."

Daggett turned quickly and walked down the steps. Andy and Bud followed. Andy said, "We'd better turn our horses loose in the wagon yard."

Daggett said, "And arrest the owner. Remember, he's on the list."

They did not find their quarry. His helper was alone, forking hay into an overhead rack. He said, "Salty Willi: came by here in a devil of a hurry. Boss saddled up and left with him. All he said to me was to take care of things till he gets back."

Andy said, "So he does intend to come back."

Daggett added, "And not by himself, I'd wager."

Sheriff Seymour sat in a chair away from his desk. He held a shotgun in his lap. He acknowledged Bud with surprised nod, then said soberly, "The telegraph office has

sent over a couple of wires. I'm afraid it's not good news."
He handed one to Andy and one to Daggett.

Andy unfolded his and read. It said: STATE APPROPRIA-
TIONS CUT. YOU ARE RELIEVED OF DUTY. REPORT BACK IM-
MEDIATELY FOR DISCHARGE.

He read it a second time before the full impact hit him.
He was not sure whether to laugh or curse. He said, "I've
been fired."

Daggett seemed in momentary shock. "Me too. All
those years, the outlaws kept tryin' to get me but never did.
Now the money counters have brought me down."

Andy looked again at the wire. "It says report immediately. But we've got these prisoners. And what'll we
do about the regulators? Are we supposed to turn our backs
and walk away?"

The sheriff said, "To me, it says you've got no authority
to do anything. You're supposed to dump it all in my lap
and leave." Anxiety came into his eyes. "I ain't got that
big a lap. I'd just as well open the cell doors and leave with
you."

Daggett faced the wall and considered the problem, his
fists clenched. When he turned, his look was fierce. "Like
hell! They sent us to do a job, and be damned if we're quittin' with it half done. We've still got all the authority that
really counts." He slapped his hand against the pistol on
his hip. His gaze fastened on Andy.

Andy said, "We could get in trouble."

"I've been in trouble since I was eight years old."

Andy nodded. "Come to think of it, so have I."

The sheriff looked hopefully from one to the other.
"Does this mean you're stayin'?"

Andy said, "It does."

Seymour reached into a desk drawer. "Since they've taken away your authority as Rangers, I'll swear you in as my deputies till this trouble is over with." He handed each of them a badge. Hesitantly he offered one to Bud, who accepted it.

Daggett asked, "What's the pay?"

"Salty was gettin' a dollar and a half a day."

"That won't hardly cover hotel expenses, but I'll take it."

Andy said, "So will I."

The sheriff said, "Now if you'll excuse me a few minutes, the judge has been after me to fetch him some cigars from his office. He's particular about the brand."

Dryly Daggett said, "Down at Huntsville, he'll smoke what they give him."

Seymour said, "I can't forget that he's been my friend."

Daggett shook his head. "Looks to me like *he* forgot it. I don't favor givin' him any slack."

"You haven't known him as long as I have." Seymour left.

Andy took another look at the wire, though by now he had it memorized. "I'd figured on leavin' the Rangers sooner or later, but this forces my hand. I reckon I'll start ranchin' a little smaller than I'd expected to. What about you, Daggett?"

"Everybody knows my name. I don't think I'll have much trouble findin' a job runnin' a cow outfit for somebody. I've got a wife to support."

Bud said, "I'll bet we can find you somethin' around here. That'd keep Carrie close to home."

Seymour returned with a box of cigars. Andy heard

the judge tell him gratefully, "Much obliged, old friend. It is often the small pleasures in life that mean the most."

Seymour said, "I just don't understand why you let yourself get into a fix like this, a man of your caliber mixed up with a band of ruffians like the regulators."

The judge bit off one end of a cigar. His voice was weary. "It was easy at first. Things here had gotten out of hand. Juries would not convict because they feared retaliation. The regulators could do what I could not, so I closed my eyes. In time, I was one of them. My court enforced the law in ways the law never intended. But the best intentions can go awry. I found myself with blood on my hands that would not wash clean. It was like being trapped on a runaway wagon and unable to jump off." He shrugged. "The truth is, they don't pay much attention to me anymore. They pat me on the head like an old dog and do what they want. They like me to be on the bench so I can rule their way when necessary."

Seymour said, "Looks to me like you could've gotten off that wagon if you really wanted to."

"I was not certain that I wanted to get off. Power can be more intoxicating than whiskey."

Andy stood in the open door for a time, watching the street. Passersby stopped for a moment and looked toward the jail. He sensed that the news was spreading around town. Though he saw nothing more tangible than that, he sensed a growing tension out there, or perhaps it was simply his own.

Daggett warned, "You better get out of that door and close it. You'd make a good target for a sharpshooter like Rodock."

Andy shut the door and barred it, then opened a small loophole at eye level so he could see out.

Seymour said, "People laughed about me puttin' up curtains in the jailhouse. None of them match. But at least nobody can climb up outside and shoot at us through the windows."

Bud seemed vaguely disturbed. He kept staring toward an empty cell. Andy made a guess. "Is that the one where Skeen was killed?"

"It is."

"From what I've heard, the regulators did your family a favor."

Bud grimaced. He looked around to see that no one was close enough to hear. In a quiet voice he said, "We never told a soul about this, not Carrie, not even Pa. It wasn't the regulators. Me and my brothers done it . . . for Carrie, and for us."

"The regulators got the blame."

"There wasn't many people blamed them. Most thought they did everybody a service. But you can see why we never wanted Carrie to know. In spite of him bein' a rattlesnake, she loved him, or thought she did. She's got a better man now."

"You'd better not ever tell Daggett. He might let it slip, or Carrie might read it in his eyes."

"I don't know why I even told *you*. Just wanted to get it off of my chest, I suppose."

Andy said, "It'll die with me. But not tonight, I hope."

Someone knocked on the door. Andy carefully approached the loophole and looked out. Editor Tolliver stood there. He said, "I bear a message."

Andy asked, "Are you heeled?"

"I never carry a gun. I do my fighting with a pen."

Andy opened the door slowly, making certain no one was waiting to rush in behind Tolliver.

Tolliver said, "The regulators out there chose me to be a go-between. They said it's because I'm neutral. I suppose that means I don't much give a damn one way or the other."

Andy said, "Do you?"

"Not enough to mention. Whichever way this all goes, I'll get a book out of it. Then I'll move to New Orleans and live the life of a rich author."

"You said you've got a message."

"Those men are in dead earnest. They say they'll lay siege to this jail until they either blast you out or starve you out."

Daggett angered. "The hell you say!"

"*They* say, not me. I'm just the messenger."

Andy asked, "Are they wearin' hoods?"

"No. I suppose they see no need inasmuch as their identities have been revealed anyway."

Andy said, "This jail has got stone walls, so they're not apt to blast us out. As for starvin' us out, tell them that if we go hungry, the judge goes hungry, too. He stays right where he's at." He paused. "And remind them that any bullets that find their way in here are as apt to hit the judge as any of us."

"I'll tell them."

Seymour asked, "Who all is out there?"

"Your deputy Willis for one. And Scanlon, who owns the wagon yard. Willis thinks he's giving the orders, but the rest appear to be looking to Scanlon for leadership. Willis is in past his depth."

Seymour said regretfully, "I'm afraid he always was. I

don't know why I thought he might be the one to succeed me someday."

Tolliver said, "He has been seduced by the prospect of easy money. It is a delusion and a snare."

Andy thought Tolliver was probably deluding himself about the prospect of getting rich from writing a book. But, each man to his own dreams, and his own delusions.

The judge yelled from his cell, "How many did you say are out there?" On hearing there were eight or nine, he was disappointed. "I thought there'd be more."

Tolliver said, "I suspect some of the regulators are busy getting ready to leave the country. Fair-weather friends aren't of much help in a thunderstorm." He told Andy and Daggett, "I'll tell them the judge is hungry. Perhaps they will allow Kennison to bring something over from that greasy café of his."

Andy closed and barred the door as Tolliver left. The regulators gave the editor time to get clear, then opened up with a fusillade. Andy could hear bullets whine off of the stone walls. A few struck the heavy wooden door but did not penetrate it.

Granger howled in fear and flattened himself on the floor of his cell.

Andy said, "They're just lettin' us know they're serious."

Daggett said, "I never had no doubt about that."

Toward dusk, Kennison brought two steaming pots. He said, "Hope you-all like beans and beef stew because I've about run out of the makin's for anything else." He seemed eager to catch a glimpse of Judge Zachary in his cell. He said, "Remember me, Judge? You sentenced me to two days in here once. Said I was drunk and disorderly. I've never been drunk in my whole life, except for a few times." He turned back to the sheriff. "Who's payin' for this grub?"

Seymour said, "The county."

"With things so uncertain, I'd like to be paid now. You might not be in a shape to pay me later."

Seymour bristled. "You don't think we can handle it?"

"No offense meant, but there's more of them than there is of you. And I remember what happened to Skeen."

The sheriff said, "This jail is like a fort."

"So was the Alamo."

The sheriff dished out a bowl of beans and stew and passed them to Judge Zachary through a narrow slot in the cell door. Pain in the sheriff's voice indicated how much he regretted this turn of affairs. "I'm afraid he didn't bring any biscuits, but I'll fetch you some coffee directly."

Zachary sampled the stew. He said, "Whatever his hygienic shortcomings, the old rascal can cook."

Just before dark, Daggett said, "Pickard, lift the bar on the door. I'll go out and look around. Might get a better idea what we're up against."

Andy cautioned, "You may not get back."

"You be ready to let me in quick."

Daggett went out. Andy closed the door but did not replace the bar. The big Ranger had been out only a few seconds when several bullets whined off the stone wall. Daggett shouted, "Open the door!"

He rushed back in, breathing hard. Andy barred the door behind him. Daggett said, "That damned Rodock and his rifle." He blinked hard. "I've got rock dust in my eyes."

Andy asked, "Did you see who-all's out there?"

"They didn't give me time for a tally."

Seymour said, "I'll stand watch a while. You'd all better try to get some sleep if you can. I have a notion they may worry us all night."

Andy stretched out on a cot in an unlocked cell, but his eyes were wide open. Sleep did not come on command. After a time he noticed a window curtain move. A hand appeared, lifting it. Andy drew his pistol, aimed above the hand, and fired. From outside he heard a startled curse. The curtain fell back into place.

As he had expected, shots were fired at irregular intervals during the night. They ricocheted off the stone walls or, a few times, thudded into the heavy door. In the wee hours, Daggett arose from his cot and walked to the door. He said, "They're tryin' to keep us from gettin' any sleep, but they're wastin' their time. I couldn't have slept noway."

He opened the loophole in the door, poked his pistol barrel though it and fired into the night. "In case any of *them* are tryin' to sleep," he said.

Time went by at a terrapin's pace. After a period that seemed long enough for three nights, the promise of daylight began to show through the curtains. Andy walked to a window and carefully lifted the curtain's corner. He saw early orange streaks of sunrise. There was no movement on the street. Usually much of the town was up and going by daylight. No regulators were in sight, but he knew they were there, biding their time.

Seymour rattled around the stove, rebuilding the fire, putting the coffeepot on. He stood in front of the judge's cell and said, "I'll have you some coffee directly, Judge. Did you get any sleep?"

"Not much," Zachary replied. "Those men out there

mean well for me, but they don't seem to realize that old men like us need our rest."

"They probably figure they've worn us down. I wouldn't be surprised if they try to rush us this mornin'."

The judge said, "That would be a mistake on their part. The war taught me that it is futile to charge an impregnable position. One must find a different course of attack."

"Like what?"

"Even if I knew, I could not divulge it to you. My neck is on the chopping block."

"I'm sorry to've had a hand in puttin' it there."

"You are doing your duty, Pete, as I have always tried to do mine, by my own lights."

Seymour returned to the front of the jail, where Andy peered beneath a window curtain. He said, "It's time I gave up this job. There's some people I hate to have to put in jail."

Daggett grunted. "I doubt you ever jailed anybody for singin' too loud in church. Most of them deserved what they got."

Seymour said, "I wish I could be like you. It's a lot simpler when you can't see but one side."

As the sun came up, a shower of bullets rattled against the walls. One penetrated the door, leaving a hole with splintered edges. Daggett said, "Rodock's rifle."

Andy said, "This thing between you and him must go back a long ways."

Daggett nodded. "We were boys together. Hunted, fished, rode over the country like two wild Indians. But as we started sproutin' whiskers, he went off in one direction and I went another. There came a time when I was sent to arrest him, and he tried to kill me. Almost did. It's hard to remember we was ever friends. I'll probably have to kill him sooner or later."

"You'll regret it like Seymour regrets havin' the judge in here as a prisoner."

"If your best dog gets the hydrophoby, you have to shoot it no matter how much you hate to. I'm afraid Rodock has turned into a hydrophoby dog."

Their conversation was interrupted by another short fusillade. One bullet came through a window and ricocheted across the room, prompting a curse from Daggett. "I'll make Rodock eat that damned rifle."

Presently Tolliver knocked on the door again. He shouted, "Is everybody all right in there?"

"Nobody's dead," Andy answered after peering through the small loophole. "You got another message?"

"I'm sorry to bring bad tidings, but the regulators have sent me to offer a trade. They want the judge. They also want Granger."

"They've got nothin' to trade that we'd want."

"I'm afraid they do. They have taken Daggett's lady hostage. Look at the hotel porch. You can see for yourself."

Andy caught a quick glimpse of Carrie standing in her nightgown, a man holding her. Daggett shoved him aside so he could see for himself. He exploded in anger, his voice wild. "Give up the judge? I'll kill him first! Him and the whole damned bunch." He brought up his rifle and tried to shove the barrel through the loophole.

Andy pushed it up so he could not take aim. He said, "It's too far, and your hands are shakin'."

"Turn aloose of me," Daggett cried.

"You're apt to hit Carrie. I don't think they'd really hurt a woman. It'd turn the whole town against them."

Tolliver said, "I wouldn't put too much stock in what they would or would not do. The hotel clerk tried to protect her. When I saw him he was lying on the floor. His head was bloody."

Daggett tore free of Andy's hold. "Stand aside. I'm goin' out. I'll hunt down and kill any son of a bitch that lays a hand on my wife."

Andy argued, "For God's sake, they'll cut you to pieces."

Daggett was a loaded cannon, on the point of firing. "If they do, I'll take a bunch of them with me." Daggett violently lifted the bar from the door and tossed it aside. Andy tried to wrestle with him, but it was like wrestling a bear. Daggett was in a frenzy. Andy swung a fist and caught him on the chin, but Daggett seemed not even to notice. He struck Andy a blow that sent him reeling backward. He lost his footing and went down on his back, hard. For a moment he could see nothing but lightning flashes playing against a stormy sky. Daggett opened the door and charged out, roaring like a wild man.

Bud took Andy's arms and brought him to his feet. He said, "Daggett's gone crazy."

"We'd better do what we can to help him. Sheriff, please let the judge out of his cell. Maybe the regulators will hold their fire if they see he's in the way."

Seymour said, "They might kill him by accident."

Andy found himself talking like Daggett. "Then it'll be their own fault. Let's do it."

His legs still unsteady, Andy went out, Bud Teal at his side. Daggett was already partway to the hotel, firing the rifle as he walked. He had surrendered himself to blind fury. The stable owner, Scanlon, fired at Daggett. Daggett fired back, and Scanlon went down on his face.

Andy saw that Deputy Salty Willis was the man holding Carrie's arm. Willis was distracted by Scanlon's fall.
Carrie broke loose from him. She bent down and came up
with a fist that struck Willis across the nose and sent him
stumbling backward against the wall. Andy heard her
shout something but could not make out the words. He suspected they were not for tender ears. She strode angrily
back into the hotel and slammed the door.

Zachary said, "I want you to know that I do not condone
the abuse of women. I shall see that Willis pays a price."

Andy admired Carrie's courage. "I think he already has.
Wouldn't be surprised if she broke his nose."

The judge said, "I trust you are gentlemen enough not
to shoot me in the back. I am taking my leave." He turned
away from Andy and Bud and the sheriff and walked
briskly toward the wagon yard.

Rodock had stepped onto the hotel porch to stand beside Willis. He cradled a rifle in his arms. He shouted,
"Daggett, you'd better stop where you're at!"

Daggett never broke his stride. Rodock moved halfway
down the steps. Daggett shouted, "Rodock, we've put this
off way too long!"

Rodock answered, "Then do your damndest." He swung
the rifle to his shoulder.

Daggett dropped to one knee. The two rifles fired at the
same time. It sounded as if but one shot echoed along the
street. Rodock dropped to his knees, then sprawled forward across the bottom steps. Daggett pushed back to his
feet. He seemed unhurt.

Carrie rushed out from the hotel, down the steps, and
into Daggett's arms. Embracing her fiercely, he asked,
"What did they do to you?"

She said, "Just dragged me out of bed. Nothing to kill a man about."

"They laid hands on you. That's enough. Thank God you're all right."

Andy saw a rip in Daggett's sleeve, and some blood. He said, "Looks like Rodock got you."

"It was Scanlon. Rodock ain't half as good a shot as he thinks he is." He turned Carrie back toward the hotel. "Come on, let's get you into some decent clothes. Can't have half the town starin' at you in your nightshirt."

Rodock was struggling to turn himself over onto his back. His right shoulder was a bloody mess. Trying to focus his gaze on Daggett, he wheezed, "Damn you, you ain't killed me yet."

Daggett picked up Rodock's rifle. "I intended to. Then I asked myself why I ought to give you an easy out. You crippled me once. I thought the fair thing was to return the favor."

"I'll come for you one day, Daggett."

"By the time you get out of the penitentiary you'll be too old to come after anybody."

Half a dozen horsemen galloped up the street. Andy squinted against the early morning sun. "Looks like your in-laws are here," he told Daggett.

Harper Teal led his sons Lanny and Cecil and two T Cross cowboys up to the hotel steps. The patriarch took in the scene with a sweeping glance. "Looks like we got here a little late."

Daggett did not reply. Andy said, "You're in time to help round up a few regulators." He pointed to Salty Willis, who held one hand to his face. "You can start with him. And yonder is Scanlon, if he's still alive."

Harper looked critically at Carrie. "What has my daughter to do with all this?"

"For one thing, she laid that bloody nose on Salty Willis."

Teal turned angrily on Daggett. "If you've done anything to put my daughter in danger . . ."

Daggett's only response was an angry stare.

Andy said, "Anybody who messes with her is in more danger than she is."

Tolliver looked down on Rodock with evident disappointment. He said, "It would have made a much more interesting story if you had killed him, Daggett."

Daggett said dryly, "You can kill him in your story. You'll make up most of it anyway." He looked down the street. "Ain't anybody sent for the doctor? Rodock could bleed to death layin' here."

Harper demanded, "Carrie, what're you doin' out here in your sleepin' clothes?"

Andy explained that the regulators had tried to use her as a hostage. He said, "She didn't take kindly to it."

Teal stood a moment, facing his daughter, then wrapped his arms around her. "Damn it, girl, we've missed you. I've missed you."

Carrie asked, "Am I back in the family now?"

Harper said, "You never was out of it. I was, for a while."

The Bar F riders appeared on the street, headed by Ethan McIntosh. Harper growled, "What're they doin' here?"

Bud said, "Same thing you are. They've come to help."

"We don't need no help from that old scoundrel."

Bud was disappointed. "I hoped when you realized what

the regulators tried to do to us, you'd bury the hatchet with Old Man McIntosh."

"You boys can, if you want to. But damned if I ever will, not in a hundred years."

Andy suspected Ethan McIntosh would feel the same way. If there was to be peace between the families, it would have to come from the younger members.

Daggett said severely, "Pickard, the judge has gotten away. You turned him loose, so you go and find him."

The sheriff said, "I think I know where he went. There's no big hurry."

Daggett put his arm around Carrie and started up the hotel steps. He said, "I hate to tell you, but I'm out of a job."

She smiled. "I'm sure you'll find plenty to do."

Andy soon realized that the sheriff was guiding him toward the judge's ranch. Seymour said, "It's where he always goes for peace and quiet. He says it's his thinkin' place."

Andy asked, "Reckon he'll give us any resistance?"

"He's a gentle man at heart, in spite of what all he let the regulators do. He always said he did enough fightin' in the big war. He never wanted to do any more."

"It's too bad that so many didn't come back feelin' the same way."

The two men rode through a scattering of cattle bearing an MC brand. Seymour said, "They're the judge's. He's always taken great pleasure in them."

"Does he own the land?"

"Just the cattle, and the section the house sits on. Like most others around here, he's a free range man. He claims the land by right of first possession, but legally the state still owns it."

"Somebody could take it from him and claim six-shooter possession."

"The regulators wouldn't have let them get away with it. They've had their good uses as well as their bad."

The judge's dog came to greet them, its tail wagging vigorously. It eagerly led them to the house, barking the news all the way. Judge Zachary stepped out onto his small porch. Andy looked for sign of a weapon but saw none. He reached down to his own pistol.

The sheriff shook his head. "You'll have no need for that. He has had shame enough without we add to it."

Zachary greeted the pair as genially as if they were on a purely social call. "Light and hitch, Pete. And you, Andy. Coffee ought to be comin' to a boil pretty soon."

Seymour dismounted and nodded in gratitude for the invitation. "Let's sit out here and talk on the porch. It'll be cooler than inside."

Zachary said, "We have a good deal to talk about." He seated himself in a rocking chair and gazed across the pasture. "I love to sit out here of an evening and just rock. I watch my cattle grazing and the calves playing yonder, and I don't feel alone. I doubt that heaven can offer much more."

Seymour said, "I envy you that."

Zachary mused. "You've always been a good friend, Pete. You don't have much to show for all those years of work and hardship, do you? You probably expect to keep working until they carry you away."

"I'm used to work."

The judge's eyes were sad. "I wouldn't mind so much

going away if I didn't worry about my cattle. They're the nearest thing to family that this old bachelor ever had."

"You could sell them to somebody who'd pet them like you have."

"You deserve some pleasure out of life. I'd like to sell them to you, Pete."

"I ain't got the kind of money it'd take."

"You don't need to pay now. While I was waiting for you, I wrote out a bill of sale. Andy, I'll need you to witness my signature."

Surprised, Andy said, "I'll be glad to."

Seymour was stunned. Zachary went into the house and brought out a paper. He signed it, and Andy affixed his own signature. The judge folded the paper and handed it to the astonished Seymour. The sheriff summoned voice enough to say, "I don't know how to thank you."

"No need to say anything. This is my way of thanking you for being a good friend through the years." His eyes were sad, but he attempted a smile. "You could retire now if you want to. You could turn the sheriff's office over to someone else, perhaps Logan Daggett."

Seymour said, "I'll sure think on it."

Zachary arose from his chair. "Now, if you two will wait for me out here, I have a thing or two to do before we leave."

Seymour seemed to remain in shock. "I never expected such as this would ever happen to me."

Andy said, "I used to know an old preacher named Webb. He always said the Lord works in mysterious ways."

From inside the house, a shot rattled the windows. Andy and the sheriff glanced at each other, then rushed through the door.

* * *

It was turning dark when Andy rode up to the little house at the edge of Fort McKavett. He half feared that Bethel might already have gone to sleep, but he saw dim lamplight through the open door. Bethel's dog came out from behind the house and sniffed suspiciously, then recognized Andy's scent and welcomed him with a violent wagging that shook its whole body.

Andy stopped on the porch to wipe his boots on a sack Bethel kept there for the purpose. He called, "Anybody home?"

Bethel appeared in the door, holding the lamp high so she could see his face. For a moment her eyes betrayed her joy. Then her voice took on an exaggerated tone of severity. "How long this time?"

He said, "I've got some bad news. I've been dismissed from the Rangers."

"And you call that bad news?" She set the lamp aside and hugged him with all her strength. "It's the best news I've heard. Well, almost the best." She pulled his head down and whispered in his ear.

Andy swallowed hard. "When?"

"It'll be a while, long enough for us to build that cabin and for you to put some livestock on the place."

He found himself trembling, momentarily overwhelmed. "It won't be easy. It's apt to be red beans and squirrel stew for a few years."

She kissed him and smiled. "I know seven different ways to cook squirrel stew."